BETTER
the feel good place

Lincolnshire
COUNTY COUNCIL
Working for a better future

KT-556-904

Lincolnshire Libraries
This book should be returned on or before the due date.

Gainsborough
Library

2 4 JUN 2021

To renew or order library books please telephone 01522 782010
or visit https://capitadiscovery.co.uk/lincolnshire/
You will require a Personal Identification Number
Ask any member of staff for this.
The above does not apply to Reader's Group Collection Stock.

EC. 199 (LIBS): RS/L5/19

Look out for the rest of The Rockwood Chronicles,

05380874

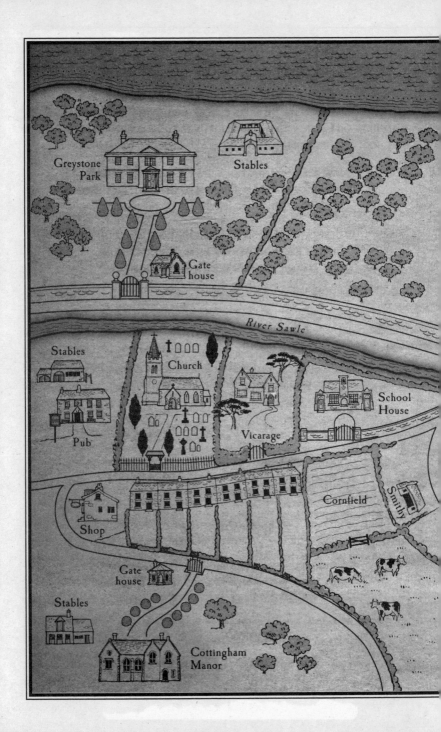

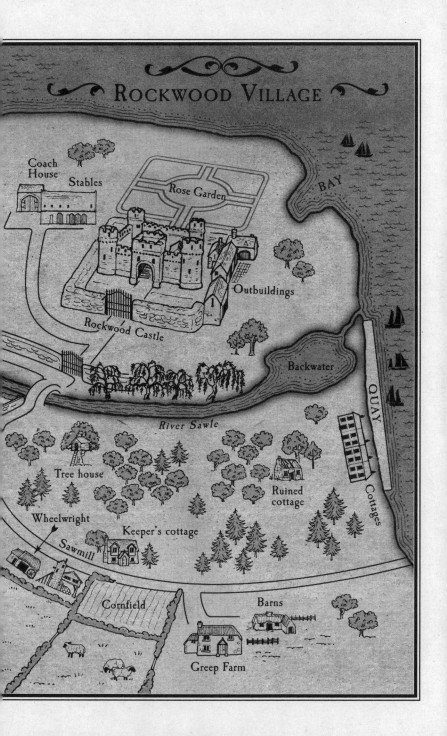

Fortune's Daughter

Book one in

The Rockwood Chronicles

Dilly Court is a No.1 *Sunday Times* bestselling author of over forty novels. She grew up in North-East London and began her career in television, writing scripts for commercials. She is married with two grown-up children, four grandchildren and two beautiful great-grandchildren. Dilly now lives in Dorset on the Jurassic Coast with her husband.

To find out more about Dilly, please visit her website and her Facebook page:

www.dillycourt.com
🔲 /DillyCourtAuthor

Also by Dilly Court

Mermaids Singing
The Dollmaker's
Daughters
Tilly True
The Best of Sisters
The Cockney Sparrow
A Mother's Courage
The Constant Heart
A Mother's Promise
The Cockney Angel
A Mother's Wish
The Ragged Heiress
A Mother's Secret
Cinderella Sister
A Mother's Trust
The Lady's Maid
The Best of Daughters
The Workhouse Girl
A Loving Family
The Beggar Maid
A Place Called Home
The Orphan's Dream

Ragged Rose
The Swan Maid
The Christmas Card
The Button Box
The Mistletoe Seller
Nettie's Secret
Rag-and-Bone Christmas
The Reluctant Heiress

THE RIVER MAID
SERIES

The River Maid
The Summer Maiden
The Christmas Rose

THE VILLAGE
SECRETS SERIES

The Christmas Wedding
A Village Scandal
The Country Bride

Dilly Court

Fortune's Daughter

Book one in

The Rockwood Chronicles

HarperCollins*Publishers*

HarperCollins*Publishers* Ltd
1 London Bridge Street,
London SE1 9GF

www.harpercollins.co.uk

HarperCollins*Publishers*
1st Floor, Watermarque Building, Ringsend Road
Dublin 4, Ireland

First published by HarperCollins*Publishers* 2021
1

Copyright © Dilly Court 2021

Map copyright © Liane Payne 2021

Dilly Court asserts the moral right to
be identified as the author of this work

A catalogue record for this book is
available from the British Library

ISBN: 978-0-00-843548-6 (HB)
ISBN: 978-0-00-843549-3 (B)

This novel is entirely a work of fiction.
The names, characters and incidents portrayed in it are
the work of the author's imagination. Any resemblance to
actual persons, living or dead, events or localities is
entirely coincidental.

Set in Sabon LT Std by
Palimpsest Book Production Ltd, Falkirk, Stirlingshire

Printed and bound in the UK by
CPI Group (UK) Ltd, Croydon CR0 4YY

All rights reserved. No part of this publication may be
reproduced, stored in a retrieval system, or transmitted,
in any form or by any means, electronic, mechanical,
photocopying, recording or otherwise, without the prior
permission of the publishers.

MIX
Paper from
responsible sources
FSC
www.fsc.org
FSC™ C007454

This book is produced from independently certified FSC™ paper
to ensure responsible forest management.

For more information visit: www.harpercollins.co.uk/green

With gratitude to those in the NHS frontline, carers and support workers during the pandemic and always.

Chapter One

Rockwood Castle, Devonshire, May 1839

'Wait for me, Bertie.' Eight-year-old Rosalind Carey stumbled over the rocks in the cove as she tried in vain to keep up with her elder brother. The moon had vanished behind a bank of clouds, throwing the beach into a sea of shadows, and a south-westerly had blown in from the Atlantic, hurling waves onto the shore. All Rosalind could see were the white soles of Bertie's bare feet as he scampered towards the cliffs, leaping across pools of salt water like a mountain goat. Suddenly he was gone and she was alone in the darkness with the waves crashing on the foreshore as the incoming tide swallowed up the strand. She could hear the shouts of men riding the waves in a small boat as they prepared to leap out and drag it onto the shore. There were flashes of light from oil lamps in the mouth of the cave that had been carved into the red sandstone by centuries of high tides, where local men prepared to receive the bounty from the sea. It had been her brother's idea to catch the smugglers red-handed, but she realised now that it had been the foolhardy boast of a twelve-year-old boy who should have known better.

The voices were getting closer and she could hear the keel of the boat grinding on the pebbles as it reached land. She glanced over her shoulder and the clouds parted, allowing a shaft of moonlight to reveal the men dragging kegs and tubs onto the beach.

'Bertie,' she cried on a sob, 'where are you?' But her brother had disappeared into the scrubby foliage that grew at the base of the cliff and she knew that she was on her own. With a last burst of energy, but hampered by her wet skirts, she tried to follow him. If she could reach the cliff path that led to Rockwood land she would be safe. Then the sudden staccato report of a gun being fired from the cliff top was followed by the barked orders of the preventive men. Rosalind made a grab for the branch of a thorn bush, but it snapped, sending her tumbling backwards onto the hard-packed sand and stones. Stunned and winded, she lay there gasping for breath.

'Don't make a sound.' A hand clamped over her mouth and she was pinned to the ground by a warm body. His face was close to hers and he smelled of the sea. 'I'll take my hand off your mouth if you promise not to scream.'

She nodded vigorously.

'Are you hurt?'

'I don't know.'

'Keep very still or they'll see us.'

Rosalind had little option but to nod again, sensing that she was not in any danger from the boy, who had appeared as if from nowhere. She could feel a trickle of warm blood running down her cheek from a cut on her head. Her rescuer edged further into the shadows, dragging her with him, and she looked up, following his gaze as he watched the men push the boat back into the foaming waves and leap on board. More shots were fired, but they missed their mark, and Rosalind found herself hoping that the smugglers would get away. The lights had been extinguished in the cave and no doubt those who had been waiting to collect the contraband would be well on their way to safety. Rosalind knew all the cliff paths, and the exploits of the smugglers were legendary. Tales of their brushes with the law circulated from below stairs to the Carey family, who had owned Rockwood Castle since the eleventh century. Hester, the housekeeper, who had been part of the household ever since Rosalind could remember, had regaled them with tales of the derring-do of the free traders, and their brushes with the preventive men. Bertie and Walter had listened avidly, as had Rosalind, although Patricia, being four years her junior, had usually been tucked up in bed with Raggy, her beloved rag doll.

'Are you sure you're all right?' the boy sounded anxious.

Rosalind blinked and rubbed her eyes. She had drifted off into a daydream and her head ached, but now she was back to reality. 'Yes, I think so.' She moved away from him so that she could study his face. The moon had come out from hiding and although they were still in the protective shadow of the cliffs, she could make out his features and she was not afraid. 'Who are you? Why did they row away and leave you here?'

'I'm just a boy – you don't need to know more. What's your name and why were you out on your own at this time of night?'

'I'll be in trouble if they discover I'm not in bed.'

'Do you live in the village?'

'Not exactly. Where are you from? You sound different to the people in Rockwood.'

He grinned. 'I'm not from here. I can't tell you more, little maid. I need to get away from here before I'm caught.'

'How will you do that without a boat?'

'I'll walk if I have to.'

'Are you a smuggler?'

'You don't need to know anything about me, maid.'

'I don't care anyway.' Rosalind scrambled to her

feet, but she swayed as she tried to get her balance and the boy leaped up to catch her.

'I'd best get you home. Do you live far from here?'

'No, not really, but the preventive men might be waiting at the top of the cliffs.'

'They'll be after those who were in the cave. Come on. You can lean on me.'

They made their way up the cliff, using a path that Rosalind and her brothers had created by scrambling down to the beach without being spotted by the gamekeeper or any of the outside staff. When they reached the top Rosalind pointed to the dark shape of the castle, which owned the landscape with its imposing presence.

'That's where I live, boy.'

'Then we'd best get you home before you're missed.'

They walked on in silence. Rosalind knew that sounds seemed to carry more easily at night, and if Abe Coaker, the gamekeeper, found them he would feel bound to tell Hester. It would be preferable to be scolded by Mama than by Hester, especially if she brought 'Slipper' into action. Hester was loving and gentle, but when pushed to the limits she invoked 'Slipper', an old leather slipper worn to a shine by its contact, first with Bertie's bottom, then Walter's. On rare occasions Rosalind had also felt its sting. Patsy, of course, was too young, and too easily moved to tears, to need such chastisement.

'Does your mother work at the castle?'

Rosalind stopped at the postern gate and opened it careful, mindful of the squeal of its hinges if pushed too hard. 'Mama doesn't work, but she used to sing at the opera.'

'That sounds very grand.'

'I've never thought about it.' Rosalind laid her finger to her lips. 'We have to be very quiet or the dogs will hear us and then there'll be trouble. Follow me, boy. Don't say a word.'

'I can't come in with you, maid. I have to start walking.'

'Your clothes are wet; you'll catch your death of cold. You must come in and get dry.'

'All right.'

'We'll go in through the kitchen. Bertie will have left the door unlocked. Just don't tread on the boot boy – he sleeps in the hall.'

Rosalind led the way across a cobbled courtyard to the rear of the castle, and, as she had predicted, the door to the kitchen had been left ajar. The vast kitchen, where little had changed over the centuries apart from the addition of a cast-iron range, was illuminated by the glow from the fire. Rosalind tiptoed across the flagstone floor and motioned her new friend to sit down while she cut bread from a loaf she found in the larder and buttered each slice, adding a spoonful of jam, which she spread lavishly. She watched the boy devour the food in seconds, and she cut her piece in half and gave it to him. She poured milk from a pitcher into two cups and handed him one.

He drank thirstily and wiped his mouth on the back of his hand. 'Oughtn't you to tidy up?'

Rosalind shrugged. 'The scullery maid will do it when she gets up. It's her job. You'd better sleep down here where it's warm. Just make sure you're gone before she starts work.'

'Thank you, maid. Just tell me one thing.'

Rosalind put her head on one side, eyeing him curiously. Now she could see him more clearly she liked the look of the boy from the boat. He was probably a bit older than Bertie and he was tall for his age, with a mop of dark hair that curled slightly round the back of his head. What struck her most were his eyes, which were slightly almond-shaped, large and a mysterious shade halfway between green and brown, with tiny gold flecks. She decided that she liked him. 'What do you want to know, boy?'

'Will you tell me your name so that I can remember the little girl on the beach?'

Rosalind smiled. 'My friends call me Rosie. Good night, boy.'

'Not so fast, Miss Rosalind.'

Rosalind found her way barred by the ample figure of Hester. 'What's going on, and who is this?' Hester grabbed the boy by the collar as he attempted to escape.

'Boy brought me home, Hester. Don't scold him. I was on the beach and the preventive men were shooting smugglers. I fell and boy saved me.'

Hester released him. 'What were you doing on

the beach in the middle of the night, Miss Rosalind? You're bleeding. Sit down and I'll take a look.'

'I'll go, miss,' the boy said hastily.

'You're not local. I haven't seen you before. You're not going anywhere, my lad. It's not safe with the smugglers roaming the cliffs.'

'I can take care of myself, miss.'

'You'll sleep here tonight, boy. You can leave in the morning when it's safe to do so.' Hester attended to Rosalind's abrasions. 'Now, off you go to bed. I'll look after your young friend.'

With a backwards glance at the boy who had come to her aid, Rosalind left the warmth of the kitchen and made her way through the dark corridors to the grand entrance hall. The sudden booming single chime from the grandfather clock, which stood next to one of many suits of ancient armour, made Rosalind jump. A shaft of moonlight filtered through an oriel window, guiding her up the sweeping oak staircase with its carved balusters and banister rail worn to a silky patina by centuries of use. Her room, which she shared with four-year-old Patricia, was in the north tower, while Bertie and seven-year-old Walter slept in the room a little further along the landing. Their old nursery, on the floor above, was now converted to a schoolroom, where Miss Brailsford tried hard to instil some knowledge into their heads. Of all the children, only Walter showed any real interest in learning, while Bertie wanted to be out of doors, climbing trees, diving from the cliffs at high tide, or riding the pony their father had bought him for his eleventh birthday.

Rosalind slipped off her damp clothes and left them in a pile on the floor for the maid to retrieve and take to the laundry room next morning. She put on her nightgown and climbed into bed, snuggling down beneath the down-filled coverlet.

She awakened early and dressed hurriedly, glancing every now and then at her sister, but Patricia was still sleeping soundly with Raggy clutched in her arms. Her pretty face had not lost its baby chubbiness and her golden hair tumbled around her head like a halo. Her eyelashes formed golden crescents on her pink cheeks, but her angelic looks belied a strong will and a determination to make everyone in the household bow to her wishes. Rosalind loved Patsy dearly, but sometimes she felt she could strangle her little sister. Then, of course, she was contrite and felt guilty for her intolerance. After all, Patsy was only little; she would soon grow up and then she would be a good companion.

Rosalind let herself out of the sunny tower room and made her way down the spiral staircase to the wide landing where the rest of the bedchambers were situated. There was a priest's hole hidden at the side of the back stairs, and there were numerous secret passages with doors leading into the main rooms, which were used by the servants so that they did not disturb the family or guests. Rosalind wanted to check that the boy had left and she used the servants' staircase to reach the kitchen. Mattie, the young scullery maid, was busy scrubbing the pine table. She stood to attention at the sight of Rosalind, averting her eyes hastily.

'Good morning, Mattie,' Rosalind said, smiling. It was only a few weeks ago that she had played hide-and-seek with Mattie and other children from Rockwood village. The older boys had constructed a tree house in an ancient oak in the woods, designed by Ossie Cottingham, the squire's son, although it had been Bertie's idea originally. He had taken over from Ossie and had organised the process with a degree of command that Rosalind admired. Mattie's father was a fisherman and at the age of ten she was the eldest of six children. She had started working at the castle just a month ago, and Rosalind could only hope that Cook did not work her too hard.

'Good morning, Miss Rosalind.' Mattie bobbed a curtsey.

'Are you settling in well, Mattie?'

'Yes, miss. Thank you.'

Rosalind eyed the sticky patches where she had spilled some of the jam the previous evening. 'I'm afraid I made a mess on the table, Mattie. I came down in the night to get something to eat because I was hungry.'

'Yes, miss. I'll clear it up before Cook gets here.'

'You get up very early,' Rosalind said cautiously. She could not ask outright if the boy had been here when Mattie came down to start her daily chores.

'Yes, miss.'

'Well, I mustn't disturb you, Mattie. I'm going for a walk but I'll be back soon. No need to tell Hester that I was here. It's our secret.' Rosalind left the kitchen before Mattie had a chance to answer and stepped out into the courtyard. The sun was shining and it was warm, even this early in the morning. She had no need for a bonnet or shawl and she strode briskly, heading for the cliff tops. Across the fields she could see Farmer Greep herding his cows towards the milking parlour, and a plume of smoke rising from Abe Coaker's cottage on the edge of the copse.

When she reached the top of the cliffs she shielded her eyes against the sunlight bouncing off the water, but the only vessels she could see were fishing boats. She could only hope that the mysterious boy had been rescued by the smugglers and that he was on his way home, wherever that might be. The waves had washed away any signs of a boat being dragged onto the shore and last night's escapade might never have happened. It could have been a dream, except that the boy was real enough. He had come into her life and now he was gone for ever. How long she stood there gazing into the distance she did not know, but eventually she turned her back on the wide expanse of ultramarine sea and walked resolutely in the direction of home.

* * *

'Miss Rosalind, where have you been?' Hester caught Rosalind by the arm. 'Breakfast is ready and they're all in the dining room. Your mama is fuming.'

'I'm sorry, Hester. I went for a walk and I must have taken longer than I intended. I thought I might say goodbye to the boy.'

'He's gone on his way. I wouldn't mention last night's escapade if I was you, Miss Rosalind.'

'I won't say a word.'

'Now hurry, or you'll be in real trouble.'

'I forgot that Bertie and I were having breakfast with the grown-ups today.'

'I don't approve of it. In my day children ate in the nursery until they were much older than you, but your mama says that you must learn how to behave in company. Anyway, it's only once a week and today is the day.'

'I'd rather eat in the nursery with Patsy and Walter.'

'It's not your choice, poppet.' Hester gave her a despairing glance. 'You look as if you've just got out of bed.' Hester produced a comb from her apron pocket and dragged it through Rosalind's unruly golden curls. 'There, that's better. You'll have a lot of explaining to do if your mama sees that cut on your head. Wait a minute, you've buttoned your blouse all wrong. Stand still and let me put it right before you go into the dining room.'

Rosalind stood very still. She loved Hester more than almost anyone in the world, but it didn't do to make her cross. Hester and Slipper were a pair to be avoided at any cost.

'Can I go now, Hester?'

A reluctant smile lit Hester's grey eyes and she leaned over to drop a kiss on the tip of Rosalind's nose. 'You are a little minx, Rosie. Go and join the family and don't forget to say sorry to your mama.'

Rosalind put her head on one side, eyeing Hester closely. 'If Mama is in one of her states, it won't be because I'm not at table. What's happened, Hester?'

'It's not up to me to say, but I think your papa is about to leave on one of his expeditions.'

'Did he tell you that?'

'No, of course not. I'm just a servant, Miss Rosalind.'

'But we tell you everything – me and Bertie, and even Walter.'

'That's as maybe, but there have been several hampers delivered from Fortnum and Mason in London – that's a sure sign that Mr Wilfred is planning a long journey. Now join the family and don't repeat what I just said.' Hester gave her a gentle shove and Rosalind opened the door as quietly as possible. Somehow she managed to slip into the oak-panelled dining room without anyone noticing and she went to sit beside Bertie. At the head of the table her grandfather was sitting very upright with a frown deepening the creases on his brow. Rosalind was in awe of her famous grandfather, who had been a captain in Nelson's navy and had played an important part in the dull old sea battles, the dates and details of which Miss Brailsford tried to drum into their heads. Vice-Admiral Sir Lucien Carey, Bt., decorated for gallantry by King George, had now retired from active service but he went up to London quite often, doing something important in the Admiralty, so Rosalind had been informed by Bertie, who knew about these things. At the far end of the table her father was looking distinctly sheepish, a bit like Bertie when he had been caught doing something very naughty.

'Really, Felicia, do we have to discuss this at breakfast?' Wilfred Carey protested mildly. 'Can we not discuss it in private later on?'

Rosalind turned her head to gaze at her beautiful mother, who had been an opera singer before she married. Mama had sung on the stage of the Royal Opera House in London, and would have been a star if she had not fallen in love with the young botanist and explorer, Wilfred Carey, and given up a promising career. Rosalind admired her mother, but she was a distant figure and often away from home, but when she did send for her children she entertained them with stories of her life before she gave up everything to live in 'a mausoleum' on the Devonshire coast. Rosalind had had to ask Miss Brailsford for an explanation but she did not agree with the definition of mausoleum that she had been given. Rockwood Castle was very old, hundreds of years old, in fact. It was a bit draughty in the winter and when the south-westerlies were blowing, but it was beautiful and romantic and it was home. Rosalind held her breath, waiting for her mother's response.

'No, Wilfred. I want to say this in front of your father and my children. I do not want you to go on another stupid expedition to the Himalayas or wherever you are planning to go this time. I do not want to be abandoned yet again and left to shoulder the responsibility for this old pile on my own.'

'Come, come, Felicia,' Sir Lucien said hastily. 'You are not on your own. I am the head of the family and you have me to sustain you. Wilfred has a reputation to keep up. You know that he has an important mission to find rare plants for the Botanic Gardens at Kew.'

Felicia threw up her hands. 'I don't care, Sir Lucien. I gave up a glittering career to marry your son and here I am now, wasting my talents in Rockwood.'

'But, my love, you are my wife and the mother of my children,' Wilfred protested. 'Surely that is enough for any woman?'

'Do you really think so?' Felicia tossed her damask table napkin onto the floor and rose to her feet. 'Well, I do not. If you go off on this trip, which you didn't tell me about until this morning, I will return to London. Claude de Marney, my former manager, has kept in touch all these years and has begged me to return to the company on several occasions. I think it is time for me to think about myself and not put others first, as I have done for all these years.'

'I say, Felicia. That's not fair.'

'I'm still a young woman. I have a God-given gift, which I need to share with the world.'

'My sainted Prudence was happy to be my wife and mother of my child,' Sir Lucien said angrily.

'She might be alive now had she not trailed round the world after you, Papa-in-Law.' Felicia turned her attention to Rosalind and Bertie. 'You should be in the nursery. Meals in the dining room are for adults. Go away now.'

'But, Mama . . .' Bertie began tentatively.

'Now, I said.' Felicia glared at him and then Rosalind, who leaped up from her seat and ran from the room with Bertie following close behind.

Hester was waiting in the grand entrance hall and Rosalind ran into her outstretched arms.

'Papa is going away,' she murmured on a sob. 'Mama says she's going to London to share her gift with the world.'

'See if I care,' Bertie said with an impatient toss of his head. 'I'm going hunting with Abe Coaker. He's going to teach me how to shoot.'

Hester reached out and caught him by the ear as he was about to make his escape. 'No you don't, young sir. You are going to the schoolroom for lessons as usual. Miss Brailsford is waiting for you.'

'But we haven't had breakfast,' Rosalind protested, wiping her eyes on the back of her hand.

'Where's your kerchief, Miss Rosalind?' Hester took a hanky from her apron pocket and handed it to Rosalind. 'If you hurry to the nursery I'll tell Cook to send up some breakfast. Then you must go to the schoolroom.'

Bertie eyed her warily. 'All right, but I'm going out with Abe after lessons have finished. I'm going to be a soldier, Hester. I need to learn how to handle a gun.'

'I wouldn't mention soldiering in front of your grandpapa,' Hester said hurriedly. 'He expects you to join the navy.'

'I don't care.' Bertie headed for the grand staircase. 'Come on, Rosie. I'm hungry.'

Lessons had just finished that morning and Miss Brailsford left the children to tidy the schoolroom. She had been unusually distracted and seemed to find it difficult to concentrate, going off into a dream while she was supposed to be teaching. Bertie had taken advantage and had spent the entire morning drawing battle scenes, which resulted in a severe scolding when Miss Brailsford realised what he had been doing. She lectured him on wasting expensive paper, although Rosalind could see that Bertie was not listening. He was used to being scolded and he always adopted the same innocent expression, with his curly blond head tilted to the side, as if he were concentrating, when in fact he had not heard a single word. What amused Rosalind most was the fact that Miss Brailsford was convinced that Bertie was taking it all in, when he was probably imagining himself roaming the woods with the gamekeeper, or running wild with Barnaby Yelland, the blacksmith's son, and Ben Causley, the landlord's son from the Black Dog.

'What's the matter with Miss Brailsford?' Walter asked gruffly. 'She was in a mood this morning. I got told off for sniffing, but I have a cold.'

'It's probably a matter of the heart,' Rosalind said with a knowing smile. She had heard Hester say the same thing when talking to Mrs Higson, the cook.

'What does that mean?' Walter closed the book on his desk. 'I saw her crying the other day.'

'Why was she crying?' Patricia slid off her stool. 'I don't like it when people are upset.'

'Miss Brailsford is in love with Mr Jarvis, the butler,' Rosalind said firmly. 'I heard Mrs Higson say that nothing good would come out of it, and Miss Brailsford would have to leave if she couldn't control her emotions. Servants aren't allowed to marry each other.'

'Oh, is that all?' Walter swept his books into his desk and closed the lid. 'She's silly.'

'Maybe she'll have to lie down in a darkened room this afternoon,' Bertie said hopefully. 'If she does I'm going to find Abe and make him keep his promise to take me shooting.' He looked up as the door opened and their father strode into the school-room.

'Papa.' Rosalind ran to him and would have given him a hug, but he held her at arm's length.

18

'Not now, Rosalind. I want you all to sit down and listen very carefully.' Wilfred Carey folded his arms and waited for his children to obey him. 'That's better. Bertie and Rosalind know that I am going away very soon, but I wanted to tell you all together. I am about to leave for the Himalayas. Do you know where they are?' He pointed at Bertie.

'India, sir?'

'Yes, but can you tell me more?'

Rosalind could see that Bertie was struggling. 'It's a mountain range, Papa,' she said hastily. 'It separates the plains of India from the Tibetan Plateau.'

'Well done, Rosalind. Anyway, I'm going on a plant hunting expedition for the Botanic Gardens at Kew. I will be gone for some time, so I want you all to be good and to study hard, and don't upset your mama.' He gazed at them each in turn and they all nodded and murmured in assent. 'Then I'll say goodbye for now, and when I return I expect to have good reports on all of you.' He ruffled Bertie's hair, and patted Walter on the head. Rosalind held her face up hoping for a kiss, but her father patted her cheek and turned away to give Patricia a kiss. 'Look after little Patsy, Rosalind. Remember that you're the big sister and you must protect her at all times. Bertie, you're the man of the house next to Grandpapa, so I trust you to take care of Walter and your sisters.' Wilfred took a handkerchief from his pocket and blew his nose loudly. 'I'm going now, children. Be good.' He left the room.

'Has Papa got a cold, like Miss Brailsford?' Patricia asked, breaking the silence.

Rosalind gave her a hug. 'Grown-ups take their hankies out when they don't know what to say. Don't worry about Papa. He'll be home again soon.'

After their midday meal in the old nursery, which was always very plain but wholesome food, unlike the lavish meals served in the dining room, Hester came to tell them that Miss Brailsford was feeling unwell and would not be teaching them that afternoon. Bertie took the opportunity to disappear, although Rosalind knew very well where he was headed, and she herself spent the afternoon entertaining Patricia. From the oriel window above the front entrance, they watched the servants load the considerable amount of baggage that their father needed for his expedition. There was no sign of their mother, but it was not hard to guess that she had taken to her boudoir and might not come out for days.

It came as a shock two days later when Hester broke the news that their mama had left for London and the lure of the opera house.

'Why didn't Mama come to say goodbye?' Rosalind asked tearfully.

'Your mama was too upset,' Hester said gently. 'Leaving you was very hard for her. She wants you to know that she loves you very much, but she needs to put her talents to good use.'

Patricia sobbed and Walter went to the library to

bury his head in a book, while Bertie claimed that it would make little difference to any of them, if the truth were to be told. 'And now I can go hunting with Abe whenever I want,' he said grinning.

Rosalind shed a few tears with Patricia, but in a way she had to agree with Bertie. They had seen so little of their parents that being apart for longer periods of time would make very little difference. At least they had Hester to love and comfort them. People came into their lives and then they were gone – like Papa and Mama – and the boy.

Chapter Two

Rockwood Castle, May 1851

Sunshine filtered through the narrow windows of the kitchen, which had been barely modernised since the castle was erected in the eleventh century. Thick stone walls kept out the wild winter weather that crossed the Atlantic to hurl itself at the Devonshire coastline, having spent some of its rage on the rugged shores of Cornwall. Now it was spring. The air was mild and filled with the scent of salty sea breezes and the bluebells that carpeted the woods nearby. Steam from the bubbling pot on the ancient cast-iron range condensed on the cold stone and trickled down the walls as if the castle itself was crying.

Rosalind was no expert when it came to cooking, but at least she had not burned the porridge, and it was almost ready. She turned with a start at the sound of running footsteps and her grandfather's voice raised in alarm.

'The French fleet have been sighted off the starboard bow.'

Rosalind sighed wearily. 'It's all right, Grandpapa. We've raised the standard – they'll know they've been spotted.' She stood back from the heat that blasted out from the fire in the range. 'Breakfast is ready.'

Sir Lucius Carey wagged a gnarled finger at his granddaughter. 'We'll be eating snails and frogs' legs if they send out a landing party. Sound the alarm, Rosalind.'

'I think you should eat your breakfast first, Grandpapa.'

'Don't answer back, young lady. Where are you manners? If you were a midshipman you would be severely disciplined for insubordination.' Sir Lucius pulled up a wooden stool and sat down. He picked up a spoon. 'Well, where's the slop you call porridge?'

She filled a wooden bowl, having learned from bitter experience not to trust her grandfather with china, and she handed it to him. 'The French fleet can wait a while longer.'

He jumped to his feet. 'I'm going to the tower. Send the bosun to me when he comes on watch.' With his dress coat-tails flying and his silver hair standing up like a halo around the bald patch on his head, Sir Lucius strode out of the kitchen, heading towards the narrow staircase that led to one of the four towers each guarding a corner of Rockwood Castle. The ancestral home of the Carey family, Rockwood had survived wars and many changes of fortune. According to legend, Simon de Carey had been granted the land by none other than King William the Conqueror, as a reward for services rendered in battle. Simon had won the hand of the heiress to the adjoining estate, and he had built the castle for his new bride. Since then the Careys' fortunes had ebbed and flowed like the waters in the estuary, and now it was definitely low tide.

Rosalind shook her head. Sometimes her grandfather seemed quite rational, but at others, such as this, he was reliving his glory days in the Royal Navy. He was in a world of his own, where the responsibilities of being a baronet and the head of the Carey dynasty meant nothing to him. Rosalind opened the door that led directly into the courtyard and took a deep breath of fresh air. The aroma of damp earth mingled with the faint scent of the bluebells that carpeted the woods on the edge of the deer park, although the herd had been sold more than a year ago. The sun had emerged from the clouds after a heavy shower, leaving the traces of a fading rainbow in the sky above the ramparts, which was a sight to gladden any heart. Rosalind breathed deeply, closing her eyes. She remembered the castle in the old days when everything was plentiful, but she loved it even now, when times were hard.

She was suddenly aware of footsteps and she opened her eyes to see Bertie crossing the courtyard with his familiar swagger. He marched into the kitchen, flinging a brace of pheasants onto the scrubbed pine table.

'We'll dine like royalty tonight, Rosie.'

'I thought the game-shooting season had ended.'

'They're our birds on our land, and we have to eat. Do you know how to cook them?'

She eyed the dead birds warily. 'I suppose so. It can't be too hard, can it? I mean Hester prepares them regularly.'

Bertie stood his precious Manton shotgun against the stone wall. 'Where is she? Why are you working in the kitchen like a common skivvy?' He seized a spoon and helped himself to some porridge. 'This isn't bad. Did you make it?'

'I did.' Rosalind tried not to look too pleased. She did not often get praise from any of her siblings, especially Bertie, who took everything for granted.

'Pass me a bowl. I'm starving.'

He could easily have reached the dresser himself, but Bertie was twenty-four, the elder son and the heir to the estate, and he was used to being waited upon. She filled a bowl and handed him a generous portion of porridge.

'That's got to last you until supper-time. I gave Hester the day off to visit her ailing aunt in Dawlish, so we won't see her until late this evening. I don't know why she stays with us anyway. We haven't paid her for six months, and there's a stack of unpaid bills in the housekeeper's room. No wonder the tradesmen refuse to give us any more credit.'

Bertie shovelled porridge into his mouth. 'Is there any tea in the pot? I suppose coffee is out of the question.'

'Bertie, we have to pay the grocer. The poor man has a wife and children to keep.'

'Tell him he'll be paid at the end of the month,' Bertie said airily.

'It's the end of April. You'll have to do something, Bertie. You're the head of the family while Papa is away. You know we can't rely on Grandpapa.'

Bertie scraped the last of the porridge from his bowl. 'How many French ships has he sunk today?'

'It's not funny.' Rosalind did not know whether to laugh or cry. 'Papa is up a mountain in Nepal or somewhere equally foreign, searching for rare plants that he always swore would make our fortune. All we have for his efforts is a conservatory filled with dead seedlings and straggly palm trees.'

'I believe Mama is appearing at the Royal Opera House in Covent Garden this season,' Bertie said thoughtfully. 'I read it in a copy of *The Times* I found in the barber's shop.'

'Then we must go to London and ask her to help us. It's two years or more since she was last here, and then she only stayed for two days.'

Bertie rose to his feet. 'There's something about this place. The family don't call it Carey's Folly for nothing. I think we should sell up and let someone else take on this crumbling pile of stone.'

'You don't mean that, Bertie.'

Rosalind turned to see their younger sister, sixteen-year-old Patricia, standing at the foot of the stone stairs, which had, until the change in the family's circumstances, been used only by servants.

'Come and have breakfast, Patsy,' Rosalind said cheerfully. 'Don't worry about what Bertie said. We're just trying to sort out our finances.'

'I heard you mention Mama. Is she coming home?'

'Maybe, or perhaps we'll go to London to see her. That would give her a nice surprise.'

'Or not,' Bertie said gloomily. 'Our mother doesn't worry about us. Why don't you girls admit it?'

'That's not fair,' Patricia said, pouting ominously, her blue eyes brimming with tears. 'Mama explained it to me the last time she came home. She said that she has a God-given talent for singing, and she would be utterly miserable if she were prevented from sharing her beautiful voice with the rest of the world.'

'And she stayed two days before sailing off for France and then Italy and goodness knows where else.' Bertie picked up his shotgun. 'I'm going to bag a few pigeons. Do you know how to make pigeon pie, Rosie?' He strolled out into the courtyard before she had time to answer.

Patricia helped herself to porridge and took a seat at the table. 'Where's Hester? Why are you doing the cooking, Rosie?'

'She's visiting her sick aunt in Dawlish, and I don't know how to make pigeon pie. Bertie will have to forgo that pleasure.' Rosalind picked up the porridge saucepan. 'There's just enough left for Walter. Have you seen him this morning?'

'I expect he was up all night writing poetry, as usual. He's probably sound asleep.'

'In that case, I'll just have to eat his portion. I'm not wasting good food.' Rosalind leaned over to pat the head of a large yellow Labrador that had suddenly appeared at her side. 'You can lick out the pan, Bob.'

Bob's pink tongue lolled out of his mouth and his eyes shone as he sat down to wait for the treat.

'What are you going to do with those?' Patricia asked tentatively, pointing to the pheasants that Bertie had left on the far end of the table.

'I'm not quite sure.' Rosalind spooned the last of the porridge into her mouth before placing the pan on the floor for her dog. 'I've never plucked a bird. I thought I'd take them to Coaker. He's sure to know what to do. That's if I can find him. He could be anywhere on a fine day like today.'

Patricia placed her spoon neatly in her empty bowl. 'What are we going to do, Rosie? All the servants have left, except Hester. My hands are raw from washing dishes and scrubbing floors.'

'I never ask you to do anything I don't do myself.'

'I know that, but why don't Walter or Bertie share the work? Walter hardly leaves his room, unless it's to spend hours in the library, and Bertie is always out shooting something, or fishing.'

'At least Bertie brings us food. And Walter is delicate. You know he suffers from his chest.'

'I suppose so, but it still isn't fair. Christina and Sylvia Greystone attend parties and balls, but if anyone invites us we have to refuse because we've nothing to wear. I hate being poor.' Patricia rose from the table and took her bowl to the scullery.

Rosalind could hear the splash of water as Patricia worked the pump over the sink and rinsed the bowls in cold water. Rosalind sighed. Sir Michael Greystone's daughters lived a life of luxury at Greystone Park, the neighbouring estate, but envying them their wealth was a waste of time and energy. If only Patsy would realise that. Rosalind pushed back her chair and stood up.

'Patsy, do you fancy a trip into town? I think a visit to Mr Mounce, Papa's solicitor, is called for.'

Patricia appeared in the doorway with water dripping from her hands. 'I'd do anything to get away from this place for an hour or two.'

'We'll go into Exeter this afternoon, but first I must find Gurney and I'll ask him to have the pony and trap ready.'

'And don't forget to take those poor dead creatures with you,' Patricia said, pointing at the pheasants. 'It's cruel to shoot living things.'

'Maybe, but I doubt that you'll refuse to eat them when they're cooked.'

'You always manage to put me in the wrong, Rosie.' Patricia tossed her head and stalked out of the kitchen, muttering beneath her breath.

Rosalind shook her head. It seemed that she was the only one who took matters in hand. The others were very good at complaining and bemoaning the fact that they might own a castle, but they were as poor as church mice. However, when it came to practicalities it was she, Rosalind Louise Carey, who was left to deal with the problems that arose daily.

She picked up the pheasants and went outside, crossing the cobbled courtyard with Bob at her heels. She walked to the stable block that had once housed some of the finest bloodstock in the county, but now there was just Ajax the sturdy Dartmoor pony, who had been the first horse that Rosalind had ever ridden. No one knew exactly how old Ajax was, but he was certainly over twenty and still fit enough to work when required.

Jim Gurney was one of the few staff remaining at Rockwood. He had been with the family since he was a child and was now approaching his sixties. Jim had never married and lived above the stables, helping out in the gardens occasionally with his old friend Abe. The pair of them could be found at the Black Dog Inn every Friday night, each nursing a tankard of ale. Rosalind had never been in the pub, but Bertie was a frequent customer and he brought home all the village gossip, or at least snippets of it that could be repeated without making his sister blush.

'Are you there, Jim?' Rosalind shouted as loud as she could, knowing that Jim was a little hard of hearing.

She could hear his footsteps on the wooden stairs and he came down, buttoning his jacket and smoothing his thinning hair over an almost bald pate.

'You wanted me, miss?'

'Yes, Jim. I have to go to Exeter. Will you harness Ajax to the trap and have it ready at noon?'

'Shall I drive you, miss?'

'That won't be necessary. You taught me how to handle the reins, Jim. I'm very happy to drive myself.'

She made her escape before he could start reminiscing about the good old days when the stables were filled with horses and the Careys employed a coachman as well as several grooms and stable boys. She could hear Ajax whinnying as if he knew that months of inactivity were coming to an end. He had been well fed during the cold winter as last year's hay harvest had been quite a good one. Rosalind had been able to sell the surplus to Sir Michael Greystone's land agent, and that had helped to eke out the money received in rent from the cottagers on the estate. But Rosalind had a soft heart and if their tenants had fallen on hard times she was not one to press them for payment. In the depths of winter, when food was short, she made sure that the elderly and the sick people on the estate always had something to eat. The family might not live like lords now, but with vegetables from the walled garden and Bertie's prowess as a marksman, they were never on the verge of starvation. The local miller was always happy enough to exchange a sack of flour for a haunch of venison, and a tenant farmer supplied milk, butter and cheese in lieu of rent for the ten-acre field where his herd could graze on the lush grass.

Rosalind quickened her pace as she made her way to the kitchen garden where Abe Coaker would most likely be hard at work. When she was a child she had often ventured through the gate in the high brick wall to watch a small army of workers tilling the soil and planting out the tender green seedlings that Abe had grown in the large greenhouse. Now he had to toil away on his own, although sometimes he had help from his eldest grandson, Noah, a boy of nine who clearly loved the work. Rosalind could not afford to pay the child, but she made a point of sneaking him a slice of Hester's seed cake or a couple of saffron buns, although with the current state of their finances any such luxuries would be off the table for the foreseeable future.

Bob raced on ahead, tail wagging with the sheer joy of living, which always made Rosalind smile, no matter how many problems she might have. Bertie had bought Bob as an eight-week-old puppy after a drunken night in Exeter, with the intention of training him to be a gun dog. However, Bob had other ideas, and his first loyalty had, from the start, been for Rosalind. Even as a small puppy he would protect her fiercely from anyone who dared to raise their voice in her presence, and he followed her like a shadow. All Bertie's efforts to train Bob proved to be a waste of time. Bob was a happy spirit, carefree and quite unable to remember an order, let alone to find and fetch anything that did not resemble a stick or a ball. Bertie had given up eventually and Bob was free to enjoy life in his own way.

Rosalind let herself into the walled garden and Bob raced on ahead to find Abe, who always made a fuss of him, and occasionally shared a piece of bread and cheese. She followed the sound of Bob's joyful bark and found him jumping up and down in front of Abe, who was leaning against the warm red bricks, eating a thick slice of bread. He threw a crust to Bob.

'Morning, Miss Rosalind.'

'Good morning, Abe.' Rosalind held up the brace of pheasants. 'I need your help.'

Abe swallowed the last of his lunch and wiped his mouth on the back of his hand. 'You want I to pluck 'em, miss?'

'Yes, please. If you show me how it's done I won't have to bother you next time my brother shoots something for the pot.'

''Tis out of season, miss. They birds should be left to breed in peace.' Abe took the birds into the greenhouse. He perched on a stool and began plucking the pheasants so that the feathers fluttered into a sack.

Rosalind watched with interest. Abe's fingers might be gnarled with rheumatism, but he worked quickly and deftly.

'You're right, of course,' she said slowly. 'But we have to eat, and money is very short at the moment.'

'I knows that, miss. I haven't been paid since last year. Not that I'm complaining. Hester gives me bread and I can live off the land as well as any man.'

'It shouldn't be like that, and I'm going to do something about it.'

'You'm just a young maid. It's not right, leaving everything to you, miss. I speak as I find because I've known you since you was a babe in arms. Sir Lucius should take charge.'

'I'm twenty, Abe. I'll be twenty-one in June, and I'm perfectly capable of managing things. My grand-papa is not well. You know that.'

'Aye, I do, miss. I found him wandering near the edge of the backwater yesterday. He couldn't remember where he was or why he was there in the first place. It took me a fair old while to get him home.'

'I'm grateful to you,' Rosalind said softly. 'We try to keep an eye on him, but it's not always possible.'

Abe finished plucking one pheasant and laid it on the wooden staging. 'Time was when his lordship had a man to take care of him and I had plenty of help, too. But I'm not complaining, miss. I got my cottage and everything I need.'

'I don't know what we'd do without you, Abe.' Rosalind leaned closer in order to get a better view of Abe's handiwork. 'I can see how you're doing it. Shall I have a go? You can tell me if I'm not going about it the right way.'

Half an hour later she was back in the castle kitchen with the pheasants plucked, drawn and prepared for cooking. She placed them on a marble slab in the larder, which was cold enough to keep them fresh for several days.

'Just look at the state of you, Rosie.' Patricia had come into the kitchen and she was staring at her sister with a frown knotting her brow. 'You look as though you've been dragged through a hedge backwards.'

Rosalind glanced down at her skirt. Damp from the long grass and mud from the walled garden had spread upwards in a dark stain. Her hands were covered in blood from the pheasants and a feather floated down from her tangled mass of fair hair. 'You won't be so critical when it comes to enjoying roast pheasant for dinner tonight.'

'Maybe, but we were supposed to be going to Exeter to see Mr Mounce.'

'Yes, of course. I don't know where the time went.' Rosalind hurried to the scullery and worked the pump over the stone sink, washing her hands in ice-cold water.

'Don't forget your face,' Patricia said crossly. 'You look as if you've been blooded at your first hunt.'

'I've never been on a hunt.' Rosalind splashed water on her face. 'And I don't want to, either.' She turned to her sister. 'Is that better?'

'Yes, but you'd better change your skirt, and hurry. Gurney's waiting outside with the trap.'

'Tell him I'll be five minutes.' Rosalind headed for the servants' staircase. It would not do to turn up at the family solicitor's chambers in such an unkempt state. Times may be hard but there were standards to maintain. The Careys never admitted defeat.

An hour later Rosie and Patricia were ushered into Herbert Mounce's office by his head clerk. Herbert rose from his seat behind a large desk. The tooled leather surface was covered in piles of documents, hefty tomes and a large brass inkstand, which stood on claw-like feet as if it were about to walk away.

'Good afternoon, ladies. Do take a seat.'

'Thank you for seeing us without an appointment, Mr Mounce,' Rosalind said, smiling. 'We are in desperate need of advice.' She pulled up a chair and sat down, leaving Patricia to perch on the edge of a wooden settle.

'What is the problem, Miss Carey?'

'Money, sir, as always, or rather the lack of it. Have we any trust funds about to mature? Or are there any shares that have not been sold?'

Herbert sank down on his seat, leaning his elbows

on the desk. 'I can answer that in one word, and I'm afraid that word is in the negative.'

'Could you perhaps look again? There must be something.'

'I had this conversation with your elder brother just a few days ago, Miss Carey. My clerk went through every document in our possession, and I believe that Bertram had already visited your bank manager. There is nothing left, I'm afraid, unless you count the rents from the various cottages on your estate, although I believe it was a poor harvest last year and monies are unlikely to be forthcoming.'

'Are you absolutely certain?' Rosalind asked in desperation. 'We weren't always poor. How did our forebears manage to live so well?'

Herbert sat back in his chair, eyeing her with a wry smile. 'There were many ways in which people living on the coast could supplement their income in times of need.'

'Do you mean free trading?' Rosalind stared at him in astonishment. 'Surely not? My grandfather is a naval hero.'

'Yes, indeed.'

'He is an honourable gentleman,' Rosalind said coldly. 'He wouldn't stoop so low.'

'Does it really matter what went on in the past?' Patricia said impatiently. 'We need money now, Rosie.'

'Yes, we do.' Rosalind managed a smile. 'Is there anything you can do to help us, sir?'

'My dear, young lady, the best advice I could give to you would be to sell the castle and the estate. Even allowing for repayment of the outstanding debts there would be enough to purchase a smaller property where you could all live in comfort. But,' he added, shaking his head, 'that is a decision that has to be taken by your grandfather, and if he is incapable of doing so, then it is your father who has the responsibility. Have you any idea when he might return to Devon?'

Rosalind shook her head and Patricia began to cry softly into her handkerchief. 'No, sir. We haven't heard from Papa for over a year.'

'I believe that your mama is at present appearing at the Royal Opera House, Covent Garden. Perhaps she could help.'

'I had intended to travel to London to see her but, to be honest, we can't afford the train fare.'

'I'm afraid I can't help you, much as I would love to, but my hands are tied. If you can't pay off some of your creditors a declaration of bankruptcy will be the only answer and you and your family will lose the castle and the whole estate.'

'What will we do, Rosie?' Patricia demanded, sniffing.

Rosalind shook her head. 'Papa sold the family silver to finance his latest trip abroad.' She fingered the gold locket she always wore. 'I suppose I could pawn this. It was the last thing that Grandmama gave me before she died.'

Herbert took a large handkerchief from his pocket and blew his nose. 'Such a shame. I'd help you from my own money, but Mrs Mounce keeps a very strict eye on our outgoings.'

'I wouldn't dream of imposing on your good nature, Mr Mounce,' Rosalind said firmly. 'I dare say we owe you a considerable amount, too. You must send your bill to my grandfather. I'll add it to the rest and you will be paid, I promise.'

'I'm so sorry, Miss Rosalind. I hate to see you and your sister in such reduced straits. Time was when—'

'I know.' Rosalind rose to her feet. 'But we have to deal with matters as they are today. Thank you for your time.'

Herbert stood up, moving swiftly round the desk. 'You won't do anything rash, will you, Miss Rosalind?'

'No, Mr Mounce. Of course not. Come, Patsy. We have things to do.'

Chapter Three

'Where are we going, Rosie?' Patricia asked breathlessly as she followed her sister down a narrow lane close to the Cathedral Close. 'What are you going to do?'

'Wait and see.' Rosalind came to a halt outside a half-timbered building with a pawnbroker's sign hanging above the doorway. 'You can stay outside if you like.'

Patricia glanced anxiously at a scruffily dressed man who was loitering on the corner. 'No. I'll come in with you.' She followed Rosalind into the dim interior of the pawnshop, and the bell above the door jangled, announcing their arrival.

A bead curtain at the rear of the shop clattered as if in tune with the bell and a small round-cheeked man, dressed more like a bank clerk than a pawnbroker, came towards them with a beaming smile.

'Well, young maidies, what can I do for you?'

Rosalind took off the locket and laid it on the counter. 'How much will you give me for this? It's solid gold.'

The man examined it closely. 'It's nice, but out of fashion. I couldn't give you a penny more than ten shillings.'

Rosalind bit her lip. 'I want more than that.'

'I'd like to help, maid. Eleven shillings and that's my final offer.'

'It belonged to my late grandmother,' Rosalind said with a break in her voice. 'I'm sure it's worth more than that.'

'Being as you asked so nicely, I'll give you twelve shillings and six pence. I'm a fair man, not like some in my trade.'

Patricia nudged Rosalind in the ribs. 'Let's go, Rosie.'

'I'll accept your offer,' Rosalind said grudgingly. 'But I'll be back to redeem it in a few days.'

The pawnbroker unlocked a strong box and took out the coins, which he laid on the counter. He wrote out a ticket and handed it to Rosalind in exchange for the locket and chain. 'You've got thirty days, maid. If you haven't redeemed the article it goes up for sale. You do understand that, don't you?'

Rosalind nodded and scooped up the coins. She put them in her purse, together with the ticket. 'I'll be back sooner than that.' She left the shop, followed by Patricia, who fell into step beside her.

'Will that be enough for our fares to London, Rosie?'

'It will have to be. Mama is our last chance. It's high time she took some responsibility for her family. I don't mean to sound unkind, but having a wonderful talent is one thing, and neglecting your offspring is another.' She tossed a coin to the small boy who had been minding Ajax and the trap. He caught it deftly and raced off.

'What do we do now?' Patricia asked as she climbed up onto the seat beside her sister.

'We'll go to the railway station and find out the time of the trains and how much it will cost to go third class to London.'

'Third class? But Papa always travels first class. What will I tell the Greystone girls?'

'Don't tell them anything. It's none of their business.' Rosalind flicked the reins. 'Walk on, Ajax.'

That evening Rosalind carried the platter of roast pheasant, surrounded by carrots, parsnips and potatoes into the dining room. Her footsteps echoed on the polished floorboards, the carpet having been removed after Sir Lucius caught his foot in a patch that was worn to the bare threads. His tumble had not resulted in a serious injury, but he was badly bruised and shaken, and Rosalind had taken the decision to roll up the almost one-hundred-year-old Axminster and have it stored in one of the towers until they could afford to have it restored by professionals. A desultory fire had been lit in the huge fireplace, designed to warm such a large room, but they were running out of logs and the coal cellar had been empty since Christmas.

Sir Lucius, in full dress uniform, sat at the head of the table with Bertram at the other end, and Patricia sat to her grandfather's left. The silver candelabra had been the first items to be sold, and now the room was dimly lit by candles in pewter candlesticks and the feeble light from the fire. Rosalind placed the platter in front of her grandfather.

'Why are you serving dinner, Rosalind?' Sir Lucius demanded crossly. 'Who gave Jarvis the night off, and where are the maids?'

Rosalind exchanged weary glances with Bertie. This was a ritual they went through every evening when Sir Lucius failed to remember that Jarvis, the butler who had served the family all his life, had retired a year ago, and now they relied solely on Hester.

'We can't afford servants these days, Grandpapa.' Rosalind served the food and placed the plate on the table in front of him.

'Where's the redcurrant jelly, Rosalind? You know I like some with my roast pheasant.'

'I'm afraid we used the last jar before Christmas.

Hester didn't have time to make more and the crop was poor last year.' Rosalind took a small portion for herself and passed the platter to Bertram with a warning look. Even Bertie, who normally lived in a world of his own, knew better than to take too large a helping. Sharing what they had fairly was probably the only thing that she and Bertie agreed upon.

'Where's Walter?' Sir Lucius demanded, looking round the table.

'He's on the dog watch, sir,' Rosalind said quickly.

'Ah! Good, it's nice to know that one of my grandchildren takes their duties seriously. Who is that pale creature sitting opposite me?'

'Grandpapa, it's me.' Patricia's voice shook with emotion. 'Your granddaughter, Patricia.'

'Oh, yes. So you are. Well, eat up girl. You're too skinny and you look as if you've been below decks too long.'

Patricia's bottom lip began to tremble and Rosalind went to sit beside her. 'Chin up, Patsy. We're going on a trip to London tomorrow – you need to look your best.'

'I might meet a handsome and charming man, who'll sweep me off my feet,' Patricia said with a watery smile.

'What's this?' Sir Lucius speared a roast potato with his knife. 'Who's going to London?'

Rosalind decided that it was best to tell the truth, even if it caused her grandfather to react angrily.

'We're going to see Mama. She's appearing at the Royal Opera House.'

'What? You're going to London to see that madam. It was a bad day when she got her claws into my son.' Sir Lucius pushed his plate away. 'I'm going to take over Walter's watch. He'll probably fall asleep anyway. I don't know what young people are coming to these days.' He stomped out of the dining room.

'He's left half his dinner,' Bertram said casually. 'Pass the plate to me, Rosie. No sense in wasting good food.'

'Get it yourself, Bertie. I'm not walking the length of the table to give you Grandpapa's leftovers.'

Bertram opened his mouth as if to argue just as Walter strolled into the room.

'Pass me Grandpa's plate, Walter old chap,' Bertram said lazily. 'The old fellow thinks he's gone to relieve your watch.'

'Don't be disrespectful, Bertie.' Rosalind frowned at him. 'Grandpapa can't help the way he is.'

Walter took a seat, ignoring his brother's request. He reached for the platter and helped himself, piling his plate up with food.

'You greedy young pup.' Bertram stood up and marched to the head of the table to pick up his grandfather's plate. 'We held back, but you stuff yourself regardless.'

Walter looked round dazedly. 'This was left to go cold. What did I do wrong?'

'You're a pig,' Patricia said crossly. 'We all took small helpings.'

'I'm sorry. I didn't think.' Walter stared down at his rapidly cooling plate of food, his shoulders hunched in a picture of dejection.

'It's all right, Walter,' Rosalind said gently. 'We're just especially hard up at the moment, but Patsy and I are going to London tomorrow to see Mama. Perhaps she can help us out financially.'

'You could go out and get a job, Walt.' Bertram popped the last piece of parsnip into his mouth. 'Maybe you should join the navy. Grandpa would love that.'

'I hate the sea,' Walter muttered through a mouthful of meat and potato. 'I don't even like looking at it from my bedroom window.'

'Your room faces the rose garden and the deer park,' Patricia said, smirking. 'You are such a ninny.'

'I can see the estuary if I lean out of the window.' Walter turned to Rosalind. 'I don't suppose there's any redcurrant jelly, is there, Rosie?'

Rosalind jumped to her feet. 'If anyone else asks for that I'll scream. I don't think any of you realise just how poor we are at this moment. I'm stewing the pheasant bones and the last of the onions and carrots for tomorrow night's supper, and you boys will have to serve it yourselves. Patsy and I will be in London with Mama.'

'Just a minute,' Bertram said angrily. 'I'm the

eldest. Why wasn't I consulted? Anyway, how did you get the money for the fares?'

'I went to see Mr Mounce. He explained our financial situation.' Rosalind turned to Bertram with an ominous frown. 'You'd already been there asking for money. He told me.'

'I have debts to repay,' Bertram said huffily. 'So what did you do to squeeze money out of the old skinflint?'

'I know exactly what he said to you. In the end I pawned my gold locket. It's the only thing of value I had. Mama took the family jewels with her when she left and she's probably sold them by now. I'm just hoping she can help us out.'

Situated in the depths of the Royal Opera House, Felicia Carey's dressing room was small and claustrophobic. The smell of the flickering gas mantle mingled with the lingering odour of stale smoke from the black cheroots that Felicia indulged in when not on stage. A rack of ornate costumes took up most of the space, leaving her barely enough room to sit in front of the mirror. She was retouching her *maquillage* from a Japanned box containing a vast array of powder makeup while Rosalind and Patricia huddled together against the far wall. Their welcome had been less than luke-warm.

'You should have given me warning of your impending visit,' Felicia said, staring into the mirror as she applied rouge to her cheeks and lips. 'I'm on stage in ten minutes.'

'I'm sorry, Mama.' Rosalind knew better than to argue with her mother when she was in this mood. She had been told that artistes were temperamental, especially when about to perform, and she could tell by the set of her mother's shoulders and the small impatient flicks of those long white fingers, that this was not a good time to ask for anything, let alone money.

'We wanted to see you,' Patricia said plaintively. 'You haven't been home for years, Mama.'

'But we understand that you have to satisfy your faithful audiences,' Rosalind added tactfully. 'Perhaps we should leave you to get ready in peace.'

'No need for that.' Felicia dismissed the offer with a casual wave of her hand. 'When the boy comes to tell me it's time for my entrance I'll instruct him to find you seats in the auditorium. I'll see you after the performance.'

'Thank you, Mama,' Rosalind said politely. 'There's just one problem. We haven't anywhere to stay tonight.'

'You're just like your father – totally irresponsible. Why would you bring your younger sister to town when you have not made any arrangement for accommodation?'

'We haven't any money, Mama. Things are very bad at home.'

Felicia yawned. 'When are they not? I suppose

you'd better stay with me, although you'll have to sleep on the sofa.'

'We don't mind,' Rosalind said hastily. 'And we'd love to watch your performance. Wouldn't we, Patsy?'

Patricia nodded, but she did not look convinced. 'I'm hungry, Rosie,' she whispered.

The door opened before Rosalind had a chance to say anything and a middle-aged man squeezed into the dressing room. He was dressed in evening clothes: an extravagantly frilled shirt and a white cravat, a black waistcoat with a gold watch chain looped over a bulging belly, and a smart black frock coat over pin-striped trousers. His silver hair was combed back and sleeked with Macassar oil, and his waxed moustache curled upwards at the tips. Rosalind eyed him curiously.

'What have I said about allowing visitors into your dressing room before a performance, Felicia?'

'Oh, Claude, don't be so silly,' Felicia said, fluttering her soot-blacked eyelashes. 'These young ladies are my daughters.'

'Oh, well, in that case they may stay. But don't allow your emotions to spoil your performance and you must save your voice – no chit-chatting.'

'Darling, I never chit-chat.' Felicia blew him a kiss. 'Now make yourself useful, Claude. Find some seats for my girls in the stalls, or a box, if there is one vacant.'

'We haven't been introduced, Mama,' Rosalind

said cautiously. She knew of Claude de Marney, her mother's manager, but this was the first time they had met.

'Of course, I was forgetting that you don't know, Claude.' Felicia turned away from the mirror, holding her hand out to him. 'This gentleman is Claude de Marney, my good friend and manager.'

'How do you do, sir?' Rosalind managed a smile, but she was not sure she liked the man, nor did she like the way he looked her up and down before his gaze travelled to Patricia.

'Rosalind is my elder daughter,' Felicia added casually. 'And Patricia is the younger.'

'Charming,' Claude said silkily. 'Of course I will find you excellent seats so that you may enjoy the performance. Come with me, ladies.'

Rosalind glanced at her mother, but Felicia was busy adding finishing touches to her makeup. 'Yes, go. I'll see you later.'

'This way.' Claude led them down a series of passages and up what felt like endless flights of narrow stairs. They emerged into a world consisting of red plush, thick carpet and gilded paintwork. Ladies in beautiful evening gowns were being escorted to their seats by gentlemen of obvious means. Rosalind was dazzled by their elegance and exquisite jewels. She felt dowdy and out of place in such a glamorous setting, but Claude seemed unimpressed and he ushered them into a box with an uninterrupted view of the stage.

'Your mama is a wonderful woman. I am proud to be her manager. I hope you young ladies appreciate good music.' He bowed out of the tiny space, closing the door behind him.

Rosalind took a seat, gazing down at the audience in awe. She wished she had brought something more appropriate to wear, and she realised that they were attracting some curious stares. Patricia, however, appeared not to notice and she leaned her elbows on the balustrade.

'Just look at the gowns the ladies are wearing, Rosie. And the jewels – I've never seen anything like them.'

'Don't stare,' Rosalind said nervously. 'It's rude. Anyway, the lights are dimming. I think the performance is about to begin.' Even as she spoke Rosalind was aware of someone staring at her. Across the auditorium, seated in a box opposite, was a gentleman in evening dress and he was looking straight at her. He smiled, but then the gaslights were dimmed and she could no longer make out his features, although she still felt as though he was watching her. She turned her head as the orchestra struck up the overture and the curtains slid back to reveal an elaborate set. During the performance Rosalind forgot about everything other than the unfolding drama, the soaring music and her mother's beautiful mezzo-soprano voice. It was only when she heard gentle snoring that she realised her sister had fallen asleep.

When the curtains came down for the interval Rosalind watched enviously as people in boxes opposite sipped champagne. The dark-haired gentleman had disappeared and she smiled to herself, thinking that their brief moment of connection must have been in her imagination. She sat back in her comfortable chair and her stomach rumbled, reminding her that she had not eaten since midday. Patricia was still asleep, and although Rosalind was tempted to wake her, it seemed unkind, and anyway, Patsy would start complaining that she, too, was hungry. Rosalind turned with a start as someone tapped on the door and it opened just wide enough for a uniformed barman to proffer a bottle of champagne and two glasses.

'I didn't order that,' Rosalind said hastily. 'It must be a mistake.'

'Compliments of the gentleman in the box opposite, miss.'

'I don't know him.' Rosalind glanced across the auditorium and saw that he had returned to his seat. He smiled and nodded, but she looked away. 'I can't accept it.'

'I have other duties, miss. I can't take it back – it's paid for.' The barman placed the glasses and the bottle on a ledge at the side of the box and then backed out, leaving Rosalind staring at it with a puzzled frown. The ways of people in London were strange to her, but perhaps the gentleman was a friend of her mother's. She sighed with relief. That must be the answer: the present was meant for her mother, the great Felicia Carey. The lights dimmed again and the second half of the performance began. Patricia was still asleep.

There was tumultuous applause as the curtains came down for the last time and Patricia finally opened her eyes.

'Is it over?'

'Yes. You slept through the whole thing.'

'I don't like opera, but don't tell Mama that I said so.' Patricia stretched and yawned. 'I'm starving, Rosie.'

'Well, I suppose even operatic stars like Mama have to eat. We'd better stay here until she sends for us. I don't want to get lost in all those narrow corridors.'

'There's a bottle of champagne and two glasses. Is it for us?'

'It was obviously a mistake, but the barman wouldn't take it back. I was going to take it for Mama, but perhaps we'd better leave it here.'

Patricia rose to her feet and made a grab for the bottle. 'No, we won't. We'll give it to Mama as a present for allowing us to stay with her. I'm sure she simply adores champagne.'

Without warning, the door opened and Claude stood there, smiling benignly. 'Come along, ladies. Your mama and I are leaving now. I have a cab waiting to take us to dinner.' He eyed Patricia curiously. 'Champagne?'

'A present for Mama,' Patricia said boldly.

Rosalind shrugged. Perhaps it was easier this way. After all, how could she explain that a man she had never met had given them a present, which must have been very expensive? She stole a quick look at the box opposite, but it was in darkness. She would have thought she had imagined the whole thing, but for the bottle that her sister was clutching to her bosom. Perhaps the champagne would put Mama in a responsive mood when she had to broach the subject of money.

Later, after a meal at Rules Restaurant in Maiden Street, they walked to the small hotel where both Claude and Felicia had rooms. Claude kissed Felicia on the cheek, acknowledging Rosalind and Patricia with a nod and a smile and he strolled off to collect the key to his room.

'I suppose you'd better come with me,' Felicia said grudgingly. 'I can't promise you a good night's sleep, but you know that already.' She led the way upstairs to her accommodation on the first floor where she had a bedroom and a small parlour.

'This looks very comfortable, Mama,' Rosalind said hopefully.

'I have to live here for the whole of the season.' Felicia tossed her reticule on the sofa. 'I believe there are extra blankets and pillows in one of the cupboards. You'll have to find them yourselves.' She reclined gracefully in an armchair by the fireplace.

'Now, tell me exactly what you want from me. I can't believe that you came all this way just to see me perform.'

'We miss you, Mama.' Rosalind sank down on the sofa, carefully avoiding her mother's reticule. 'You hardly ever get down to Devon these days.'

'We bought you champagne.' Patricia placed the bottle on the table at the side of her mother's chair and pulled up a chair.

'No, you didn't. I don't know how you came by it, but you didn't have that bottle when you arrived in my dressing room. Anyway, it doesn't matter.' Felicia reached for a silver case and took out a cheroot, which she lit with a spill placed in the dying embers of the fire. 'I want the truth now, girls.'

'We need money or the castle will have to be put up for sale.' Rosalind was too exhausted to flatter her mother into helping them. 'You are our last hope.'

'It's not up to me.' Felicia blew a plume of smoke up the chimney. 'Your grandfather holds the title and your father is next in line. You should go to them.'

'But we haven't seen Papa for such a long time, and Grandpapa isn't himself,' Patricia said sadly. 'We have to rely on Bertie to bring game in for us to eat. Rosie has to do horrible things like plucking pheasants and cooking them. Walter's no use either. He spends all his time writing poetry, and I have to wash dishes like a common skivvy.'

Felicia tapped the ash from her cigarillo into the grate. 'The men in our family are a disgrace. I'm so glad I made a break for freedom when I did, but I can't help you, girls. I might be famous but I'm not rich.'

'You have the family jewels, Mama,' Rosalind said cautiously.

'They are my insurance against a lonely old age. Unless, of course, I marry again, but I am still shackled to your father, so that's out of the question.'

Rosalind could see that they were getting nowhere and she sighed. 'Don't trouble yourself, Mama. I expect we'll manage somehow. We'll leave first thing in the morning.'

'So you came just to ask for money?' Felicia's beautiful hazel eyes filled with tears. 'Am I such a bad mother that you feel nothing for me?'

'No, of course not.' Rosalind gazed at her mother in dismay. 'You know we love you, but you are so far away from us now.'

'I do love you, Mama.' Patricia reached out to clutch her mother's hand. 'Why don't you come home and live with us?'

Felicia shuddered dramatically. 'I couldn't live in that draughty old pile with a mad father-in-law, and an absent husband who spends all his time climbing mountains or hacking his way through jungles.' She lifted Patricia's hand to her lips. 'Of course I love all my children, but please get up, dear. You're creasing my gown.'

'I'm sorry, Mama.' Patricia scrambled to her feet. 'I'm being selfish – I know you belong to your public.'

'That's very true, for my sins.' Felicia dashed a tear from her cheek. 'I have a God-given talent that has to be shared with the world – that's what Claude says, and he's always right. Anyway, we're leaving for Vienna at the end of the season. Now, I must get my beauty sleep.' She stood up and headed for the bedroom, pausing in the doorway. 'As a special treat, perhaps you could stay for another day? The Great Exhibition has just opened and I have been given several tickets. You must come with me. It will broaden your outlook and you may learn something. However, Claude isn't really interested in that sort of thing, so it suits me to be accompanied by my handsome daughters.' Felicia stepped into her room and closed the door.

'I don't know what to say.' Rosalind rose slowly from her seat. 'I promised Bertie we would return as soon as possible.'

'Bother Bertie,' Patricia said with a mischievous grin. 'Let's do something exciting. Christina Greystone told me they would be coming up to London to see the exhibition. She said she'd tell me about it, but if we go with Mama tomorrow I'll beat her to it. I like Christina and Sylvia, but they think they're so superior.'

Rosalind laughed. 'We can't have that, Patsy. We've wasted the money I got for my locket, so we might as well enjoy ourselves. Anyway, I'm worn out. I'll see if I can find some bedding.' She went round the parlour, opening cupboards until she found one that contained a couple of blankets and two pillows. 'At least you'll have something to talk about. I have no idea what I'm going to say to Bertie when we return home with nothing. I'll never hear the end of this.'

Patricia undressed, sighing with relief as she took off her stays and tossed them on the floor. Oh, bother it. I forgot to pack my nightgown.'

'Then you'll have to sleep in your shift. You can have the sofa.' Rosalind handed her a blanket and a pillow. 'I'll take the armchair.'

'All right. But I'm so tired I could sleep on a rock.' Patricia wrapped herself in the woollen blanket and subsided onto the horsehair sofa with a groan. 'Maybe a rock would be softer,' she muttered, closing her eyes.

Rosalind settled herself as best she could in the armchair by the fire, which had burned down to ashes. She could imagine what Bertie would say when they had failed to return home this evening, but the prospect of a day out in London was too exciting to resist. She could only hope that Hester would have returned from Dawlish and taken charge. It had been a long day, and she was exhausted.

Next morning they breakfasted in the dining room with Claude, as Felicia was still asleep, and apparently rarely rose before midday. However, she was awake, although still in her nightgown when Rosalind and Patricia went upstairs, having enjoyed a hearty meal. Claude had said he liked to see young ladies with good appetites, although Rosalind suspected that it gave him an excuse to gorge himself on ham and eggs, toast and two pots of coffee.

Felicia paced the room, sipping tea from a delicate china cup. 'You girls cannot go to a fashionable event looking like scarecrows.'

'I'm sorry, Mama,' Rosalind said humbly. 'But we travelled light because we planned to return last evening, and we should really go home today.'

'I can't think why. The men can look after themselves for once. Surely you have servants?'

'We only have Hester, and she had to visit her sick aunt in Dawlish. I don't know when she'll return.'

'Well, the boys will have to fend for themselves. As to Sir Lucius, the last time I saw him he didn't even recognise me.' Felicia placed her cup and saucer on the table. 'I have gowns that should fit both of you. I've managed to keep my figure, thank goodness. Come into my boudoir and I'll find something suitable for both of you.'

Patricia pushed past Rosalind. 'How exciting. I haven't had a new gown for ages, Mama. And you have such lovely clothes. May I be first?'

Felicia smiled proudly. 'You are so like me, my darling. I always wanted nice things, and now I have them. Your papa was never interested in anything other than his wretched plants. I could have worn a sack and he wouldn't have noticed. Now Claude is another matter. He loves to see me wearing nice clothes.' She hesitated in the doorway. 'Come along, Rosalind. You hide your light under a bushel, but you could be very pretty if you only took more trouble with your appearance.'

'Yes, Mama.' Rosalind tucked her work-worn hands behind her back as she followed her mother into her bedchamber.

The Crystal Palace covered seventeen acres of Hyde Park and it was the most amazing sight that Rosalind had ever seen. Constructed of steel and glass, it was a magnificent edifice with fountains playing outside, creating the impression that the whole world was sparkling in the reflected sunlight. Flags of all countries fluttered in the breeze and there was a constant stream of vehicles drawing up outside to deposit crowds of well-dressed, well-off visitors at the entrance. Escorted by Claude, they entered the vast exhibition hall. Rosalind gazed around in awe. It was so light and very warm, like being in the greenhouse at home on a hot summer's day, but the things on show were truly breathtaking. There were huge trees growing beneath the glass roof, an enormous pink glass fountain, and a model of an elephant, complete with a canopied howdah. Rosalind was dazzled by the colours and richness of everything she saw. In the exhibit from

India were the Koh-i-Noor diamond and the Daria-i-Noor, a beautiful pink diamond, plus countless other gems.

There were marvels on show from all over the world, involving every type of modern invention. There was even a machine that could manufacture cigarettes, the latest fashion in smoking, patented, so the ticket read, by a French inventor. There were Cossack uniforms and furs from Russia, and a gigantic lump of gold from Chile, weighing over a hundred pounds. In fact there were so many amazing sights that after an hour of edging through the crowds Felicia declared herself exhausted and dying of thirst. Claude, who had come under sufferance, suggested that they visit the central tea room for refreshments. Patricia accepted instantly, but Rosalind said she wanted to see as much as she could before they had to leave. They arranged to meet later and Rosalind was left to her own devices.

She was admiring a life-sized plaster statue of Richard the Lionheart on horseback when she realised that someone was standing closer than felt comfortable. She turned her head and was astonished to see the man from the opera house. He met her gaze with a nod and a smile.

'I believe we have met before.'

'No. I don't think so.' Rosalind edged away from him.

'You were at the Royal Opera House last evening. I sent you champagne.'

'So it was from you.'

'It was a form of introduction, Miss Carey.'

'You know my name?'

'I made it my business to discover the identity of the beautiful young lady who attended the opera without an escort.'

'My mother . . .'

'She is the celebrated opera singer, Felicia Carey.'

'I don't accept gifts from strangers, sir.' The handsome young man seemed genuine enough, but Rosalind had the feeling that he was laughing at her. 'Please leave me alone.'

'It's not the thing for a young woman to be on her own. Even in this illustrious crowd there are pickpockets, and people who are ready to prey on those who are not so well versed in the ways of the world.'

'I am not on my own. I'm going to join my family in the . . .' She turned away. 'Please don't follow me,' she added as he fell into step beside her.

'I'm not following you, Miss Carey. I merely want to pay my respects to your mama.'

'You are acquainted with my mother?'

'Yes, of course. Would I be speaking to you like this if I were a complete stranger?'

There seemed little point in arguing with someone who was so determined to accompany her to the tea room, but Rosalind marched on, keeping slightly ahead. She was beginning to realise that people in London thought and behaved in quite a different manner to the people she knew at home. Or perhaps she had led such a sheltered life in the old castle that she herself was out of step with the rest of the world. She came to a halt as the gentleman, for it was obvious that he was a man of some breeding and substance, opened the door to the noisy refreshment room. It was crowded but she could see her mother, Claude and Patricia seated beneath a potted palm. Rosalind made her way between the packed tables to join them. She knew the man was following her and it made her uneasy, but to her surprise her mother looked up and smiled with genuine pleasure.

'Piers! How lovely to see you here. If you'd told me you were coming you could have accompanied us.'

He bowed over her hand. 'Good afternoon, Felicia. It's always a pleasure to be in your company.' He nodded to Claude. 'I'm surprised to see you here. I didn't think you were interested in this sort of show.'

Claude flushed uncomfortably. 'I'm not a philistine, Blanchard.'

'Of course not, Claude.' Piers smiled urbanely.

'Who are you?' Rosalind demanded crossly. 'Everyone seems to know you, apart from my sister and myself.'

'I'm sorry, my dear.' Felicia's eyes sparkled with mischief. 'This gentleman is Piers Blanchard. He might just have the answer you've been seeking.'

Forgetting her manners, Rosalind stared at him in surprise. 'I don't understand.'

'Piers is a distant cousin, and he is the heir to the family estate.' Felicia smiled and raised her teacup in a toast. 'I would love to see my husband's face when he finds out that he is dispossessed.'

Chapter Four

Rosalind sank down on a chair next to Claude. 'But that's impossible, Mama. I know the family history only too well. It was drummed into us by our last governess.'

'Yes,' Patricia added eagerly. 'Giles Blanchard was given the land by King William after the Conquest. He married heiress Bertha Chaldon, who died in childbirth and her son was stillborn. Giles never remarried and he willed the estate to his cousin, Simon de Carey.'

Felicia patted the empty seat next to her. 'Do sit down, Piers. Tell my girls what really happened all those years ago.'

He nodded but remained standing, fixing his gaze on Rosalind. 'Of course we can never know exactly what occurred, but the documents I discovered prove that Bertha gave birth to twin boys, and one of them survived.'

'That doesn't make sense,' Rosalind said, frowning. 'If one child lived, why did our ancestor leave everything to his cousin, Simon?'

'Bertha had a younger sister, Mathilda, who was plain and cursed with a crookback.' Piers pulled up a chair and sat down. 'Mathilda was jealous of her beautiful sister and she took the surviving baby, bribing the midwife to keep silent. As far as the grieving father was concerned he had lost both his wife and son.'

'What happened then?' Patricia leaned forward on her seat, agog with anticipation. 'Did she flee the country, taking the baby with her?'

'No, but she did leave the county. She was wealthy in her own right and she moved to Cornwall, where she bought a manor house on the coast. She changed her name to Mathilda Blanchard, and had the child christened Piers. It seems that she might have wanted her adopted son to claim his birthright, but for some reason we'll never know, that didn't happen.'

'So you say that you are related to us.' Rosalind gave him a searching look. 'What do you want?'

Felicia shook her head. 'That's not very polite, Rosalind.'

'We are distant cousins,' Piers said, smiling. 'Does that bother you?'

'No. Why should it? But Mama said you own Rockwood, but that can't be true.'

'Mathilda might have been crippled but she was

66

no fool. She had everything documented, including registering Piers' father as Giles Blanchard in the parish records.'

'Why didn't Piers claim Rockwood when his father died?' Rosalind said warily. 'It sounds very far-fetched.'

'As I said before, there's no way of knowing. Piers already had Trevenor, his estate in Cornwall, and a large inheritance from Mathilda. Maybe she didn't reveal his true identity or maybe he was satisfied with what he already had.'

Rosalind gave him a searching look. 'If you knew that you were the heir to Rockwood, why didn't you come forward sooner?'

'A good question.' Piers eyed her with a lazy smile. 'I stumbled on the secret by chance when going through old documents after my father died. I couldn't understand why Mathilda, who had never married, changed her name from Chaldon to Blanchard, and so I did some research, which led me to the Careys and Rockwood. I'd read an article about Felicia Carey in *The Times* and as I'm rather fond of opera I decided to make myself known to her – and here we are.'

'You might be able to prove that you are the heir to Rockwood,' Rosalind said coldly. 'But do you really want a bankrupt estate?'

'Rosalind, you're being tiresome,' Felicia said crossly. 'Piers will be doing the family a huge favour if he takes Rockwood off our hands.'

'Are you speaking for Papa?' Rosalind demanded. 'Or is this of some benefit to you?'

'Don't speak to your mama in that tone,' Claude said stiffly.

'I can handle this, Claude.' Felicia dismissed him with a wave of her hand. 'Rosalind, you will apologise at once. You've insulted both Piers and myself by inferring that there has been some sort of collusion between us.'

Rosalind met her mother's angry gaze with a stubborn lift of her chin. 'No, Mama. I stand by what I said. Since Papa isn't here to defend himself and his property, I feel I have to speak on his behalf.'

'Surely Sir Lucien is the landowner?' Piers looked to Felicia for an answer. 'I believe he holds the title of baronet.'

'My esteemed father-in-law is very eccentric,' Felicia said bitterly. 'Or in common parlance, he's mad as a hatter.'

'He's an old man, Mama.' Rosalind loved her grandfather, in spite of everything, and the last thing she wanted was for his name to be bandied about in public. 'My grandfather was a hero of the Napoleonic naval battles, sir.'

'And Papa is abroad, hunting for rare plants that will restore our fortune,' Patricia added, inching closer to Rosalind. 'He'll come home and then everything will be as it was when I was little.'

Felicia shot her a pitying glance. 'Poor deluded girl. Your papa is a dreamer, as is Walter, and I'm

68

afraid Bertie is little better. I suppose he's still hoping for a commission in the army, which will never happen.'

Rosalind rose to her feet. 'I don't think there is any point in continuing this conversation, Mama. I think it's time that Patsy and I made our way to the railway station.'

A look of genuine surprise flitted across Felicia's beautiful face. 'But I thought you would stay a little longer. You've only just met Piers. There will be family matters to discuss.'

Piers shook his head. 'I've no intention of upsetting the Carey family in any way. Rockwood Castle might belong to me legally, but I have no plans to take it from you, Rosalind.'

'Do you expect us to live there as if we were tenants on the estate?' She faced him angrily. 'That will never happen.'

'Did I say anything about demanding rent?' Piers' tone was serious although there was a glint of mischief in his eyes. For a brief moment Rosalind felt drawn to him as a person, but the feeling was gone in an instant.

'Don't laugh at me, Mr Blanchard,' she said with as much dignity as she could muster. 'Come along, Patsy. It's time we were on our way.' She turned to her mother, who was clutching Claude's hand. She seemed genuinely upset, but Rosalind knew that her mother was a consummate actress who could summon up tears and just as quickly turn them into laughter.

'You left your valise at the hotel, Rosalind,' Felicia said with a pitiful break in her voice.

'Does that mean we have to give you back your gowns, Mama?' Patricia asked wistfully.

'No, of course not, my darling. I've been able to do little enough for my girls, so if it pleases you they are yours to keep.'

Patricia's face brightened. 'Thank you, Mama.'

'We brought very little with us, so perhaps you will send the valise to Rockwood by carrier,' Rosalind said firmly. 'We really should get a cab to the railway station.'

'I'll find you a cab, Miss Carey.' Piers rose to his feet.

Patricia gave her mother a hug. 'Goodbye, Mama. Please come and visit us at home when you get time.'

'My darling child, of course I will.' Felicia reached into her reticule for her hanky. 'Claude, make sure you keep a day or two free before we travel to Vienna. I want to see my boys before we leave.'

'Thank you for putting us up last night, Mama,' Rosalind said stiffly. 'Thank you for the dinner, Claude, and for bringing us to the exhibition. It's something I'll never forget.'

Claude made a half-hearted attempt to stand, but seemed to think better of it and sank back on his chair. 'It was nice to get to know you, Rosalind, and you, too, Patricia. We will definitely visit Rockwood before we go on our next tour.'

'Goodbye, Mama. Goodbye, Claude.' Rosalind

followed Piers from the refreshment room with Patricia hurrying after them.

Piers came to a halt outside and with an imperious wave of his hand he caught the attention of a cabby, who had been about to drive off. 'Would you like me to accompany you to the station, Rosalind?' Piers handed her into the cab.

'Thank you, but we can manage perfectly well on our own.'

'Perhaps it would be a good idea, Rosie?' Patricia said nervously. 'It's so busy in London.'

'If you have the time, then perhaps it would help if you accompanied us, Piers.' Rosalind did care to admit that her purse was extremely light. If Piers Blanchard was a gentleman he might offer to pay the cabby. 'If you're sure it's not too much trouble.'

He climbed in and sat down opposite them. 'I expect you both want to know more about me. I can understand that.'

Rosalind met his humorous gaze with a direct look. 'I don't know why you find all this so amusing. It's not funny at all. What do I tell my brothers?'

'I am not the enemy.'

'What are you then, Mr Blanchard?' Rosalind leaned forward in an attempt to distance herself from the smell of stale tobacco and cheap pomade that lingered in the worn leather squabs. She did not want to appear hostile, although she was struggling to make sense of the man who seemed prepared to turn their lives upside down simply to prove a point.

'Are you going to save us from destitution?' Patricia asked plaintively. 'I'm so tired of being poor.'

'We're not poor,' Rosalind said hastily. 'We are rich compared to some of the people in the village.'

'But we haven't got much money.' Patricia protested. 'You wouldn't have had to visit that horrible little shop in Exeter where you pawned Grandmama's locket if we were well off.'

'I'm sure that Mr Blanchard doesn't want to know things like that,' Rosalind said hastily.

Piers glanced out of the window. 'It's a lovely spring day. Perhaps I'll accompany you to Rockwood.'

'But you can't do that,' Rosalind said in dismay. 'You'll upset Grandpapa, and I need to speak to my brothers before you descend upon us.'

He laughed. 'You make me sound like one of the plagues of Egypt. I'll probably be the best thing to happen to your crumbling castle in many a year.'

'You can't travel without your luggage.' Rosalind clutched her hands tightly in her lap. 'See us off, by all means, but you will meet with considerable opposition from my family. Careys have lived at Rockwood for centuries. What happens to us affects the whole village.'

'Now that is impressive. I can't wait to get acquainted with my long-lost relatives and the castle where my ancestor was born. As to my personal effects, I'll send a message from the station. My man, Trigg, will bring my luggage.'

'You have a valet?' Patricia's eyes widened. 'Do

you have many servants at Trevenor? That is the name of your home, isn't it?'

'Yes, I suppose I have quite a few people looking after me.'

'But you aren't married.' Patricia leaned forward, her eyes alert with interest.

'Patsy, you don't ask questions like that,' Rosalind said hastily. 'It's rude.'

'But honest.' Piers turned to Rosalind, smiling. 'No, I am not married. I have yet to meet a woman who can put up with me.'

'That I can believe,' Rosalind said with feeling. 'We're very grateful for the cab ride to the station, but I wouldn't dream of putting you out by asking you to leave London in such a hurry. We really can manage on our own, and if you wish to visit Rockwood, it would help if you gave us some warning.'

He held up his hands. 'I understand, and I do have some business to complete in London, so if you're sure you can cope . . .'

'I'm very sure,' Rosalind said firmly. 'Thank you.'

It was almost dark by the time Farmer Greep's cart bumped its way along the lane that led to Rockwood Castle. Rosalind had felt every rut and stone on the road since they left the railway station in Exeter. She was stiff, sore, and exhausted. It had been a long journey and at times she wished that she had accepted Piers' offer to accompany them. He would almost certainly have paid for them to travel first-class instead of third, and they had suffered accordingly. At times the compartment had been packed with travellers of all ages, shapes and sizes, including a few animals, and the wooden seats had been unforgiving, although not quite as uncomfortable as the farmer's wagon. However, they were almost home, and riding in Farmer Greep's ancient vehicle was better than walking.

The cart rolled to a halt. 'I can't take you maids no further. I need to get home meself.'

Rosalind lowered herself to the ground, followed by Patricia, who stumbled and would have fallen if her sister had not caught her.

'Thank you, Mr Greep,' Rosalind said breathlessly. 'Are you sure I can't pay you for your trouble. You have come out of your way to bring us home.'

He tipped his billycock hat. 'No, Miss Carey. You'm all right. I recall many times in the past when your pa helped us out, so I'm more than happy to give 'ee a lift.' He flicked the reins and his horse ambled off into the darkness, which had fallen on them like a velvet cloak.

Accompanied by the gentle sound of the waves lapping the shore at high tide and the occasional hoot of an owl, Rosalind and Patricia walked hand in hand, quickening their pace as the castellated towers came into view against a starlit sky. Rockwood Castle stood squarely in the landscape, a symbol of security and defiance against the outside world.

Rosalind felt a surge of emotion as they approached their home. The Royalist Careys had successfully defended the castle against Cromwell's Roundheads, withstanding a long siege. If they could do that then surely she and her family could protect their heritage from someone like Piers Blanchard.

Patricia staggered, tripping over her own feet. 'I just want to go to bed and sleep, Rosie.'

Rosalind opened the massive iron gates that led into the bailey and the rusty hinges groaned in protest. There was a flicker of candlelight in the east tower, which meant that their grandfather was still on watch. She sighed, thinking of the conversation they had had in London, and her mother's careless assumption that Grandpapa was insane. He was definitely eccentric and often deluded when memories of the past overcame his sense of reality, but at other times he was his old self: kind, amusing and very wise. Rosalind braced her shoulders – she was home now and she would protect her family, no matter what.

'Why have you stopped?' Patricia demanded peevishly.

'It's late and if I knock on the door it will disturb everyone. We'll go round the kitchen entrance, Patsy. You can go straight to your room, if you like, and I'll bring you some bread and butter and a cup of tea.'

'I hope Hester is back.'

'So do I. She'll have a kettle on the hob and

something tasty for us to eat.' Spurred on by that prospect, Rosalind led the way. The kitchen and the outbuildings containing the wash house were reached through a door in the wall, and the courtyard was in darkness. If Hester was at home there would have been light pooling on the cobblestones. Rosalind feared the worst. The back door was unlocked, but the kitchen was cold and there was no fire in the range. She felt along the mantelshelf for the metal tin where Hester kept the matches, and lit a candle. As she had suspected, nothing had been done since they left for London. The stone sink was piled high with unwashed dishes, cups and bowls, the pine table was covered in crumbs, empty bottles and crumpled newspapers, and ashes spilled out of the grate.

'It will take a while to get the fire going, Patsy.' Rosalind lit another candle. 'Take this and go to bed. I'll be up as soon as I can.'

'I should stay and help you. Bertie and Walter are useless.'

Rosalind laid her shawl over the back of a chair and took off her bonnet. 'I hope they've been looking after Grandpapa. Anyway, don't worry. I'll sort it out. You get some rest.'

'Thank you.' Patricia blew her sister a kiss as she mounted the stairs. 'You're too good to me, Rosie.'

Rosalind smiled to herself as she rolled up her sleeves and set to work to clean the grate and light the fire. She had fallen into the role of mother by default when Mama decided that she had to follow her career 'or die' – Felicia's words exactly. It had not been a hardship, but now Rosalind was beginning to lose patience with her idle brothers. She went into the larder and found that the loaves she had baked before her trip to London had disappeared, leaving nothing but crumbs. The boys had also consumed all the butter and eggs. She was not in a mood to be tactful when Bertie swanned into the kitchen, followed by Bob, who hurled himself at her, trying to lick her hands and face.

'You're home, Rosie,' Bertie said, smiling stupidly. 'We've missed you.'

'You've been drinking.'

'Just a couple of pints with Barnaby Yelland and Tom Nosworthy. You and Patsy were having a wonderful time in London, so you can't begrudge me a drink or two.'

Rosalind petted the dog, but her attention was focused on her brother. 'You were supposed to be looking after Grandpapa and keeping an eye on Walter. There isn't a crust of bread left.'

'We had to eat, and you're the only one who can cook.' Bertie sank down on the nearest chair. 'Hester sent a message saying she'll be back tomorrow, so we had to look after ourselves. Anyway, you should have returned sooner.'

At that moment the kettle on the hob emitted a gust of steam and Rosalind busied herself making a pot of tea. 'This is the last of the tea leaves, Bertie.

My trip to London was to try to raise money to get us out of trouble.'

'Well, did you? Did our famous mother pay up?'

'No, she didn't. What's more, I was introduced to a man who says he's the rightful heir to Rockwood and he can prove it.'

'He's a trickster. Careys have owned Rockwood for centuries.'

'You'll be able to decide for yourself, Bertie. He's planning to visit us, so you'd better be prepared because he has a very believable story.' Rosalind filled a cup with tea and passed it to him. 'Drink this. Maybe it will clear your brain.'

'There's no milk.'

'Did you go to the farm to collect some?' Rosalind sighed. 'No, of course you did not. How do you think we manage every day, Bertie?'

He shook his head. 'I don't know.'

'That's the trouble. You spend all your time hunting or fishing.'

'I put food on the table,' Bertie said crossly. 'What else can I do?'

'You could try to find work and earn some money. We need pounds, shillings and pence, Bertie. We can't survive on air, and this man Piers Blanchard is obviously wealthy. We don't stand a chance of keeping Rockwood if he decides he wants to turn us out.'

'I'd join the army, but I haven't the money to buy a commission.'

'You could enlist.'

'I suppose you think that's hilarious. A Carey of Rockwood enlisting with the commoners.'

'Can you think of any other way, Bertie? I'm deadly serious. We have to do something or we'll lose Rockwood through bankruptcy anyway.'

'It's getting late and my head is aching. I'm going to bed. We'll talk about it in the morning.' Bertie drank his tea and stood up to make his way somewhat unsteadily from the room. 'Stop worrying, Rosie. We're Careys, we'll be all right.'

Rosalind filled a cup with tea and took it upstairs to Patricia, Bob trotting along at her heels, but Patricia was stretched out on her bed, sound asleep. Rosalind covered her with a quilt, and drew the curtains before going to her own room. She was tired, but she was too agitated to sleep and she sat on the window seat, sipping the rapidly cooling tea, Bob curled up at her feet. She gazed out onto the shadowy rose garden with the estuary twisting like a silver ribbon towards the sea. This was home and she would do anything she could to stop Piers Blanchard from taking it away from them.

Hester arrived in style next morning, seated in a trap beside her gentleman friend, Jacob Lidstone. Jacob had been butler to Lady Jane Patterson until her death, when the estate near Teignmouth was sold, and the new owners had brought in their own servants. Rosalind had never been able to understand why a smart, well-spoken man like Jacob had not found a new position, but she suspected that it was his devotion to Hester that prevented him moving too far away. He had, to Rosalind's knowledge, been courting Hester for twelve years and yet he had not proposed marriage.

Rosalind went into the yard to greet them with Bob at her side.

'Good morning, Hester. How is your aunt?'

'Fair to middling, Miss Rosalind. But no worse, thank the Lord. She's cheerful as ever, bless her soul. My cousin Mary is going to look after her from now on, so that's a weight off my mind.' Hester climbed down from the trap. 'Thank you kindly, Jacob.'

He tipped his hat. 'I'll call on Mrs Penrice tomorrow, Hester. I'll let you know how she's faring.'

'Thank you, my dear. 'Tis very much appreciated.'

'I'll see you in church on Sunday, Hester.'

'Yes, indeed. Goodbye, Jacob.' Hester gave him a beaming smile before bustling into the kitchen. She set her carpet bag down on the table. 'I'm sorry I've been away so long, Miss Rosalind. My aunt was quite poorly when I got there, but she's perked up a lot now and Mary is very capable.'

'You were missed, but if you need to look after her in the future you must feel free to do so,' Rosalind said firmly. 'I've been away myself, which explains why not much cleaning has been done. I've started off the bread dough, and I've left it to prove, but I must go to the farm to get milk, eggs and butter.'

Hester took off her bonnet and shawl, tut-tutting as she glanced around the kitchen. 'You shouldn't be doing this sort of work, Miss Rosalind. It isn't right. You should send one of they idle boys to run errands for you.'

Rosalind turned away to hide a smile. Hester had started work at the castle when she was little more than a child herself, and she had watched them all grow up. It was obvious that she still thought of Bertie and Walter as small boys who needed a firm hand.

'I would enjoy the walk,' Rosalind said mildly. 'Bertie has gone out with his gun, so he might bring home something for dinner. Patricia and Walter are going through the rare editions in the library, trying to find some that might fetch a good price. We've precious little else to sell.'

Hester shook her head and attacked the dough, punching it down with her fists as if it were her worst enemy. 'I don't know what the world is coming to. I remember the days when I first came here and this was the finest house in the county. The parties your grandparents gave when Sir Lucius came ashore were the social events not to be missed by anyone who was anyone.'

'That was part of the trouble,' Rosalind said, sighing. 'Anyway, I'd better be off. We all have our work to do.' She picked up a wicker basket and was about to walk out of the kitchen when Hester called her back.

'You've forgotten your bonnet, Miss Rosalind. You'll ruin your complexion if you go out in the sun without a hat or a parasol.'

Rosalind plucked her straw bonnet from a peg at the back of the door and rammed it on her head. 'Anything to keep you happy, Hester.' She chuckled as she walked out into the warm May sunshine. With Hester working away in the kitchen it felt as though things were normal once again and the threat from Piers Blanchard had faded with the morning mist. What would a man like him want with a run-down castle miles away from London, and one that was on the verge of bankruptcy?

Swinging her basket, Rosalind strolled across the deer park, which was now empty of all livestock, the herd having been sold to Sir Michael Greystone over a year ago. She missed seeing the newborn fawns with their mothers, but she knew they were well cared for on the Greystone estate. The money raised by their sale had kept them throughout a long hard winter, and now she must think of something else. Piers Blanchard might think them an easy target if he discovered the true state of their finances. She did not trust him and she did not like him, and yet there was something about him that seemed vaguely familiar. She sighed; he would have a fight on his hands if he tried to take Rockwood away from them.

She walked on in a more hopeful mood, skirting the backwater and enjoying the clean air redolent of clover and the tang of salt from the marshes on the far side of the estuary. A short cut through the woods to the south of the estate would take her to Greep's farm, and she loved to see the carpet of bluebells beneath the ancient oaks. Their fresh green leaves created dappled shade and it was much cooler beneath the trees. The undergrowth thickened and brambles shot out long prickly tendrils as they invaded new territory. Rosalind made her way around a particularly large holly bush and found her skirts snagged on broken branch. She bent down to unhitch the material and was suddenly aware that she was not alone.

Chapter Five

'I didn't expect to see you here, Rosalind.'

She snatched her skirt free. At any other time she would have been careful not to tear the material, but she was startled and angry. 'Mr Blanchard! I could say the same about you.'

'Piers, please. I think we should agree to be less formal.'

Rosalind straightened up. 'Why have you come here? I asked you to give me some warning.'

'I had to satisfy my curiosity. I did tell you that I'd pay you a visit.'

'Yes, you did, but why didn't you come to the castle and announce yourself instead of creeping around like a thief?'

He laughed. 'I can't steal what's legally mine.'

'So you do intend to take our home from us?'

'You seem determined to cast me in the role of

villain. As I said before, I have no intention of evicting you or your family. I wanted to get an idea of the exact layout of the estate before I made my presence known.'

'Why? What difference does it make if you don't intend to live here?'

'I am not the enemy, Rosalind. I might even be able to help you out of your present difficulties. From what you said in London and from the remarks that your mother let slip, I gather that the estate is facing bankruptcy.'

'I really don't understand any of this, Piers. What do you expect from us?'

'I could say that it was the satisfaction of knowing I had regained my birthright, but I am a businessman, Rosalind. I might find some benefit from having a property in this area.'

'What sort of business?'

'I inherited the family china clay mine near St Austell and I hope one day to own a small fleet of ships, which will transport the clay all over the world.'

'If you're so rich and successful, why on earth would you want to saddle yourself with Rockwood?'

'Call it sentiment, if you like.'

She eyed him curiously. 'You don't look like a man who's led by his emotions. If you're a hard-headed businessman I would have thought that saving Rockwood Castle would be the last thing on your mind.'

'Perhaps I have a softer side to my nature.'

'I think you're playing games with us, and I have an errand to run, so you'll have to excuse me.'

'Maybe I could accompany you?' He picked up the wicker basket she had dropped and handed it to her. 'You could tell me more about your family. I've met Patricia but I believe you have two brothers.'

'Yes, and you'll meet them later, if you decide to stay on.'

'I do indeed. I haven't come all this way just to pass the time of day, Rosalind. Now where are we going on this fine May morning?' He fell into step beside her.

'I'm going to the farm to collect eggs, milk, butter and cheese.'

'That sounds as if it might be expensive.'

'I have an agreement with Farmer Greep. He lives rent free in return for some of his produce.'

'That sounds like a very good arrangement for the farmer.'

'You know nothing of our circumstances. It has served us well in the past.' Rosalind quickened her pace and they emerged from the cool shade into brilliant sunshine.

She shot him a sideways glance. 'Why don't you tell me more about yourself? I find it very odd that you chose to visit my mother in London when you discovered that you were the rightful heir to Rockwood. Why didn't you come here and speak to Grandpapa?'

'Your mother told me that he isn't in command of his full senses.'

'You weren't to know that when you decided to claim your inheritance. I'm not sure I believe your story, Piers.'

'It's true that I had business in London, and I did intend to come here afterwards, but when I discovered that your mother was appearing at the Royal Opera House, I couldn't resist the temptation to meet her. I had seen her once before when she appeared at the Paris Opera.'

Rosalind was still suspicious, but it was obvious that he was not ready to divulge his true reason for making himself known to them. She decided to change the subject.

'You're a businessman and you like opera. That much I know, but what about your family? Do they live with you in Cornwall?'

He smiled. 'I love the way you get straight to the point, Rosalind. Most women ask things in a round-about manner, but not you.'

'It's more or less the question you asked me. Are your parents still living? Have you any brothers and sisters?'

'My parents are both dead, but my grandmother, Lady Pentelow, lives with me at Trevenor, as does my sister, Aurelia, who has all the eligible young men in the county competing for her hand. My brother, Alexander, is a captain in the 32nd Regiment of Foot.'

87

'I see.' Rosalind had not imagined Piers Blanchard to be a family man. He had admitted that he was unmarried when they met in London, and she had not given his situation at home much thought. However, the knowledge that he looked after his grandmother and sister had done something to soften his image in her mind.

'I leave running the household to my grandmother, who rules the family with a rod of iron. Aurelia is much in demand when it comes to assemblies and balls, and I try to avoid the young men who follow her like devoted spaniels.'

They lapsed into silence as they crossed a field where cows grazed peacefully, and a startled skylark rose into the air warbling its beautiful song in an attempt to guide them away from its nest amongst the clumps of grass. They came to a stile and Rosalind was about to negotiate it, as she had done more times than she could count, when Piers came to her aid. To refuse would make her look childish and petty, and reluctantly she accepted his help.

'The farm is just over the rise,' Rosalind said casually. 'Do you still want to accompany me? Or would you rather explore on your own?'

'I want to get to know Rockwood village and its inhabitants, but that can wait. I'd like to meet your tenants.'

'I dare say that Farmer Greep is out in the fields somewhere, but his wife is a pleasant soul. Her family have lived in Rockwood for as long as the Careys, or maybe even longer.'

'I suggest you don't mention my reasons for being here. Just say I'm a visitor. There's no need to tell them anything else, as yet.'

Rosalind laughed. 'You obviously don't live in a village, Piers. I imagine word has gone round already. But I won't say anything, not yet, anyway.'

An hour later Rosalind entered the kitchen at Rockwood, followed by Piers. She placed her full basket on the table and Piers added a pail of milk, some of which had been spilled on the way home. Mrs Greep had taken an instant liking to Piers and had insisted on lending them the milk pail, suggesting coyly that he might like to return it when empty. Rosalind had teased him all the way home, and to her surprise he had taken it good-naturedly. She realised that Hester was staring pointedly at Piers with her lips pursed and her arms folded tightly across her bosom.

'Who is this, Miss Rosalind?'

'This gentleman is Mr Blanchard, Hester. He's a friend of Mama's.'

'You didn't say we was expecting a visitor,' Hester said huffily. 'Will he be staying for dinner?'

Rosalind drew her aside. 'He's a guest in our home, Hester. Be polite.'

'The spare rooms haven't been used for years. A bed will need airing if he's going to stay. What will we feed him on? He looks as if he's got a good appetite, and judging by his clothes he's a gentleman, used to the finer things.'

'We were just discussing practicalities, Piers,' Rosalind said apologetically. 'Hester has such a lot to do. We have the bare minimum of help.'

'We have none.' Hester faced Piers with narrowed eyes. 'We manage on our own.'

'Please don't go to any trouble on my account, Hester,' Piers said with a disarming smile. 'I came uninvited so I don't want to put you to any inconvenience. 'My valet, Trigg, will be here soon. We'll put up at the local inn.'

'I'm sure we can manage.' Rosalind sent a warning glance to Hester.

'Your man can sleep in the servants' quarters, sir,' Hester said reluctantly. 'I expect we can make a room ready for you, as long as you don't mind a damp mattress and a bit of mould.'

Rosalind glanced out of the open door and saw Bertie striding across the yard with his gun over his arm. 'You wanted to meet the rest of my family, Piers. My brother Bertie is the provider of an endless supply of game.'

Bertie breezed into the kitchen, grinning broadly as he tossed his trophies on the table. 'I have a fancy for rabbit pie for dinner tonight, Hester.' He shot a curious glance in Piers' direction. 'I didn't know we were expecting company, Rosie.'

'Piers Blanchard.' Piers stepped forward, holding out his hand. 'How do you do?'

'Bertram Carey.' Bertie shook hands. 'My friends call me Bertie.'

'I met Piers in London, Bertie. He knows Mama.' Rosalind made an effort to sound casual, but she could see that Bertie was not going to be fobbed off easily. 'Why don't we go to the drawing room? Will you bring us some coffee, please, Hester?'

Hester gave her a meaningful look. 'The grocer hasn't delivered yet, Miss Rosalind.'

'Will you show Piers to the drawing room, Bertie?' Rosalind turned to Hester, frowning. 'I need to have a few words with Hester.'

Bertie strolled off with his Manton shotgun broken over his arm. 'Are you a shooting man, Piers?'

Piers' response was lost as Rosalind closed the door. 'Why are you being like this, Hester?'

'Who is this man? I don't like the cut of his jib.'

'That's as may be, but you'll have to try harder. I can't go into it now but he comes from Cornwall and he claims that he owns Rockwood Castle and the whole estate.'

Hester's eyes widened and she sank down on the nearest chair. 'I don't believe it.'

'I find it hard, too. I'm not going to accept his word on it, but if it is true he could throw us all out onto the street, if he so wished.'

'The villagers won't let that happen, Miss Rosalind.

If I tell Ned Causley at the Black Dog he'll muster everyone in the county to support us. We fought off the Roundheads – we can do the same to an upstart from the other side of the Tamar.'

'There won't be any need for that, but I must find out if Mr Blanchard's claim is genuine. In the meantime we have to get some groceries. Tell Jim Gurney to take Ajax and the trap to Hannaford's shop with a list of everything you need.'

'But Joe Hannaford won't give us any more credit. You know that.'

'Tell Jim to promise Mr Hannaford that his bills will be settled in full before the end of the week.'

Hester rolled her eyes. 'We've tried that one before. Joe won't be fooled a second time.'

'Jim should say that a wealthy relative is visiting us. It will be common knowledge in the village by now if I know Dora Greep. She's the biggest gossip in Rockwood.' Rosalind was about to open the door but she hesitated. 'Have you seen my grandfather this morning?'

'I took him his breakfast in the morning parlour about half an hour ago. Miss Patsy said she wasn't hungry, which is just as well because I used the last of the oats to make porridge for Sir Lucius, and Master Walter finished off what was left.'

'Where is Walter?'

'I think he went to the library. He spends nearly all his time there – it ain't natural for a young man to have his head stuck in a book all day.'

'That's the least of my worries. Write that list, Hester, and I'll help you to get the solar in the west tower ready.' Rosalind made her way to the drawing room, where she found Piers and Bertie chatting away like old friends.

Bertie looked up and grinned. 'Piers has a brother in the 32nd Foot. He thinks he could help me to get a commission. What do you say to that, Rosie?'

She stared at her brother in amazement. 'But you know a commission is out of the question, and I thought you'd changed your mind about joining the army if you had to enlist, Bertie.'

Bertie turned to Piers. 'The trouble is, as I mentioned, we're a bit financially embarrassed at the moment.'

'You needn't worry about that, Bertie. If your heart is set on a career in the military, I would be happy to help.'

'I'd be very grateful, of course, but why would you do that for me? I hardly know you, Blanchard.'

Piers turned to Rosalind. 'Shall I tell him, or will you?'

'Tell me what?' Bertie demanded angrily. 'I'm not a child. What is it that Rosie knows but I do not?'

'He'll have to know sooner or later,' Rosalind said reluctantly.

'I only discovered the truth about my ancestry very recently, Bertie. As I said earlier we are distantly related.'

'Related? How?' Bertie shrugged. 'We haven't got

any relatives, have we, Rosie? You're the one who knows about these things.'

Rosalind sank down on a damask-covered sofa that was sadly faded and threadbare in large patches. 'I didn't think we had any living relatives until I met Piers. But, it's a long story and I suggest we wait until all the family are together at dinner tonight, and then I'll introduce Piers to everyone, including Grandpapa.'

'That's not good enough,' Bertie said firmly. 'What are you keeping from me, Rosie?'

'Piers seems to have a genuine claim to Rockwood. He'll tell you in more detail.'

Bertie gave Piers a searching look. 'Can you prove it?'

'I could get copies of the documents substantiating my claim, but before we go any further I want you to know that I have no intention of evicting any of you. As far as I'm concerned we are all part of the same family.'

'Of which you are now the head.' Rosalind could not keep a hint of bitterness from her tone. 'You will have control over us whether we like it or not.'

'I have no intention of exerting my will over anyone. I have to say that I like what I've seen of Rockwood Castle and the estate, and I look forward to furthering my knowledge. I'm here to help, not to hinder.'

Bertie stared at him, frowning. 'I don't know what to make of all this.'

'We should give him a fair hearing,' Rosalind said hastily. 'That's why I suggested we discuss it over dinner tonight when we are all together. It affects each one of us.'

Bertie rose to his feet and picked up his gun. 'I need time to think. If it's true it means that I forgo my inheritance. Is that why you offered to purchase a commission for me, Blanchard? Were you trying to buy me off?'

'Certainly not. I think the army would be the making of you, Bertie.'

'You don't know me,' Bertie said stiffly. 'You can't just walk into our home and tell us that you're the legal heir.'

'I know how this must seem, Bertie, but I promise you that I'm not trying to rob you of your inheritance.'

'So you say now, but why else would you come here? Does it please you to patronise your poor relations?'

'Bertie! That's not fair.' Rosalind protested. 'At least we should give Piers a chance, and with our financial situation as it is, we need help.'

'I do my best to feed my family.' Bertie lovingly fingered the stock of his gun. 'What else can I do?'

'I must say that's a fine gun,' Piers said smoothly. 'Do you always bring it into the drawing room?' he added with a wry smile.

'No, but I don't want to leave it lying around. It's worth a small fortune and I'm lucky to have kept hold of it. Rosie went and pawned Grandmama's locket just to pay the fare to London. I suppose I should have sacrificed my Manton, but it provides us with food.'

'I'm only just beginning to realise the true extent of your financial problems,' Piers said thoughtfully.

Rosalind met this gaze with a challenging look. 'Perhaps you should think again about taking on our debts. They are quite considerable, and the roof leaks in so many places I've lost count.'

'If it's not an inconvenience, I'd like to stay for a few days so that I can take a proper look at the castle and the estate. I won't get in your way, and of course it depends upon what Sir Lucius says.'

'Have you seen Grandpapa today, Bertie?' Rosalind asked anxiously.

'He went out earlier. I expect he's gone to the cliffs to look for enemy vessels.' Bertie shrugged. 'I'm sorry, Rosie. I'm not going to pretend that the old fellow is sane, when clearly he is not.'

'After the experiences he went through during the sea battles, I think that Sir Lucius is entitled to be eccentric,' Piers said calmly. 'I would very much like to meet him. Perhaps you'd like to introduce me to him, Bertie?'

'Yes, I will, but don't expect too much.'

'Maybe we could take him for a glass of ale at the village inn,' Piers suggested, smiling. 'Sometimes it's easier to talk away from home.'

Bertie nodded. 'All right, I'll lock this away in

the gun room and then we'll be off. And don't worry about luncheon, Rosie. I'll take Piers to the Black Dog – Mrs Causley makes wonderful beefsteak pies. I haven't had one for ages and as he's so well-heeled I assume he'll be paying.'

'I'm sure Grandpapa would enjoy a pie and a glass of rum, but don't tell him everything, Piers.' Rosalind tried not to sound too relieved. At least that would give her time to decide how best to break the news to her grandfather.

Piers hesitated in the doorway. 'Would you like to join us?'

She laughed. 'That really would give the gossips something to talk about. No, thank you. I have plenty to do here.'

Rosalind waited until they had left before making her way to the library where Walter was studying one of the leather-bound tomes while Patricia sat on the window seat, gazing out across the deer park. She looked round with a start when Rosalind called her name.

'You were miles away, Patsy. I need your help.'

'I wasn't deliberately avoiding you,' Patricia said sheepishly. 'But I get so tired of sweeping and dusting. Could we hire a cleaning woman at least once a week?'

Walter looked up from the text he was studying. 'When my book of poems is published we'll have plenty of money.'

'Really, Walter?' Rosalind shook her head, smiling. 'Could you leave that for a moment and take a message to Abe Coaker? We need vegetables for dinner tonight, the best he can find, if there are any left in the clamp. We have a guest.'

'No, really?' Patricia jumped to her feet. 'Who is it? We haven't had any visitors for ages.'

Walter groaned. 'I'm really busy here, Rosie. Can you send someone else?' He sent a pleading look at Rosalind, but, meeting her stern gaze, he rose to his feet. 'All right, I'll go, but you've disturbed my train of thought.'

'You were reading, Walter, you weren't writing anything down, so a breath of fresh air will do you good. Anyway, it's an important meal this evening. Our guest is a man called Piers Blanchard and he claims to be a distant relative, so it's important that we're all here together.'

'That's the charming man we met in London,' Patricia said excitedly. 'I can't believe that he's travelled all the way to see us.'

'I'm not sure I believe everything he says, but he's a guest and we must treat him as such. I need you to help me to make a room ready, Patsy. Hester will see that Mr Blanchard's valet has accommodation in the servants' quarters.'

'He must be rich if he has a manservant.' Walter closed the book. 'I'll go, if it means so much to you. Let's hope this fellow is generous. He might help me to get my book published.'

'If you impress him with your best manners he might do just that,' Rosalind said with as much conviction as she could muster. Walter's education had ceased abruptly when his last tutor had left because he had not been paid for six months. By rights Walter should have gone to university, but with funds non-existent, there was no possibility of that – unless, of course, Piers Blanchard could be persuaded to help.

'There's something more, isn't there, Rosie?' Walter said slowly. 'Why has this man turned up now? What does he want?'

'He says that he's the rightful heir to the estate.'

'How do we know he isn't making it all up? Why should we believe him?'

Rosalind shook her head. 'Why would anyone want to take on a run-down castle and a pile of debts? I don't know if he's genuine or not, but we have to give him a chance to prove himself. I think we need to hear him out.'

Walter closed his book with unnecessary force. 'We'll see what Bertie has to say about this.'

'Bertie is taking Piers to the Black Dog. You may join them if you so wish, Walter. In the meantime we must treat him as we would any guest,' Rosalind said firmly. 'Come with me now, Patsy. If you go to the linen cupboard and take out the best sheets and pillowcases, I'll fetch the blankets from the cedar chest. By the way, Walter, on your way back from the kitchen garden, would you fetch kindling and any coal you can scrape up for a fire in the west wing solar.'

'Do you think that's necessary? It's too warm for a fire,' Walter said grudgingly.

'The fire is to air the room. I can't remember the last time we entertained anyone at Rockwood.'

The room reserved for special guests had been the solar in the original part of the castle. It was a large echoing space with stone walls and a tall window overlooking the backwater and the estuary. Rosalind and Patricia worked tirelessly to get it ready for their visitor. They dusted the ancient oak coffer and the clothes press and swept the floor, having first shaken the feather mattress until it was plumped up and welcoming. They made up the bed with clean linen, adding a thick coverlet to ward off the chills of the night air.

Walter lit a fire, which smoked a bit until a bird's nest tumbled into flames. After that the blaze roared up the chimney, warming the cold stones. As a finishing touch Rosalind picked a bunch of rosebuds from the garden and put them in a glass vase on a table at the side of the four-poster bed. Satisfied that they could do no more, she went downstairs to join Patricia and Hester in the kitchen.

There was a stranger seated at the table, enjoying a bowl of Hester's soup, but he stood up the moment he saw Rosalind.

'You must be Trigg,' Rosalind said, smiling. 'Mr Blanchard's valet.'

He bowed from the waist. 'Yes, ma'am.'

'I'm Rosalind Carey. Mr Blanchard has gone into the village with my brother, so you have plenty of time to unpack and find your way around.'

'I'll take you to your accommodation when you've finished your meal, Mr Trigg.' Hester ladled more soup into his bowl. 'I made up a bed in the tower room, just above the solar where Mr Blanchard will sleep.'

'Thank you, ma'am. I'm much obliged. I hope you don't mind, but I left the carriage and horses in the care of your head groom.'

Rosalind's lips twitched. Jim Gurney was the one and only groom. He would be flattered by his sudden promotion. 'That's quite all right. Gurney will take care of the horses. But you couldn't have driven down from London.'

'No, Miss Carey. I came by train and collected the horses and carriage from the livery stables. Mr Blanchard likes to travel by carriage, but it's too far to drive all the way to London.'

'I understand. Anyway, we will do our best to make you comfortable during your stay at Rockwood.'

'Thank you, Miss Carey. This is a very fine castle.' Trigg turned to Hester with a smile. 'And you make excellent soup, Mrs Dodridge.'

'Thank you, Mr Trigg.' Hester puffed out her chest. 'You're right about Rockwood Castle – it is one of the finest in the south-west.'

'But Trevenor is also a very historic house,' Rosalind said tactfully. 'So I believe, anyway.'

'It is, Miss Carey. Successive generations of the family have added extensions and made many improvements. I'm proud to be a member of the staff.'

'Are there many people employed there?' Patricia put the question that Rosalind would like to have asked.

'I haven't counted, but there a considerable number of servants both indoors and outdoors.'

Rosalind could see that Piers Blanchard's valet was not going to be drawn into comparisons. 'Well, enjoy your meal, Trigg. Hester will show you round. I expect Mr Blanchard will return quite soon.'

Patricia opened the door that led out into the courtyard. 'Someone is ringing the bell on the postern gate, Rosie. It might be the postman. Maybe it's a letter from Papa.' She raced off in the direction of the curtain wall that surrounded the bailey, with Rosalind close on her heels. It was over a year since they had heard anything from their father and news of his imminent return would be more than welcome. Grandpapa might be the nominal head of the family, but Wilfred Carey was the next in line to inherit the baronetcy, and he might be in a position to challenge Piers Blanchard's claim.

Patricia reached the gate first. The brass bell was still clanging loudly. She pulled back the bolts and opened the door.

The postman took a letter from the pack attached to his horse's saddle. 'This is addressed to Sir Lucien.'

Rosalind held out her hand. 'I'll see that he gets it, thank you.'

'It's a hot day,' Patricia said shyly. 'Would you like a cup of water?'

He tipped his cap. 'Thank you, miss. Much obliged, I'm sure, but Mrs Greep gave me a cup of tea. I've got a delivery for Sir Michael at Greystone Park so I'd best be on me way.' He vaulted on to his horse and was away before Patricia had time to close the gate.

Rosalind held the neatly folded and sealed document in her hand. 'This can't be from Papa. It's come from London.'

'Best open it then,' Patricia said eagerly. 'You know that Grandpapa won't pay any attention to anything it says, unless it's orders to rejoin his ship.'

Rosalind hesitated. 'Bertie's the eldest, so really it should be up to him, but he's not here.' She broke the seal, unfolded the letter and focused with difficult on the distressing contents. 'Oh, no. There must be some mistake. It can't be true.'

Chapter Six

'What is it, Rosie? You're white as a sheet. Are you all right?' Patricia clasped her sister's hand. 'Say something, do.'

'It's from the Horticultural Society of London.' Rosalind took a deep breath, blinking back tears. '"It is with great sadness that we write to inform you that we have received a report of a fatal accident to a plant hunter in Nepal."' Her voice shook and she dashed her hand across her eyes. She took a deep breath and continued to read slowly.

Documents on his person revealed his identity to be Wilfred Carey of Rockwood Castle in the county of Devonshire. Mr Carey was a plant hunter par excellence who had added greatly to our collection and our knowledge of the flora in other countries. Please accept our sincere condolence on your tragic loss.

She allowed the piece of paper to flutter to the ground as she fumbled in her pocket and brought out a hanky.

'Don't cry, Rosie. If you cry I will, too.' Patricia slipped her arm around her sister's shoulders.

'I'm all right. It's a shock, but in an odd sort of way I suppose I've always been expecting news such as this. Papa has been absent for most of my life, and certainly for the greater part of yours, but in spite of that I will miss him.'

'I'm not sure if I will or not,' Patricia said pensively. 'That makes me sound horrible, but you know what I mean, Rosie.'

Rosalind linked arms with her sister. 'Yes, of course I do. We've had to rely on each other so much. But I don't know how Grandpapa will take the news, especially with the arrival of Piers Blanchard. He couldn't have come at a worst time.'

'Do we have to tell Grandpapa? I mean he never remembers anything we say.'

'We'll talk it over with Bertie and Walter.' Rosalind cocked her head on one side. 'I can hear someone singing and it sounds like Grandpapa – it can't be, can it?'

Momentarily forgetting the terrible news, she broke away from Patricia and hurried across the courtyard. Through the open main gate she could see three figures strolling along, arm in arm. 'Patsy, look at this.' Rosalind pointed to their grandfather, being supported on either side by Bertie and Piers. 'They've got him drunk. Would you believe it?' She walked slowly towards them. Sir Lucien was singing a sea shanty at the top of his voice. Rosalind had never seen him look so happy and Bertie was obviously amused by his grandfather's antics.

Piers met her accusing gaze with a guilty smile. 'Sir Lucien was enjoying himself.'

'I can see that,' Rosalind said drily. 'You'd better take him to his room and put him to bed, Bertie.'

Sir Lucien gave her a tipsy salute. 'Don't look so cross, Rosalind, my dear. We've had a splendid time, but I think I need to rest in my cabin.'

'I think you do, Grandpapa.'

'You look so much like your grandmama when you're angry, Rosie.' Sir Lucien patted her on the cheek. 'She was a beautiful woman, just like you.'

'At least he knows who you are,' Patricia whispered. 'The other day he really thought you *were* grandmama.'

Rosalind laid her finger to her lips. 'Shhh – he'll hear you.'

'Don't worry, Rosie. We'll take care of him,' Bertie said hastily.

'I need to speak to you urgently, Bertie. But it can wait until you've taken care of Grandpapa. I'll see you in the library when you're done.'

'I'll make him comfortable first.' Bertie hitched

his grandfather's arm around his shoulders and they wandered off crabwise in the direction of the main entrance.

Rosalind turned to Piers with an apologetic smile. 'I'm sorry, this is family business. Your man, Trigg, has arrived. I left him in the kitchen having a meal, but your room is ready. If you care to wait in the main hall I'll ask Hester to show you to the solar.'

'Is there anything I can do?' Piers gave her a searching look. 'You seem upset. Is it bad news?'

'It's not good.' Rosalind could not bring herself to talk about their loss to a comparative stranger, let alone a man who was about to turn their lives upside down.

'I'll show you to your room, Piers,' Patricia said eagerly. 'We worked so hard to make it ready for you, my hands are quite raw.'

Piers frowned. 'I can't think why your father left you all in such straits. You can't continue like this.'

'We'll see,' Rosalind said evasively.

'I know I'm an interloper, but sometimes it takes an outsider to see what's necessary.' He turned to Patricia with a genuine smile. 'Lead on, Miss Patricia.'

Fifteen minutes later Patricia returned to the library followed by Bertie.

'What is it now, Rosie?' Bertie asked impatiently. 'If it's about Blanchard, we all know the reason for his visit.'

'But we don't know his claim is genuine,' Walter said gloomily. 'He could tell us anything and we would have difficulty in disproving it.'

'I like him.' Patricia looked from one to the other. 'What? I'm sixteen – aren't I allowed to have an opinion of my own?'

'Of course you are.' Rosalind took the crumpled letter from the pocket in her skirt. 'I don't want to talk about Piers for the moment. There's something else. We've had terrible news.' She handed the document to Bertie. 'Read it and you'll understand.'

'It's addressed to Grandpapa.' Bertie looked up, frowning. 'You shouldn't have opened it.'

'Read it, Bertie.'

He unfolded the letter and read it, a frown furrowing his brow. 'So much for all the rot he used to come out with about restoring Rockwood's fortunes. His jaunts abroad have virtually bankrupted us.'

Walter snatched the document from him and studied it for a moment. 'Hold on, Bertie. That's not fair. The old man was trying to improve our lives, and he died in the attempt. I can't honestly say that I'll miss him, but at least he was doing something he believed in.'

Bertie shook his head. 'This spells the end of my hopes for a career in the military. With Grandpapa being as mad as a March hare, that makes me the head of the family.'

'Unless you believe Piers Blanchard's story,'

Rosalind said gently. 'Perhaps he would be doing you a favour if he took control, Bertie. He has promised to let us live here as we've always done. Maybe his arrival is opportune.'

'I need to think this over,' Bertie said stiffly. 'I'm going for a walk.' He strode out of the library, slamming the door behind him.

'I thought he liked Piers.' Patricia sighed. 'They seemed to be getting on so well.'

'He's upset.' Rosalind took the letter from Walter and put it back in her pocket. 'We all are, of course, but someone has to be practical. What we have to decide now is if we give Grandpapa the bad news.'

'Even if we do, will he understand?' Walter met Rosalind's questioning look with a shrug.

'Maybe he's the lucky one,' Patricia said miserably. 'Now you'll never get your locket back, Rosie.'

Rosalind gave her sister a hug. 'Don't worry about that. We've got more important things to think about.' She brushed a stray curl back off Patricia's forehead. 'Why don't you visit Christina and Sylvia tomorrow? You deserve to do something nice.'

'Really? Do you think I could?'

'Of course you can, but you'd better write a note to Christina asking if it's convenient. Jim will take it for you. After all, you don't want to arrive there and find that they've gone out for the day.'

'No, you're right. I'll do that now and take it to the stables. Are you sure you won't need me?'

Rosalind smiled. 'We'll manage.'

Patricia rushed from the room, almost knocking over Piers as he was about to enter.

'I'm sorry,' Patricia gasped. 'I have an important note to write.' She hurried on without giving him a chance to respond.

'Piers, I have something to tell you,' Rosalind said slowly. 'We've just had some very bad news.'

Walter rose from his seat. 'I have things to do.' He shot Piers a sideways glance as he left the room.

Rosalind motioned Piers to take a seat by the fireplace and she handed him the letter. 'It's probably best if you read this.' She sat down opposite him, folding her hands in her lap. 'I suppose I should write to Mama and let her know,' she said half to herself.

Piers looked up from reading the letter and handed it back to her. 'I'm so sorry. I don't know what to say, Rosalind.'

'It is tragic,' she said slowly, 'but Papa died doing what he loved best. Plant hunting was his life and we all knew that we came a poor second. The difficult part, as far as we're concerned, is how to break the news to Grandpapa.'

'Sir Lucien lives in a world of his own. I doubt if anything you tell him will alter that, but I won't complicate matters by revealing my relationship with Rockwood, at least for the present.'

'Thank you for that at least.'

He gave her a searching look. 'Who deals with the family finances, Rosalind? Somehow I can't imagine Bertie paying much attention to such details.'

'I do, but the income we've had from the estate for the past couple of years has been used by Papa to fund his expedition, and there were some repairs to the roof and a flood in the cellars last winter. We still owe money to some of the tradesmen.'

'A heavy burden for someone so young.'

'I'm almost twenty-one, Piers.'

He smiled. 'I'm not casting aspersions on your ability, Rosalind. You've been faced with an impossible task. I can at least help with funding.'

'What possible benefit could it be to you to spend money on a crumbling castle that you don't intend to occupy?'

'I understand that you're suspicious, but you are my family, too. We may only be distantly related but Rockwood is in my blood as well as yours. One day I might claim my inheritance, but this is not the right time.'

'I don't know what to say.'

'Say nothing, there's no need. Give me the name of your bank and leave the rest to me. I'll give you a monthly allowance, which will enable you to live more comfortably.'

'There's really no need to go that far,' Rosalind said hastily. 'We've managed for quite a while now.'

'I can see that, but you and your sister shouldn't have to work your fingers to the bone looking after the men in the family. I wouldn't allow Aurelia to do such menial work.' He laughed. 'She wouldn't know where to start anyway. I'm afraid to say it but, much as I love her, my little sister has been spoiled by everyone, and I dare say I am partly to blame. I hope you will meet her one day.'

Rosalind smiled. It was obvious from his expression and tone of voice that, despite his words, Piers Blanchard loved his sister. It made him suddenly seem more human and less of a threat. 'I hope so, too. And thank you for coming to our rescue. If you don't take Rockwood from us, I'm afraid our creditors will, and I'd rather keep it in the family.'

Piers rose to his feet. 'My horses will be rested by now. Will you come for a drive with me and show me the rest of the estate? I'd like to get to know the village, too.'

'They will have made their minds up about you by now.' Rosalind rose to her feet. 'I'll show you the best and the worst of Rockwood and its surroundings. There's considerable poverty in parts of the village and I'd like to do more for those in need, but it's been almost impossible in recent years. We share as much as possible, especially when there's a good harvest.'

'I wish I were as philanthropic,' Piers said wryly. 'I'm afraid I give very little thought to those who work for me.' He walked to the door and opened it. 'Maybe you can give me some advice as we drive round.'

'Maybe.' Rosalind shot him a sideways glance.

'Although I'd be surprised if you're the sort of person who takes kindly to being told what to do.'

'It depends who is handing out the wise words. Shall I bring my carriage round to the front entrance?'

'It will be easier if we walk to the stables. I'll just get my bonnet and I'll tell Hester where we're going.'

'Do you always have to let your cook know your whereabouts?'

Rosalind smiled. 'I dare say it sounds odd to you, but Hester is the mainstay of our family. If any one of us has a problem we take it to her, knowing that she will hand out a dose of common sense or, in the case of illness, one of her homemade remedies. Hester's mother had the second sight as well as a sound knowledge of medicinal plants and herbs. Hester has mothered us all, and she's so much more than a servant. She can even calm Grandpapa down when he gets upset and angry. He thinks the world of her and so do we.'

'Then I should seek her approval. I have a feeling she doesn't like me.'

'Give her time – she'll come round.'

Rosalind could remember when Rockwood was the centre of society in this part of Devonshire, and they had a full complement of servants both indoors and outside. There had been a smart barouche in the carriage house, a chaise and a governess cart, as well as a hay wagon. The stables had been filled with thoroughbred horses and sturdy shire horses that worked the land. However, she could not fail to be impressed by the comfort of Piers' spanking-new curricle and the pair of thoroughbred horses, which waited eagerly to be off again on the open road. Piers took the reins and with Rosalind's guidance they toured the country lanes in and around the estate. As she had expected, people emerged from their cottages to stare curiously at the expensive equipage. Women wearing aprons over their simple frocks bobbed curtseys, while their young children waved shyly. Men stopped work in the fields to lean on their hoes or spades and tip their caps to the stranger and Miss Rosalind Carey.

The village itself was picturesque, with rows of thatched cottages, a smithy and a Norman church with a rambling eighteenth-century vicarage. One of the cottages had been converted into the shop run by Joe Hannaford and his wife, which was situated opposite the village inn, the Black Dog. Lazing in the late spring sunshine, Rockwood seemed idyllic, but Rosalind knew that behind many of the doors there was crippling poverty. The main occupations of the male inhabitants were fishing and working on the land, with a few employed at the saw mill on the edge of the village. If ill health prevented any of them from going to work there was no one to help their families unless the local landowners were charitably minded. Old age and infirmity were the things that people dreaded most, and common ailments could carry off even the strongest. The children were the most vulnerable and it broke Rosalind's heart to see young ones running round barefoot and in rags, especially in winter. She had done what she could when harvests failed and the cottage gardens did not produce enough to feed the families that depended on them for vegetables and fruit. The children were encouraged to pick up windfalls in the Rockwood orchard, and Abe Coaker, a full-time gamekeeper before he turned to gardening, had been instructed to turn a blind eye to poachers. Rosalind deemed it more important to feed families with rabbits or even pheasants than to provide for shooting parties of the rich and privileged.

They drove out of the village, past the smithy, the wheelwright's cottage and the saw mill, heading for the quay.

'How does this compare with your land at Trevenor, Piers?' Rosalind asked eagerly. 'What is the village like?'

Piers drew the horses to a halt. 'It's not as picturesque as Rockwood, if that's what you're asking.' He turned to her with a wry smile. 'You have all the points for serenity and beauty, even if behind closed doors the reality is rather different.'

'That's probably the case everywhere. I meant, what does the countryside look like? Is it beautiful?'

He shook his head. 'I wouldn't call it beautiful.

Open mining leaves scars on the landscape as well as mountains of white clay. But we're on the coast, like Rockwood, with a wide sandy bay surrounded by gently rolling hills. It has its own special appeal.'

Rosalind shielded her eyes against the sun. 'The fishing boats are returning. I hope they've got a good catch. The mackerel should be running soon, so I've been told, anyway. I know very little about fishing, except for what Bertie catches in the river, when he's in the mood, that is.'

'It seems to me that Bertie's talents are being wasted while he kicks his heels in Rockwood.'

Rosalind turned on him angrily. 'You have no right to criticise us, Piers. You've only known us for five minutes.'

'First impressions are often correct. I see a young man with very little to occupy his mind or his considerable energy.'

'Bertie will inherit the baronetcy when Grandpapa dies. It was granted to the Carey family in 1663 for supporting the Royalist cause, so you can't take that away from us.'

'Nor would I wish to, and I would like to help your brother to get into the military, which seems to be his ambition.'

'You will have to talk that over with Bertie. It's his decision.' Rosalind shivered as a chilly breeze rippled the waters of the inlet. 'I think we should head for home. The others will be wondering where I am.'

'I'm sure Hester will have told them. Hester seems to occupy a very special position in your household.' Piers flicked the reins. 'Walk on.'

When they arrived back at the castle Rosalind left Piers in the stables, where he was keen to talk to Jim, and she strolled round to the kitchen, hoping to find Hester.

'The fresh air has brought the roses back to your cheeks,' Hester said approvingly. She dropped the last peeled potato into a large black saucepan. 'I haven't cooked for so many people for an age.'

'The pigeon pie smells delicious.' Rosalind undid the ribbons on her bonnet and took it off. 'What can I do to help?'

'Nothing, as it happens. Your cousin, or whatever relative he is to you, has been busy. He must have mentioned our lack of servants to Ned Causley at the Black Dog because young Tilly Madge turned up shortly after you left on your jaunt. She said she'd been told we needed a kitchen maid and she was more than eager to start right away.'

'Widow Madge's daughter? But she's only about ten or twelve.'

'The child is twelve, but she's more than willing and she's quite capable of following instructions. She's worked her little fingers to the bone with no complaints, so I'm more than happy. I made sure she was fed well, and I sent her home with one of the loaves of bread that she helped me make.'

'Poor child. Wasn't her father lost at sea just before Christmas?'

'Him and his only boy, who was just thirteen. Dora Madge was left with five little maids, all under twelve.'

Rosalind shook her head. 'I've been so busy worrying about this family that I'm afraid I've neglected some of our tenants. I should have done better.'

'That's enough of that talk, Miss Rosalind. You've done your very best with little or no help from those who ought to be taking more responsibility, naming no names.'

'Well, I'll try to do better for young Tilly and her family. If Piers keeps his word we'll have a much easier time in the future.'

'I know you like him, but I don't trust him,' Hester said gloomily. 'I think he's keeping something from you.'

'He seems genuine enough, Hester.'

'Just be watchful and don't believe everything he says.'

'I'll be careful,' Rosalind said guardedly.

Dinner that evening went off pleasantly enough. Sir Lucien had sobered up from his visit to the Black Dog and was in a jovial mood. He entertained them all with stories of his life at sea from the age of eleven when he was a midshipman, to his glory days battling against Napoleon's fleet. With encouragement from

118

Piers he related tales that Rosalind had never heard before, and she could tell from the rapt expression on Bertie's face that he was living every moment of the victories as well as the defeats. For once, their grandfather seemed like his old self, but he grew tired and left them when Hester brought in a pot of coffee and a jug of cream. These were luxuries that the family had been forced to forgo, and both Bertie and Walter made the most of the unexpected treat.

Rosalind handed a cup to Piers. 'I'm afraid we can't offer you brandy.'

'That's quite all right. The coffee smells delicious and Hester's pie was magnificent. I wish my cook at Trevenor had such a magic touch with pastry.'

'I suppose Patsy and I should retire to the drawing room,' Rosalind said, smiling, 'but we don't follow society's rules at Rockwood.'

'I understand. I've always thought it rather boring when the ladies leave us gentlemen to our brandy and cigars.'

Rosalind sipped her coffee. It had been ground from the best beans, which meant that Joe Hannaford must have heard the rumours about their wealthy new relation, and had been keen to supply the order that Hester had sent to him. There was even some sugar to sweeten the rather bitter drink. Rosalind could not remember the last time they had been able to afford to use sugar for anything other than preserving fruit. If entertaining Piers was supping with the devil, as Hester had hinted, perhaps it was worth the trouble.

Rosalind eyed him over the rim of her coffee cup, wondering why he had come into their lives. If Hester was right – and she almost always was – then Piers Blanchard had an ulterior motive for making himself known to them.

Piers looked up and smiled. 'Excellent coffee. I must congratulate Hester on a wonderful meal.'

Bertie reached for the bowl of sugar lumps. 'What is the plan for tomorrow, Piers? Would you like to come shooting with me? There are several shotguns to choose from in the gun room. We used to have shooting parties here in the old days. I can remember them when I was very young.'

'Thank you, Bertie, but I have business in Exeter tomorrow.'

'Maybe the day after, then?'

'If I conclude my business tomorrow there's nothing I would enjoy more. What about you, Walter? Do you share your brother's enthusiasm for hunting?'

'I'm more of a studious sort of fellow. I should have gone to Cambridge, but funds wouldn't stretch that far.'

'That's a shame. But you never know – things might change.'

Walter pulled a face. 'Not with the Careys' luck, Piers. Rockwood isn't nicknamed Carey's Folly for nothing.'

'That's just a silly joke,' Rosalind said hastily. 'All families have a certain amount of ill fortune. I doubt if we've had more than anyone else.'

Piers drank the last of his coffee and placed the delicate bone-china cup on its saucer. 'Thank you for an excellent meal and delightful company, but if you'll excuse me I'll retire to my room. I have some letters to write before I go to bed.'

'Can you find the way?' Patricia half rose to her feet. 'I could show you again, if you wish?'

He smiled and shook his head. 'You're very kind, Patricia, but I have a good memory, and the castle already feels like home.' He pushed back his chair and stood up. 'Good night, everyone. It's been a most pleasant evening.'

'He's a jolly decent fellow,' Bertie said appreciatively when the door closed behind Piers. 'He's the only one who's listened to me when I talk about joining the military.'

'He seems all right,' Walter added, nodding.

'I think he's very handsome.' Patricia looked away, her cheeks suffused in a blush.

'Well, Rosie?' Bertie gave her a quizzical glance. 'You're very quiet. What do you think?'

'He's very presentable,' Rosalind said carefully. 'He's quite charming and he always seems to say the right things. I can't put my finger on it, but I'm not entirely sure about Piers Blanchard.'

Chapter Seven

Next morning Rosalind was up early and she went straight to the kitchen where she found Hester giving young Tilly another lesson in bread-making.

'Good morning, Tilly,' Rosalind said, smiling. 'How is your mother? Is she keeping well?'

Tilly nodded, wiping her hand across her face and leaving a smear of flour on the tip of her snub nose. 'Yes'm. Thank you, ma'am.'

'It's Miss Rosalind to you,' Hester said sternly. 'Just remember that you must never speak until you're spoken to. I hope your ma taught you that.'

'Yes'm.' Tilly stared at the dough as if expecting it to rise of its own accord.

'Something smells good.' Rosalind went to the range and lifted the lid on a pan of stew. 'You must have got up very early this morning, Hester.'

'I couldn't sleep, so I thought I'd get a head start,

what with having extra mouths to feed, but his lordship took off very early. He left you a note. I put it on the dining-room table.'

'The dining room? But I always take my breakfast with you,' Rosalind said suspiciously.

Hester ladled porridge into a bowl and handed it to her. 'Not any more. It's time we went back to the old ways. Master Bertram will inherit the baronetcy soon enough and we have standards to keep up.'

Mystified by Hester's sudden change in attitude, Rosalind took her breakfast to the dining room. The table had been laid and there was a folded sheet of paper in her place. She sat down and started to read the note written in elegant copperplate.

Dear Rosalind

Thank you for your wonderful hospitality. I have business to conclude in Exeter and I hope to return this evening. However, as this might not be possible I will visit your bank and arrange to transfer sufficient funds to keep Rockwood from sinking into the sea!!

If you need anything I beg you to keep me informed. A letter addressed to me at Trevenor, near St Austell, will find me.

Yours truly

Piers Blanchard

It was quite obvious that he had no intention of returning that evening, if ever, and that made him even more of a conundrum. There was nothing she could do other than to carry out her normal daily routine, but she had a feeling that things would never be the same again. They might have been comparatively poor, but they were the Careys of Rockwood Castle. Now it seemed that this certainty had been built on a falsehood. The arrival of Piers Blanchard had changed everything. Rosalind folded the note carefully and tucked it into her pocket.

It seemed strange sitting at the dining table on her own. She had grown used to the homely comfort of the kitchen with Hester bustling about and chatting as she worked, but in her heart Rosalind knew that Hester was right. It was time that she and her siblings shook off the habits of the nursery and took responsibility for their own lives. Owing to their grandfather's state of mental confusion, Bertie was head of the family now. She would help him to run the estate, even though taking on the responsibility was the last thing that Bertie wanted, and he in turn would have to forget his ambition to join the military. Rosalind sighed and ate her rapidly cooling porridge.

She had just finished when Patsy burst into the room with her bowl clutched in her hands.

'Hester said you were here. Why are we eating in the dining room?' She flopped down onto her chair. 'Well?'

'It was Hester's suggestion and she's right, Patsy. We can't act like children now. Papa is gone for ever this time, and we have to face the fact that there are people who depend on us. We have to act responsibly.'

'But Piers is the rightful owner. He said so and I believe him.'

'I'm not sure if I do or not. After all, we have only his word on it. In any event, I doubt if we'll see him again.' Rosalind took the note from her pocket and tossed it across the table. 'He left early this morning, according to Hester. I don't think he'll be coming back.'

Patricia studied the contents of the letter. 'He says he hopes to return, Rosie. Why do you think the worst of him?'

'We know nothing of him, except what he's told us. He charmed Mama, and Claude seemed to like him, but that doesn't mean that Piers Blanchard is telling us the whole truth.'

'What will you do?'

'There's nothing much we *can* do at the moment. Anyway, you wanted to spend the day at Greystone Park. Did you get a reply from Christina?'

Patricia nodded enthusiastically. 'Yes, I did. Jim brought it back while you were out driving with Piers. I meant to tell you.'

'It will do you good to have a day with your friends. Jim can take you there and pick you up later.'

'Yes, I told him I'd be ready at ten o'clock. I know that Chrissie and Sylvia don't rise early. May I borrow your green sprigged muslin? My gowns are all so old and I can't wear one of Mama's cast-offs. The girls are always dressed in the height of fashion.'

'My dress is not exactly in the latest mode, but you can wear it if you like. Take my best straw bonnet with the green satin ribbons, too, but please don't lose it.'

'My lace shawl is torn,' Patricia said cautiously. 'And there is a blackberry stain on it that won't come out.'

'All right.' Rosalind rose to her feet. 'You can borrow my lace shawl, too. You always get your own way, Patsy. I don't know how you do it.'

'You love me, that's why.'

'Spoilt brat,' Rosalind said, smiling. 'Go out and enjoy your day. I have plenty of things to keep me occupied.'

Rosalind was not surprised when Piers and his valet did not return that evening. Bertie and Walter were disappointed. What Patricia thought, Rosalind didn't know, as Patsy was staying at Greystone Park overnight. She had sent a message with one of their coachmen, and Rosalind sent him back with a valise containing everything Patricia might need for a short stay. Rosalind was pleased to think that her sister was enjoying herself away from the gloomy atmosphere at Rockwood.

Sir Lucien kept asking plaintively where the interesting fellow had gone, and Rosalind tried to convince him that urgent business matters had been the reason for Blanchard's sudden departure. However, Sir Lucien seemed unconvinced and he retreated to his tower to relieve the non-existent officer on watch. Rosalind knew from past experience that her grandfather would spend the best part of the night using his telescope to scan the mouth of the estuary for enemy vessels. She decided that it was a good thing they had chosen to keep Piers Blanchard's claim on the Rockwood estate to themselves. With her grandfather's fragile mental state, it was possible that such information might prove too much for him.

Two days later Rosalind received a letter in the post from the manager of their bank in Exeter, requesting that she attend a meeting the next day. Even though she had been handling the family finances since their father left on his last fatal plant hunting trip, Bertie was surprisingly angry when she told him that she had been summoned to the bank.

'I'm the head of the family now that Papa is no longer with us,' he said crossly. 'Why does the manager want to speak to you, Rosie? You're a woman.'

'Thank you, Bertie. I'm surprised you've noticed. I've been doing all the bookkeeping, such as it is, and I've dealt with the bank for the past two years. Grandpapa isn't capable, and you simply don't want to, so it's been left to me.'

'Have it your own way. I've no head for figures.

Anyway, there's no money in the account, so I don't know what there is to talk about.'

'I'll find out when I see Mr Salter tomorrow, Bertie. I'll get Jim to drive me to Exeter.'

Bertie shrugged. 'I wish Blanchard had stayed on for a while. It was good to have a man to talk to, and he understood why I want a commission in the army. I think he'd have helped me if he hadn't had to return home so soon. What am I supposed to do, Rosie? Tell me that.'

'You've kept us fed all winter, Bertie, and we still need meat. Could you go out and bag some pigeons or rabbits?'

'That's all I'm good for,' Bertie muttered as he walked away. 'I might as well be a gamekeeper.'

'We depend on you, Bertie,' Rosalind called after him. Dealing with everyone's moods seemed to come naturally to her these days. Walter was the only member of the family who plodded on regardless of the chaos around him. Sometimes Rosalind envied the cosy little world of books that her brother inhabited. She would like to escape there herself, but tomorrow she would have to face Mr Salter, yet again. Despite his cordial manner, she suspected that he disliked doing business with a woman.

Septimus Salter rested his elbows on his desk and steepled his fingers. It was obviously a look that was intended to intimidate customers with large over-drafts, but all Rosalind saw was a small man, who had once been a counter clerk and whose starched shirt points threatened to pierce his double chin. He cleared his throat as if he were about to preach a sermon, and his gold watch chain seemed to stretch to breaking point over his corpulent belly.

'Good morning, Miss Carey. Won't you take a seat?'

Rosalind perched on the edge of a chair placed strategically in front of the impressive mahogany desk, and she met his stern look with a steady gaze. She had no intention of being intimidated by a mere clerk who had risen to the position of bank manager only because the previous incumbent had died of apoplexy.

'Good morning, Mr Salter.'

'What can I do for you today, Miss Carey?'

'I believe it was you who requested to see me.'

His plump cheeks reddened and he glanced at the notes on his desk. 'Yes, it's about your family's finances.'

'Of course.' Rosalind folded her hands in her lap, making an effort to look calm, when she was trembling with anxiety. Mr Salter had the power to bankrupt them if he demanded repayment of their overdraft. A word from him could snatch Rockwood from the family for ever.

'There has been a change in your circumstances, Miss Carey.'

Rosalind clenched her gloved hands in her lap as she waited for the death blow to everything she held dear. She wished now that she had accepted Sir Michael's offer to purchase Rockwood, even though it would have barely paid off their debts, but now it was probably too late. Bankruptcy, disgrace and maybe even prison might be the outcome.

'What has changed, Mr Salter?' Rosalind held her breath as she waited to hear the worst.

'All your debts have been settled in a most surprising turn of events.'

'Really?' Rosalind stared at him in disbelief. 'Are you sure?'

'I had a visit from Mr Piers Blanchard of Trevenor China Clays, a businessman of some repute. He told me that you are related, and due to the sudden tragic demise of Mr Wilfred Carey, Mr Blanchard has taken responsibility for your family's finances.'

Rosalind was at a loss for words. Piers had said he would do something to help them, but she had not expected him to pay off their considerable debts in one fell swoop. To have that much money was unimaginable. She could see that Salter was waiting for her to respond, but she had to be certain that it was not simply a cruel joke.

'Are you sure that we are debt free?'

'Completely, Miss Carey. Moreover, Mr Blanchard has put a sum at your disposal, which, if used sensibly, will keep you and your family until the next harvest, which we all hope will be a good one.'

Rosalind nodded wordlessly.

'I'm not surprised that you are stunned by this

news, Miss Carey. I've done my best in the past to help you and your family, especially in the light of Sir Lucien's most successful career in the Royal Navy. Now you will be independent.'

'Thank you, sir.' Rosalind could think of little else to say. Septimus Salter was, however, mistaken in one thing: far from being independent, they now depended entirely on Piers Blanchard's charity. She rose to her feet. 'Am I able to withdraw money today?'

'Yes, of course.' Salter handed her a document. 'This details the exact amount you have in your account, which Mr Blanchard insisted was to be in your name only.' He sniffed and pursed his lips. 'I might say it is a highly unusual arrangement. One would normally expect the head of the family to be the beneficiary of such munificence.'

Rosalind bit back a sharp retort. It would not do to make an enemy of the bank manager. They might need his goodwill in the future. She managed a nod and a weak smile.

Salter opened a drawer in his desk and took out a small linen pouch. 'Mr Blanchard left this, which he stressed must be given only to you. He said you know what it is.'

Feeling as though she was in a dream, Rosalind took the pouch from him. 'Thank you, Mr Salter.'

'Don't mention it, Miss Carey.' Salter rose to his feet and hurried past her to open the door. 'It's always a pleasure to deal with such an illustrious family. Now tell me how much you wish to withdraw and I will see to it myself . . .'

Still in a daze, Rosalind left the bank and climbed into the chaise. She could hardly believe that the burden of debt had been lifted so suddenly, or that their financial struggles were over, for the time being, anyway.

Jim gave her a searching look. 'Are you all right, Miss Rosalind? You look a bit peaky, if you don't mind me saying so.'

'I'm perfectly fine, thank you, Jim. Drive on, we'll collect my sister on the way home.'

He tipped his hat. 'Yes, Miss Rosalind. Of course.'

As the chaise pulled away from the kerb Rosalind opened the pouch and tipped the contents into her hand. Grandmama's locket. She stared at it in disbelief. Piers had not only remembered that she had pawned it, but had gone to the trouble and expense of redeeming something that he must have realised meant so much to her. Once again she was baffled by his actions, but she was also a little touched, and she could not resist the temptation to fasten the chain around neck. Fingering the delicate locket she sat back against the worn squabs, staring out of window, still dazed by the sudden turn of events.

Unlike Rockwood, which had the natural boundaries of the River Exe estuary and its lesser tributary, the River Sawle, Greystone was surrounded by a high brick wall. The gatekeeper hurried out of his cottage to let them in and they entered the long drive, lined with fiery copper beeches. At the far end the carriage sweep curved to reveal the Jacobean mansion, which never failed to impress Rosalind with its grandeur. The building itself was modern in comparison with the ancient stones of Rockwood, and the mellow red brick gave out a warm welcoming glow. Sunlight reflected playfully in the leaded glass panes of the mullioned windows, and the tall chimneys reached up into the sky almost touching the fluffy white clouds. The moment the chaise drew to a halt outside, the iron-studded oak door opened and a liveried footman hurried down the steps to assist Rosalind to alight. As she entered the house she was greeted by Sir Michael's butler.

'Good morning, Miss Carey. May I say it's a pleasure to see you again?'

She smiled. 'Thank you, Foster. I've come to take my sister home.'

'Would you care to wait in the drawing room, Miss Carey? I believe the young ladies are playing croquet.'

'I'll join them on the lawn, thank you, Foster. I know my way.'

'Shall I inform Sir Michael of your presence, Miss Carey?'

'I don't wish to disturb him,' Rosalind said hastily. She walked on before Foster had a chance to argue. It was not that she disliked Sir Michael, but at their last meeting she had felt slightly uncomfortable in his presence. He was tall and handsome, a wealthy widower, who for many years had successfully evaded local matchmakers and designing women. He was always impeccably dressed, courteous and often very amusing, but recently she felt that his manner towards her had changed subtly. There was a warmth in his eyes and the tone of his voice changed when he spoke to her. He singled her out from the other people in the room when they attended the same functions, and he called at Rockwood on the slenderest of excuses. Added to all that, he had purchased their hay last autumn at well above the going rate. Sir Michael Greystone was old enough to be her father and Rosalind had never thought about him in a romantic way, but it seemed that he might have other ideas.

She had been to the house often enough to know the way to the garden and she made her way there now, walking quickly without stopping to admire the antiques and paintings. She wanted to avoid a meeting with Sir Michael, if at all possible, and she hoped that he was occupied elsewhere. Her intention was to find Patricia and leave as soon as possible. She had left Jim Gurney waiting for her with the chaise so that they could get away quickly.

Sounds of merriment from the garden grew louder as Rosalind opened the double doors that led from the room that had been Lady Greystone's parlour. Christina, Sylvia and Patricia were engaged in a game of croquet, although from what Rosalind could see they were not bothering too much with the rules. Their straw bonnets bobbed up and down and their muslin dresses fluttered in the warm breeze as they moved like brightly coloured butterflies around the lawn.

'Patsy.' Rosalind called her sister's name, but Patricia was laughing so loudly that she did not appear to hear. Rosalind tried again, waving her hand in an attempt to attract her sister's attention. 'Patsy – it's time to leave.'

Christina turned and acknowledged her with a warm smile. 'Why don't you join us, Rosie? We're having a cracking game.'

Sylvia came to a halt, staring at her sister with disapproval written all over her pretty face. 'Don't let Papa hear you saying such common words, Chrissie. He won't think it's funny.'

'You are such a killjoy, Sylvia.' Christina tossed the croquet mallet aside and ran across the velvety grass to meet Rosalind. 'Come and sit on the terrace. It's uncommonly warm for May. Would you like some lemonade?'

'Thank you, but we really should go home.'

'I'm sure you could spare time to chat with old friends,' Christina said, smiling. 'Or is there someone special waiting for you at home?'

Rosalind frowned. 'If you are referring to Mr Blanchard, he and his valet left three days ago.'

'Oh, how disappointing. Patsy told us all about him. He just turned up out of the blue and told you that he owns Rockwood. That must have been such a shock. Was he telling the truth, do you think?'

'Patsy shouldn't have said anything. I don't know if he is genuine or not, Chrissie.'

Christina led the way to the terrace and sank down on one of the chairs. She patted the seat of the one next to her. 'Do stay for a while, Rosie. I can't wait to hear all about Mr Blanchard. Is he handsome?'

'Is he married?' Sylvia rushed over and pulled up a chair. 'Patsy says he's very charming.'

'I didn't say that exactly.' Patricia perched on the balustrade. She shot a wary glance in her sister's direction. 'I said he was nice to me, that's all, Rosie.'

Rosalind could see that both Christina and Sylvia were eager to learn more of the stranger who had arrived in their midst and she knew that they would not be satisfied until she had given them more information. 'He seemed a decent sort of fellow,' she said guardedly. 'Grandpapa liked him, although we haven't told him why Piers came to Rockwood.'

'Piers.' Christina gave Sylvia a meaningful nod. 'So you're on first-name terms already, are you, Rosie?'

Rosalind peeled off her gloves and laid them on a seat next to her. 'You're obviously making his visit out to be much more significant than it was. What exactly has my sister told you?'

Sylvia snatched a silver bell from the table and rang it energetically. 'You tell us your version of the story, Rosie. You know that Patsy likes to exaggerate.'

'I do not,' Patricia protested. 'That's unfair, Sylvia. All I said was that we met this man in London. He sent us a bottle of champagne in the interval of the opera.'

'Did he come to the box to speak to you?' Sylvia asked eagerly. 'You never mentioned the champagne, Patsy.'

Before Patricia had a chance to respond, a maid-servant emerged from the house. 'You rang, Miss Christina?'

'I did,' Sylvia said firmly. 'We'd like lemonade, please, Ivy.'

'Yes, Miss Sylvia.' Ivy bobbed a curtsey and hurried off towards the kitchens.

'Well, go on, Patsy,' Sylvia said eagerly.

'Patsy is making more out of it than necessary.' Rosalind made an effort to sound unconcerned. 'Mr Blanchard knows Mama, or at least he had made himself known to her and to her manager. We happened to meet him again at the Great Exhibition, which was wonderful. I could have spent a week there and still not seen everything.'

'Never mind the exhibition,' Christina said dismissively. 'Tell us more about the charming man you met in London, who turned up in Rockwood and announced that he is a long-lost relative. It's so romantic.'

'If you say so.' Rosalind shifted uncomfortably in

her seat. 'Although *I* wouldn't say that someone claiming they are the rightful heir to Rockwood and the estate is romantic. However,' she added hastily, 'Mr Blanchard seems a reasonable sort of person and he said he doesn't want us to leave our home.'

'He's going to pay our debts,' Patricia said, grinning.

'We don't discuss our financial matters.' Rosalind could see that Christina and Sylvia were eager to learn more. 'I don't mean to be rude, but it's our business.'

'Papa would have helped you,' Christina said sympathetically. 'Papa always speaks very highly of Sir Lucien.'

'And he likes you—Ouch!' Sylvia glared at her sister. 'Why did you kick me?'

'You are so tactless, Sylvia Greystone.' Christina sat back in her chair as the maid returned with a laden tray. 'Lemonade, that's just what we need, and I see that Cook has put some of her lemon biscuits out, too. How thoughtful. Thank her for me, Ivy. You may go. I'll ring if we need anything else.'

'Yes, Miss Christina.' Ivy curtsied and backed away.

Christina picked up the cut-glass jug and filled glasses with lemonade before handing them round. 'Do help yourselves to the biscuits. Now, what were you saying about Mr Blanchard, Rosie? You don't seem too upset that a stranger is claiming to be the rightful heir to Rockwood.'

Patricia stared at her sister, eyebrows raised. 'You've redeemed Grandmama's pendant, or did Piers buy it back for you, Rosie?'

'Did he really pay off your creditors?' Sylvia asked, ignoring the black looks from her sister.

'Really, Sylvia, that's not the sort of question you ask anyone, least of all a guest in our home.' Sir Michael walked slowly towards them. 'Foster informed me that you were here, Rosalind. You and Patricia will stay for luncheon, of course.' It was a statement rather than an invitation.

Rosalind met his steely gaze and she knew she could not refuse without offending him. The Greystone estate bought all their surplus crops and provided help at harvest time. It was one thing for Piers Blanchard to descend upon them and hand out largesse, but he had returned to Cornwall and life had to carry on as before.

'Of course they'll stay for luncheon, Papa,' Christina said, smiling. 'Rosie hasn't finished telling us the whole of the story.'

Chapter Eight

Rosalind found herself seated on Sir Michael's right at luncheon. She had thought of all possible excuses why she and Patricia had to return home immediately, but abandoned them as being too far-fetched. However, the food was delicious and Sir Michael skilfully steered the conversation away from the embarrassing topic of Piers Blanchard, although it was obvious to Rosalind that Christina would have loved to ask more questions. It was a relief when the meal came to an end and everyone rose from the table. Rosalind was about to ask if Jim Gurney could be sent for to take them home when Sir Michael suggested that she might like to accompany him to the stables to see his latest acquisition. Once again it would have been impossible to refuse without appearing rude.

The stables at Greystone Park were built around

a large courtyard with accommodation above the main buildings for the dozen or so stable boys, grooms and two coachmen. They were greeted by the head groom.

'Miss Carey would like to see Apollo, Jones.'

'Yes, Sir Michael. I'll see to it right away.' Jones hurried off, beckoning to a younger man as he headed into the stable block. They reappeared moments later leading a magnificent chestnut Arab stallion.

'What do you think, Rosalind?' Sir Michael asked eagerly. 'Isn't he beautiful?'

'He is very handsome indeed.' Rosalind inched away from Sir Michael, who was standing too close to her for comfort, but he edged even closer. 'I have a surprise for you, my dear.'

She eyed him warily. 'Oh!'

'Don't you want to know what it is?'

'I can't imagine what it could be, sir.'

'Jones, saddle Gypsy and bring her here. You may take Apollo back to his stall.'

'Yes, Sir Michael.' Jones led the spirited animal away.

'I don't understand,' Rosalind said anxiously. 'Gypsy is Christina's horse, isn't she?'

'Not any longer. I purchased a faster animal for Christina, and Sylvia already has a grey mare that she adores. I want you to have Gypsy, Rosalind. I know you only have Ajax in your stables, and it's a disgrace that Miss Carey of Rockwood Castle is seen riding a work horse.'

'Wait a minute.' Rosalind rounded on him angrily. 'I can't accept such a gift. You must realise that, Sir Michael.'

He grasped her hand in his. 'I would give you a great deal more, if you would let me, my dear.'

She felt the colour rush to her cheeks and she snatched her hand free. 'It's time I left for home.'

Sir Michael took a step backwards. 'I apologise, Rosalind. I didn't mean to offend you. I have the greatest respect for you – more than that, I . . .'

Rosalind spotted Jim Gurney standing by the door of the tack room and she waved frantically. 'Jim, we're going home.'

He tipped his cap. 'I'll bring the chaise round to the front entrance, Miss Rosalind.' He disappeared into the coach house, shouting instructions to one of the stable lads.

'Thank you for the offer, Sir Michael,' Rosalind said hastily. 'I realise it was well meant, but I have to go now. I can find my own way back to the house.'

'May I call on you in the next few days? I would like to pay my respects to Sir Lucien and your family.'

To refuse would have been rude, but to accept made it difficult to remain aloof if he called at Rockwood. 'I'm sure my grandfather would be delighted to welcome you whenever you wish to call.'

'But what about you, Rosalind?' Sir Michael fell into step beside her.

She came to a sudden halt and turned to face him. 'Sir Michael, I am only a year older than Christina.'

'You are almost twenty-one, my dear. You are no longer a child and you've grown into a charming and beautiful young woman. I might be a few years your senior, but I am still a relatively young man.'

Rosalind glanced over his shoulder. 'I can see my sister. She's waiting for me on the terrace.'

'Must you leave so soon? I didn't mean to alarm you, Rosalind. Stay for a while longer, please.'

'Bertie will be wondering what's happened to me. I'm sorry, sir, but we really have to leave now.' Rosalind edged past him. 'Patsy, it's time to go home.'

'What's the matter with you, Rosie?' Patricia demanded as Ajax plodded along the carriage sweep, heading for the massive iron gates. 'You're very flushed. Are you going down with a fever?'

Jim grunted and flicked the whip above Ajax's head.

'I'm perfectly well, Patsy,' Rosalind said sharply.

Patricia shot a wary glance in Jim's direction and lowered her voice. 'What's going on, Rosie? What did Sir Michael want?'

'He wanted to show off his Arab stallion.'

'You looked very flushed when he was talking to you,' Patricia said slyly. 'Sylvie thinks that her papa wants to marry you.'

'Don't be ridiculous. Sir Michael is old enough to be my father.'

Patricia pulled a face. 'Penelope Warner married

a man who was nearly thirty years her senior. Mind you, he was very wealthy and he didn't survive long, so she inherited a fortune.'

Rosalind laughed. 'Sir Michael isn't in that category and neither am I. I wouldn't marry anyone for their money. I'd rather end up an old maid than sell myself to the highest bidder. As to Sir Michael, I don't know what's got into him. He's always been nice to me, but that's all.'

Patricia moved closer. 'What did he say? Tell me everything.'

Rosalind nodded pointedly at Jim, who was no doubt listening eagerly. 'Nothing of note, but he did offer to give me Gypsy because Christina has a new horse.'

'That would be so wonderful. I could ride her, too. I could go out visiting again. Did you accept?'

'Certainly not.'

'I would have, had he wanted to give me a horse of my own. Sometimes I think you are too proud, Rosie. You know what they say about beggars not being choosers.'

'Well, we aren't in that category any more. Our so-called cousin has paid off our debts. We'll say no more about it now, but I'll tell everyone when we're all together at dinner.'

'Did Piers redeem your pendant, Rosie? You didn't answer my question earlier.'

'Yes, he did, but if I remember correctly it was Sir Michael who put a stop to that discussion.'

'I think he was jealous,' Patricia said triumphantly. 'I told you that he had taken a fancy to you, Rosie.'

'Next time you visit the Greystone girls I'll leave you to find your own way home. I really don't want to talk about it, Patsy.'

'We'll see.' Patricia smiled mischievously. 'I'll lay a bet that Sir Michael pays us a visit at Rockwood within the next few days.'

They arrived home to find the household in a panic because Sir Lucien was missing yet again, and no one had seen him for several hours.

'He seems to have gone out not long after you left this morning,' Hester said worriedly. 'We've all been looking for him. I can usually guess where he might be, but not this time.'

Rosalind took off her bonnet and shawl. 'Has anyone checked the stables and the keeper's cottage?'

'Master Bertie did that first, and he said he would visit Greep farm. If he can't find Sir Lucien there he'll go on to the village to organise a proper search party.'

'What about Walter? Is he looking for Grandpapa?'

'Oh, yes. He's been all along the beach, and he came back to say that he'll wait for the fishing boats to come in. He seems to think that Sir Lucien might have persuaded one of them to take him out on the water. You know how he misses the sea.'

'He might have fallen in,' Rosalind said anxiously. 'Anything could have happened.'

Patricia retied her bonnet strings. 'I'll go to the smithy and ask Barnaby if he's seen him.'

'Just remember that Barnaby Yelland is engaged to the wheelwright's daughter, Miss Patricia,' Hester said pointedly.

'I know.' Patricia tossed her head. 'I wouldn't look twice at a common blacksmith's apprentice, I can assure you of that. I'm going to look for Grandpapa.' She stalked out of the kitchen, wrapping Rosalind's best shawl round her shoulders as she went.

'She can't pull the wool over my eyes,' Hester said with a disapproving frown. 'She's been seeing Barnaby on the sly. Dora Greep knows everything that goes on in the village and she told me that she'd seen them together.'

'Patsy's known Barnaby for years, Hester. They're friends, that's all.'

'I warned your mama against allowing you girls to mix with the village children when you were growing up. It's lucky that you didn't form an attachment to any of the boys who flocked around you.'

'I'm sure there's nothing untoward going on between Patsy and Barnaby, but I've got more important things to worry about at the moment. Grandpapa's memory is getting worse and he could be anywhere by now, or he might have fallen and hurt himself. I'll take a walk through the woods, just in case Bertie missed something.' Rosalind hurried from the kitchen with Bob trotting at her side.

She searched every inch of the wooded area without

any success, although Bob found a broken branch that seemed to appeal to him and he insisted on carrying it, despite the fact that it kept catching in the undergrowth and hindering his progress. When they finally emerged from the cool greenness beneath the trees, Rosalind threw the stick for him and he retrieved it with obvious pleasure. She threw it again, but even as she did so she was aware of two figures walking slowly towards the castle. With a heartfelt sigh of relief, she quickened her pace, breaking into a run as she reached the bridge that spanned the tributary. She stopped for a moment to catch her breath.

'Jarvis.' She walked to meet them, holding out her hand to the man who had been the family butler until his retirement. 'You found Grandpapa. Where was he?'

'I was visiting my sister. You remember her, Miss Rosalind?'

'Yes, of course I do. Minnie used to work in the sewing room when I was a child.'

'I saw Sir Lucien walking along the lane outside Minnie's cottage and I went out to speak to him.'

'I was going to rejoin my ship, Rosalind,' Sir Lucien said feebly. 'This man said I am needed at home.'

Rosalind nodded. 'Yes, Grandpapa. We were worried about you.'

'You're wearing the pendant I gave you for your twenty-first birthday, Prudence. I'm glad you like it.'

'I'm Rosalind, Grandpapa.'

Jarvis stepped in between them. 'Lady Prudence is waiting for you in the solar, Sir Lucien. I think we should hurry. It looks like rain.'

Sir Lucien gazed up into the cloudless azure sky. 'I do see clouds gathering on the horizon, Jarvis. Perhaps we had better quicken our pace.'

Jarvis tucked Sir Lucien's hand in the crook of his arm. 'This way, sir. If you please.'

Rosalind was amazed to see her grandfather falling into step beside Jarvis as if it were the most natural thing in the world. She followed them at a discreet distance with Bob at her heels, still carrying his prized stick. As they reached the main gates they were met by Bertie.

'Jarvis, you've found him.'

'I wasn't lost, Bertram,' Sir Lucien said coldly. 'I was on my way to my ship when I met Jarvis.' He turned his head to glare at Rosalind. 'Although I can't think why Lady Carey was walking without her maid in attendance. Prudence, my dear, you'd better go indoors out of the sun. You know it's damaging to a fair complexion.'

Rosalind managed a weak smile, fighting back tears. It broke her heart to see her beloved grandfather in such a confused state.

'Perhaps you would like to go to your cabin, sir?' Jarvis suggested gently. 'I will bring you some refreshment.'

'Yes, good man, Jarvis. I am rather peckish.' Sir Lucien allowed Jarvis to lead him into the hallway and they made their way towards the east tower where Sir Lucien had his suite of rooms.

'How did Jarvis find him, Rosie?' Bertie demanded. 'We've looked everywhere for the old fellow.'

'Jarvis was visiting his sister and he spotted Grandpapa strolling along the lane. Jarvis guessed that there was something amiss, luckily for us.'

'He always knew how to handle Grandpapa, even before the old man went off his head.'

'He's not mad, Bertie. Don't say things like that.'

'He's not normal either, Rosie. And he's getting worse.'

'I wonder if Jarvis would consider coming out of retirement,' Rosalind said thoughtfully. 'Someone has to look after Grandpapa, and we haven't managed very well on our own.'

'That's true. It's odd the way he does whatever Jarvis suggests.' Bertram sighed. 'Can we afford to pay his wages, Rosie? What happened at the bank today?'

'Come into the study, Bertie. I was going to wait until dinner and tell you all then, but I have some good news.' She fingered the locket, smiling. 'You see I have it back?'

'You redeemed it from the pawnbroker?'

'No, I didn't. It was Piers. He left it at the bank with instructions to return it to me.'

'That was decent of him.' Bertie ushered her into the study and closed the door. 'So how do we stand financially?'

'Piers has settled our debts and he's deposited quite a considerable amount in the Rockwood Castle account at the bank. We should be able to living comfortably until the next harvest, if we're careful.'

Bertie paced the room. 'Why would he do that? What does the fellow hope to gain?' He came to a halt, staring at his sister. 'Is he interested in you, Rosie? Do you think all this is a way of making you feel beholden to him? The next thing we know he'll be asking you to marry him.'

'Don't be ridiculous, Bertie. I hardly know him, and he doesn't know me. A man of his standing could have anyone.' She smiled reluctantly. 'Besides which, he'd have to fight off Sir Michael. He tried to give me Gypsy, Christina's horse, earlier this afternoon.'

'Sir Michael! But he's an old man.'

'Quite! Which is what I more or less told him, although it seems a little cruel now I come to think about it. But he's too old for me, and that's the truth.'

'He's very wealthy, Rosie,' Bertie said, frowning. 'His land abuts ours it would be a convenient marriage.'

Rosalind shook her head, laughing. 'For you, maybe, but not for me. He's a charming man but I don't love him. Anyway, I don't fancy having Christina and Sylvia as my stepdaughters. Can you imagine their faces if I married their papa?' She went to open the door in answer to scratching on the bottom panel. 'It's all right, Bob,' she said, chuckling. 'I'm done here. We'll go to the kitchen and give Hester the good news that Grandpapa has been found.'

'He's a dog, Rosie. He doesn't understand what you're saying.'

'Of course he does. Bob is more intelligent than most people.' Rosalind hesitated in the doorway. 'It would be wonderful if Jarvis would agree to come back to Rockwood and take care of Grandpapa. Anyway, the least we can do is to give him a meal. I'll let Hester know to lay another place in the servants' hall.'

'Don't let Hester hear your referring to her as a servant,' Bertie said, grinning. 'She thinks she runs this place.'

'She's not far wrong.' Rosalind left the room, followed, as always, by Bob.

'Mr Jarvis is a good man,' Hester said slowly. 'I think he's been lonely since he retired. At least, that's what Minnie told me when I met her in the village shop. He devoted his whole life to Rockwood and the Carey family.' She took a deep breath. 'But if he comes back he'd better not tell me how to run my kitchen. I've grown used to doing things my way.'

'I'm sure he will realise that.' Rosalind tasted the rabbit stew that was simmering on the range. 'This is delicious, Hester. You are a superb cook.'

'You always know how to get round me, Miss

Rosalind. I suppose you want me to make up a bed for Mr Jarvis.'

'I haven't asked him if he'll come back, but I'm hoping he will. Mr Blanchard has settled our debts and we're reasonably well off again, Hester.'

'That's good news, but are you sure you can trust that man?'

'No, but he's done what he promised, and I'm not going to argue with that. It means that I can afford to pay someone to take care of Grandpapa. You should have seen how Jarvis handled him. Grandpapa went up to his room without a word of argument.'

'In that case I'll do what I can to make Mr Jarvis comfortable.' Hester nudged the scullery door open with her foot. 'Tilly, stop lurking in there. I need you to help me.'

Tilly emerged, wiping her hands on her apron. 'I'm here, Mrs Dodridge. Just tell me what to do.'

'Fetch cleaning cloths, a mop and a broom and some of my lavender polish. You'll find that in the still room.'

'I'll sort out some clean bed linen,' Rosalind said, smiling. 'I'm sure that Mr Jarvis is very particular in his requirements, but first there's the matter of luncheon for my grandfather. If you would see to that, Hester, I'll show Tilly what to do.'

Hester frowned. 'It's not right, Miss Rosalind. It was one thing when we were poor, but you say we're all right for money now. You're the mistress and should be treated as such.'

'That's as maybe, but have you a better idea? We want Mr Jarvis to stay, so I'm prepared to do what I can to persuade him to return. Come with me, Tilly. We'll do this together.'

Henry Jarvis agreed to take up his old position as butler with special duties where Sir Lucien was concerned. He accepted gracefully and Rosalind suspected that he was pleased to be back in charge of the servants' hall, even though the indoor staff numbered only two, and Hester was beholden to nobody, so Mr Jarvis's rule only really extended to Tilly. However, Rosalind was adamant that she would be taking on more servants, starting with the daily cleaning woman and a housemaid, if funds permitted.

However, the return of the man who had ruled the servants' hall for more than twenty years did not work out exactly as planned. After a few days it was evident to Rosalind that all was not well between Hester and Mr Jarvis, who was a stickler for everything being done by the book. There were no more meals taken in the kitchen by family members. Jarvis suggested firmly that everyone should change for dinner, and, much to Bertie's amusement, he attempted to train Tilly to wait on table. Matters came to a head one evening at dinner.

Tilly staggered into the dining room, clutching a tureen in both hands, but it was obviously very hot and her small face was screwed up with pain. Unable to see where she was going, she tripped over a frayed patch on the carpet, and dropped the tureen with a cry of distress. Soup pooled on the floor and shards of broken china were scattered all over the Persian carpet. Jarvis forgot himself enough to shout at Tilly, who fled the room in tears.

'It really wasn't her fault, Jarvis,' Rosalind said crossly. 'The tureen was hot and too heavy for her to handle. She's just a child – far too young to train as a parlour maid.'

'Begging your pardon, Miss Rosalind, but in my day young people were more disciplined. They knew their place and respected their elders. That girl is hopeless.'

'Nevertheless we can't afford to take on experienced staff, Jarvis. I'm afraid you will have to be patient, and I suggest that Tilly is kept in the kitchen to help Hester.'

'Yes, Jarvis,' Bertie said casually. 'There's no need to make a fuss. Tilly can clean up the spill and we'll say no more about it.'

'Very well, sir.' Jarvis backed away from the table and left the room, shoulders hunched.

'You've offended him, Bertie,' Walter said, chuckling. 'I hope there's some more soup or something to follow it, because I'm famished.'

'You always think about your stomach, Walter.' Patricia tossed her head. 'They don't have this trouble at Greystone Park. Do they, Rosie?' She shot a mischievous smile in her sister's direction.

Rosalind chose to ignore this remark and she rose to her feet. 'I'll go and see what's happening in the kitchen. I don't want that poor child made miserable because of a broken dish and some spilled soup.'

'Leave it to Jarvis, Rosie.' Bertie pushed his chair back from the table and stood up. 'That's what he's paid for. You don't have to take responsibility for everything that happens below stairs.'

'Where are you going?' Rosalind demanded suspiciously.

'To the Black Dog. At least I know I'll get something to eat and drink there. Are you coming with me, Walter?'

Walter shot a wary glance at Rosalind. 'Do you mind, Rosie? It means there's more food for you and Patsy.'

Rosalind sighed, shaking her head. 'It's all right, Walter. Go with Bertie and make sure he comes home sober. We don't want any more mishaps.'

'You shouldn't be so soft with them,' Patricia said crossly as the door closed on their brothers. 'Why do they get away with such bad behaviour?'

'I'd rather they went out than have them sit opposite me with long faces. I'm going to speak to Hester, regardless of what Jarvis thinks.' Rosalind made her way to the kitchen to find Jarvis and Hester in the middle of an altercation, while Tilly sobbed in the scullery.

'It was an accident,' Rosalind said firmly. 'There's no need to fall out because of it. I suggest you bring whatever food is left to the dining room, Jarvis. Tilly can clear up the mess when we have finished our dinner.' She looked from one startled face to the other. 'And my brothers have gone to the Black Dog where they hope to eat a meal in peace.' She fixed her gaze on Jarvis, who was standing stiffly to attention. 'I'm surprised at you, Mr Jarvis. You were always so calm and professional. Now I find you and Hester behaving like a couple of costermongers. Shame on you both.' Rosalind turned on her heel and marched out of the kitchen, but when she returned to the dining room there was no sign of Patricia.

Rosalind went to the window and looked out over the rose garden. It was a lovely May evening and it was not hard to guess where Patricia had gone. It was impossible to tell whether the relationship between her sister and Barnaby Yelland, the blacksmith's son, was serious, or merely a continuation of their childhood friendship, but Rosalind suspected it had gone much further. Patricia was only sixteen, too young to know her own mind, and Barnaby only a year or two older. What was evident was the scandal their relationship would cause if they were discovered. Not only that, but Lucy Warren, the wheelwright's daughter, was a nice girl and she would be heartbroken if she discovered that her fiancé was seeing someone else.

Ignoring the pangs of hunger that cramped her stomach, Rosalind fetched her shawl from the morning parlour and slipped out through the doors that led into the rose garden, with Bob bounding on ahead. She did not want Hester or Jarvis to see her leave the castle grounds. Some secrets were best kept within the family. The sun was low in the sky, turning the backwater into a shimmering silver lake, but Rosalind did not stop to admire the view. She crossed the bridge and was about to enter the orchard, where the apple blossom showered the grass with pink and white petals as if a wedding had taken place, when she heard a distant peal of laughter. She knew instantly where Patricia and Barnaby had chosen to meet, and she cut through the orchard, heading towards the wood, which was Bertie's favoured hunting ground. In the densest part of this was a glade, which in late spring was carpeted with bluebells, and it was here that they had all played when they were children. Barnaby and Lucy had been privileged to join them, and some of the other village children had braved Abe Coaker's wrath if he found them trespassing on Carey land.

'Find Patsy, Bob,' Rosalind said in a low voice.

He looked up at her, his topaz eyes shining with excitement and his pink tongue lolling out of his mouth, his tail wagging so fast it made his whole body shake.

'Find,' Rosalind repeated, and Bob raced off into the densely wooded area with Rosalind following him.

Bertie and Walter with the assistance of Ossie

Cottingham, the squire's son, had built the tree house in the ancient oak tree at the edge of the glade with probably more help from Barnaby than any of them would admit, and it was here that Rosalind suspected she would find the errant pair. Bob seemed to share her opinion, and he crashed through the undergrowth, coming to a halt beneath the tree house. Rosalind made her way over a carpet of green leaves and delicate white flowers that exuded the pungent aroma of wild garlic. She could hear Patricia's laughter, followed by Barnaby's deeper tones.

'Patsy, I know you're up there. Come down at once.'

There was silence and then Patricia poked her head out. 'Rosie, what are you doing here?'

'I know that you're with Barnaby. Come down, now.'

Barnaby appeared first. He leaped to the ground, holding his arms out to catch Patricia as she climbed down more slowly.

'We weren't doing anything wrong, Miss Carey,' Barnaby said gruffly.

Rosalind met his anxious gaze, finding it difficult not to smile. He treated her now with a deference that had not existed when they were younger. Barnaby had Romany blood somewhere in his ancestry, which was evident in his dark-haired, dark-eyed looks and the raffish charm that most of the local girls seemed to find irresistible, including Patricia.

'Why can't you leave us alone?' Patricia demanded crossly.

'You are engaged to be married, Barnaby. What do you think Lucy would say if she knew that you two were meeting in secret?'

Barnaby shrugged, but he avoided meeting Rosalind's angry gaze. 'Lucy is all right. Anyway, she can't stop me seeing my friends.'

'This is more than that, isn't it? I've known you most of my life, Barnaby, and I can tell when you're lying.'

He slipped his arm around Patricia's shoulders and hugged her close. 'You won't tell anyone, will you?'

'She won't, but I'm not going to keep quiet about this, boy.' Abe Coaker burst through the trees brandishing a shotgun. 'I thought you was poachers, but now I see I've come across something worse. Lucy is my niece. What have you to say for yourselves?'

Chapter Nine

Rosalind gazed at Abe in dismay. She had quite forgotten that Abe's sister, Mary, had married Daniel Warren, the wheelwright, and that Lucy was his niece.

'It's all right, Abe. I can handle this,' Rosalind said with more conviction than she was feeling. Abe was a loyal and devoted servant, but he was known in the village for his sudden outbursts of temper, and she feared for Barnaby if Abe became violent. He might be a much older man but he was fit and strong, and been known to take on bare-knuckle fighters when the fair came to the village.

Abe took a step closer to Barnaby. 'If I find out that you've been going behind my Lucy's back I'll make you rue the day you was born, boy.'

Patricia broke away from Barnaby. 'That won't be necessary, Mr Coaker. Barnaby and I are just good friends. We were . . .' she paused.

Rosalind could see that her sister was at a loss for words. 'I believe they were planning a surprise for Lucy,' she said hastily.

'That's not how it sounded, Miss Rosalind.' Abe eyed her suspiciously. 'You wasn't too pleased to find them together, from what I heard just now.'

'I'd forgotten that Lucy's birthday is in a few days' time,' Rosalind said casually. 'We've had a lot of problems, as you know, Abe. Anyway, Mr Jarvis has returned to the castle and things will get better. In the meantime, you'd best come home with me, Patsy. We don't want people to get the wrong impression.'

Patricia shot an imploring glance in Barnaby's direction, but he was keeping his distance both from her and from Lucy's uncle. 'Perhaps we'd better forget our plan, since people seem to think the worst.'

Rosalind grabbed her by the hand. 'Come, Patsy.' She dragged her sister unceremoniously through the tangle of undergrowth, stopping only when they emerged into the field on the edge of Greep farm. 'What were you thinking of? You're not a child, but you are acting like one.'

'That's not fair,' Patricia said, pouting. 'I love Barnaby and he loves me. He doesn't want to marry that wispy streak of nothing Lucy Warren.'

'Then why did he ask her to marry him?'

Patricia dropped her gaze. 'I don't know.'

'Yes, you do. Tell me, Patsy.' Rosalind threw up her hands. 'She's in the family way, isn't she?'

'So she says, but it could be a ploy to get Barnaby to marry her. She's a scheming little minx.'

'Look at me, Patsy. Stop staring at the ground and look at me.'

Patricia raised her head. 'What else can I say?'

'You will give me your word not to see Barnaby Yelland again. This is his problem, and if you continue to meet him in secret it will be you who comes off worst. Do you understand what I'm saying?'

Patricia shrugged and started off across the field. 'You don't understand. Nobody understands.'

Rosalind followed more slowly. She knew that there was no reasoning with Patricia when she was in this mood. They arrived home within minutes of each other but Patricia stormed off to her room, leaving Rosalind standing at the foot of the grand staircase. This was one problem that she could not share with Hester, or with anyone, if it came to that. Rumours flew round the village in ever-increasing circles and it would only take the smallest hint to send news of a scandal spinning out of control. Rosalind decided to leave Patricia to cool down before she did anything, but she knew that Patricia would not give up easily.

Rosalind was about to make her way to the kitchen when the door in the panelling flew open. It was one of several such doors in the castle that had been used by generations of servants to ensure the privacy of those above stairs. Jarvis emerged into the hall, brushing a cobweb from his forehead.

'Excuse me, if I startled you, Miss Rosalind, but I was in the tower with Sir Lucien when I spotted a carriage heading this way.'

'Did you recognise the vehicle, Jarvis?'

'No, but it seems to have arrived. Shall I investigate, Miss Rosalind?'

'Please do.' Rosalind stood back as he opened the door. She was curious and her first thought was that Piers had returned. It was even more of a surprise when she saw her mother alight from the carriage, assisted by Claude.

'Welcome home, madam,' Jarvis said solemnly.

Felicia rushed into the entrance hall, her arms open wide. 'Rosalind, my darling, I promised to visit you and here I am.'

Half smothered by her mother's expensive French perfume and her warm embrace, Rosalind took a step backwards. 'Mama, Claude, we weren't expecting you.'

'Darling girl, I promised to visit this hideous pile of old stones before Claude and I left for Vienna, and here we are.' She turned to Jarvis, thrusting her parasol into his outstretched hand. 'You're still here, Jarvis? I thought you had retired.'

'I came out of retirement at Mister Bertram's request, Mrs Carey.'

Claude handed his top hat, cane and gloves to Jarvis, acknowledging him with a slight nod, as he turned his full attention to Rosalind. 'My dear

Rosalind, what have you done to yourself? Is that a leaf in your hair? If I might say so, you are in desperate need of a lady's maid. Your hair is in quite a tangle.'

'I've just been for a walk.' Rosalind brushed a stray curl back from her forehead. 'We live very simply, Claude.'

Felicia glanced over her shoulder. 'Where is Smithers?'

'I believe she's helping Heslop to unload some of your baggage, my dear,' Claude said patiently.

'Jarvis, send someone to help them, if you please.' Felicia glanced round the hall, frowning. 'This mausoleum doesn't change, more's the pity. We haven't eaten since midday, Rosalind. We'll go to the drawing room and wait for your cook to make us a meal. Nothing elaborate, you understand. Perhaps some soup followed by baked trout or roast chicken, but a glass or two of sherry wine would be most welcome. I don't suppose there is any champagne in the cellar?'

'No, Mama. The cellar has been empty for quite some time, but I'll go and speak to Hester about a meal.'

'I'm not fussy, Rosalind. But where are my boys? Do send them to me, darling.'

'I will when they return from the Black Dog, Mama.'

'Perhaps we should have called there first, Felicia, my sweet?' Claude said warily. 'We don't want to be a nuisance, after all.'

'Nuisance? Nonsense. This is still my home and I am the mistress of the house when I am in residence.' Felicia hesitated at the sight of Patricia, who came running down the stairs.

'Mama, you came! You said you would.' She flung her arms around her mother and burst into tears.

'My darling, what's the matter?' Felicia held her at arm's length. 'Don't cry on my best silk travelling gown, my love. Are those tears of joy?'

'No, Mama. Rosalind has been horrid to me.'

Rosalind met Claude's amused gaze and she rolled her eyes. 'I'm going to sort out a meal and rooms for you both. Please go to the drawing room and I'll see if I can find some sherry, although it might be Hester's home-made blackberry wine, if my brothers haven't drunk it all.'

Hester, as always, rose to the occasion and in less than an hour had created food that was tasty and filling, although Felicia made it quite clear that vegetable soup and bread still warm from the oven, was what peasants ate, and she herself was used to the finer things in life. However, two bottles of blackberry wine that Hester had been saving for a special occasion turned the homely meal into something of a celebration, and Claude ate two helpings of apple pie, swearing that it was the best he had ever tasted. Patricia toyed with her food and Rosalind had lost her appetite, but she ate enough not to draw attention to herself.

Felicia was much more cheerful after three glasses of blackberry wine, and she regaled them with London gossip, although most of the people she mentioned were unknown to Rosalind. They had just finished their meal and Tilly had brought coffee to the drawing room when Bertie and Walter returned from the Black Dog in very good spirits. At that point Claude produced a flask of brandy from his coat pocket, which he shared with them. Patricia was more cheerful now and seemed to have forgotten the episode in the tree house. Now that her family were comfortably at ease with each other, Rosalind made her escape unnoticed. She met Jarvis in the entrance hall.

'Is my grandfather still in his room?'

'Yes, Miss Rosalind. He's eaten quite well and he's had a couple of tots of rum. He should sleep until morning.'

'Where did you get the rum? I thought the cellar was bare.'

Jarvis tapped the side of his nose. 'When I retired I put several bottles aside for Sir Lucien. It seems that my hiding place was a good one, and he's gone to bed quite happy.'

'You're a marvel, Jarvis. I don't know how we managed without you. I'd really prefer it if we could keep Grandpapa in his suite of rooms while my mother is visiting. They never did get on, and I'm afraid there'll be a terrible row if they meet.'

'Of course, Miss Rosalind. I understand.'

Rosalind smiled and walked away, heading in the direction of the kitchen. She could not go to bed without thanking Hester for providing a meal at such short notice, and it was high time Tilly went home to her family. Although the evenings were drawing out nicely it would soon be dark and Tilly was just a child. However, when Rosalind reached the kitchen she found Hester and Miss Smithers, Felicia's maid, glaring each other across the pine table.

'Please tell this person that I am in charge of domestic arrangements, Miss Rosalind,' Hester said angrily.

'I am Madame Carey's personal maid and I deserve the respect due to that position,' Miss Smithers said stiffly.

'Of course you do, and I'm sure there has been a misunderstanding.' Rosalind sent a warning look to Hester. 'But Mrs Dodridge is quite correct. We have a very small household here, Miss Smithers, and Mrs Dodridge has been with my family for many years. She will offer you any help and assistance you need. Won't you, Hester?'

Hester's full lips twisted into a vinegary smile. 'Of course, Miss Rosalind.'

'Then I wish to have my meals in my room,' Miss Smithers said with a triumphant smile. 'I don't eat in the kitchen like a common servant.'

Rosalind could see that Hester was fuming, and she sympathised with her, but she knew she must make an effort to keep the peace. 'As you can see, Miss Smithers, we have very few servants at present, so I suggest that you collect your food here and then you may take it to your room, if you so wish. That is the best I can offer you, but you look like a reasonable woman to me.'

'I count myself as a lady, Miss Carey. I can't say that this is an ideal solution, but it will have to do.'

'How about a nice hot cup of tea, Miss Smithers?' Hester said through clenched teeth.

Next morning Rosalind was up early, as usual, and after a quick word with Hester she went to the dining room to lay the table for breakfast. There was only so much that Hester could do on her own and Tilly was kept busy with the tasks that had been allotted to her.

'What on earth are you doing, Rosalind?' Felicia stood in the doorway, staring at Rosalind as if she were doing something extraordinary.

'You're up early, Mama.'

'Why are you doing menial work? Where are the servants?'

'There's only Hester, Mama. I have employed a young girl from the village, but she's untrained and I doubt if she would know how to set a table.'

'You said that things were bad, but I had no idea that you had sunk to this level.' Felicia walked over to the window. 'It was late when we arrived last evening, but I can see now that the rose garden needs some attention. My bed wasn't properly aired and Smithers complained about her accommodation. She was decidedly put out this morning, and I had to wash in cold water.'

'I tried to tell you about it when Patsy and I visited you in London. I knew you didn't believe me.'

Felicia turned her head to give Rosalind a long look. 'I'd believe anything when it comes to this terrible place. The years I spent here were the unhappiest time of my life.'

'But that's all behind you now, Mama.'

'Yes, thank goodness. But Patricia isn't happy and you look worn out. I thought that Piers was helping you. He told me that he would.'

'He's paid off our creditors and he's put quite a generous sum at our disposal, although I hate accepting money from a virtual stranger.'

'But he's related to you, my love. Even if it's a very distant connection, that makes him part of the family. No woman can manage on her own, unless of course she has independent means.'

'I've had to accept his help, but I don't entirely trust him, Mama. He might decide to evict us all on a sudden whim.'

'He could have done that from the start had he wanted to be difficult.'

Rosalind shrugged. 'He might change his mind. Besides which, I have other problems that are far more pressing.'

'It really isn't fair that you've had to bear so much responsibility at such a young age, Rosie. I know I haven't been a good mother,' Felicia said slowly. She moved away from the window and took a seat at the head of the table. 'Sit down, my dear. I want to talk seriously.'

Rosalind did as she asked. 'What is it, Mama?'

'Claude and I will be leaving for Vienna in a few days' time. I know you are very capable, much more so than I ever was, but it's Patsy who worries me.'

'Did she say something to you last evening, Mama?'

'She came to my room and sobbed as if her heart would break. You know she thinks she is in love with a young man from the village.'

'Yes, Mama.'

'She told me that you had forbidden her to see him again, which of course was the right advice, but likely to have the opposite effect.'

'What else could I say?'

'I'm afraid Patricia takes after me. I was always headstrong and I suppose I'm selfish, in a way. Although, of course, with my undoubted talent that is only to be expected.' Felicia paused, fixing Rosalind with an expectant look.

'Yes, I suppose so, Mama.'

'There is no "suppose" about it, my dear. I have a God-given gift, which must be shared with the world. I have said so on numerous occasions. However, we're talking about your sister, and I can see she is heading for a disaster, not to mention creating a terrible scandal.'

'Do you think she intends to elope with Barnaby?'

'It wouldn't surprise me.'

'She won't listen to me. Maybe you could talk sense into her, Mama?'

'She imagines herself to be in love and in her mind she's the heroine of some Gothic novel. She's very young, Rosie, and she needs protecting from herself. Besides which, I refuse to have an artisan as a son-in-law. I won't have my beautiful child throwing herself away on a mere blacksmith.'

It struck Rosalind forcibly that this was the first time her mother had shown such passionate interest in any of her children. 'What do you suggest we do about it, Mama?'

'I can't do anything, my dear. I will be far away from Rockwood and I have my public to consider, so I'm afraid the onus is on you and your brothers.'

'Then it's down to me, I suppose. But I confess I'm at a loss to know how to handle this. I can hardly lock Patsy in her room.'

'I think the time has come for more drastic action,' Felicia said thoughtfully. 'I think it would serve your purpose well to take Patricia to Cornwall.'

'To Cornwall? Why?'

'Don't be obtuse, Rosalind. When I say Cornwall, of course I mean Trevenor. Piers Blanchard claims to be family, so why not visit him at home. I mean, he sought you out in London and he told me that he planned to come here. I think a month or two on the Cornish coast would take Patricia's mind off the blacksmith.'

'I can't just arrive at Trevenor without an invitation,' Rosalind protested.

'I will write a letter to Piers. After all, he claims to be one of my devoted admirers. I will tell him that you and Patricia are about to visit Cornwall and would love to make yourselves known to his family. What could be wrong with that?'

'But Patsy will refuse to accompany me, I know she will.'

'Leave your sister to me.'

'She won't agree to leave Rockwood for one simple reason. Barnaby is engaged to Lucy Warren, the wheelwright's daughter, and she is in the family way. Not only that, she's Abe Coaker's niece and he won't stand by to see her humiliated, so the wedding will be very soon.'

'Then a little subterfuge is needed. I'll write to Piers now and Gurney will post it. We won't tell Patricia until the last minute, and we won't wait for a response either. Leave the arrangements to me.'

Felicia managed to keep Patricia busy for the rest of the day, and Claude went out hunting with Bertie. Rosalind had no idea whether Claude really enjoyed poetry but, later, when she ventured into the library to announce that dinner was served, it seemed that

Claude was showing a genuine interest in Walter's work.

Felicia rose from the window seat where she had been leafing through an old copy of *Household Words*.

'I've spoken to Claude and he's more than willing to help. I'm going to suggest that you, Patsy, Claude and myself spend a day or two in Plymouth. We can explore the city shops and visit the theatre, where I had my debut more years ago than I care to remember. Then we will return here, leaving you and Patsy to travel on to Cornwall.'

'Are you sure about this, Mama?'

'My dear, if I remain here for more than two days at a time I fear I will lose my mind. I know now why I left Rockwood, although, of course, it's delightful to be with my children again.'

Despite her lovelorn state, Patricia was easily tempted by the promise of a new bonnet and anything else that she might fancy in Plymouth. The prospect of a visit to the theatre made the trip even more attractive, and two days later Felicia, Claude, Rosalind and Patricia set off on the road to Exeter. Miss Smithers travelled on the box with Claude's coachman, having refused point-blank to remain in the castle with Hester. No matter how many times Rosalind intervened and tried to make peace between them, Hester and Smithers did not get along. From Exeter they caught the train and after several changes, they arrived in Plymouth where Claude booked them into a hotel on the Hoe. Rosalind and Patricia shared a room overlooking Plymouth Sound and Drake's Island. Rosalind could have looked out of the window, gazing at the view, until sunset, but Patricia was eager to explore the city and Claude had promised to purchase tickets for the theatre that evening.

In the end, Rosalind gave herself up to enjoying the freedom and excitement of doing something new and unexpected. They dined early and spent the evening at the Theatre Royal watching a play that everyone seemed to enjoy, with the exception of Claude, who fell asleep during the second act. Felicia nudged him in the ribs when he began to snore, and Patricia giggled, hiding her face behind her fan. The fact that her sister actually found something amusing came as a relief to Rosalind after the emotional ups and downs of the past few days. It seemed to confirm their mother's suggestion that time spent away from Rockwood might bring Patricia to her senses. Rosalind could only hope so.

Next morning Felicia took them shopping, leaving Claude to amuse himself. They spent an hour or so in a milliner's shop, where Felicia treated them to new bonnets, and they went on to an emporium that seemed to sell everything a young woman would want or need. They came away with packages and bandboxes filled with exciting luxuries. But time was short and Rosalind was only too well aware that her mother and Claude would have to leave very soon to begin their journey to Vienna. It was no surprise when Claude took her aside before dinner that evening.

'I've hired a carriage to take you and your sister to Trevenor tomorrow, Rosalind,' he said in a low voice.

'What will I tell Patsy?' Rosalind asked anxiously. 'I haven't told her that we're going to Cornwall.'

Claude shot a wary glance at Felicia and Patricia, who were seated side by side on one of the sofas. 'I suggest that we say you are going to visit Mount Edgcumbe House on the other side of the Tamar. It isn't open to the public, but I've spoken to the concierge and I believe the housekeeper occasionally allows visitors, providing the family are not in residence.'

'Won't Patricia wonder why we're going on our own?'

'I think subterfuge is necessary in the circumstances, Rosalind. I will tell her that we're all going, but your mama will feign a headache, as she often does on such occasions. We will wait until you've gone and then we will return to Rockwood, and on to Vienna in our own good time.'

'What are you two whispering about?' Patricia demanded suspiciously.

'We're planning an excursion for tomorrow, my dear,' Claude said glibly. 'You'll find out in the morning.'

*

Next morning Felicia put on the performance of her life, feigning a headache that left her prostrate on the bed. Patricia was reluctant to leave her at first, but Felicia fluttered her hand and ordered her to enjoy the outing.

'It will make the pain more bearable if I know that my girls are making full use of their time. I can't expect you to sit in a darkened room with me. In fact I insist that you go on this trip and you can tell me all about it when you return.'

'Mama is right,' Rosalind said firmly. 'Come, Patsy. She needs peace and quiet above all.'

'Oh, very well, but I'm not sure that I want to see around a stately home. It will only make Rockwood look more shabby and old-fashioned.'

'Perhaps it will give us some ideas on renovating the furniture.' Rosalind led the way downstairs to the vestibule. 'Mama has insisted that we go without her, Claude,' she said pointedly. 'You could accompany us, if you wish.'

He shook his head. 'I'll stay at your mother's side, Rosalind. I'm sure she'll feel better quite soon.'

Patricia stepped outside into the sunshine. 'Come on then, Rosie.'

'Just a minute. I want a word with Claude.' Rosalind drew him aside. 'Where did you put our baggage?'

He smiled. 'Don't worry. They're on the box with the coachman.'

'You will explain everything to Bertie, won't you?'

Rosalind asked anxiously. 'I wanted to tell him before we left, but Mama thought it best to keep our plans secret.'

'Your mother is a wise woman.' Claude glanced at Patricia, who was looking distinctly rebellious. 'You'd better go now, my dear. Who knows when we'll meet again, but I hope all goes well in Cornwall.' He took a leather pouch from his inside pocket and placed it in Rosalind's hand. 'This will pay for your return journey should you not receive a warm welcome.'

'I have to admit I'm not comfortable about simply turning up at Trevenor, but I can't see any other way out of the present situation.'

'What are you talking about?' Patricia leaned out of the carriage.

'I must go.' Rosalind stood on tiptoe to plant a kiss on Claude's whiskery cheek. 'Take care of Mama.' She ran down the steps and climbed into the carriage. 'Move over, Patsy.'

'What were you two talking about?' Patricia demanded. 'You're keeping something from me, Rosie. I know you.'

Rosalind settled in the corner seat just as the carriage moved forward. She waved to Claude as they drove away. 'I was just telling Claude what Hester did for us when we were unwell. I suggested a chamomile tisane, or feverfew. Anyway, Claude is perfectly capable of looking after Mama. He's done so for years and he knows her better than anyone.'

'Do you think they'll get married now that Mama is a widow?'

'Mama is officially in mourning, but who knows? She never follows the rules set down by society.'

Patricia sighed. 'Do we have to visit the old mansion? I'd much rather go shopping.'

'What with, Patsy? We haven't any money to spend on ourselves. We were lucky that Mama was in a generous mood yesterday.' Rosalind fingered the ribbons on her new bonnet.

'What is the point of having pretty things if there's no one to admire them?' Patricia gazed out of the window. 'When are we going home, Rosie?'

'I wasn't going to tell you until later, but we planned a surprise for you, Patsy.'

Patricia turned her head and her eyes lit up with anticipation. 'A surprise? How lovely. What is it?'

Chapter Ten

'What?' Patricia's voice rose to a shriek. 'We're going to Cornwall?'

'Mama wrote to Piers. She told him that we would be in the area and we would like to call upon him and his grandmother, Lady Pentelow.'

'You did this on purpose.' Patricia turned away. 'You planned this thinking that keeping me apart from Barnaby would change things.'

'Barnaby is engaged to be married – you know that. He has to marry Lucy. He has no choice now.'

'She planned it to trap him.'

'I don't believe that for a moment. However, let's not argue about it, Patsy. We need to get to know Piers and his family, if only for the simple reason that he has the power to take away everything we hold dear. I'm still not sure I believe his story, and I want to find out if his claim is all that it seems to be.'

'Maybe you should marry him,' Patricia said sulkily.

Rosalind chose to ignore this remark. 'He has a younger sister called Aurelia. I think you might get on very well together, from what he told me.'

'I don't care. I'm going to tell the coachman to take us back to the hotel.' Patricia tried to open the door, but the vehicle was tooling along at speed and Rosalind pulled her back.

'Don't be silly. You'll kill yourself if you fall out of the carriage while it's moving. We're on our way now and there's no turning back. We might as well make up our minds to enjoy ourselves.'

'I'm going to tell Piers that you tricked me into coming with you.'

'I doubt if he would be interested.'

'I really hate you sometimes, Rosalind Carey.' Patricia moved as far away from her sister as she could in such a confined space, staring moodily out of the window.

Rosalind sighed. 'Have it your own way, Patsy.'

Patricia played the martyr all the way to Cornwall, despite several stops to change horses and an overnight stay at a rather shabby inn. It was midday when they finally arrived at Trevenor, which was situated on the cliffs above St Austell Bay.

'Is this the right place?' Patricia turned to Rosalind. 'Are you sure?'

Rosalind opened the door as the carriage drew to a halt. 'Is this Trevenor?'

The coachman, who had barely spoken a word to them during the whole journey, climbed stiffly down from the box. 'Yes, miss. This is it.' He put down the step and helped Rosalind to alight, followed by Patricia. 'I've got another job in St Blazey, so I'll have to leave you now.' He reached under the driver's seat and pulled out their two rather small valises, which he dumped at their feet.

Rosalind watched him drive away with a sinking feeling. She turned to gaze at the house, which seemed to have impressed Patricia, who was staring at it open-mouthed.

'It's much larger than I imagined,' Rosalind said cautiously. Piers had said that the original building dated back to before the Norman Conquest, and it was not hard to believe. Part of the mansion did look like a fortified manor house, with an entrance high above ground level, presumably to keep marauders at bay. The rest of the impressive building seemed to scan several centuries, as if each successive generation had added to it in the architectural style that was fashionable at the time. The different periods were brought together by a wide veranda with climbing roses and wisteria trailing over its roof in delicate pastel shades.

'What do we do now?' Patricia asked nervously. 'What happens if they're not expecting us?'

Rosalind was thinking the same thing, but she managed a smile. 'We'll soon find out.' She marched purposefully across the gravelled forecourt and tugged at the bell pull. She could hear the sound echoing inside the building. Then after a few moments she could hear footsteps and the door was opened by the butler, who gave her a cursory look.

'Good morning. I believe we're expected,' Rosalind said with more confidence than she was feeling. 'Miss Carey and Miss Patricia Carey.' For a dreadful moment she thought that he was going to send them away, but he nodded and held the door open for them.

'Come this way, if you please, Miss Carey.' He clicked his fingers and a footman appeared as if from nowhere to take their baggage.

Rosalind was about to follow him when she realised that Patricia was not paying attention. She seemed to be rooted to the spot and was gazing around the spacious entrance hall, wide-eyed. 'Patsy,' Rosalind tugged at her hand, 'come along.'

'It's so beautiful,' Patricia breathed, gazing up at the ornate plasterwork on the coving, and the ceiling roses that surrounded the brass chandeliers. The walls were papered in expensive hand-painted paper, which Rosalind suspected had been imported from China. The design of exotic birds and delicate foliage was something she had noticed at the Great Exhibition, and now she was seeing it in all its glory.

She did not blame her sister for being impressed, but they must not appear to be country bumpkins and she quickened her pace to keep up with the butler. He led the way along a wide corridor with tall windows facing the gardens at the side of the house. In between each window there was a large terracotta tub containing a tree with shiny green leaves, and what appeared to be oranges hanging from the branches.

'They can't be real,' Patricia breathed, and before Rosalind could stop her, Patricia had plucked a fruit and was holding it to her nose. 'It's an orange,' she whispered. 'A real fruit, growing indoors.'

'Put it in your pocket,' Rosalind hissed as the butler came to a halt and turned to them, and although it was obvious that he had seen Patricia pluck the fruit, his expression remained impassive. 'If you would wait in the Chinese room, I'll inform Mr Blanchard that you have arrived.'

Rosalind sent a warning look to her sister and she entered the room with as much dignity as she could muster, which was not easy in the circumstances.

Patricia burst out laughing as the door closed on the affronted butler.

'What is so funny?' A pretty, dark-haired girl leaped up from a chair by the window. 'I've never seen anyone who found Patterson amusing.'

'I'm sorry, we didn't know there was anyone in the room,' Rosalind said awkwardly. 'Your butler asked us to wait here for Mr Blanchard.'

'I'm not supposed to be in here. I'm hiding from Grandmama. You must be the sisters from Rockwood Castle. Piers told me that you were coming.' She held out her hand. 'I should introduce myself. I'm Aurelia Blanchard. Piers is my brother.'

'How do you do?' Rosalind decided that Piers had described his sister accurately. Aurelia was a beauty with large hazel eyes. Her hair was dark and curled extravagantly around her face, even though it was tied back with a pink ribbon, and her soft cheeks dimpled when she smiled. It was obvious from her demeanour that Aurelia Blanchard knew she was attractive, and she exuded confidence. Rosalind found it easy to believe that she was what Hester would have called 'a handful'.

'How do you do, Miss Carey?' Aurelia inclined her head graciously. 'Welcome to Trevenor. We seldom have visitors so I will make the most of your company.' She turned to Patricia. 'Piers tells me that we are distant cousins, whatever that means. I hope you will stay long enough for us to get to know each other.'

Patricia managed a smile. 'I don't know. I wasn't expecting to come here today.'

'You weren't?' Aurelia's eyes shone with excitement. 'I wouldn't do anything that went against my wishes. So why are you here?'

'We wanted to get to know you,' Rosalind said hastily. 'It was a surprise to find out that we had relations in Cornwall, and it seemed the right thing to do to come here and introduce ourselves to you and your grandmother.'

'And you're afraid that my brother will turn you out of your home,' Aurelia said, chuckling. 'I know it's not funny, but I would feel the same if the situation was reversed. Anyway, Piers wouldn't do that to anyone. Don't tell him I said so, but he's a good brother.' She glanced over her shoulder as the door opened and Piers strolled into the room.

'Patterson told me that you'd arrived. I hope your journey wasn't too tedious.'

'We're here now, and that's all that matters,' Rosalind said firmly. 'You have a beautiful home, Piers.'

'I think she means that we are well suited here, so you don't need to take Rockwood from them, dear brother.' Aurelia held her hand out to Patricia. 'Come with me. I'll show you to your room. I'm sure you want to change out of your travelling costume. Are you hungry? We haven't had luncheon yet, so you're just in time.' She led Patricia from the room, still chattering.

Piers waited until the door closed on them before turning back to Rosalind with a questioning look. 'I must admit I was surprised to receive a letter from your mother, but you are very welcome, nonetheless.'

'Thank you. I know it must seem odd, but I had my reasons for coming here.'

'Something serious must have occurred. Take a seat and tell me about it, Rosalind.'

It had seemed so easy when she made the decision to visit Trevenor, but face to face with Piers Blanchard she was assailed with doubts. What had sounded so reasonable in her head now felt like a pathetic excuse. She walked over to the window and gazed out onto a wide terrace with a stone balustrade and stone urns filled with geraniums. The gardens stretched as far as the eye could see and were bordered by woodland on one side and the sheer drop of the cliffs straight ahead, with an uninterrupted view of the bay.

'If I'm perfectly honest I think I wanted to see how you live in Cornwall. You can't blame me for being curious.' She turned to give him a searching look. 'You appeared out of nowhere, claiming to be the rightful heir to Rockwood.'

'So you wanted to make sure that I am who I say I am.' He smiled and he seemed genuinely amused. 'Quite right. I would have done the same myself.'

'You have all this,' Rosalind said with an expansive wave of her hands. 'And yet you want more. Why? What possible good would come of taking Rockwood from us?'

'I've told you that I have no intention of evicting you or your family. You have to believe me, Rosalind.'

'Then why did you go to all the trouble of introducing yourself to us in London? And a question that's been bothering me for ages – we'd never met and yet you appeared to recognise me that night at the opera. How did you know that my mother was Felicia Carey?'

'The fact that I was there at the same time was a coincidence, but I'd met Claude and I saw him escort you to the box. Besides which, you are very like your mother in appearance, so it was an educated guess.'

'Or had you been spying on us at Rockwood?' Rosalind said thoughtfully. 'Were you planning to descend upon us and claim the estate for yourself?'

'You've had a long journey in a hired hack and you must be tired and hungry. Shall we have this conversation later, when you are settled in and rested?'

'Don't treat me like a child, Piers. You're evading the question, as usual. I simply want to know your real motive.'

'Maybe I don't have an answer to that.' He walked over to the mantelshelf and pulled the bell rope. 'Since my sister has spirited Patricia away, I've rung for a servant to take you to your room. Luncheon will be served in half an hour and then you'll meet my grandmother.'

'I do feel slightly travel stained after a day and a half on the road, but we will talk again, Piers. That's why I came to Trevenor. I'm obligated to you now because of your generosity, but I need to know exactly where my family stands in all this.'

Rosalind gazed around her room in a mixture of delight and amazement. The inspiration for the décor had been the apple blossom depicted on the wallpaper, and this was carried through in the pale pink, white and green colour scheme. Everything was coordinated, from the delicate pattern of the curtains and the matching coverlet, to the deep pile of the carpet. There was even a dressing room all to herself, and the china on the washstand was decorated with apple blossom. She strolled back into her bedroom, which was so light and airy that she might well have been standing in a scented orchard.

'Shall I help you to change, miss?'

Rosalind came out of her reverie and turned to the young maid with a smile. 'I can manage, thank you. But I will need someone to show me to the dining room in time for luncheon.'

'Just ring the bell and I'll come, but you'll soon find your way around. I know I did.'

'What do I call you?'

'I'm Ada, miss.'

'Thank you, Ada. That will be all for now.' Rosalind walked over to the window and found herself gazing over the sweep of St Austell Bay. Sunlight shimmered on the calm turquoise water, which deepened to ultramarine at the horizon, and ships were moored in the harbour ready to take on loads of china clay. The mine stood out sharp and white against the background of green fields. All this and the beautiful old house made Rosalind even more curious about Piers' motive for coming into their lives, but then she realised that she would have to make haste or she would be late for luncheon and that would be very rude.

After a quick wash she changed into her best and only gown, having first shaken out the creases. She brushed her blond hair and secured it in a chignon at the back of her neck. Aurelia and Lady Pentelow were sure to have the luxury of their own personal maids. Yet again Rosalind was assailed by doubts. Lady Pentelow would see straight through her and would be quite within her rights to ask them politely to leave. Having done the best she could, Rosalind was about to ring for Ada when Patricia burst into the room followed by Aurelia.

'Rosie, you must come and see my room. It's so beautiful but very grand. I feel quite overwhelmed.'

'Don't worry,' Aurelia said casually. 'You'll soon get used to it, Patsy. I've stayed in far grander houses than this. Grandmama parades me round to all the country house balls and soirées in the hope that I'll catch a wealthy husband. She's determined to see me married and off her hands.'

'Do you really attend balls and such?' Patricia asked breathlessly. 'My friends Christina and Sylvia Greystone get invited to all the local functions, but Greystone Park isn't as fine as Trevenor.' Patricia turned to Rosalind with an excited giggle. 'Aurelia says that Trevenor used to be the haunt of smugglers when her grandmother was a girl. Isn't that exciting?'

'As was Rockwood.' Rosalind felt bound to champion their home, even if it did mean exposing the darker side of the castle's history. 'In fact, it was so common along the south coast that almost everywhere has something they don't mention in polite society.'

'Let's change the subject, shall we?' Aurelia made for the door. 'Grandmama is a stickler for punctuality.' She raced off with Patricia on her heels and Rosalind following more slowly, although she had to quicken her pace in order to keep up with them.

The dining room was surprisingly homely with wainscoted walls and leaded windows overlooking a parterre garden. The table was set for five and Piers was already seated at the head, but he rose to his feet as Aurelia entered the room with Rosalind and Patricia close behind.

'You're just in time, Aurelia. Grandmama will be here at any moment.' He pulled out a chair for Rosalind.

'You can sit here, Patsy.' Aurelia pointed to the chair next to her, but at that moment the door opened to admit Lady Pentelow and everyone froze, standing by their places in respectful silence.

Rosalind tried not to stare, but Clarissa Pentelow must have been a beauty in her youth. Although she was probably on the wrong side of sixty, she was still a strikingly handsome woman with a neat figure and imposing bearing. Her silver hair was coiffed in an ornate fashion that complimented her long neck and classic profile. Gold earrings hung from her ears but she wore no other jewellery than her wedding ring. Her gown in lavender silk was simple, but Rosalind suspected that it had come from one of the London fashion houses. She could not help but be impressed.

Piers stepped forward. 'Grandmama, may I introduce our guests? Miss Carey from Rockwood Castle and Miss Patricia Carey.'

Rosalind bobbed a curtsey and Patricia copied her.

Lady Pentelow smiled graciously. 'Welcome to Trevenor. It's a pleasure to meet you both, but please do sit down. We can get to know each other over luncheon.' She seemed to glide towards her place at the end of the table and Patterson held her chair for her. She sat down, motioning everyone to follow suit.

Rosalind felt as though she were in the presence of royalty and she shot a sideways glance in Piers' direction, wondering whether she ought to say something.

He seemed to understand and he gave her a reassuring smile. 'I would feel privileged to show both of you around the house and the estate this afternoon, Rosalind. If you are not too tired after your long journey.'

'Thank you, I would like that very much.' Rosalind turned to Patricia. 'I'm sure you would like to see everything, wouldn't you, Patsy?'

'I'll take Patsy on a tour of the house,' Aurelia

said firmly. 'Piers will only bore you with the history of the building. I can tell you the scandalous secrets of our ancestors.'

Lady Pentelow shook her head. 'That's enough of that talk at table, Aurelia.' She turned to Rosalind with a gracious smile. 'How is your grandpapa, Miss Carey? I believe I met him once at a ball in Plymouth, but that was many years ago. I remember him as a very charming gentleman.'

Rosalind sent Patricia a warning glance. There was no need for the whole world to know of their grandfather's problems. 'He is well, thank you, Lady Pentelow.'

'He must be quite senior in years now,' Lady Pentelow said, thoughtfully. 'If I remember correctly he was quite a mature man when we met all those years ago.'

'Sir Lucien carries his years well, Grandmama.' Piers nodded to Patterson, who was standing to attention by the door. 'You may serve now, Patterson. I'm sure our guests must be very hungry.'

'I am famished . . .' Patricia blushed rosily. 'I mean, thank you. I am very hungry.'

'I haven't seen much of Trevenor, but it is a very imposing residence, Lady Pentelow,' Rosalind said hastily. 'And the setting is idyllic.'

'I believe it is.' Lady Pentelow nodded graciously. 'You must make the most of your visit here, Miss Carey. There are some delightful walks along the cliff tops.'

'There are smugglers' caves, too,' Aurelia added with a mischievous smile. 'I believe much of the family fortune came from free trading.'

'Aurelia, if you continue to prattle like a child, you will take your meals in the nursery,' Lady Pentelow said firmly. She sat back in her chair as the maids brought the dishes to the table, supervised by Patterson.

The food was excellent and Rosalind enjoyed every bite, but she was glad when the meal ended. Conversation had been stilted, despite Piers' attempts to make everyone feel at ease. It was obvious that Aurelia and Patricia were eager to leave the table as soon as they had eaten enough to satisfy their appetites, and for once Rosalind agreed wholeheartedly with her sister.

After what seemed like an eternity, Lady Pentelow rose from her seat. 'I am going to my room to rest for a while, but I will see you at dinner. Piers will make sure that you have everything you need.'

Patterson leaped to attention and held the door open for Lady Pentelow. A lingering waft of expensive lavender cologne remained even after the door closed behind her. The atmosphere in the room relaxed and Aurelia leaped to her feet.

'Come along, Patsy. I'll give you a guided tour of the house and the dungeons.'

'You have dungeons?' Patricia gasped.

'Don't you? I mean you live in a proper castle, so surely you have dungeons and probably an oubliette.

You know, the place where they throw prisoners and leave them to die a horrible lingering death.'

'We have cellars,' Rosalind said, laughing, 'but if there is an oubliette, I've never found it.'

'Well, you wouldn't, would you? I mean it's supposed to be secret. There's probably one somewhere in the depth of Rockwood Castle, filled with whitened bones of old enemies.'

Piers pushed back his chair and stood up. 'Come with me, Rosalind. We'll leave my sister to terrify Patricia with ghoulish stories.'

Patricia tossed her head. 'I'm not scared.' She followed Aurelia from the room. 'It's not true, is it, Aurelia? You don't have bodies buried in your cellar?'

Rosalind met Piers' amused look and she smiled. 'I have a feeling that Patricia will be sleeping with me tonight, thanks to your sister's vivid imagination.'

He laughed. 'I apologise for Aurelia. She spends too much time reading Gothic novels, but it's good for her to have a friend close to her own age to talk to. How old is Patricia?'

'She's nearly seventeen, although she behaves like a twelve-year-old at times.'

'Aurelia is just eighteen and, as I told you before, is a confirmed flirt. In fact there's a ball at Knighton Hall tomorrow evening. Perhaps you and your sister would like to come with us?'

'I'm afraid we haven't come prepared for social occasions.'

'I'm sure that Aurelia has gowns enough to clothe an army of charming young ladies.' He walked to the door and opened it. 'Shall we follow the girls' example? I'll show you around and then you won't get lost in the maze of corridors.'

'Thank you, I'd like that.' It came as a surprise, but Rosalind realised that she meant what she had said. Her reservations about Piers were slowly fading, but she was not entirely won over. He was so genial and accommodating yet she still didn't understand why, when he had such a beautiful home, he would wish to own a crumbling pile like Rockwood.

Moving from room to room and from one part of the many-faceted building to another was like a walking tour of history, from the ancient fortified manor house to the Tudor part of the building, then the Jacobean wing and the beautifully proportioned rooms designed in the style of Robert Adam. Rosalind decided that she would need a map if she were to negotiate the corridors and passages, but she managed to memorise the way to the Chinese room and the blue drawing room, as well as to her own bedchamber. When Piers had completed the guided tour of the house he suggested a walk in the grounds.

A small army of gardeners were hard at work in the different parts of the garden. The parterre garden, with its neat box hedges and geometric beds filled with flowers, was as delightful as the rose garden.

Early flowering varieties competed with wisteria that clambered over a pergola and shrub roses were in bud, promising a breath-taking display in the coming months. The scent of wallflowers filled the air and Rosalind found herself wishing that she could work the same magic on the overgrown formal gardens at home. But that was a dream and this was reality: Piers Blanchard was wealthy and the Careys were poor; there was no getting away from the fact.

'You look sad, Rosalind,' Piers said softly. 'What's wrong?'

She managed a smile. 'Nothing. I was simply wishing that I could do something similar at home, but that's out of the question. Your gardens are beautiful, as is the house. What has Rockwood Castle to offer that you do not have here?'

'It may seem odd to you, but there are other things in life than money and possessions.'

'You have both.'

'Yes, I do and I'm not apologising. I have worked hard to make the Trevenor mine pay. It was quite run down when I took it over, and now it's thriving and providing work for half the village.'

'I'd love to visit the mine.'

'Would you really?'

'Why do you find that surprising?'

'My sister seems to think that the mining business is slightly less interesting than a lesson in Greek or Latin.'

'We had a governess who taught us Latin, and I

found it quite absorbing, although I doubt if I can remember much of it now. However, I would genuinely like to see the mine.'

'Tomorrow morning, then. I leave here after an early breakfast. Would that suit you?'

'I can't wait.'

That evening, after a delicious dinner, Rosalind had little choice other than to accompany Lady Pentelow to the blue drawing room, where they sat on either side of the ornate marble fireplace. Piers had excused himself, saying he had papers to go through in his study. Patricia and Aurelia were entertaining themselves with a game of loo, which seemed to cause a great deal of merriment.

'Now then, Miss Carey,' Lady Pentelow lowered her voice. 'Perhaps you would like to tell me the real reason for your visit to Trevenor.'

Chapter Eleven

There seemed no escape other than to tell the imperious lady the truth. Rosalind glanced over her shoulder to make sure that Patricia was not listening, but the girls were too involved with their card game to pay any attention to her. Rosalind lowered her voice. 'There were good reasons why I needed to get my sister away from the village for a while, Lady Pentelow.'

'That's not what you told my grandson, Miss Carey.'

'Won't you call me Rosalind? It would make me feel a little less like someone on trial.'

'That wasn't my intention, but I would like a straight answer.'

'My sister has become involved with an unsuitable young man, someone from the village whom we've all known since childhood, but he is already engaged to be married.'

'I see.' Lady Pentelow's expression softened just a little. 'Your sister is very young for her age, as is Aurelia. They seem to be getting along so well.'

Rosalind smiled. 'Yes, they are, and it's a pleasure to hear Patricia laughing and enjoying herself.'

Lady Pentelow put her head on one side, giving Rosalind a searching look. 'But that's not the only reason for your visit here, is it? You told Piers that you wished to know him better. How am I supposed to interpret that?'

'I admit I was suspicious of his motives when we first met. As I think you yourself might be if someone arrived on your doorstep, claiming that he was the true owner of Trevenor.'

'Yes, I dare say I would feel like that.'

'I still don't understand why anyone would want to take on an ancient castle, especially when your grandson owns Trevenor. I don't know if he told you, but Piers paid off our debts and has made us an allowance, which, I might add, I am loath to accept.'

'Piers is a very generous man, and he must have his reasons for helping you, not least because of the injustices his ancestor suffered, even if it was long ago.'

'He told me something of the Blanchard family history, Lady Pentelow. But that isn't in itself a reason for giving financial assistance to virtual strangers. You can't blame me for suspecting his motives.'

'And you fear he might evict your family, is that why you came here?'

'That is always at the back of my mind, even though Piers promised that he would never do that to us. We haven't told our grandfather about any of this. He is in a fragile state of health.'

'I can't speak for Piers, but I can assure you that he is an honourable man. And I can tell you with certainty that financial gain is not his motive.'

Rosalind nodded, glancing round the elegantly furnished room. 'That I can see for myself, ma'am.'

'Then it seems to me that you need to talk this over with him.'

'Yes, ma'am.'

'As to your sister, I understand your problem only too well. Aurelia is a dear girl, but impulsive, and we had a similar situation not so long ago. I think having a companion like Patricia will do her good.'

'Are you talking about us, Grandmama?' Aurelia asked, giggling. 'What are you telling Rosalind?'

'We were discussing the ball tomorrow evening.'

'Do you mean that Rosalind and Patsy will accompany us, Grandmama?'

'I do indeed.'

'But, as I told Piers, we haven't come prepared for a long stay, and we quite literally have nothing suitable to wear,' Rosalind said urgently.

Aurelia jumped to her feet, sending the cards flying. 'Don't worry about that, Rosalind. I have plenty of lovely ball gowns that you may choose from, and we are about the same size. Come with me, Patsy. You can have first choice.'

Patricia hesitated. 'What about Rosie?'

'You go first, Patsy,' Rosalind said, smiling.

'All right, but if I see something that might suit you better I'll ask Aurelia to put it aside. You never know, Rosie, we might find you a rich husband and then all our problems will be solved.' Patricia dashed from the room. 'Wait for me, Aurelia.'

'Are you on the lookout for a suitable husband, Rosalind?' Lady Pentelow's eyes narrowed. 'Is that perhaps the real reason for your visit to Trevenor? Do you hope to charm my grandson into a proposal of marriage?'

Rosalind jumped to her feet. 'Lady Pentelow, I know I am a guest in your home, and I am grateful for your hospitality, but I have told you my reasons for coming here today. I am not in the least interested in your grandson as a prospective husband. That was not my motive at all.'

'Then I accept your word on it and the matter is closed. Do sit down and stop looking so affronted. You were suspicious of Piers and I think I was entitled to ask you a few searching questions.'

Rosalind was about to obey when the door opened and Piers strolled in. 'Is anything wrong? I sense an atmosphere.'

'I was just going to my room,' Rosalind said hastily. 'It's been a long day and I'm tired.'

'Yes, you must be exhausted. We'll talk further tomorrow, Miss Carey.' Lady Pentelow smiled benignly.

'Good night, Piers,' Rosalind edged past him.

'Grandmama, what have you been saying?' Piers demanded.

Rosalind slipped out of the room and closed the door without waiting to hear her ladyship's response. She almost bumped into Ada, who was carrying a tray. 'I'm sorry,' Rosalind murmured. 'I'm going to my room.'

'I have her ladyship's chamomile tisane here, but if you would care to wait I could show you the way, miss. If you've forgotten it, that is.'

'Thank you, Ada. It's not quite the same after dark. Everything looks different.'

'I'll be with you in two ticks, miss.' Ada knocked on the door and somehow managed to juggle the tray and open the door without spilling a drop of the fragrant tisane.

She reappeared moments later minus the tray. 'If you'd care to follow me, miss.'

'Thank you,' Rosalind said with feeling. Suddenly the house, which had seemed so welcoming in daytime, felt cold and unfriendly. Although she understood Lady Pentelow's reservations, the comments she had made were hurtful. Rosalind followed the young maidservant. Perhaps a good night's sleep would make things look better.

She was just getting ready for bed when Patricia erupted into the room clutching an armful of shimmering material. 'Look what Aurelia has given me, and there's one for you, too.' She laid one gown on the bed and held the other up against herself. 'See? Isn't it just beautiful?'

'Yes, it's lovely, and I'm sure you'll look wonderful in it. Sprigged muslin is just right for a girl of your age.'

'Yes, I know.' Patricia did a twirl. 'Look at the other one. It's such a lovely shade of green, which always looks good on you, Rosie. Do try it on.'

'In the morning, Patsy. I'm really tired now and you ought to get some sleep.'

'Are you all right?' Patricia was suddenly serious. 'You do look a bit pale.'

'I'll be fine when I've had a rest. After all, we have the ball to look forward so, and tomorrow morning I'm going to see the china clay mine.'

Patricia giggled. 'You're getting on very well with Piers.'

'I'm still trying to understand why he has been so generous. Something isn't quite right, and I'm determined to find out what it is before we return home, but you needn't let that worry you.'

'I know why you brought me here,' Patricia said, frowning. 'You wanted to keep me away from Barnaby.'

'That is one reason.' Rosalind did not bother to lie. 'But as I've said before, I like Piers – who wouldn't? Yet I don't trust him, and that's the truth. I want to discover his real motive for coming into our lives.'

'I don't know about that, and staying here for a while won't make me change my mind about Barnaby. However, as we're here, I intend to enjoy myself.'

'Good night, Patsy.' Rosalind climbed into bed.

'May I sleep with you, Rosie? I'm afraid the ghosts of the dead from the oubliette might come and haunt me.'

'Of course, but if you kick you'll have to sleep on the floor.'

Piers was waiting for Rosalind in the chaise and a footman assisted her to climb into the vehicle.

'It's a lovely day,' Piers observed as he flicked the reins. 'Walk on.'

Rosalind settled herself down beside him as they moved forward. 'Yes, it is. I'm looking forward to seeing your clay mine.'

'Really?' He gave her a quizzical glance. 'Most young ladies of my acquaintance say that and then their eyes glaze over if I try to explain the business to them.'

'You won't have that problem with me,' Rosalind said airily. 'I want to see everything. I have to admit I know nothing about commerce, but I'm eager to learn. It's a whole new experience for me.'

'Then I hope it will be an enjoyable one.'

They drove on, descending slowly from the top of the cliffs, down narrow country lanes with high banks covered in frothy white cow parsley. As the road twisted Rosalind caught glimpses of the sea and at other times she could see the white expanse of the open-cast china clay mine surrounded by pyramids of what Piers described as waste material.

On arrival Piers showed Rosalind into the offices where she met Pedrick, the site manager, after which they went on a tour of the mine itself. Piers explained the method of spraying water onto the hard walls of the pit to remove the clay, and the processing of the material, then transporting it to ships moored in the harbour for export to all parts of the world. Piers was an enthusiastic guide and Rosalind was fascinated. The morning passed so quickly that she could hardly believe it when the whistle blew and the men downed tools to take their short break for lunch. Piers sent for the chaise and suggested that they take their midday meal at the local pub, which was noted for its good food.

When they arrived at the Anchor Inn, Piers gave the reins to a stable boy and tossed him a coin. They were about to enter the building when a gentleman dressed in black, with a top hat pulled down low over his forehead, stepped out of the shadows.

'A word, Blanchard.'

'Later,' Piers snapped. He ushered Rosalind into the smoky taproom.

'Who was that? He obviously wanted to speak to you.'

'A business acquaintance, nothing more. He can wait.' Piers guided her between the packed tables. 'Good morning, Jed. Is your private parlour available? I'd like my guest to sample Minna's cooking.'

'Yes, Mr Blanchard,' the landlord said hurriedly. 'Come this way, if you please.'

'Why didn't you want to go home for luncheon?' Rosalind asked as she sipped a glass of cider, while they waited for their food.

'I love my family, but it's impossible to have a private conversation at home. I trust the servants, but they're only human, and secrets have a way of escaping.'

Rosalind smiled. 'We're lucky to have Hester, who is entirely to be trusted. She has been with us ever since I can remember. She's more like a member of the family than a servant. We all think the world of her.'

'Yes, I saw that. She's a good woman.'

'So what is it you wish to tell me that you don't wish the servants at Trevenor to hear?'

Piers gazed into the amber liquid in his pint mug. 'You want to know why I came forward to claim my inheritance, especially now you've seen Trevenor and you realise that we are very comfortably off.'

She nodded. 'Yes, indeed. You live a life of luxury,

even if you have to earn it. Although, as I see it, you have plenty of workers to make the money for you.'

'That's true.' Piers looked up as the door opened and the landlord walked in carrying two bowls of stew, which he placed on the table in front of them.

'My wife's finest,' he said cheerfully. 'I'll send the girl in with some bread.'

'Thank you, Jed. I'm sure the stew will be excellent as always.'

Jed puffed out his chest. 'Minna is the best cook in the county, sir.'

Piers waited until he had left the room. 'I don't think you'll be disappointed.'

'It smells delicious,' Rosalind said eagerly. 'I'm really hungry after all that walking.'

Another tap on the door preceded a young girl who brought the bread and a slab of yellow butter. She shot Rosalind a cursory glance before leaving them to their meal.

'It will be common knowledge that Mr Blanchard is entertaining a young lady to luncheon in less time than it will take us to eat our meal,' Piers said, smiling. 'They'll be agog with curiosity as to your identity.'

'It was probably the same at Rockwood when I showed you round the village.' Rosalind put her fork down. 'You were going to tell me something, Piers. What was it?'

'I think I told you that Rockwood is in a useful

place for me. I'll be able to break my journey to London there on business trips.'

'Yes, and I didn't believe you then. Quite soon there will be a railway link all the way to Cornwall, and you won't need to travel by road.'

'That's true, but it won't be for a few years yet.'

'Even so, I wouldn't call Rockwood Castle a good investment. You must have better things to do with you money.'

He smiled, shaking his head. 'I can see that you remain unconvinced.'

'I'm trying hard to work out exactly what it is you want.' Rosalind buttered a slice of bread and took a bite. 'The stew is excellent, by the way.'

'We are related, Rosalind. I know it's a tenuous link to the past, but if Mathilda Chaldon hadn't abducted her dead sister's baby, my family would still be living in Rockwood Castle, and I wouldn't be running a china clay mine in Cornwall.'

'But you grew up knowing that you would one day take over the business,' Rosalind said calmly. 'If you hadn't been going through archived papers you would never have known about us.'

'And I would be the poorer for it. I feel a responsibility for you and your family, especially after your father's untimely death. If the Rockwood estate had proved to be prosperous and your brothers were established in their careers I would probably have made myself known, and moved on. But what I saw when

I visited the castle convinced me that my help was needed.'

'So you lavished money on us. What did you expect in return?'

'Gratitude seems hard to come by when dealing with the Carey family.' He held up his hand. 'Don't look like that, Rosalind. I understand why you're wary, but today I brought you here to tell you what I would like to do.'

Rosalind put her fork down. 'I knew there had to be a catch.'

'Not at all. I wanted to suggest that I purchase a commission in the army for Bertram, and I will pay for Walter to attend a university of his choosing.'

'Why would you do that? Would you like to go further and settle dowries on Patsy and myself? No doubt you would like to see us both married off and then, with the boys away, you could walk into Rockwood and claim it for yourself. Grandpapa is too old and frail to put up any resistance.' Rosalind rose and pushed her plate away. 'The stew was excellent but I've lost my appetite.'

'Please sit down and finish you meal. That's not what I meant. You seem intent on suspecting every suggestion I make as being something underhand, which is not the case.'

Rosalind rested her hands on the table, leaning over to give him a straight look. 'Yes, you're right, Piers Blanchard. It simply doesn't make sense. I'm sure you have an ulterior motive and I won't rest until I find out what it is. Can you give me a straight answer as to why you're doing all this for my family?'

'I've explained my reasons.'

'No, you have not. There's something more and I want to know why Rockwood is so important to you.'

'I can't tell you anything more.'

'Then, if you'll excuse me, I think a walk in the fresh air will be very beneficial.'

Ignoring his protests, Rosalind left the snug and edged her way between the tables in the taproom. The men who were drinking and smoking their clay pipes stared at her and mumbled comments, but she was too angry to care. She slammed out of the pub and started walking in the direction of Trevenor, which stood out in all its glory on the top of the cliffs.

The sun was high in the sky and although there was a slight breeze off the sea, it was very warm for the time of year. After only a few hundred yards she could feel trickles of sweat running down between her shoulder blades, and the tightness of her stays made it difficult to breathe. However, she was not one to give up and she marched on, nodding curtly to several women who moved respectfully aside to allow her to pass. Small boats skimmed in and out of the harbour and large ships were at anchor in the bay, no doubt waiting to be loaded with cargoes of china clay. Other vessels were moored alongside, unloading barrels, crates and boxes, but Rosalind took little interest in the activities of the small port. She was convinced that this visit had been a terrible error of judgement, and the sooner she and Patricia were on their way back to Rockwood, the better.

She was on the edge of the village when she heard the sound of a horse's hoofs and the rumble of carriage wheels. She knew it must be Piers even before he reined in the horse.

'Please get in, Rosalind. Allow me to take you back to the house.'

She was about to refuse when he drew the chaise to a halt, but it was a long uphill walk to Trevenor and reluctantly she accepted his offer.

'I think we've outstayed our welcome, Piers. Patsy and I will leave tomorrow.'

'All right, if that's your wish. I won't try to stop you.' Piers flicked the reins. 'Walk on.' He turned his head to give her a searching look. 'But you are quite wrong about my intentions. I don't blame you for being suspicious, but please don't say anything about our conversation to my grandmother.'

'I won't, of course. Lady Pentelow has been very gracious, considering the fact that we turned up on her doorstep uninvited.'

'And you will attend the ball tonight, I hope. There's no need to involve your sister and mine in our disagreement.'

'I won't say anything, but I will tell Patricia that we must return home.'

'That's your choice, although I wish it were different. I would like the opportunity to prove you wrong.'

Rosalind had no answer to this. They could go round in circles for ever, and she was tired of arguing. They completed the rest of the journey in silence and she managed to enter the house without anyone seeing her other than Patterson. She went straight to her room where she sat on the window seat gazing out over the grounds to the turquoise sea, dotted with white sails.

She lost track of time as she sat there, staring absently at the view as she considered Piers' offer to help her brothers further their careers. Perhaps she had been too hasty. After all, it was vital for Bertram and Walter to make something of themselves. Had the family fortunes been secure there would not have been a problem, but there was no knowing what Bertie might do if he had to remain tethered to Rockwood for much longer. Walter was a worry, too. It was not natural for a young man to spend all his time reading or writing poetry. Both her brothers needed to be out in the world. Rockwood came second to their health and happiness. Then there was Patsy, the most worrying of all. Without a suitable dowry her sister might never find a husband, and it would be almost impossible to keep her safe from Barnaby Yelland's undoubted charms.

Rosalind turned with a start at the sound of her sister's voice.

'What are you doing skulking in your room?' Patricia asked peevishly. 'Why didn't you join us for luncheon? It was quite delicious.'

'I had a meal at the village in with Piers.' Rosalind tried hard to sound casual.

'Did you, indeed? That will be the latest gossip, I've no doubt, especially if Trevenor is anything like Rockwood.'

'I was merely trying to ascertain his motives, but without success.'

'Personally, I really don't care why he wants to help us. I'm having such a lovely time here. I wish it would go on for ever.'

Rosalind sighed. Patricia was not going to leave willingly, but to stay on for much longer would be difficult. 'What time is it?'

'I don't know. I suppose it must be about three o'clock. Anyway, it doesn't matter. We've ages before we need to get ready for the ball. Aurelia says that Knighton Hall is even grander than Trevenor. Can you imagine that? Anyway, we're going to have a game of croquet. Why don't you join us, instead of moping in your room?'

'I've never really mastered the game.'

'Then you need some practice. I've had plenty of

practice at Greystone Park, so I'm quite good at it. Come on, Rosie. Don't be a misery. Let's enjoy ourselves before we have to go back to drudgery at home.'

Rosalind would have liked to remain in her room, but it was so good to see Patricia pink-cheeked and happy again that she had not the heart to refuse. Reluctantly she accompanied her sister to the croquet lawn, where Aurelia was waiting with a mallet in her hand and a determined expression on her lovely face. Rosalind knew she was going to be beaten and she was. Aurelia was an excellent player and Patricia came a good second, which led to much laughter on their part as they teased Rosalind about her lack of skill at the game. She knew that she was never going to live it down as far as Patricia was concerned. Rosalind Carey's clumsiness and lack of ability with a croquet mallet would be the subject of conversation at the dinner table when they returned home for days, if not weeks, to come. However, the exercise and fresh air took her mind off her problems.

Eventually it was time to get ready for the ball. Aurelia had her own personal maid to help her, but Rosalind and Patricia were left to assist each other. It was fortunate that they had grown used to getting dressed without the aid of a personal maid and, from sheer necessity, they had become adept at creating hairstyles for each other.

'You look lovely, Patsy.' Rosalind had plucked a couple of rosebuds from the garden and she pinned them in Patricia's hair. 'There, that's the finishing touch.'

Patricia admired her reflection in the dressing-table mirror. 'Yes, I think this dress looks quite splendid on me. I think I'll be a match for Aurelia.'

'You will outshine her completely,' Rosalind said, smiling. 'But for heaven's sake don't let her know that. I think Miss Blanchard is used to being the centre of attention.'

'Then she had better move over a little.' Patricia jumped to her feet. 'Sit down, I have just the thing to finish your coiffure.'

Rosalind fingered her gold locket as she took Patricia's place. 'What is it? You've already done my hair beautifully.'

Patricia produced a sparkling hair comb from the pocket of her day dress. 'Aurelia said I could have this – honestly, Rosie, she has a jewellery box the size of a . . .' she hesitated, 'of something very large, and it's full of jewels and hair combs. She gave me this to wear, but it will suit you much better.'

Touched by Patricia's generosity, Rosalind met her sister's intense gaze in the mirror, and she blew her a kiss. 'That's very sweet of you, Patsy. Thank you.'

Patricia placed the comb in her sister's hair, securing the knot of curls on the top of Rosalind's head. 'There, you'll be the heartbreaker tonight, Rosie. Aurelia is lovely, but you have style and poise. You might catch the eye of a wealthy lord and you can throw Piers' money back in his face.'

Rosalind reached for the long white gloves that Aurelia had be kind enough to lend her. She stood up. 'Come on, Patsy. We'd better go downstairs or they'll go without us.' She would try to put on a brave face; after all, it was just one more evening in Piers' company. Tomorrow she would make arrangements to return to Rockwood.

Knighton Hall was as grand as Rosalind had anticipated. It was almost dark when the Blanchards' carriage drove up the wide avenue lined with flambeaux. The white stucco classical façade of the mansion was tinged with golden light from even more flaming torches, and liveried footmen stood on either side of the front entrance, ready to rush forward and assist the guests to alight from their carriages.

'It looks like a good turnout,' Lady Pentelow said with a satisfied smile. 'I hope you girls will behave with decorum this evening, and that means you in particular, Aurelia.'

'I'll be a perfect lady, Grandmama.' Aurelia turned her head to glance out of the window. 'There's Piers. I don't know why he insisted on riding. We could have made room for him.'

'Perhaps he wants to distance himself from your idle chatter, my dear.' Lady Pentelow made ready to alight as the carriage door opened and a footman put down the steps.

Rosalind was next and as she stepped down from

the vehicle she saw Piers hand his horse to a groom. He strode across the gravelled carriage sweep, to join them at the front entrance.

'I'm glad you decided to come with us, Rosalind.' His face was in shadow but Rosalind sensed that he was smiling.

'Why would she not, Piers?' Lady Pentelow demanded impatiently. 'You do talk nonsense at times.' She accepted his proffered arm. 'Let's go inside. There's a definite chill in the air.'

Chapter Twelve

Rosalind had been impressed by Trevenor, but Knighton Hall was so grand that it made the Blanchards' residence seem quite ordinary. The entrance hall with its sweeping staircase and galleried landing was lit by five crystal chandeliers and a blaze of candles. The scent of hot wax mingled with the fragrance from the flower arrangements, which would not have been out of place at a royal wedding. Guests were arriving in a steady flow and the heady perfumes worn by the ladies vied with the scent of the expensive pomade used by the gentleman, tempered just a little by a faint aroma of cigar smoke. Chubby cherubs and scantily clad Grecian maidens gazed down at the arrivals from a painted ceiling, and well-trained servants were at hand to take care of capes, top hats, canes and gloves.

Rosalind forgot her worries and stood behind

Lady Pentelow and Piers as they queued, waiting to be greeted by Lord and Lady Knighton.

'Charming,' Lord Knighton said when Lady Pentelow introduced Rosalind to him and his wife. 'I hope you enjoy your stay in Cornwall, Miss Carey.'

Rosalind inclined her head. 'Thank you, sir.'

Lady Pentelow went on to introduce Aurelia, whom they obviously knew very well, and lastly Patricia.

'Are you out in society already, Miss Carey?' Lady Knighton asked, peering closely at Patricia.

Rosalind could see that Patricia was taken aback and she took her sister by the hand. 'Not officially, my lady. But our father died in a tragic accident abroad quite recently, and our mother is in Vienna.'

'Good gracious!' Lady Knighton stared at her as if she were speaking in a foreign tongue. 'Vienna?'

'Our mother is an opera singer, my lady,' Rosalind said firmly. 'She is one of the best.'

'I can vouch for that.' Piers moved closer to Rosalind. 'Perhaps you've heard of Felicia Carey?'

'Of course,' Lady Knighton said vaguely. 'Delightful.' She turned away to greet the next couple.

'She's never heard of her,' Piers said, chuckling as they moved on. 'I think I've touched her ladyship's Achilles heel. The Knightons are not known to be patrons of the arts.'

Lady Pentelow raised an eyebrow but she did not comment and she strolled away to speak to a group of people who were obviously known to her.

Piers took two glasses of champagne from a tray that a footmen offered them and he handed one to Rosalind. 'Let's find a table.'

'You put her in her place, Piers.' Aurelia hurried after them. 'Lady Knighton is a mean woman. She's always looking to find fault, and today it was your turn, Patsy. What does it matter if you've endured a London season, or not? She knows very well that I haven't and she usually makes catty remarks about my gown or my hair.'

'Why doesn't she like you?' Patricia asked, frowning. 'That seems odd.'

'The old witch knows that her darling son is in love with me.'

'Really? Which one is he?' Patricia clutched Aurelia's hand, looking to left and right as they made their way to one of the tables set around the edge of the vast ballroom.

Aurelia pointed to a handsome young man, who was talking to an older lady. 'That's Hugo.'

'He looks very nice,' Patsy said approvingly. 'You should ignore anything that his miserable mother says.'

'You're right. It's up to Hugo whom he chooses to marry.' Aurelia tossed her head.

'Don't cause any trouble, Aurelia,' Piers said firmly.

Rosalind drew her sister aside. 'Don't interfere, Patsy. Let's have a pleasant evening as it might well be the last one before we return home.'

Patricia gazed at her sister in horror. 'We're leaving so soon?'

'We should get back to Rockwood, Patsy. Who knows what has been going on while we're away?'

'But you don't want me to go home, do you?' Patricia put her head on one side. 'I thought you wanted to keep me away from Barnaby.'

Piers pulled up a chair for Rosalind. 'If you'll excuse me, I see someone I need to speak to about business.'

'Are you going to be boring all evening, Piers?' Aurelia sat down, arranging her satin skirts around her like the petals of a pink flower. 'Business is for the office.'

'Remember what I said. Behave properly for once.' Piers shot an apologetic smile in Rosalind's direction and he walked off to speak to a man at the far end of the room.

'Who is that gentleman, Aurelia?' Rosalind stared at the stranger, who was loitering in the shadows at the far corner of the room. There was something vaguely familiar about him.

'I don't know,' Aurelia said peevishly. 'He's probably talking about china clay. It's always commerce as far as Piers is concerned.'

Rosalind was not so sure. It was obvious that the conversation was heated and when Piers returned to their table his expression was not encouraging.

'Is anything wrong?' she asked in a low voice, not wanting to alarm Aurelia and Patricia, although their attention was firmly fixed on Hugo Knighton.

Piers gave her a steady look. 'It's rather close in here. Perhaps you'd like to take a look at the conservatory. It will be cooler in there.'

'Wouldn't it look odd if we left the girls on their own?' Rosalind glanced at Lady Pentelow, who was chatting amicably with an impressive dowager whose jewels winked and shone in the candlelight. 'Your grandmother doesn't entirely approve of Patsy and me. I don't want to offend her.'

'This is important. Grandmama will be even more put out when she hears what I have to tell her, but that will have to wait until we get back to Trevenor.'

The orchestra in the gallery had struck up the music for the grand parade and couples were already gathering on the dance floor. Rosalind nodded. 'All right. I doubt if she'll notice, and your sister has her sights set on that young man.'

Piers glanced over his shoulder. 'That's the Honourable Hugo Knighton, who will one day inherit all this.'

'Aurelia told me that he's in love with her,' Rosalind said, tucking her hand in the crook of Piers' arm. 'Is that true?'

A wry smile curved his lips. 'Possibly, but I'm afraid such a match will be out of the question now.' He led the way to the conservatory, which was delightfully cool after the heat of the ballroom, and he came to a halt by a stone bench surrounded by exotic palms and ferns. 'You were right to be suspicious, Rosalind.'

She sank down, feeling the cold granite strike through her silk gown, and a shudder ran down her spine. 'What are you trying to tell me?'

'The plain fact is that I've lost the business and Trevenor.'

She stared at him aghast. 'I don't understand. You showed me round today and the mine seemed to be in full production.'

'It is, and it will be so, but I don't own it any longer. The man you saw this morning is the same person who came here tonight. I have no choice other than to sign everything over to him.'

'Why? How can that be?'

Piers sat down beside her, staring into the distance. 'His name is Ewart Blaise. He turned up in my office some months ago and he told me that my father had an affair with his mother. When her husband returned from two years at sea, he discovered that she had given birth to a child, and she was forced to name the father.'

'So you're saying that Ewart Blaise is your half-brother?'

'Yes, that's it exactly. He threatened to reveal the family scandal unless I gave him a job at the mine. He also knew things about my father that would prove more than embarrassing if they became public knowledge, and he threatened to tell the authorities. I can't say more than that at present, but Blaise's demands have increased almost daily, and now he wants half the business and Trevenor. A scandal that he could reveal would effectively ruin Aurelia's chances of making a good match.'

'So you agreed to his terms?'

'I had very little choice. I couldn't put my grandmother through the humiliation and disgrace, and Aurelia claims to be in love with Hugo Knighton. His family would never agree to their marriage if the truth were known, and my brother, Alexander's, chances of promotion would be adversely affected. I couldn't allow that to happen.'

'But surely a scandal would blow over eventually? Wouldn't that be preferable to losing your home and your business?'

'Grandmama gave up everything to move to Trevenor and run the house after we lost both our parents. She put all her fortune into the mine and now she depends solely on me.'

'You said that you'd lost Trevenor as well. Surely your half-brother won't take your home?'

'Blaise has no legal claim to the estate, but he is ruthless in his determination to take everything that he considers to be his by rights.'

'Was that why you went through your family's records?'

He nodded. 'Yes, I was desperate to find something that would disprove his story.'

'And the reason why you've laid claim to Rockwood Castle is because you knew you were about to lose your home and business?'

'That was my original reason for seeking you out, but when I visited the castle and got to know you and your family, I was genuinely concerned for your welfare.'

'But you were using Rockwood as an insurance against bankruptcy?'

'Yes, I suppose I was. I had to do something, Rosalind. Besides which, Blaise is only interested in the mine and Trevenor itself. I'm not a poor man, but I haven't enough funds to buy him off, even if he would consider such a thing.'

'What I don't understand is why he left it until now? Why didn't he make his claim sooner?'

'From the little he told me, his mother kept the secret of his birth until she lay dying. It was only then that she told him that my father had paid her handsomely for her silence.'

'You could expose him as a blackmailer.'

'He knows I won't do that.'

'So you're just going to walk away from everything you hold dear?'

'What would you do in similar circumstances?'

'I would probably do the same, but he ought not to get away with it.'

'Maybe I should challenge him to a duel.'

Rosalind rose from the cold stone seat. 'Do you find this situation amusing?'

'Not at all, but I'm doing what I consider best for my family.'

'You're standing by and allowing them to be made homeless.'

'No, that's not true. I'm going to tell Grandmama and Aurelia what's happened, and I'll rent a suitable property, maybe in Bath or even in London.'

'That won't be necessary.' Rosalind faced him with a steady look. 'You saved Rockwood, probably with this in mind, but that doesn't matter now. It seems that the least I can do is to offer you a home, if your grandmother can bear the thought of living in a draughty old castle. We have so few servants that we can house as many of your staff as you wish to bring with you, providing you pay their wages.'

Piers took both her hands in his. 'Thank you. The invitation had to come from you, but I was hoping you would feel that way.'

'I believed you when you told me that you are the rightful heir to Rockwood Castle, Piers. But I do have one condition.'

'And that is?'

'You must keep your promise to purchase a commission for Bertie, and I want you to send Walter to university.'

He raised her right hand to his lips. 'That's something I can do, and I will.'

'Then all you have to do is to convince your grandmother and your sister that this is the only way.'

'Ewart Blaise and I might have the same father, but he's no brother of mine. I won't rest until Trevenor and the mine are restored to my family, however long that might take.'

'When will you break the news to your grandmother and Aurelia? I can't imagine Lady Pentelow giving up without a fight.'

'I'll allow them to enjoy their evening, especially as it will be the last one here for the foreseeable future. I'll gather everyone together tomorrow morning, after breakfast.'

'I won't say a word to Patsy.'

'I'm forever in your debt, Rosalind.' He smiled and closed his fingers over her hand. 'I hear a waltz. May I have this dance, Miss Carey?'

Next morning Piers called the family to a meeting in the blue parlour, where he gave his grandmother and Aurelia the bad news. There was a shocked silence and Rosalind laid her finger on her lips when Patricia opened her mouth to speak.

Lady Pentelow rose majestically to her feet and began to pace the floor. 'This is preposterous,' she said at last. 'What absolute nonsense.' She came to a halt in front of her grandson. 'You can tell Ewart Blaise, whoever he might be, that the Blanchard family have lived here for centuries. I used my own fortune to keep the business going through difficult times. The mine belongs to me as much as to you.'

'Grandmama, I know this is hard to accept, but

I've checked everything, even the birth records in the parish church. Blaise is my half-brother and he is prepared to reveal all if we don't give in to his demands.'

'Then let him. We've lived through worse scandals.'

'Blaise has discovered something that my father did, which would be very hard to live down, and the family name would be blackened for ever.'

'This is all too much,' Lady Pentelow said faintly.

Piers took her hand in his. 'I know this is difficult to accept, but do you really want everyone to know that your daughter was married to an adulterer and worse? What do you imagine it would do to Aurelia's chances of making a suitable match if such a story became public? Alexander would never achieve promotion and you yourself might find your position in society jeopardised.'

'This is so unfair.' Aurelia burst into tears, sobbing into her handkerchief.

'Surely there must be a way to get round this, Piers.' Lady Pentelow sank down onto her chair. 'Tell him that you need time to make arrangements.'

'This has been going on for six months or more, Grandmama. I've even set a private detective to look into his affairs, but nothing has come to light that would disprove his claim.'

'You can't allow him to do this to us, Piers,' Aurelia cried passionately. 'You must stop him at all costs.'

'He won't wait any longer, Aurelia,' Piers said patiently. 'I can do no more for the moment, but that doesn't mean that I will stop trying.'

'But we'll be homeless. We'll have to go to the workhouse, like common people.' Aurelia bowed her head and sobbed on Patricia's shoulder.

'Is there no other way, Piers?' Lady Pentelow clasped her hands tightly in her lap. 'We can't allow this to happen.'

'I know it's hard, Grandmama, but we have very little choice, unless you want Blaise to blacken the family name. I've spoken to him many times and I know he isn't prepared to give way. He's a bitter man and he's determined to carry out his threats if his demands are not met.'

Rosalind had kept quiet until now, but she could see that Lady Pentelow was not about to give in easily. 'If you'll allow me to speak, ma'am . . . I would like to say that you are very welcome to share Rockwood Castle with me and my family. But for Piers we would have lost our home to our creditors, so it's the least I can do.'

Lady Pentelow turned on her with an arrogant toss of her head. 'Do you really expect me to leave my home to live in a ruin of a medieval castle? I suppose this is your doing, Piers. I should have been consulted before you came to any such arrangement.'

'Piers may or may not be the rightful heir to Rockwood, but without his aid we would have faced bankruptcy,' Rosalind said earnestly. 'I can sympathise wholeheartedly with you and Aurelia, but my offer is genuine. You would be very welcome.'

'Don't I have any say in this?' Aurelia demanded, wiping her eyes on a hanky that Patricia produced from her pocket. 'I don't want to move away from here. This is my home.'

'I came here as a bride,' Lady Pentelow added, frowning. 'Why should I give it all up to a criminal? You say you've checked his credentials, but he might be an imposter, Piers. Why give in so easily?'

'I've done everything I can to find a way to challenge him without success. Could you really face society if the scandal came to light, Grandmama?

'Last evening, Hugo told me again that he loved me,' Aurelia said miserably. 'Now he'll never propose. You've ruined my life, Piers.'

Patricia slipped her arm around Aurelia's shoulders. 'It doesn't sound as if it's your brother's fault.'

'Hugo wouldn't care about a scandal,' Aurelia said, sniffing. 'He's too good a person to be swayed by tittle-tattle.'

'I very much doubt that.' Lady Pentelow heaved a sigh. 'The Knightons are parvenus, whose wealth came from trade. I hate to admit it, Piers, but I think you're right. If this gets out we won't be able to hold up our heads. I was descended from a long line of aristocracy where such affairs would be overlooked, but my husband was in trade and this could ruin us.'

'That was my conclusion, Grandmama. If you are

agreeable we will take Rosalind up on her kind offer, and we'll move to Rockwood Castle. However, there must be a way to disprove Blaise's claim, and I promise you that if there is I will find it, no matter how long it takes.'

'It breaks my heart, but I can see there is little choice.' Lady Pentelow spoke slowly, as if each word she uttered cost her pain. 'I accept your offer, Miss Carey.'

'Thank you, Lady Pentelow. I'm sure it will only be temporary and then you'll be able to return to your own home.'

'There's one proviso, however. I wish to bring my most loyal servants with me.'

'We have plenty of room for everyone, although the accommodation won't be luxurious.'

'Are you sure about this, Grandmama?' Piers asked anxiously. 'The servants might wish to remain in Cornwall.'

Lady Pentelow brushed off this suggestion with a wave of her hand. 'I insist on bringing Patterson. A good butler is hard to come by these days, and I won't go anywhere without Cook and Mrs Witham, my housekeeper. Of course my maid, Miss Simms, will accompany me.'

'I'm taking Grainger,' Aurelia said sulkily. 'I can't manage without a maid.'

'Of course not.' Lady Pentelow nodded in agreement. 'It will take several days for the servants to pack what we need for an extended stay, and then all the treasures and furnishings will have to go into store, apart from the articles I wish to take with me. I'm not allowing an interloper to snatch everything this family owns. He may take the bricks and mortar, but he is not having the heart of Trevenor – that goes with us. Am I making myself clear, Piers?'

'Yes, Grandmama, and it will only be a temporary measure. I promise that, hand on heart.' Piers stood up. 'Are there any more questions? Then I'll start making the necessary arrangements.'

He beckoned to Rosalind who was more than willing to escape from the room. Tension had built to a dangerous level, and one wrong word might cause an angry outburst.

Piers came to a halt in the entrance hall. 'I'm afraid this move will be as difficult for everyone at Rockwood as it is for us, Rosalind. You can still change your mind. You don't have to make this sacrifice.'

'You saved us, so it's the least I can do, but you saw how we live, Piers. There's plenty of room for everyone and for any belongings that your grandmother wishes to bring with her. You helped us, but in the process you've lost what is most dear to you.'

'What I did for Rockwood has no bearing on the situation here. I'm being forced to comply with Blaise's demands, and I can't fight him through the courts without bringing the whole sordid story to light, but I will find a way to regain what's rightfully mine.'

'I believe you,' Rosalind said earnestly. 'You and your family are welcome to stay at Rockwood for as long as it takes, although I don't know how I'm going to break the news to Hester that she will have to work with the servants from Trevenor. She was not very keen on your man, Trigg. They didn't get along very well.'

'That's all right. I had to sack Trigg when I discovered that he'd stolen a few personal items of mine. So Trigg won't be a problem.'

'I understand. You must have been very upset to think someone you trusted could behave that way.'

Piers glanced over his shoulder to where Patterson was winding one of the grandfather clocks, which stood sentinel in almost every room. It seemed to Rosalind that the Blanchard family had always been obsessed with timekeeping.

Piers lowered his voice. 'It will take several days to arrange our move to Rockwood. You might like to go on ahead of us to warn your family.'

'Yes, I think that's eminently sensible. There's very little I can do here, and I feel as if we're rather in the way.'

'Not at all, but I dare say there will be many more tears and tantrums before all this is over.'

Rosalind glanced at Patterson, whose back was turned to them, but she sensed that he was straining his ears to listen to their conversation. 'I think you'd better inform the servants very soon, Piers. You know how rumours fly round.'

'You're right. This sort of thing is beyond me.'

She smiled. 'Don't underestimate yourself. You handled the situation very well just now. Anyway, I expect you have work to do in the mine office. The men there will also need to know very soon. I don't know Mr Blaise, but I suspect he will be eager to take over.'

'I need to see my lawyer in Plymouth urgently to make sure everything is done legally, and perhaps he can work out a way to give me some control of the business.' Piers frowned thoughtfully. 'I can take you are far as Plymouth and make sure you get the train from there to Newton Abbot, where you could hire a carriage to take you the rest of the way.'

'I thought perhaps the stage coach might be cheaper,' Rosalind said warily. 'Even with your generosity we still have to be careful with money.'

'Don't worry about that. I'll make sure you have enough funds to cover everything.' He grasped her hand and held it in a warm clasp. 'You've been wonderful, Rosalind. I wouldn't blame you if you hated the sight of me, considering the fact that I've turned your life upside down.'

She felt the warmth of his fingers entwined around hers and was oddly comforted, even though what he said was true. He had appeared suddenly and with what might have been a devastating effect on their lives, but she was oddly grateful to him. He had lifted the burden from her shoulders to his own, and he had saved her beloved Rockwood, even if he were to lay claim to it for himself one day. But having seen him with his family, and watching him deal with the even worse situation in which they found themselves, she had nothing but respect for Piers Blanchard.

'When do you want to leave for Plymouth? We can be ready in less than an hour.'

Chapter Thirteen

Hester gazed at Rosalind in horror. 'Tell me that again.'

'You heard what I said the first time, Hester.' Rosalind picked up the Brown Betty teapot from the table and filled a cup, which she handed to Hester, who had collapsed onto the nearest chair. 'Sip this and you'll feel better.'

Hester gulped down a mouthful of tea. 'Wasn't it bad enough to have that man claiming Rockwood for his own, without having to put up with his family, too?'

'We almost lost Rockwood and the entire estate, don't forget that, Hester. It was Piers Blanchard who saved us from ruin, so the least we can do is to help him and his family in their time of need. You keep telling me that you need more help than poor little Tilly can provide, so perhaps we should be grateful that Lady Pentelow wishes to bring some of her servants with her.'

'I've run this household for more years than I care to remember. It's bad enough with Mr Jarvis back here, always telling me what to do; let alone having to cope with complete strangers in the servants' hall.'

'I want you to promise me that you'll try to get along with them, Hester. You're part of the family so please don't let me down.'

Hester sniffed. 'Well, if you put it that way I suppose I could make an effort.'

'Piers has promised to buy a commission in the army for Bertie, and he's going to pay for Walter to attend university.'

'That's all well and good, but what is the gentleman going to do for you and for Miss Patricia? And what will the families round here think of the arrangement? They'll want to know why these people have come to live with us.'

Rosalind knew that Hester was right. It was something that had not occurred to her until now and she frowned thoughtfully. 'I'll think of something. In the meantime we'd better get the castle ready to receive our guests. If you can organise help from the village I have the means to pay them now. We'll concentrate on giving Rockwood a rather belated spring clean.'

Hester placed her cup back on the table and rose to her feet. 'I'll go down to the village and call on Maud Causley at the Black Dog. She knows everyone's business and she'll be able to tell me who's available for work.'

Stifling a sigh of relief, Rosalind nodded. 'Thank you, Hester. They'll be here in a few days' time, so the sooner they can start, the better.'

Hester took her bonnet from a peg behind the door and rammed it on her head. 'It's lucky I told Jacob not to call for a week or two. That man pesters the life out of me. He keeps asking me to marry him, but I like things the way they are. I don't know I could put up with having a man around all the time.' She wrapped her shawl around her shoulders and marched out into the sunlit courtyard.

Rosalind could only hope that Hester would keep her word when faced with Lady Pentelow's house-keeper, who had been used to running a much larger household. She sighed; that was something she would have to face soon enough, but there were other matters that needed her attention. Patricia had not put in an appearance at breakfast, so presumably she was still in bed. Rosalind had had a long talk with her sister during their journey home, and Patricia had promised that she would not see Barnaby again – but with Patricia one could never be sure. She was capricious at the best of times, and after the considerable upset at Trevenor, and Aurelia's obvious distress at the prospect of losing Hugo Knighton's affection, it would not have surprised Rosalind to find Patricia heading straight for the smithy. She was about to go in search of her sister when Hester put her head round the door.

'Sir Lucien has got out again, Miss Rosalind. I've just seen Mr Jarvis chasing after him.'

'Oh dear!' Rosalind rushed out of the kitchen. She saw her grandfather moving extremely quickly for someone who claimed to be riddled with gout. He had reached the entrance to the bailey and he opened the heavy gates with apparent ease. Jarvis was calling out to him, but Sir Lucien did not appear to hear. Rosalind joined in the chase, her hair curling wildly round her head as the pins she had used to confine it into a chignon flew in all directions. She caught up with Jarvis, who was red in the face and panting heavily.

'How did this happen, Mr Jarvis?'

'I turned my back for a minute, Miss Rosalind – quite literally a minute – and he slipped out of the door before I had a chance to stop him.'

'He's headed for the stables. Why would he be going there?'

'I don't know, Miss Rosalind,' Jarvis said breathlessly. 'I can't run any faster.'

'Stop and catch your breath. I'll get him.' Rosalind picked up her skirts and raced on, forgetting everything other than the need to bring Grandpapa home before he was lost or had fallen and hurt himself.

She had not gone much further when she saw Jim Gurney emerge from the stable block. 'Jim.' She waved and called his name again. 'Jim, stop Sir Lucien, please.'

Jim Gurney was a burly man, fit and healthy. He approached Sir Lucien as warily as if he had been a runaway horse. 'Hold fast there, Admiral.'

Sir Lucien came to a sudden halt, staring at Jim as if he had never seen him before in his life. Rosalind hurried up to them, breathless but relieved. Her main fear when Grandpapa escaped from the castle was that he would stumble into the back-water or fall into the fast-flowing currents of the estuary itself.

'Who are you?' Sir Lucien demanded angrily. 'Do you know who I am, sir?'

Jim dropped his hands to his sides. 'Seaman Gurney reporting for duty, Admiral.'

Sir Lucien turned away. 'Who's this fellow addressing a Vice-Admiral in such a familiar manner.' He stared hard at Rosalind. 'And who are you? Have you had permission to come aboard?'

Rosalind took him by the hand. 'Good morning, Grandpapa. It's me, Rosie, your granddaughter. I've come to take you home.'

'What's the matter with you, Rosalind? Why are you talking to me as if I were a five-year-old? And why are you running about the countryside without your bonnet and gloves. Just look at the state of your hair. What will your grandmama say about this when I tell her?'

Rosalind exchanged weary glances with Jim. 'It

will be our secret, Grandpapa. Let's go home now, shall we?'

'Yes, we will. You're a very naughty girl, Rosie. Running away from your governess is not good behaviour.'

'You're right, of course. I won't do it again.'

Rosalind turned to Jim as she led her grandfather away. 'Thank you, Jim. There's no need to mention this to anyone else.'

He tipped his cap. 'Of course not, Miss Rosalind. Will you be needing the trap today?'

'Yes, I will, but not until this afternoon.' She hesitated as Jarvis came towards them, puffing and panting. 'We're expecting guests in the coming week or so, Jim. There'll be horses to stable and a carriage or two to house. If you need more help you can take on a couple of lads from the village.'

'Really, miss?' Jim's face lit up with pleasure. 'It will be like the old days.'

Jarvis tucked Sir Lucien's hand in his arm. 'Come along, Sir Lucien. Let's get you back to your cabin. I'm sorry, Miss Rosalind,' he added in a low voice. 'I'll take extra special care while he's in this mood.'

'I know you will, Jarvis. Thank you.' She followed them back to the castle, keeping at a distance so that her presence did not distract her grandfather. He was limping slightly and it was not hard to guess that his race for freedom had exacerbated his aches and pains. She sighed: it was going to be very difficult to keep his condition a secret from Lady

Pentelow and Aurelia. She had considered revealing the extent of her grandfather's mental confusion, but somehow it seemed wrong to tarnish the good opinion that her ladyship had of a man who had once been such a hero.

Rosalind had almost reached the main gates when she spotted Bertie strolling towards her with his shotgun broken over his arm and Bob trotting along beside him. She had wondered where her dog was that morning when she came down to breakfast, and the couple of brace of pigeons that Bertie was carrying were proof that they had been out hunting. At a word from Bertie the dog broke away from him and bounded towards Rosalind, barking joyously. She stooped down to make a fuss of him.

'I've really missed you, Bob, old chap.'

He responded by licking her face and rubbing his head against her arm. She straightened up. 'You went out early, Bertie.'

'Best time of day to catch these little darlings. There'll be pigeon pie for dinner this evening. By the way, what time did you get home last night?'

'It was about nine o'clock. Where were you and Walter?'

'At the Black Dog, of course. What else would we do?'

She smiled. 'I thought maybe you were visiting Greystone Park? I know you like Christina.'

'She's a nice enough girl, but I'm hardly in a

position to pay court to anyone. Who would allow their daughter to associate with a penniless fellow like me?'

'If you'd been at home last evening I could have given you some good news, Bertie.'

'That would be a welcome change. What is it?'

Rosalind leaned against the parapet of the ornamental bridge that led to the main gates. 'Piers Blanchard has agreed to purchase a commission for you in whichever regiment you choose, but there's something else, which might not be so agreeable.'

Bertie sighed. 'I knew there would be a catch. What is it?'

'It's a long story, but the Blanchard family have to leave their home. Piers is being blackmailed by a man who claims to be his half-brother. Ewart Blaise demanded Trevenor and a share in the mine in return for his silence about a scandal that occurred more than twenty years ago.'

Bertie frowned. 'I don't understand. He saved Rockwood but he's lost Trevenor?'

'Yes, that's it really. I've invited Lady Pentelow, Piers and his sister, Aurelia, to stay here until the matter is resolved.'

'You have?' Bertie shrugged. 'I suppose I can put up with them if Piers is really going to buy me a commission. I fancy the infantry, myself. I'm an excellent marksman.'

'That's something you'll have to discuss with Piers. Anyway, I need to find Walter.'

Bertie grinned. 'Is Piers going to have Walter's poems published?'

'Not exactly, but he's going to use his money and influence to get Walter into Oxford or Cambridge.'

'If Piers is so wealthy, why doesn't he use his money to get the better of the fellow who's blackmailing him?'

'That's just the trouble,' Rosalind said, sighing. 'If you pay off a blackmailer they simply come back for more at a later date. Besides which, it sounds as if Ewart Blaise isn't too interested in money. He has a personal grudge against the Blanchards and he wants to see them dispossessed and humbled.'

'Nice chap,' Bertie observed casually. 'I'll just take these birds to the kitchen and then I'm going for a ride, if old Ajax can manage it. Maybe Blanchard will buy us a couple of young horses, too. I quite like having a wealthy benefactor.' He strolled off, whistling a tune that Rosalind did not recognise. Bob looked up at her, his pink tongue lolling out of his mouth and his liquid brown eyes shining. She patted him on the neck.

'I'm home now, boy. We'll go for a walk later and it's so hot I might have a swim in the cove.'

Bob wagged his tail furiously as if he understood, although despite his breed he was not keen on going into the sea. He would rescue her if he thought she needed it, but otherwise he would amuse himself by moving large pebbles from the water's edge and lining them up on the sand. Rosalind smiled, and ruffled the thick fur on his chest. 'Good boy.' Let's go and find Walter, and then we'll see what Patsy's up to, shall we?'

Bob jumped up and down and barked excitedly.

Walter, as usual, was in the library, reading one of the leather-bound editions that their late father had bought in a house sale.

'Walter, will you put that book away for a moment, please?' Rosalind walked over to the window seat where he sat cross-legged. 'You'll ruin your eyesight if you keep on like this.'

He looked up and greeted her with a smile. 'Where have you been, Rosie? You haven't been at dinner lately.'

'I'm surprised that you noticed. Patsy and I have been away for several days.'

'I thought I hadn't seen either of you. Where did you go?'

Rosalind snatched the book from him and laid it on the library table. 'Just concentrate on what I'm going to tell you, Walter.'

'All right, but there's no need to get cross. You'll appreciate me one day when my poems get published and I start earning money.'

'Well, that might not be such a fantasy after all. Do you remember Piers Blanchard?'

'Rosie, it's me you're talking to, not Grandpapa. Of course I remember him. Jolly decent fellow.'

'Yes, well, you won't be disappointed in him when

I tell you that he's prepared to pay your way through university.'

'No! That's wonderful.'

'There's something more.' Rosalind pulled up a chair and sat down with Bob sprawled on the floor at her side. 'It's about the Blanchard family, Walter. They'll be moving in with us for the foreseeable future, but I doubt if you'll even notice the difference.'

'Probably not, unless they like reading.'

Rosalind stood up. 'You really do need to go to university. A change of scene will do you the world of good. You might even make some friends of your own age.'

'I have friends,' Walter said huffily. 'I have a drink with Barnaby sometimes, and there's Tom Nosworthy, the schoolmaster's son. Although I haven't seen so much of him since he went to Cambridge.'

'Then perhaps you'd like to try for that university? You would have at least one friend there, Walter. Anyway, I mustn't stop here chatting to you. I need to find Patsy.'

'You're too late,' Walter said casually. 'I saw her through the window. She was heading towards the village. She'll be on her way to the smithy.'

Rosalind stared at him in amazement. 'How do you know that?'

He shrugged. 'Everyone knows that she and Barnaby are sweet on each other.'

'But you must know that he's engaged to Lucy Warren.'

'Of course I do.' Walter sighed dreamily. 'My sister and Barnaby are star-crossed lovers. I've written a poem about them.'

'How long have you known about it?'

'I can't remember, exactly. They've always liked each other, even when we were very young. I think it's romantic.'

'Romantic!' Rosalind headed for the doorway. 'I don't think that's the word Mr Warren would use if he discovered that Barnaby has his eye on Patsy, when Lucy is in the . . .' She paused. 'Never mind.'

'I do understand these things,' Walter said vaguely. 'I'm not a hermit.'

Rosalind slammed out of the library with Bob bouncing along at her side. So much for Patricia's promises. Rosalind set off for the village without bothering to put on her bonnet. The sun would bring out her freckles and give her an unfashionable tan, but her mother was not here to reprimand her, and this was an emergency.

She had only just crossed the bridge when she saw Hester leading a group of women towards the castle. It was not possible to avoid them and Rosalind came to a reluctant halt.

'Don't go anywhere,' Hester said sharply. 'I've brought willing workers, and you need to give them instructions.'

Rosalind was about to refuse, but the martial gleam in Hester's grey eyes was enough to make her hesitate and she could see that the women from the village were watching her eagerly. She retreated into the courtyard and led the way through the kitchen to the servants' hall, which was rarely used these days. Mr Jarvis lit a fire in the evenings and sat smoking his pipe after Sir Lucien was in bed asleep, but otherwise it was a large echoing room with a long oak table surrounded by chairs. A dresser took up most of the wall on the far end of the room, on which the plain white china used by the servants was displayed.

'Now then,' Hester said, when the last woman had shuffled into the room. 'Miss Carey will tell you which rooms are to be made ready for the guests, and those of you who are able to live in will be given rooms in the north tower.'

Rosalind cleared her throat. 'I appreciate your coming here at such short notice. We are expecting guests to arrive within the next few days. Many of our rooms have been shut up for a very long time, and they will need cleaning thoroughly, and the beds aired and made ready. The drawing room and the music room will also have to be cleaned and the carpets taken outside and beaten on the line, if possible. You will all know Mr Jarvis, if only by sight, and he will take your particulars later today. You will be paid at the end of each week.'

Hester cleared her throat. 'Where would it be best for them to start, Miss Rosalind?'

'I think the ground-floor reception rooms today. I'll make a list of the bedchambers we will be using, and preparing those can begin tomorrow. Mrs Dodridge will tell you when meals will be served. That will be in here, so this room will have to be cleaned as well. Maybe you could start here.' Rosalind waited to see if anyone had any questions, but they seemed to be more interested in surveying their new surroundings.

Rosalind turned to Hester, lowering her voice. 'I'll leave you to it.' She walked away before Hester had a chance to raise any objections. Life with two house-keepers and a rival cook was going to be interesting.

It was too late to stop Patricia from visiting the smithy, if indeed that was where she had gone, although Rosalind was in no doubt about that. She decided that she had better go up to the east tower to speak to Jarvis and warn him that Patterson would be descending upon them, but that it was only a temporary arrangement. She could imagine Jarvis's reaction if he heard the news from anyone else, especially Hester. There had always been an element of friction between them in the old days, but they would have to put past rivalries aside if they were to survive the introduction of strangers into their midst.

Rosalind made her way through the echoing corridors to the east tower, where she found Jarvis standing outside the closed door to Sir Lucien's day room clutching a large iron key in his hand.

'What's the matter, Jarvis?' Rosalind asked anxiously.

'It's Sir Lucien, Miss Rosalind. He's determined to escape even though I gave him a dose of laudanum to calm him down. He's convinced that he must rejoin his ship and nothing I can say will make him see sense.'

As if to confirm his statement, Sir Lucien hammered on the door. 'Let me out. I'll have you keel-hauled for this, you insubordinate knave.'

'Grandpapa.' Rosalind leaned her forehead against the wooden panelling. 'It's all right. The danger is past.'

'Prudence, my dear, is that you?'

Rosalind exchanged worried glances with Jarvis. 'He thinks I am my grandmother.'

'She was a great lady, Miss Rosalind.'

'Prudence, tell that fellow to open the door.'

'I will, but only if you promise to remain where you are. We have received a signal to say that the enemy has been routed, Sir Lucien.'

There was a moment of complete silence and Rosalind held her breath. She nodded to Jarvis. 'Unlock the door.'

'Are you sure, Miss Rosalind?'

'Quite sure. I'll go in and talk to him.'

Jarvis turned the key in the lock and Rosalind opened the door. She stepped into the sunny room, closing the door behind her. 'Good morning, Grandpapa. How are you today?'

Sir Lucien eyed her warily. 'Where is my wife?'

'Grandmama had a domestic matter to attend to, sir.'

'I remember now. My dearest Prudence has passed away.' Sir Lucien sank down on the sofa, holding his head in his hands. 'Sometimes I forget things, Rosalind.'

She sat down next to him and put her arm around his shoulders. 'We all do that, Grandpapa. I forget things quite often.'

'I dreamed that I was rejoining my ship, Rosalind. It was just a dream, wasn't it?'

'Yes, Grandpapa.'

'I think I should rest for a while, my dear. Where's Jarvis? Tell him I'd like a glass of Madeira and a slice of cake. You know, the one that Hester bakes specially for me. I want to see her. Will you send her to me?'

Rosalind helped him to relax against the cushions and she rose to her feet. 'Of course, Grandpapa. I'll tell Jarvis to fetch the wine and cake right away, and I'll tell Hester what you said.' She backed towards the door but her grandfather had closed his eyes and appeared to have fallen asleep. She let herself out of the room and almost bumped into Jarvis, who leaped back a couple of steps. 'Were you listening at the keyhole, Jarvis?'

He gazed down at his feet. 'I was anxious, Miss Rosalind. Sometimes the admiral can get rather violent.'

'He would never harm me, Jarvis. However, I expect you heard his request for a glass of Madeira wine and some cake?'

'I have his bottle of wine in my makeshift pantry next door.'

'I'll send Tilly up with some cake, if my brothers haven't eaten the last slice.'

The aroma of cooking welcomed Rosalind as she entered the kitchen, where Hester was hard at work.

'Is that cake I can smell baking?' Rosalind asked hopefully.

'I know how fond Sir Lucien is of my Madeira cake, so I thought I'd better make one. At least I don't have to go begging for eggs and butter at the farm these days. Dora Greep sends me my regular order once a week, but we'll need more when they foreigners from Cornwall invade us.'

Rosalind stifled a giggle. 'They are not foreigners, Hester. They are just like us. Try to remember that we might not still be here in Rockwood if it weren't for Piers Blanchard. You will try to get on with the servants from Trevenor, won't you?'

Hester sniffed and thumped the rolling pin down on a lump of dough she had just lifted from a china bowl. 'I'll play fair just as long as they do, but if they want to take over my kitchen they'll have a fight on their hands.'

Chapter Fourteen

Patricia returned from the village later that morning and went straight to her room, but Rosalind was not going to allow her sister to get away with such wayward behaviour and she demanded an explanation.

Patricia was unrepentant. 'Yes, I did go to the smithy. You can't stop me seeing Barnaby. Anyway, he was working and Mr Yelland was there all the time, so no one can say it was improper.'

'I want you to be happy, Patsy. I know how you feel about Barnaby and I'm afraid it will break your heart when he marries Lucy Warren.'

'I can look after myself,' Patricia said sulkily. 'Leave me alone. Anyway, you've got enough to do with all this cleaning and getting rooms ready. At least I don't have to mop the floors now.'

'Perhaps you'd like to choose which room Aurelia

will have, and you can make sure that she has everything she needs.'

'Wherever we put her isn't going to match her beautiful bedchamber at Trevenor. I think Lady Pentelow will regret her decision to make a move to draughty old Rockwood Castle.'

'It's not going to be easy for any of us, but you could try to make it a little better for them, Patsy. Just think of the hospitality we received at Trevenor when we arrived uninvited. They have very little choice.' Rosalind sighed. 'Are you listening to me, Patricia Carey?'

Patricia had run to the window and opened the casement. 'I recognise that carriage. I think your suitor has come to visit you, Rosie.'

'I don't know what you're talking about.' Despite her scornful response, Rosalind was intrigued and she crossed the floor to look over hers sister's shoulder. 'Don't be silly, that's the Greystone carriage. I expect Christina and Sylvia have come to see you.'

Patricia closed the window, giggling. 'Don't play the innocent with me, Rosie. I know that Sir Michael is sweet on you. Everyone in Rockwood village knows that.'

'Then they are all wrong.'

'Really? If that's so, why are you blushing?' Patricia danced across the room and opened the door. 'I'm going downstairs to welcome them, whoever it is. Are you coming?'

Rosalind glanced in the mirror on the dressing

table and automatically smoothed her tumbled curls. 'I'm not in a fit state to receive visitors.'

'I'm sure that Sir Michael won't care.'

Rosalind followed her sister down the wide oak staircase to the entrance hall where Jarvis was already stationed by the front door.

'I heard the carriage approaching, Miss Rosalind, so I took it on myself to leave Sir Lucien for the moment. He's sound asleep, and unlikely to awaken for a while.'

'Thank you, Jarvis. I'll be in the morning parlour.' Rosalind caught Patricia by the hand. 'And so will you, Patsy. You'd better start exhibiting some decorum when Lady Pentelow is here, so now is a good time to begin.'

'Bother decorum,' Patricia said crossly, but she followed Rosalind into the morning parlour anyway.

Moments later Jarvis appeared to announce the arrival of Sir Michael Greystone and his daughters.

Sir Michael strolled into the room. 'My dear Miss Carey, I hope you don't mind us calling on you like this?'

'Of course not. We're always pleased to see you and your daughters, sir.' Rosalind managed a smile, but she dropped her gaze. The memory of their last meeting was still fresh in her mind and she was not sure how she was expected to respond to the warm look in his eyes.

Christina hurried past her father and wrapped her arms around Patricia. 'We heard that you've been to Cornwall, Patsy. Why didn't you tell us you were going away?'

'Yes,' Sylvia added. 'We sent you an invitation to luncheon and received the reply that you were not in residence. Shame on you, Patsy. I thought we were friends.'

'Now, now, girls,' Sir Michael said mildly. 'Allow Patricia to explain before you scold her.'

'It was all so sudden.' Patricia lowered her voice dramatically. 'Mama and Claude arrived unexpectedly and took us to Plymouth. It was supposed to be a shopping expedition but really it was an excuse to take me away from . . .' she paused, eyeing Rosalind warily, '. . . you know who.'

Christina's eyes widened. 'No, really?'

'Perhaps you had better continue this conversation in the drawing room,' Rosalind suggested hastily.

'All right,' Patricia said meekly. 'Come with me. I have such a lot to tell you.'

Rosalind waited until the girls had left the room and she moved to the fireplace, putting a safe distance between herself and her unexpected guest. 'May I offer you some refreshment, Sir Michael? It's a hot day and you must be thirsty.'

He shook his head. 'I came because I wanted to see you, Rosalind. I believe we have some unfinished business to discuss.'

She tugged automatically at the bell pull. 'I'm not sure what you mean, sir.'

'Yes, you do. I think I made my feelings perfectly clear when last we met.'

'I hold you in very high regard, Sir Michael, but not perhaps in the way you wish me to feel.'

'I called here one day not long after our last meeting to apologise for stating my case so boldly, only to be told that you had left for Plymouth with your mother and her manager. Now I hear that you are preparing to entertain visitors, a family from Cornwall, which I must assume includes Mr Blanchard.'

Rosalind turned to face him. 'Where did you get such information?'

'You know how it is in Rockwood. It doesn't take long for gossip to reach even as far as Greystone Park. Is it true?'

'Sir Michael, you have always been a good friend to my family and myself, but is this really any of your business? I'm sorry to be blunt, but this has nothing to do with you.'

He was at her side before she had a chance to move away and he grasped her hand in his. 'I want it to be my concern, Rosalind. I'm offering you the protection of my name and my worldly goods – in fact I'm asking you to marry me. I can't put it any plainer than that, and I think I deserve an answer.'

The door opened suddenly and Hester marched into the room, arms folded. 'You rang, Miss Rosalind?' She fixed Sir Michael with an unblinking stare.

'Would you like tea or coffee, Sir Michael?' Rosalind snatched her hand free. She could see that Hester had summed up the situation accurately. Over the years Hester had developed an amazing sixth sense when it came to anything that concerned the family, and she was always ready to take on anyone who threatened one of her own.

'I was hoping that champagne would be more appropriate,' Sir Michael said silkily. 'You may leave us, Mrs Dodridge.'

Hester puffed out her chest. 'What I also came to say is that Mr Blanchard has just arrived, Miss Rosalind. Shall I show him in?'

'No, you will not.' Sir Michael took a step towards her. 'Miss Rosalind and I were having a private conversation.'

Rosalind was about to protest when Piers walked into the room. 'Thank you, Hester,' he said, handing her his top hat and gloves. 'A tray of tea would be more than welcome. It's a long journey from Trevenor.'

'Tea it is, sir.' Hester beamed at him. 'I've just made a nice Madeira cake. Perhaps a slice of that would go down well, unless you would prefer a glass of Madeira wine?'

'Bah! This is impossible.' Sir Michael turned to Rosalind. 'I will have an answer, but I'll leave you to think over my offer very carefully. I meant every word I said. You must believe that.' He strode past Piers. 'Good day to you, sir.'

'Shall I fetch the young ladies, sir?' Hester asked innocently.

'You can go to hell, woman.' Sir Michael stormed out of the room.

Piers patted Hester on the back. 'Well done, Hester. If you go to hell, I'll be happy to join you there.'

Hester burst out laughing. 'I didn't think much of you in the beginning, Mr Blanchard, but maybe I'm changing my mind.' She left the room, still chuckling.

Rosalind sank down on the sofa. 'I don't know what to say. He shouldn't have spoken to you or Hester in that manner.'

'The poor fellow is in love with you,' Piers said dispassionately. 'That is obvious for anyone to see.'

'I've known him since I was a child. In fact, he's old enough to be my father.'

'He obviously doesn't see it that way, Rosalind. I'm sorry if he's upset you, but he's gone now.' Piers took a silver hip flask from his coat pocket. 'Would you like a tot of brandy to calm your nerves?'

She looked up and laughed. 'I'm not a fragile little woman, Piers. I don't like unpleasantness, but I don't need brandy. A cup of tea will be fine. Anyway, I wasn't expecting to see you so soon. Are your family on the way, too?'

'No, not quite. Grandmama refuses to move until all the valuables are safely in store, and Aurelia is overseeing the packing of so many trunks that we'll need an army of removal carters to bring everything here.'

'What about Blaise? Has he been to see you again?'

'No, it's all being done through solicitors now, which is much better. I don't wish to have anything to do with him. In fact, I refuse to recognise him as my half-brother.'

'I'm not surprised. I can sympathise with you because of our current situation. You could have taken Rockwood from us, but you have chosen to be generous.'

'That's one promise that I intend to keep. I'm having my solicitor draw up a document that gives you and your family the right to live here for the rest of your lives, if that is what you so wish. Rockwood belongs to you and your brothers and Patricia as much as it does to me.'

'Thank you, Piers. That puts my mind at ease.' Rosalind looked up as Tilly entered, carrying a tray of tea. 'Thank you, Tilly. Put it on the table, please.'

Tilly hesitated, juggling the heavy tray as she attempted to bend over the low table. Piers stepped forward and took it from her. 'Allow me, Tilly.'

She giggled and blushed rosily. 'Thank you, sir.'

'That will be all, thank you, Tilly.' Rosalind picked up the teapot and began to pour. 'Maybe I will add a tot of brandy, Piers, but it's not because I need to calm my nerves.' She handed him a cup of tea. 'Forgive me for asking, but why have you left your family to manage without you?'

He unscrewed the top of his flask and added a generous tot to her cup and to his own. 'You're right. This isn't what I intended, but I had to warn you in person. I think Blaise might come here.'

'Why would he do that?'

'He's sly and he's determined to take as much from me as he possibly can. I couldn't think how he discovered my connection to Rockwood, but then I found out that Trigg had been in his pay. That man had been spying on me for months.'

'I'm sorry about Trigg, but surely Blaise has no claim on Rockwood?'

'I've notified my solicitor and asked him to make certain that Blaise doesn't try to insert a clause in any legal agreement that gives him any rights over Rockwood, however unlikely.'

'He sounds like a horrible person.'

'He's embittered and greedy – a bad combination. But if he should have the face to turn up here I want you to be on your guard. He might imagine that Rockwood Castle is filled with art treasures and valuables.'

'He would be very disappointed, but thank you for coming all this way to warn me.' Rosalind frowned thoughtfully. 'I've seen him twice, but he was always in the shadows. However, I think I might recognise him.'

'He can be very charming if he wants to be, so you'd better warn Patricia and the servants. Although I'd back Hester against him any day.'

'You can tell Patricia yourself at dinner. I assume you'll be staying here for a while, at least.'

'I will stay for tonight, if that's not too inconvenient, but then I intend to return to Cornwall. I need to be at Trevenor to make sure that the move goes smoothly. I can't expect Grandmama to handle things on her own, even though she's a very resourceful woman.'

'What about the mine? Isn't there any way you can keep control?'

'My solicitor is working on that. I'm not going to give up without a struggle, but I have to protect Grandmama and Aurelia from a scandal that would ruin them far more than the loss of a few possessions.'

'I don't call the loss of Trevenor trivial. It's your family home.'

'If there's a way to get it back from that scoundrel you can rest assured that I will find it. When you get to know me better, Rosalind, you'll know that I never give up willingly.'

'I can believe that.' Rosalind replaced her cup on its saucer and rose from her seat. 'I'll make sure a room is made ready for you and I'll tell Hester there'll be one more for dinner tonight.'

'I think Hester has already seen to that,' Piers said, smiling. 'She took my valise and she told me it would be pigeon pie for dinner.'

'Then it seems I have nothing to do.' Rosalind eyed him thoughtfully. 'Are you still willing to put Walter through university?'

'Of course. I never make promises that I don't intend to keep.'

'Then perhaps you'd like to tell him in person. I did mention it but I'm not sure he believed me. Walter lives in a little world of his own. It will do him good to widen his horizons.'

'I'd like to see him again. He's a sensitive soul and needs to be handled with care and consideration.'

Rosalind met his intense gaze with a puzzled frown. 'You continue to surprise me, Piers.'

'I take that as a compliment. I might have come into your lives unexpectedly, but believe me, I never intended to do you any harm.'

'I realise that now, although I'm not sure I did at the beginning. Follow me. I'm sure we'll find Walter in the library.' She hesitated in the doorway. 'I should warn you that Walter writes poetry and he thinks he can restore the family fortunes if his book is published.'

'Thank you, I'll bear that in mind.'

Rosalind left Piers in the library with her brother and she was about to go to the kitchen to speak to Hester when Patricia erupted from the drawing room and barred her way.

'What did you say to Sir Michael? He practically dragged the girls away and he was obviously in a really bad mood. I've never seen him look so angry.'

'It was nothing. A simple misunderstanding.'

'That's not how it seemed to me. Christina thinks

that he's sweet on you, Rosie. Is that what it was? Did he propose to you?'

'You mustn't mention this to the girls, Patsy. It would embarrass their father if they said anything to him.'

'So he did ask you to marry him.' Patricia did a little dance. 'You must have refused, but you should have said "yes". I would love to have Christina and Sylvia as my sisters. Our money worries would be over. Sir Michael is as rich as Croesus.'

'Money isn't everything, and I don't want to talk about it.'

Patricia's smile faded. 'Aside from Sir Michael's broken heart – did I see Piers in the courtyard? I thought I spotted him through the window as I was taking the girls to the drawing room.'

'Yes, he's staying for the night. He says we need to be vigilant in case Blaise turns up.'

Patricia shrugged. 'If I see any strangers in the village I'll be sure to tell you.'

Rosalind caught her sister by the wrist as she was about to walk away. 'You are not to go to the village, Patsy. There is no need for you to go there now that we have servants to run errands for us, and I don't want you to go anywhere near the smithy. Do you understand?'

'Of course,' Patricia said with a smug smile. 'I understand perfectly.' She slipped free from Rosalind's grasp and sauntered off in the direction of the library.

Rosalind stared after her. She knew from Patricia's

tone that her words had fallen on stony ground. Patricia might be young, but she was stubborn and wilful, and once she had made her mind up to something it was almost impossible to make her see sense. Rosalind sighed and made her way to the kitchen. At least Hester was on her side. Hester could always be relied upon to speak her mind and to put matters into perspective.

Bertram was seated at the scrubbed pine table in the kitchen with a cup of coffee in front of him and a large slice of Madeira cake in his hand. He looked up, grinned and swallowed a mouthful. 'This is one of Hester's best, Rosie. You should try some.'

'Maybe later.' Rosalind glanced anxiously at Hester. 'I haven't had a chance to check that the new servants are doing as they should.'

'It's my place to oversee their work, Miss Rosalind. You are the lady of the house now and should be treated as such.' Hester glared at Bertram. 'Where were you when Sir Michael was making a nuisance of himself this morning? You're the man of the house while your grandpapa's mind is wandering.'

Rosalind bit her lip to prevent herself from laughing. Hester had a way of coming out with things that no one else would dare to say. 'Grandpapa is not mad, Hester.'

'No, Miss Rosalind, of course not. I know that, but others are quick to judge.' Hester sniffed and turned away to stir a pot on the range.

Bertram finished his cake and stood up. 'I saw Blanchard arrive not long ago. Hester tells me that he's come to stay for a while.'

'Just for tonight,' Rosalind said cautiously. 'He came to warn us that Ewart Blaise might turn up suddenly. Apparently he's discovered that Piers has a claim to Rockwood and he might try to prove that he also has a right to our property.'

'The man is a bastard,' Bertram said with feeling.

'Master Bertram, you might be a grown man but I won't have that sort of language in my kitchen,' Hester said, brandishing her wooden spoon in his direction.

'I'm sorry, Hester.' Bertram walked round the table to give her a hug. 'But you know it's true.'

Twin spots of colour stood out on Hester's plump cheeks and she pushed him away. 'Get on with you, Master Bertram. You were always a cheeky boy, but watch your language when there are ladies present. You'll have a proper lady staying here soon and her impressionable young granddaughter.'

'I'll always be a boy to you, Hester. Even when I'm a grey old man, you'll still be telling me off as you did when I was young.'

'Leave poor Hester alone,' Rosalind said, smiling. 'If you want Piers to purchase a commission for you then you'd better go and speak to him now. He's in the library.'

'No doubt Walter is reading his poems to him. I'd better rescue the poor devil. Walter could bore anyone to death.' Bertram strolled out of the kitchen, snatching a jam tart that had been left to cool.

'Is it true that someone else wants to take Rockwood from us?' Hester demanded when Bertram was out of earshot.

'He claims to be Piers' half-brother,' Rosalind said wearily. 'I wish I'd never heard of the Blanchards, although this man is called Blaise – Ewart Blaise. He says he can prove his claim to Trevenor and the mine, even though he was born on the wrong side of the blanket.'

'That can't be right.'

'He's blackmailing Piers, threatening to make the scandal public if he doesn't get what he wants.'

'Then he is a bastard, and I'm sorry I told Master Bertram off for using a bad word.'

'Piers thinks he might come here, although heaven knows what the man thinks he might gain from a visit to Rockwood. It seems that he's greedy and determined to make the family suffer for past wrongs. If you see a stranger lurking anywhere near the castle I want you to tell me. I'll warn Abe Coaker and Jim Gurney, too. We can't be too careful, especially if this man discovers that Grandpapa is not quite himself these days.'

Hester nodded in agreement. 'It would be dreadful if it got about that Sir Lucien had lost his mind, which is nonsense. We have long talks about the old days whenever I have a reason to go to his room.'

'I don't care for myself, but Grandpapa is as

helpless as a baby at times. It's up to all of us to keep him safe.'

'Every family has something they want to hide, but I agree, Miss Rosalind. Your grandpapa was a hero, and a hero he should remain until the end of his days, not a laughing stock.'

'What would we do without you, Hester?' Rosalind blinked tears from her eyes. 'You've practically brought us up and now you're still looking after us.'

'It's been my privilege, Miss Rosalind. I hope I will continue to be here for a great many years to come.'

'Amen to that. And now I'd better pass the word round to Jim and Abe.' Rosalind left the kitchen, taking a jam tart from the plate as she walked past. Hester's pastry was always light and delicious, and the strawberry jam had been made from fruit grown in the walled garden. If there were to be a competition in the village for the best jam tarts, Hester would win by a mile.

'I saw that, Miss Rosalind.' Hester's voice rang out as Rosalind stepped into the courtyard. A sudden shower had left the cobblestones clean and shining like pebbles on the beach, and Rosalind took deep breaths of the salt-laden air. The scent of roses from the formal gardens was intoxicating and the mellow stones of the castle walls glinted with a multitude of colours in the late spring sunshine. For all its drawbacks, Rockwood was her home and she loved every crumbling piece of masonry and every worm-eaten wooden beam. Piers knew how much the castle meant to her, but now there was danger from another source, and Ewart Blaise did not sound like the sort of man who would be so considerate. She quickened her pace, heading for the walled garden where she was reasonably certain of finding Abe. Rockwood Castle had withstood the threat from the Spanish Armada and from Napoleon's navy – she was not going to let it fall into the hands of a blackmailer.

Over dinner that evening everyone seemed to be in good spirits. Sir Lucien sat at the head of the table, with Jarvis hovering close at hand, but Rosalind was delighted to see her grandfather almost back to his old self as he chatted to Piers. Patricia seemed to have forgotten their previous disagreement and Bertram was visibly excited about the prospect of a commission in the 46th Regiment of Foot. Walter was more animated than usual and clearly delighted to have the opportunity to study at Cambridge. When Piers produced a bottle of cognac at the end of the meal, Rosalind decided it was time to observe the niceties and retire to the drawing room.

Patricia yawned and rubbed her eyes. 'If you don't mind, Rosie, I think I'll go to my room. I'm really tired.'

'Are you feeling unwell?'

'No, not at all. It's been an exhausting day, and I really do need to get some sleep.'

'Of course. Good night then, Patsy. I'll see you in the morning.'

Patricia managed a weary smile. 'Good night, Rosie.' She turned on her heel and headed for the stairs, leaving Rosalind to make her way to the drawing room. She sat by the window, gazing out as long purple shadows enveloped the rose garden. It had been an eventful day, and it seemed that her brothers would soon be setting out on their own in their different ways. The quiet life at Rockwood Castle would change irrevocably with the arrival of Lady Pentelow and Aurelia. However, the biggest change of all would occur below stairs. Rosalind could only imagine how it might be when the staff from Trevenor invaded the servants' hall. She sipped her rapidly cooling coffee. Piers Blanchard had come into their lives so suddenly and she had been suspicious at the outset, although now he seemed to be their saviour. She could only hope that Ewart Blaise would stay in Cornwall and leave them in peace.

Next morning, Rosalind was up early as usual. It was a fine June morning and from her bedroom window she could see the sun sparkling off the waters in the estuary. She washed, dressed and tied her hair back with a blue ribbon that Patsy had given her for her birthday, saying that it exactly matched the colour of her sister's eyes. Thinking of Patsy, Rosalind could not help wondering if she had been sickening for something. Patsy never admitted to feeling tired, and she rarely went to bed early. She left her room and went along the corridor to knock on Patsy's door. When there was no response she let herself into the room, then came to a sudden halt. It looked as though Patsy's bed had not been slept in and a quick inspection of the clothes press and chests of drawers confirmed Rosalind's suspicions. There was only one explanation that came to mind.

Chapter Fifteen

'Hester, I think Patsy has run away from home,' Rosalind said breathlessly as she leaned against the kitchen table.

'The silly little maid. It's obvious where she'm headed. I knew no good would come of her seeing the Yelland boy. He was always trouble.'

'Do you think she's eloped with Barnaby?'

'Where else would she go?'

'Maybe she went to Greystone Park. She was a bit upset that I refused Sir Michael's offer of marriage.'

'Quite right too, in my humble opinion, Miss Rosalind. You'm too good for him, even if he's filthy rich.'

'Money doesn't come into it, as far as I'm concerned. I wouldn't marry a man I didn't love. I'd rather die an old maid.' Rosalind looked up at the sound of footsteps and a shadow moved across the flagstones.

'Is anything wrong? You sounded anxious, Rosalind?' Piers entered through the door to the courtyard. 'It's such a beautiful morning I went for a stroll.'

'You didn't happen to see my sister, did you?'

'The only person I saw was Abe and we had a chat about strawberries. Apparently the fruit is almost ready for picking.'

'Never mind the strawberries,' Rosalind said impatiently. 'I think Patsy has run away.'

'Where would she go?'

'That's what we want to know, sir.' Hester poured boiling water into the teapot. 'Have a nice cup of tea, Miss Rosalind. It'll calm your nerves.'

'Thank you, Hester,' Rosalind said absently. She met Piers' gaze with a steady look. 'At best she might have gone to Greystone Park to see Christina, but I'm afraid she might be planning to elope with the blacksmith's son.'

Piers laughed. 'It sounds like something Aurelia would do.'

'It's not funny. Barnaby is engaged to Lucy Warren, the wheelwright's daughter, and she's in the family way, not to put too fine a point on it. If you think you might have a scandal on your hands you ought to understand why I'm so worried.'

Hester poured the tea and handed them each a

cup. 'Miss Patricia is under age. No vicar in his right mind would perform the service.'

'Patsy was reading a novel where the hero and heroine eloped to Gretna Green. She's very romantic.'

'And very young.' Piers placed his cup back on the table. 'There's only one solution. I'll go after them.'

'I'm coming with you,' Rosalind said hastily. 'Greystone Park must be my first call. I'll have Ajax saddled and I'll go there now.'

'And if she isn't there? What will you do then?'

'I'll think about that later.'

'I have a better idea. I'll have my tilbury made ready. It's not as fast as the curricle, but I left that at Trevenor. If your sister isn't at Greystones we'll drive on and try to catch them up.'

Rosalind could see the sense of this argument and she nodded. 'All right, if you're sure?'

'I'm quite sure.' Piers hurried from the kitchen.

'If I was a betting woman I'd put my money on Gretna Green,' Hester said grimly. 'Miss Patricia wouldn't get much sympathy from Sir Michael. I reckon he'd send her home straight away if only to get into your good books, poppet.'

'I think you're right about that, Hester.' Rosalind smiled in spite of her worries. Hester must be very anxious to have lapsed into using her old terms of endearment. 'We'll call at Greystones because the road north passes the estate, but I'm almost certain that Barnaby has persuaded Patsy to elope.'

'If it's money he's after he'll be unlucky. I hope Miss Patricia has told him that she has no dowry.'

'I'm going to pack a few things in a valise, Hester. I don't know what time Patsy left. It could have been last night, so we might have to go a long way before we catch up with them.'

'I don't approve of you gallivanting around the countryside with a gentleman, but under the circumstances I don't suppose there's much choice,' Hester said grudgingly. 'I'd suggest you took Master Bertram, but he'd probably want to shoot young Yelland.'

'I wouldn't put it past him. I'll leave you to tell my brothers what's happened, Hester. You're in charge of the household while I'm away, but Grandpapa mustn't be told. I want you to make that clear to Jarvis.'

'Leave everything to me, Miss Rosalind. I'll keep them all in order.'

Half an hour later Piers drew his horse to a halt outside the front entrance of Greystone Park. Foster opened the door and a footman hurried down the steps to help Rosalind alight from the carriage. Throwing decorum to the winds, she took the steps two at a time.

'Foster, have you seen my sister? Is she here?'

He shook his head. 'No, Miss Carey. I haven't seen her since you were both here last month.'

'You are sure?' Rosalind said anxiously. 'I mean she couldn't have crept in surreptitiously?'

Foster raised her eyebrows. 'Certainly not, Miss Carey. I know everything that goes on in this house. Besides which, Miss Christina and Miss Sylvia have gone to Exeter, I believe on a shopping expedition. Would you like me to see if Sir Michael is receiving visitors?'

Rosalind backed away. 'No, thank you, Foster. Another time, maybe.' She turned and ran down the steps to where the footman was standing patiently by the carriage. 'We're leaving.'

'One moment, if you please.' The footman stood stiffly to attention. 'Miss Patricia was here very early this morning, miss.'

Rosalind stared at him in surprise. 'But, Foster said . . .'

'She went straight to the stables, miss. My brother is one of the grooms. Miss Patricia told Mr Jones that you had changed your mind and you wanted her to collect Gypsy.'

'Are you certain about that?'

'Mr Foster is watching me, miss. I can't say any more.' He helped Rosalind to climb onto the gig. 'She rode off on Gypsy, miss. That's all I know.'

'Thank you,' Rosalind said earnestly. 'I won't forget this. Drive on quickly, Piers.'

He flicked the whip and urged the horse to a brisk walk. 'I assume that Gypsy is a horse?'

'Sir Michael had purchased a new animal for Christina and he offered me Gypsy. I refused, of course.'

'It looks as if Patricia took advantage of the situation. Is Gypsy a fast horse?'

'Yes, he's an Arab stallion and much too strong for Patsy to control, so I can only hope that Barnaby was waiting for her and that he will take charge.'

'It sounds as though they had this elopement well planned, but at least we can be fairly certain that they will be heading for Scotland.'

'We must hurry, Piers. Can't we go any faster?'

'Another minute or two won't make much difference. They have a good start on us.'

'I want to get away from here before Sir Michael sees us. I don't want to tell him that my sister has virtually stolen one of his horses and that she's eloping with the blacksmith's son.'

'I thought Sir Michael was an old friend.'

She shot him a sideways glance. 'You know what passed between Sir Michael and me at Rockwood yesterday. You were there.'

Piers laughed. 'I was teasing you, Rosalind. It does have a funny side, although I doubt if Sir Michael will be amused. Hold on tight, we'll soon pick up speed.' He flicked the whip above the horse's ears and the carriage shot forward. Rosalind clung to the side with one hand while holding her bonnet in place with the other. Once they were outside the village boundary Piers slowed the horse to a trot.

'They will have to allow their mounts to rest. I'm guessing that the Yelland boy will have borrowed or stolen a horse from somewhere, unless both of them are riding Gypsy, in which case they won't be able to go very far without exhausting the animal.'

'Barnaby's work at the smithy means that there are always horses waiting to be attended to. I think he will have taken the fastest and fittest one he could lay his hands on.'

'Even so, they will have to stop for rest and refreshment. Don't worry, Rosalind. We'll catch up with them.'

They drove on in silence. It was a beautiful June morning but Rosalind was too preoccupied to pay much attention to the glories of nature or the pretty villages they passed through. They called in at several wayside inns, where Piers made enquiries, but there were no apparent sightings of the errant couple. At midday they stopped to feed and water the horse and Rosalind sat outside on a bench. Piers ordered food and two glasses of cider, but Rosalind had little appetite, and they left when Piers judged that the horse had rested long enough, heading north.

The further they went, the lower Rosalind's spirits became, until, at mid-afternoon, they stopped at an inn where the landlord said he remembered a young couple passing through a couple of hours earlier. Rosalind was elated and, at the same time, despondent. With two good horses they could have covered several miles in that amount of time, making it even more difficult to catch up with them. Patricia's reputation would be damaged beyond repair if she spent the night with Barnaby. The later it became, the more desperate Rosalind was to find them, and the weather had taken a sudden turn for the worse. Dark clouds had gathered and it began to rain – lightly at first, and then the air turned a sulphurous yellow and flashes of lightning zigzagged across the sky.

Piers encouraged the horse to go faster. 'We'll try to outrun the storm,' he said breathlessly. 'The land-lord at the last inn said there was another place where they might decide to break their journey and it can't be more than a mile or two distant.'

Rosalind held on to her bonnet as a strong wind attempted to rip it from her head. The trees over-hanging the country lane bowed and creaked as if being torn limb from limb, and the rain lashed down on them, despite the fact that Piers had raised the tilbury's hood. It was early evening and, being midsummer, there should have been a few more hours of daylight, but they were in semidarkness with no time to stop to light the carriage lamps. The tilbury was a sturdy vehicle and its large wheels were designed to cope with rough going, but the rutted road surface was now sticky with mud and the horse was clearly struggling to maintain its pace. Rosalind clung to Piers as each time they hit a rut she was in danger of being flung from the gig. But eventually, she could see the glimmer of lights ahead, and as they drew nearer she realised with a sigh of relief that it was a hostelry.

Despite the driving rain an ostler emerged from

the stables and took charge of the horse and carriage. Piers tossed him a coin.

'Take good care of him. We've come a long way today.'

'Seems like the whole world is on the road today, sir. You'll be lucky to get a room for the night.'

Piers nodded. 'Thank you. We can but try.'

'We can't go any further in this weather,' Rosalind said through chattering teeth.

'Let's get you inside. A hot meal and a warm bed will make things seem better.' Piers led the way into the smoky taproom. The bad weather did not seem to have deterred the locals and the rough-hewn tables were packed with men drinking ale, smoking clay pipes and chatting. There was a moment of silence as all heads turned to see who had just entered, and then they went back to their conversations. Piers walked over to the bar where the landlord was busy filling jugs with ale.

'Have you two rooms for the night, landlord?'

'We're full, sir. The storm has brought us more trade than we can cope with.'

'Have you *anywhere* we can lay our heads for the night?'

The landlord scratched his bald pate. 'Well, now. There's the attic room, but it ain't suitable for a lady, although I dare say you could make it up to her in other ways, sir?' He winked suggestively.

'The lady requires a decent room to herself, landlord.' Piers took a leather pouch from his pocket and jingled it. 'I'm a generous man when the situation requires it.'

'I'd like to oblige, sir. But the truth is another young couple got here an hour or more ago. They had the last room available.'

'Do you have their names?' Rosalind asked eagerly.

'Mr and Mrs Smith, so I believe, ma'am. They're taking supper in the private parlour.' He jerked his head in the direction of a door at the back of the room.

Rosalind did not wait to hear any more. She pushed past a group of men and burst into the parlour without knocking. She came to a sudden halt.

'Patricia Carey. I knew it would be you.'

Patricia jumped to her feet, dropping her knife and fork on the floor in her haste. 'What are you doing here?'

'What do you think?' Rosalind glared at Barnaby, who had half risen from his seat. 'Sit down, both of you. Do you realise what you've done?'

'We're going to be married,' Patricia said stubbornly. 'You can't stop us now, Rosie. We're spending the night here and Barnaby will have to marry me.'

'I intend to anyway, Miss Rosalind.' Barnaby slipped his arm around Patricia's waist. 'We love each other.'

'You loved Lucy Warren, too. What do you think will happen to her and her baby if you desert her for my sister?'

'I'm sorry for her, but it was never my intention to wed the maid.'

Piers had entered the room and he stood beside Rosalind. 'That's no excuse and you know it. Do you think you can go round ruining the reputation of respectable young women? You, sir, need to face your responsibilities.'

'That's right,' Rosalind said, nodding. 'Lucy is a nice girl and she deserves better than you, Barnaby Yelland, but you will do right by her. Your father will see to that, I'm sure. As to you, Patsy, I'm taking you home.'

'I won't go with you. Barnaby and I are leaving for Gretna Green tomorrow. I'll be a married woman then, and you will have to do as I say.'

Rosalind fixed Barnaby with an icy gaze. 'How do you think you will support a wife, Barnaby? Patricia has no dowry and the family will cut her off from any financial help if she married you.'

'I – well, I suppose I'll go back to the smithy and work with Pa.' Barnaby shot a wary glance in Piers' direction. 'I'm not a shirker, sir.'

'And you will live in the cottage with Mr and Mrs Yelland and Barnaby's four younger sisters, will you, Patsy?'

A shadow passed over Patricia's pretty face and her cheeks reddened. 'I don't know. I suppose there must be a house on the estate we could have.'

'This isn't a romantic fairy story with a happy ending, Patsy. You complained often enough about having to help me run the castle before our fortunes took a turn for the better. Do you see yourself washing your clothes in the millstream? Or fetching water from the village pump? Do you think that Christina and Sylvia would still be your friends if you were married to the blacksmith's son?'

Patricia's blue eyes filled with tears. 'You're being horrible, Rosie. It won't be like that.'

Piers stepped forward. 'There is a way out of this. You, Yelland, will share the attic room with me tonight, and you will leave for home at first light in the morning.'

Barnaby opened his mouth as if to argue but he seemed at a loss for words.

'Say something,' Patricia cried, clutching his arm with both hands. 'Tell them that we love each other, Barnaby. Tell them you'll marry me.'

He shook his head slowly. 'They're right, Patsy. I've led you astray and I've betrayed Lucy's trust. I do love you, but I love her, too. I'm sorry.'

Patsy took a step backwards as if he had slapped her face. She was white with shock and trembling violently, her blue eyes brimming with unshed tears. Rosalind felt a surge of pity for her sister. Patsy was an innocent and she had been taken in by a young man who thought only of himself.

'Come with me.' Rosalind slipped her arm around Patricia's shoulders. 'We'll leave Piers to sort out the details. You and I will share a room and no one can say anything to the contrary. Tomorrow we'll go home and put this behind us.'

Patricia turned her head to give Barnaby a despairing look. 'Is this what you want?'

'Of course not, maid. But your sister is right. I didn't think about the details. All I knew was that I wanted to be with you, and I do love you.'

'Don't say that,' Patricia said vehemently. 'You can't love me and Lucy Warren at the same time. You lied to me and I hate you.' She burst into tears.

Rosalind opened the door. 'I'll see you in the morning, Piers.'

'We haven't eaten yet,' he said ruefully. 'I don't know about you, but I'm starving.'

'I'll ask the landlord to send something to the room. I'll leave you to take care of Barnaby. Good night, Piers, and thank you.'

Next day Barnaby was left to make his own way back to the smithy and Rosalind rode Gypsy, leaving Piers to drive Patricia in the gig.

It was late afternoon by the time they arrived home, but the next morning, as soon as they had finished breakfast, Rosalind insisted that Patricia must return the horse to Greystone Park. Patricia protested, wept and begged to be excused the onerous task and the admission of guilt, but Rosalind was not going to let her get away with what amounted to theft. Piers was ready to leave for Cornwall and Rosalind thanked him again for helping to save her sister from making a terrible mistake.

'I'd have done the same thing had it been my sister,'

he said, raising her hand to his lips. 'I'll be back soon with my family. Thank you for offering us a home, Rosie. It means more to me than I can ever tell you.' He walked away in the direction of the stables, leaving Rosalind staring after him. There had been a break in his voice and there was no doubting his sincerity, leaving her confused and wondering if her suspicions regarding Piers Blanchard had been unfounded. But there were more pressing matters to attend to and she went in search of her sister.

When they arrived at Greystone Park they went straight to the stables. Patricia apologised to Jones, the head groom, with tears in her eyes.

'That was well done, Patsy.' Rosalind watched as Jones led Gypsy back to his stall. 'Now all you have to do is to say you're sorry to Sir Michael.'

'Can't we just go home now? Please.'

'You want to see the girls, don't you? I'm sure they'll be eager to hear your side of the story.'

'I suppose so.'

'Then come along.' Rosalind set off for the main entrance, clutching Patricia's hand in case her sister decided to bolt like a nervous filly.

'Is Sir Michael at home, Foster?' Rosalind asked when the butler opened the door.

'If you'd care to wait here, I'll make enquiries, Miss Carey.'

'I wish you'd let me off this,' Patricia said in a whisper. 'I've returned the wretched animal – isn't that enough?'

'You stole Sir Michael's property, Patsy. You'll be very lucky if he hasn't informed the parish constable.'

'He wouldn't do that, would he?'

'He would be perfectly entitled to report a stolen horse. You took Gypsy without his permission and you lied to the head groom.'

Patricia glanced over her shoulder as if she were looking for an escape route, but Rosalind had her firmly by the hand, and Foster returned moments later to say that Sir Michael would see them in the Chinese room.

Sir Michael was seated by the window, reading a copy of *The Times*. He put it aside and rose to his feet. 'Good morning, ladies. This is an unexpected pleasure.'

'Patricia has something she wishes to say to you, Sir Michael.' Rosalind gave her sister an encouraging nod.

'Well, Patricia?' Sir Michael's lips curved in a smile but his eyes were cold.

'I took Gypsy under false pretences, Sir Michael. I came to tell you that I'm very sorry for what I did. It was wrong of me.'

'You realise, of course, that it was stealing?'

'Yes, Sir Michael. I didn't intend to keep him, but I do apologise.'

'She is very sorry,' Rosalind added. She could see that Patricia was struggling to hold back tears and Sir Michael was obviously angry.

'I am, sir. I've been very foolish,' Patricia said tearfully.

'I'm glad you realise that, Patricia. I accept your apology. You may go and find my daughters,' Sir Michael said with a wave of his hand. 'I think they're in the morning parlour, or else you'll find them in the garden. I want a quiet word with your sister.'

'Yes, go,' Rosalind said reluctantly. 'I'll join you in a few minutes.' She waited until Patricia had left the room before turning an enquiring gaze on Sir Michael. 'What was it you wish to say, sir?'

'Please take a seat, Rosalind. I suppose I wanted to apologise for upsetting you when we last met. I probably ought to have stated my feelings more romantically, but I'm a straightforward sort of fellow. I come straight to the point and I don't waste words. Although in your case, and in view of your youth, I should have known better.'

Rosalind remained standing. 'Sir Michael, let me be very clear about this. I like and respect you as a friend and a mentor, but that is where it ends. I hope you understand.'

'I do appreciate your reticence, and I think it most commendable. I wouldn't want to marry a woman who was without principles.'

'I wish you well, but I'd be grateful if we could put this behind us.'

'Of course, my dear. From now on I will pay court to you like any other man, and I promise not to dwell on the fact that my financial assistance has helped Rockwood through a difficult time.'

'That's not what I meant, Sir Michael. I believe you know that.'

He smiled. 'I'm hoping that in time you will come and to my way of thinking, Rosalind. I can offer you a way of life you can only have dreamed of, and a place in society that most women would envy. I'm thinking of putting myself forward as a candidate for Parliament in the next election and, being a major landowner, I have every chance of success.'

Rosalind clasped her hands tightly in front of her. 'I don't doubt it, Sir Michael. Now, if you'll excuse me, I'll go and find my sister. We need to get home as I have much to do.'

'Ah, yes, you are expecting visitors from Cornwall, or so I hear.'

'It never fails to amaze me how news travels so quickly, but yes, that's right.'

'Might I know the names of your guests? Or is it a secret?'

'The Blanchard family from Trevenor, and Lady Pentelow with some of their household. You've already met Piers, a distant relative of mine.'

'And the rightful owner of Rockwood Castle, I'm told.'

'Really, Sir Michael, If you knew all this before, why ask me to repeat it now?'

'Because I wanted to hear it from your own lips,

my dear. And anything to keep you in my company for a little longer. However, I can see that you wish to leave, so I won't detain you any longer. Please give my regards to Sir Lucien.' He was about to ring the bell for a servant but Rosalind moved swiftly to the doorway.

'I'll see myself out, sir. And I will pass your good wishes on to my grandfather.' She left the room before he could say anything that would need an answer. The palms of her hands were damp with perspiration and she had to take a moment to collect herself before she went in search of Patricia. Sir Michael was not the sort of man to be put off easily, and she realised that he was going to pursue his suit, no matter how many times she told him that it was hopeless.

She tried the morning parlour, but there was no one there and she could only guess that the girls were in the garden, playing croquet or tennis on the new grass court that Sir Michael, a keen tennis player himself, had had constructed. Rosalind realised that Sir Michael was a force to be reckoned with, and someone to be avoided, if she were not to be overwhelmed by him.

She found the girls, as she had suspected, attempting to play the game on the grass court. Their shrieks of laughter as they tried to control the bouncing tennis ball gave them away. Patricia was red in the face from exertion, and gasping for breath, as no doubt the tightness of her stays made strenuous exercise all but impossible. But it was good to see her laugh again and Rosalind smiled.

'Time to go home, Patsy.'

Patricia bent double as she caught her breath. 'We've only just begun, and tennis is such a good game. I feel so much happier now.'

'Yes, do let her stay.' Christina leaned on her racquet. 'We'll send her home in the carriage after luncheon.'

'I want to hear more about your adventures,' Sylvia added. 'An elopement cut short – how romantic.'

'Be quiet, Sylvie,' Christina said sternly. 'I don't suppose Rosalind finds it amusing.'

'You may stay for luncheon, Patsy. There's not much you can do at home anyway, but please be back in time for dinner.'

It was mid-afternoon and Rosalind, with Bob trotting along at her side, had called at Greep Farm to collect eggs, butter and cheese from the dairy. She was walking back to the castle at a leisurely pace when she spotted a stranger standing at the castle gates. His well-cut garments and stylish beaver top hat indicated a man of means, and he was not dressed for riding, so he must have arrived in a carriage, although there was no sign of any vehicle.

'This is private property, sir,' Rosalind said icily. 'Might I ask who you are?'

The stranger turned slowly to face her. He doffed

his hat, revealing a fine head of dark brown hair, then replaced his hat with a flourish. He was clean-shaven and at first glance he was good-looking without being handsome, but there was something about him that made her instantly alert.

'Good morning, ma'am. I believe this is Rockwood Castle?'

'Might I ask who you are, sir?'

'You have every right to be cautious, ma'am. There are some people who are prepared to cheat and lie their way into the confidence of others. I can assure you that I am not one of those.'

Rosalind edged past him, standing in the gateway ready for flight, if necessary. His presence was unset-tling and she could not help but be suspicious. 'What is your business here, sir?'

'I am, I believe, the legal owner of this ancient pile.'

Chapter Sixteen

Rosalind stared at him in disbelief. 'Is this some kind of a jest? If so, it isn't at all amusing.'

He inclined his head, eyeing her with a hint of a smile in his steel-grey eyes. 'I believe you've met my half-brother, Piers Blanchard?'

'You are Ewart Blaise?'

'I see my reputation has gone before me. Might I come in and we can discuss this like civilised human beings? Or are you going to set your dog on me?' His gazed travelled to Bob, who had come to stand protectively at Rosalind's side.

'What do you want, Mr Blaise?' Rosalind said warily. 'I don't believe for a moment that you are a legal heir to the estate, so what brings you here?'

'Is Piers here? I was told that he had left Trevenor and was heading for Rockwood.'

'That is none of your business, sir.' Rosalind leaned

down to hold Bob's collar. He seemed to sense her inner anxiety and he was growling softly at Blaise.

'I can assure you that it is. I do hate speaking to someone whose name I don't know. Are you Miss Rosalind Carey, by any chance?'

'I am, but that need not concern you. I'm asking you politely to leave my land.'

'I have already told you that it belongs to me now, Miss Carey. Piers Blanchard is an imposter, a liar and a cheat.'

'I think he would say the same of you, sir.'

'I've no doubt that he would, but the fact remains that I am the eldest son, and I can prove it.'

He seemed so certain that for a moment Rosalind almost believed him, but then she remembered Piers' warning, and she hardened her resolve. 'If there is any truth in your allegations, Mr Blaise, I suggest you take this matter to the courts. Now I'm asking you once again to leave.' She could see Bertie striding towards them with his gun slung over his arm.

Blaise followed her gaze. 'Ah, that must be Bertram, your elder brother. You see I've done my research, Miss Carey. I know that Walter is a year or so younger than you and then there is Patricia. I'm looking forward to getting to know my new family.'

'Bertie.' Rosalind made a supreme effort to sound calm as she called her brother's name.

'What's the matter, Rosie?' Bertie quickened his pace. 'Is this fellow bothering you?' He looked Blaise up and down with an aggressive set to his jaw.

'This is Ewart Blaise, Bertie. He claims to be Piers' elder brother and heir to the castle. I've asked him to leave but he won't go.'

Bertie took a cartridge from his belt and made as if to reload the shotgun. 'I suggest you do as my sister says, sir. You're not welcome here.'

Blaise held up his hands and backed away. 'No need for violence, Bertram, old chap. We're family, after all. I'm going now, but you'll hear from me again, and you'll realise eventually that Piers Blanchard is not who he says he is.' Blaise turned on his heel and strolled off in the general direction of the main road.

'How the hell did he get here?' Bertie demanded. 'If he came in a carriage there's no sign of it.'

'I don't know and I don't care. He was obviously lying.'

Bertie tucked the cartridge back in place. 'I believe Piers above that scoundrel. I doubt if that fellow would give us the time of day.'

'I don't like him,' Rosalind said, shivering even though the sun was high in the sky and it was a hot day. 'There's something about him that makes my flesh creep. I hope that Piers and Lady Pentelow get here before you have to leave for London, Bertie. Assuming that you are still going to join the military.'

Bertie nodded. 'I have decided exactly when I'm going. Are you scared, Rosie? That's the first time you've ever admitted to being afraid of anything.'

'I don't know about that, but maybe I'd better

get in some shooting practice before you go, Bertie. I mean it. After all, Grandpapa is not himself and Jarvis is an old man. Walter would be no use if it came to a fight.'

'Don't worry, Rosie. Before I leave I'll make sure that Coaker and Gurney keep a lookout for Blaise, and maybe Jacob Lidstone might care to move in with his brother, who has a cottage on the quay. Jacob might not be young but he's a big fellow. Unless, of course, Hester has sent him packing again. I don't know why he still hankers after her when she obviously isn't interested.'

'You mean rather that we couldn't manage without her,' Rosalind said with a wry smile. 'Hester has devoted her life to this family. You should show her some respect.'

'I love Hester like a mother.' Bertie was suddenly serious. 'D'you know, Rosie, I think I love Hester more than Mama. Does that sound awful?'

'Not really,' Rosalind said, sighing. 'Hester is the one who's looked after us since we were born. Mama comes and goes, and even before she became famous she was never particularly interested in what we did. She can't help it, that's just the way she is.' She turned her back on the distant figure of Blaise and walked into the bailey with Bob at her heels. Bertie caught up with her as she was about to enter the castle.

'When I find someone to marry I'll make sure she'll want to be with me always, even if I'm posted to the other side of the world.'

'Let's go inside, Bertie. That man has unsettled me more than I care to admit. I wish Piers hadn't gone back to Trevenor. There are so many questions I want to ask him.'

A week later, after an anxious wait on Rosalind's part, the family from Trevenor arrived at the castle gates. Since the unexpected appearance of Ewart Blaise, Rosalind had given instructions that the huge, wrought-iron gates must remain closed at all times. Hester had unearthed and cleaned up a rusty old padlock to make sure that the gates could only be opened by the key, which hung on a chatelaine around Rosalind's waist. The fact that Rockwood Castle had been built to withstand attack and siege made it reasonably easy to defend, and Rosalind was taking no chances. She had been dreading the invasion from Trevenor, but now she welcomed it and she hurried to unlock the gates and allow the procession to enter.

Jarvis directed the staff from Trevenor to the servants' entrance, and the wagons stacked with the priceless articles that Lady Pentelow could not bear to leave behind were sent to one of the barns, which had been set aside for their storage.

Rosalind walked back to the main entrance where she waited to greet the family. Tilly hovered in the background with young Noah Coaker, ready to take the small items of luggage up to the guest rooms. Rosalind had told them several times which room was allocated to each guest, and she could only hope that the young pair remembered her instructions. Tilly was coming along nicely as a housemaid, but Noah was happier in the gardens with his grandfather and obviously uncomfortable indoors.

Piers handed his grandmother up the steps to the main entrance. 'Good morning, Rosalind.'

She smiled and nodded. 'I hope you had a good journey.'

Lady Pentelow rolled her eyes expressively. 'My dear, don't let us talk about it. I'm black and blue from being jolted around for three days, and I won't speak of the dreadful inns we stayed at on the way. We should have come by sea. It might have taken longer, but I'm sure it would have been more pleasant.'

'I'm sorry, Lady Pentelow. I hope we can make you comfortable here at Rockwood.'

'Piers warned me not to expect too much.' Lady Pentelow stepped into the entrance hall. 'It's tolerable. I was expecting worse.'

'I'm sure you'll find that every effort has been made to make you welcome, Grandmama,' Piers said hastily.

'I don't doubt it,' Lady Pentelow said with a sigh. 'I'd like to go to my room for a rest, Rosalind. I suppose there will be washing facilities, or do we have to take a daily swim in the sea to cleanse ourselves?'

Rosalind turned to Piers with a questioning look.

She was not sure if her ladyship was serious, but a warning look from him confirmed her suspicion that Lady Pentelow was not going to be an easy house guest.

'Tilly, please show Lady Pentelow to her room. If there's anything you need, Tilly will fetch it for you, my lady.'

'Simms will look after me.' Lady Pentelow shot a withering look at Tilly. 'Send her to me as soon as she makes an appearance, and have my luggage sent to my room.' She pointed at Tilly. 'What are you waiting for, girl?'

'Oh dear,' Rosalind said in a low voice. 'I thought your grandmother might be rather upset, but it seems worse than I imagined.'

Piers shrugged. 'She's tougher than she looks. She'll come round when she's rested.' He stood aside as his sister strolled into the hall, arm in arm with Patricia.

'Look who I met outside, Piers. Patsy and I are going to be like sisters.' Aurelia beamed at Rosalind. 'It's very good of you to put up with an invasion from Cornwall, Rosie. I may call you that now, mayn't I?'

'Of course, you may. I hope you'll be very comfortable here. You must treat Rockwood as your home.'

Aurelia threw back her head and laughed. 'Well, it is my home, isn't it? I don't wish to sound unfeeling, but the romantic old castle belongs to my brother.' Her smile faded and a frown creased her smooth brow. 'Although, of course, he says that you may all live here for as long as you want. Isn't that so, Piers?'

'Yes, it is, Aurelia. Why don't you let Patricia show you round? That will give the servants time to sort out the baggage and unpack.'

'I don't mind what I do. This is quite an adventure,' Aurelia said happily. 'Are there any resident ghosts I should know about, Patsy?' She slipped her hand through the crook of Patricia's arm. 'Do show me the oubliette, if you've found one. Trevenor is quite boring compared to this old castle.'

'I haven't actually found it,' Patricia said carefully. 'However, there is supposed to be a secret passage that leads down to the cove. I've never found that either, although Bertie has tried.'

'I've yet to meet your brothers.'

'We'll go and find Walter. I don't know where Bertie is. He wants to be a soldier.'

'Really? How exciting. My brother Alexander is a captain in the 32nd Regiment of Foot.'

Rosalind waited until the sound of the girls' conversation died away before turning to Piers. 'There's something I must ask you.'

'What is it? You look serious.'

'Are you really the heir to Rockwood, or is it Ewart Blaise? He came here a week ago, claiming that you lied to us, and that he is the elder brother and legal owner of Rockwood.'

'He came here? That was ill-advised.'

'Is that all you can say?'

'Ewart Blaise is a man who can wheedle his way into a person's confidence and then use that trust to trick them into doing precisely what he wants.'

'How do I know which of you to believe? He might be telling the truth and you could be lying.'

'Ask yourself this, Rosalind. Have I taken anything from you? Or have I done my best to help you to save Rockwood from your creditors? Would I do that if I were trying to cheat you out of everything you hold dear? Blaise has already taken Trevenor from us, but he can't do anything about the shares I hold in the company. It's hard to believe, but it seems that man is out to destroy my family.'

'Why would he do that, Piers? What has he got against you?'

'I can only assume that he is driven by malice born out of jealousy. I can't put his attitude down to anything else. I'd never heard of him until recently, and I wish that he'd kept his distance.'

'Do you think he will come back now that you're here?'

Piers shrugged and shook his head. 'I can't speak for Blaise. However, if he does show his face I will be ready to deal with him. This is your home, Rosalind. I won't allow him to cause trouble for you and your family.'

'I never thought I'd say these words, but I'm glad you're here.'

He smiled. 'Thank you, that means a lot to me,

and we'll try to behave like good house guests.
Believe me, Rosalind, I'm trying hard to find a solution to the problem of Ewart Blaise, and I want to
restore my grandmother to her rightful home as
quickly as possible.'

'Amen to that,' Rosalind said with feeling. 'I'll do
my best to make her feel welcome.'

'I know you will and I'm more than grateful to
you for taking us in.'

'You helped me when I turned up on your doorstep with my sister. This is the least I can do in
return.'

'We'll get through this somehow, but in the meantime I'd better go to the stables and make sure that
Gurney isn't overwhelmed by all the extra work.
My stablemen will do their bit, but I want to keep
an eye on all the servants from Trevenor. They need
to remember that we are here as guests.'

'I'd better make sure that Hester and Mrs Witham,
your housekeeper, start off on the right foot. A battle
below stairs would be very unsettling for everyone.'

Rosalind left Piers to visit the stables while she
went to the kitchen to find Hester, but when she
walked into the room she knew instinctively that
the transition was not going to be easy.

Mrs Witham stood on one side of the kitchen
table with Patterson, the butler from Trevenor. They
were facing Hester, who was suspiciously red in the
face and bristling like an angry hedgehog.

Rosalind sensed trouble. 'Welcome to Rockwood,

301

Mr Patterson and Mrs Witham,' she said brightly. 'You are very welcome here. I see that you've met Hester.'

Mrs Witham turned to Rosalind with an ominous frown. 'Since when has a mere cook taken precedence over a butler and a housekeeper?'

'I understand that your butler, Mr Jarvis, is also in residence, Miss Carey,' Mr Patterson added. 'I need to know which of us will be in charge of the servants. Do we have to share the butler's pantry and office? I've never come across such an arrangement before.'

Rosalind sent a warning glance to Hester, who looked as if she was about to explode. 'Mrs Dodridge has been in charge of everything below stairs for a good many years. We couldn't manage without her, but I'm sure she will do her best to make you all feel at home during your stay at Rockwood. With a little give and take on both sides, I'm sure that the housekeeping duties can be divided fairly, and I should add that Mrs Dodridge is an excellent cook.'

'Lady Pentelow will eat nothing unless it is prepared by her personal chef,' Mrs Witham said haughtily. 'Monsieur Jacques, is a chef of the highest calibre.'

'I've been cooking for the family for twenty years or more.' Hester leaned her hands on the scrubbed pine table top. 'I don't want a foreigner in my kitchen.'

'I dare say he wouldn't want to work in conditions

like this, anyway.' Mrs Witham folded her hands in front of her. 'What have you got to say to that?'

Mr Patterson stepped forward. 'Ladies, please. You're forgetting that Miss Carey is present. These arguments should be conducted in the privacy of the housekeeper's parlour or the butler's office. We do not argue in front of our employer.'

'Thank you, Mr Patterson,' Rosalind said, forcing herself to sound calm and in control of the situation, even though she knew she was walking a metaphorical tightrope. 'I understand how you are all feeling. However, I suggest that when it comes to the cooking arrangements we can work something out so that neither of our excellent cooks clash in the kitchen. I'm sure I can leave you, Hester, and Mrs Witham to sort that out between you, and I'm just as certain that Mr Patterson and Mr Jarvis can share the butler's office and pantry. In fact, Mr Jarvis spends almost all his time looking after my grandfather. Sir Lucien rarely leaves his rooms in the east tower these days. His health is not what it was.'

'I'll do my best, Miss Carey,' Hester said reluctantly. 'I can't say more than that.'

Mrs Witham tossed her head. 'Never let it be said that I, Hilda Witham, behaved in anything other than a manner befitting my situation.'

'These are extraordinary times,' Mr Patterson added sonorously. 'A period of adjustment will be required, but I will do my utmost to maintain a professional approach to my duties.'

Rosalind stifled a sigh of relief. 'Thank you all. I know I can rely on you, and if you have any problems please come to me first. In the meantime, Hester, I suggest that you lay out a cold luncheon for the family in the dining hall. I'll leave you and Tilly to organise that, while Mrs Witham and Mr Patterson go to their rooms to sort out their belongings.' Rosalind left the kitchen before any of them could start another argument.

There were numerous disagreements and minor quarrels amongst the servants during the next few days. Rosalind seemed to spend all her waking hours arbitrating between one member of staff or another, but the main differences of opinion occurred in the kitchen. Monsieur Jacques was a middle-aged man with set views and was obviously used to having everything his own way. Hester, on the other hand, was also used to ruling the household and the kitchen unquestioned, and it seemed inevitable that they would clash on almost every topic. Mrs Witham was little or no help; in fact she appeared to enjoy setting one against the other, and Mr Patterson did nothing to calm the situation. Mr Jarvis was wise enough to keep out of it entirely. He devoted himself to caring for Sir Lucien and keeping him in his quarters, but, even so, Rosalind lived in constant fear that her grandfather would escape and head for the cliffs, risking serious injury in order to watch for enemy ships. Even worse, he might decide to put on his dress uniform and insist on taking his seat at the head of the table for dinner. Underlying all these concerns, there was the matter of Ewart Blaise. He had not returned, as yet, but Rosalind had a feeling that he had not finished with them and that he might reappear at any moment. All the servants, both indoor and outdoor, were warned to be on the lookout, but she remained in a state of awareness both day and night.

Despite Rosalind's fears that Blaise might upset their lives even more, she just had to make the best of things. She had her family to think of and Hester to support her in everything she did. Rosalind made a point of visiting her grandfather in his suite of rooms at the same time every day. She realised that routine meant a great deal to him, and she sat patiently listening to his accounts of naval battles that she already knew by heart. In a combined effort she and Jarvis had kept him away from their guests, and although Lady Pentelow had asked after Sir Lucien, she had been happy to accept the excuse that he was still unwell and confined to his room. Rosalind did not know how long she could keep up this fiction, but she could not bear to think of her beloved grandfather being regarded as a figure of fun by anyone.

The days passed and everyone settled in to an uneasy truce, which included the family and guests as much as those below stairs. Lady Pentelow was obviously unsettled by the move and very demanding, and this seemed to have brushed off on her maid, Miss Simms, who found fault with everything. Miss Grainger, Aurelia's maid, was less vocal but she went around with a sour look on her face that brought sharp reprimands from Aurelia, who seemed determined to enjoy everything.

She spent her time with Patricia, either roaming the castle in search of the secret passage or traces of the castle's dubious past, or exploring the grounds. They appeared to have reverted to childhood and often returned from their walks with muddy shoes and the hems of their gown wet and grass stained. Lady Pentelow lectured her granddaughter on her behaviour, but Piers merely laughed and said he would rather see Aurelia with rosy cheeks and a smile on her face than a prim little miss who sat around all day waiting for a rich husband to claim her. Lady Pentelow did not agree, and Rosalind kept her thoughts to herself. She could only be glad that Patsy had something to think about other than Barnaby. Hester had told her that his wedding to Lucy Warren had been arranged rather hastily, and the first of the banns would be read on the coming Sunday.

Rosalind waited for the right moment to pass the news on to her sister and she managed to catch her on her own after breakfast on the fifth day after the Blanchards had arrived at Rockwood.

'What's the matter, Rosie?' Patricia demanded impatiently. 'I was just about to go to Aurelia's room and see if she's awake. I've never known anyone quite as lazy at Aurelia, but she is such fun to be with.'

'Patsy, I have to tell you something, which I know will be hard for you to take.'

'If it's about the skirt I tore climbing down the cliff, I'm sorry. I know that we are still short of funds.'

'It's not that. Hester is very clever with her needle and she's going to mend it.'

'Then what is it? Don't you want me to enjoy myself with Aurelia? We're not doing any harm.'

'It has nothing to do with Aurelia,' Rosalind took a deep breath. 'Hester told me that the first of the banns announcing the marriage of Lucy Warren and Barnaby Yelland is being read on Sunday. I thought I should warn you in case it came as a terrible shock when you heard it in church.'

The colour drained from Patricia's cheeks but she held her head high. 'He still loves me, Rosie. Barnaby might marry that silly girl, but I am the one he cares about most.'

'I'm sure he is genuine in his feelings for you, Patsy, but you know it could never be.'

'No, to be honest I can't see why girls like us have to marry someone of our own class. Look at you, for example. I'll wager you will end up marrying Sir Michael whether you love him or not. He's rich and important, and our land abuts the Greystone estate, and you'll do what's expected of you.'

'That will never happen, and don't change the subject. I know how you felt about Barnaby. Are you telling me that you no longer love him?'

Patricia shrugged, but she averted her gaze, avoiding meeting Rosalind's questioning gaze. 'I do still love him, but I think staying the night in the horrid inn made me see sense. If I married Barnaby that is the sort of place we would be forced to patronise in the future. Barnaby has never been further than Exeter in his whole life. What we did was an adventure to him.'

'Really? Is that how you feel now?'

'I talked it over with Aurelia, who is set on marrying Hugo Knighton, and she made me see that I can't change the way things are, so don't worry about me, Rosie. I will be in church on Sunday and I will smile when the banns are read and if I see Barnaby outside, I will congratulate him and Lucy.' Patricia strolled off in the direction of the grand staircase, leaving Rosalind staring after her in amazement. She could hardly believe that the passionate love affair between her sister and Barnaby Yelland had ended so abruptly. Even so, it was a relief and she went to the kitchen to find Hester.

'Do you believe Miss Patricia?' Hester frowned. 'She can be a little minx when it suits her.'

'I know my sister better than anyone, even you, Hester. I don't think she was pretending. Maybe her friendship with Aurelia has been a good thing.'

'Miss Aurelia is flighty, if you ask me.' Hester

shrugged. 'I know it's not my place to criticise my betters, but that young lady is trouble.'

'I think you're being too hard on her,' Rosalind protested. 'We saw a lot of her in Trevenor and she communicates with my sister in a way that I can't.'

Hester pursed her lips. 'Time will tell,' she said tersely. 'And talking about time, I must hurry if I'm to make a terrine of rabbit for luncheon. I've only had to put up with that damned Frenchie for a few days and already I could stick a carving knife between his pompous foreign ribs.'

'Really, Hester, I've never heard you speak so harshly about anyone.'

'You don't have to put up with him, Miss Rosalind. He twirls his moustache and prances about the floor like a circus performer, pointing at my efforts and making mock of me.'

'I'll speak to Mr Patterson, Hester. He should be in control of Lady Pentelow's servants. I won't allow anyone to upset you. I promise you that.'

Hester merely clicked her tongue against her teeth and bent her head over the task of preparing the meat for the terrine.

Rosalind walked away, knowing that she had an uphill task if she were to run a household with so many dissimilar people living in close quarters.

Two weeks after the family's arrival from Trevenor a horseman was spotted approaching the castle at a gallop. Rosalind was convinced that it must be

Blaise, returning to follow up his claim to Rockwood, but when Piers joined her at the gates he laughed away her fears.

'I know that figure and I recognise the horse. Unless I'm very much mistaken that's my brother, Alexander. I never know when his regiment will arrive back in England.'

'That's wonderful, but how would he know where to find you?'

'I suppose he's come from Trevenor. Someone will have told him that we had to leave suddenly. Unlock the gates, please, Rosalind. Let him in.'

She took the large iron key from her chatelaine and did as he asked, and the gates swung open on newly oiled hinges. She stood aside as the horseman slowed his mount to a trot, reining in as he drew nearer.

'So there you are, Piers. I've ridden for three days to find you.' Captain Alexander Blanchard dismounted and handed the reins to a boy who had come running from the stables. 'Look after my horse, and there'll be a florin for your trouble. He's had a long and tiring journey. Best walk him for a while until he cools down.'

The boy pocketed the coin with an appreciative grin and led the horse away.

Piers enveloped his brother in a hug, which seemed completely out of character for a man who usually kept his emotions under control. 'It's good to see you, Alex. Why didn't you let us know that you were back in England?'

'We only arrived in Plymouth a week ago, and I arrived at Trevenor to find that you'd sold up and there was a new owner.'

'We haven't sold Trevenor,' Piers said carefully. 'Have you met Blaise?'

'Yes, I have. He was very hospitable and he invited me to stay for the night. He seems a decent chap.'

Piers and Rosalind exchanged wary glances, but Alexander seemed oblivious to anything other than his pleasure on seeing his brother again. He slapped Piers on the shoulder. 'Ewart told me that he only recently discovered that he'd inherited a castle. It was decent of him to offer you and Grandmama and Aurelia accommodation until you'd found somewhere more permanent.'

Piers shook his head. 'That's not how it was, Alex.'

'You can tell me all about it later,' Alex said cheerfully. 'Ewart said that it was a delicate matter – I mean the fact that you had to sell up to pay off your creditors – I can see that's something you wouldn't want broadcast.'

Rosalind sensed that Piers was seething with suppressed anger, and it was obvious that his brother was blissfully unaware of the traumas they had all suffered. She cleared her throat nervously. 'Won't you introduce us, Piers?'

'I'm sorry, Rosalind.' Piers inclined his head. 'May I introduce my brother, Captain Alexander Blanchard of the 32nd Foot?'

Rosalind held out her hand and Alexander raised

it to his lips. 'You can only be the fair Rosalind. I've heard all about you from Ewart.' He looked up and his smiling hazel eyes were so like those of his brother that they might have been twins. However, Piers was the taller of the two and his dark hair waved back from a high forehead, whereas Alexander's hair was straight and the colour of honey.

'How do you do, Captain Blanchard?' Rosalind said hastily. 'I'm Rosalind Carey. Welcome to Rockwood. Will you be staying with us for a while?'

'I was hoping it would not prove inconvenient. I have a month's leave and I find myself temporarily homeless.'

'You have a home here for as long as you wish to stay,' Rosalind said smiling. Despite the obvious misunderstanding that had arisen, thanks to Ewart Blaise, she had taken an instant liking to Alexander Blanchard. 'Do come indoors. I'll have a room made ready for you, but you must be in need of refreshment after such a long journey.'

Alexander eyed her curiously. 'Forgive my ignorance, but I understood that the castle belongs to Ewart Blaise.'

'Alex, come with me,' Piers said firmly. 'We need to have a serious conversation. We'll be in the morning parlour, Rosalind.' He led his brother into the house, leaving Rosalind standing in the courtyard. She looked over her shoulder at the sound of voices and she saw Patricia and Aurelia running towards her.

312

'Did I just see my brother Alex?' Aurelia cried breathlessly.

'He's just arrived.' Rosalind barred their way as they tried to enter the hall. 'Give them a few moments, Aurelia. Piers has some explaining to do. I think Captain Blanchard is in for something of a shock.'

Chapter Seventeen

The reunion between Alexander and his sister brought a lump to Rosalind's throat. There seemed to be genuine affection between them, and Lady Pentelow revealed an almost tender side to her nature when she greeted her younger grandson. Alexander seemed to have the power to charm everyone he met, including Bertie and Walter. Patricia was clearly impressed by the dashing young army officer, and Hester blushed like a girl when Alexander complimented her on her rabbit terrine.

At dinner Bertie listened avidly to Alexander's accounts of his experiences during the battles in the Punjab. Walter appeared to be interested, but it was obvious that he was more appalled than excited by the vivid descriptions of the skirmishes and the injuries inflicted upon the soldiers. When they became too graphic Lady Pentelow decided it was time for the ladies to retire to the drawing room, as the conversation was not fit for the ears of young girls. Rosalind could have listened to Alexander all evening but she was forced to agree with Lady Pentelow.

In the drawing room Patricia and Aurelia grumbled quietly to each other until Lady Pentelow lost patience with them, and it was then that Rosalind decided she had had enough for one day. She had already diffused an argument between Hester and Monsieur Jacques when they had fallen out over which of them would make the dessert, and Mrs Witham had argued with Jarvis, who insisted on having his meals taken to the east tower with those prepared for Sir Lucien. It had been a day of mixed emotions and fraught tempers, and the arrival of the charismatic Alexander Blanchard had stirred her emotions and made her feel unsettled. She left everyone to sort themselves out and went for a walk with Bob at her side.

The sun was setting and the backwater was on fire with reflections of the scarlet, crimson and purple clouds tinged with molten gold. The soft June air was filled with the scent of roses and clover, mingled with the briny smell of the sea and a hint of tar from the caulking of the fishing boats tied up at the quay. The silence, broken only by the lapping of the waves on the foreshore and the occasional cry of a gull, was welcome after the constant clash of personalities below stairs. Rosalind took deep breaths of the fresh air and closed her eyes. If only she could turn back time to before Piers had arrived to turn their lives upside down. It was not a personal vilification of the man himself, but of what he claimed to stand for that had shaken her to the core, and she was still not entirely convinced by his story.

The castle, her beloved home, was filled with people who had been strangers until very recently, including Alexander. It was he who had had the most disturbing effect on Rosalind. She had never before experienced an attraction to a man so great that it had left her shaken and unsure of herself. Alexander Blanchard was a charmer, and he was obviously aware of the effect he had on women; she had seen for herself how he had beguiled his difficult grandmother and had sent Patricia into a fit of nervous giggles whenever he spoke to her. Aurelia seemed to hero-worship him and it was easy to see why. Rosalind felt herself slipping into an emotional maelstrom that she could never have imagined, and she was angry with herself. She, of all people, needed to keep a clear head when their very existence was threatened, and yet here she was, acting like a silly young girl or a love-struck heroine in one of her mother's operettas.

She had walked further than she had intended and she found herself standing on the cliff top overlooking the bay. The mysterious dark holes in the red sandstone were deep caves where once smugglers had hidden their illegal caches. Rosalind had never forgotten the time she and Bertie had been caught up in the altercation between the preventive men and the free traders who had attempted to land on the beach. She still had a faint scar at her hairline caused by the injury she had received in the fall, and only a hazy recollection of the boy who had come to her aid, but it had all happened a long time ago. She glanced round at Bob, who had been following various scent trails when he came to a halt at her side, growling deep in his throat.

The sound of approaching footsteps made her spin round and her heart missed a beat when she saw Alexander strolling towards her. Bob ran to him, wagging his tail, and Alexander bent down to pat him.

'I imagine we're here for the same reason, Rosalind.' He straightened up, shielding his eyes against the rays of the setting sun. 'My family are a bit overpowering when they get together, aren't they?'

'No more than mine, I suspect.' Rosalind looked away quickly. Alexander had a smile that would have melted steel, and a twinkle in his eyes that made him almost irresistible.

'Are you sure you don't mind my turning up out of the blue? I can see that the Blanchards have invaded the castle without firing a shot. Trust Grandmama to bring her retinue, too. It must make life difficult below stairs.'

Rosalind had a feeling he was teasing her, but when she turned to face him and she realised that he was serious. Unlike her family, Alexander seemed to understand how she felt without asking. She nodded. 'It's not easy but I'm sure we'll manage.'

He came to stand beside her, gazing out over the sea. 'Blaise must be stopped. I understand now why Piers gave in to his demands, but I think our grandmother would prefer a blot on the escutcheon to losing her home.'

'Piers was concerned for Aurelia, too. He seems to think that Hugo Knighton would walk away if Blaise decided to blacken the family name.'

Alexander was silent for a moment. 'Aurelia is very young. She'll find someone else.'

'A scandal could ruin her chances of making a good match.'

'And a generous dowry is a great incentive to overlook such matters.'

'You are very cynical, Alexander.'

'I've seen a lot of the world, and I've listened to my fellow officers. It's not just the ladies who have their hearts broken.'

'What about you? Have you suffered in that way?'

He laughed. 'There was a girl once. I thought I was deeply in love with her, but it ended badly.'

'What happened?'

He turned his head to look at her and his hazel eyes were alight with amusement. 'I was sent away to school. I believe she went into service and eventually married her widowed employer, who was many years her senior. I think I had a lucky escape.'

It was Rosalind's turn to laugh. 'I thought for a moment you were being serious.'

'But I made you smile. That's the main thing. You have a lovely smile, Rosalind. You should always be happy.'

'I think I should get back to the castle,' Rosalind said hastily. 'It will be dark soon and they'll wonder where I am.'

He proffered his arm. 'I'll do anything I can to help. In a month's time I'll be back with my regiment and probably on my way to India, but in the meantime let's see if we can beat Ewart Blaise and restore our respective family fortunes.'

'Piers has never said much about it, but surely it must be hard for you to learn of your father's infidelity?' Rosalind said, tucking her hand in the crook of his arm.

'Our mother died quite young,' Alexander said with a sigh. 'Papa was never at home. He was either at the mine or he was travelling on business and we were never close. He passed away some time ago and it was Grandmama who brought us up. I'm just sorry she has suffered so badly because of my father's indiscretions.' He shot her a sideways glance. 'And you, Rosalind. What do you feel about my brother claiming the castle as his own and displacing Bertie as heir?'

'I was shocked at first, but we were in a terrible fix financially. If Piers had not turned up when he did we might have lost Rockwood to our creditors.

Everything of any value had been sold, and we were living from hand to mouth. I suppose Bertie will inherit the title regardless of whether he owns Rockwood or not, and anyway, all he wants is a career in the army. Piers has made it possible for us to live here and to be comfortable again.'

'It's very generous of you to see it that way.'

'Not at all. One thing the hardship of the past has taught me is to be practical.'

They walked back to the castle in companionable silence. Bats swooped overhead against a darkening sky and Bob lolloped on ahead, leading the way home.

They were met at the gates by Bertie, who was holding a lantern. 'Where've you been, Rosie? I was just coming to look for you.'

'Your sister and I have been enjoying the wonderful view from the top of the cliffs,' Alexander said, smiling. 'I'm sorry, Bertie. I meant to stay behind and talk about the regiment, but I needed to clear my head.'

Bertie chuckled. 'It's all right, I understand. Anyway, the girls have gone to their rooms and Lady Pentelow has retired for the night, but I'm afraid Grandpapa escaped from the tower.'

'Oh, no!' Rosalind's hand flew to cover her mouth. 'How did that happen?'

'It's all right. Piers and Walter found him in the cellar, looking for a bottle of rum, or so he said. Apparently Jarvis was in the servants' hall arguing with Patterson, over what I don't know. Grandpapa fancied a tot before bedtime and decided to help himself.'

'Lady Pentelow didn't see him, did she?'

'No, she had gone to her room and Grandpapa must have used the back stairs, which was fortunate because he was wearing only his nightshirt.'

'I'll have a word with Jarvis,' Rosalind said firmly. 'It mustn't happen again.'

'You're shivering.' Alexander took off his jacket and wrapped it around her shoulders. 'Let's get you inside before you catch cold. Is there anything I can do, Bertie?'

'No. We've got everything under control, but I could do with a tot of brandy.'

When they reached the great hall, Rosalind slipped off the warm jacket and handed it back to Alexander. 'Thank you for that. I'm tired so I think I'll go straight to my room, but I'll speak very firmly to Jarvis in the morning.' She left them at the foot of the stairs and taking a chamber candlestick she made her way up to her room. As she walked past Patricia's bedchamber she could hear low voices and giggling, and she smiled. At least Patsy was happier now that she had Aurelia to confide in. Perhaps it was not so bad having to share with the Blanchard family for a while, at least. She went to her own room and lit more candles, but she did not get undressed immediately. She sat on the wide stone window seat, gazing out over the park to the backwater, which was just visible, shimmering like a pool of silver in the moonlight. She knew now that she would do anything to protect and preserve Rockwood. It might belong to Piers when Grandpapa was no longer with them, but she was confident that Piers would keep his word and allow them to live in their home for as long as they wished. Ewart Blaise was a danger to them all, but there must be a way to stop him from ruining their lives. Somehow Alexander's arrival and his positive attitude had made anything seem possible.

Next morning Rosalind went to the kitchen first thing to make sure that Hester was coping, but she found Tilly in floods of tears and Hester red in the face and breathing heavily. Mrs Witham and one of the scullery maids from Trevenor were standing side by side and the atmosphere was tense.

'What's going on?' Rosalind demanded. She had not slept well and she would rather not start the day with arguments below stairs.

'I'm not going to be told what to do by her,' Hester said angrily. She jerked her head in Mrs Witham's direction. 'This is my kitchen and it was agreed with the Frenchman that breakfast is my affair. She doesn't seem to think so.'

Mrs Witham puffed out her chest. 'I won't be spoken to like that, Mrs Dodridge. I am Lady Pentelow's housekeeper and she has given me complete authority in the kitchen area.'

'What exactly is the problem?' Rosalind asked cautiously.

'Lady Pentelow is very particular about the way her food is prepared, and this woman isn't a proper cook.'

'Take that back,' Hester snapped. 'I've been cooking for this family for more years than I care to remember. My gentleman friend, Jacob, will back me up on that. I've devoted my whole life to this family.'

'Surely breakfast is a relatively simple meal?' Rosalind said calmly. 'What could Lady Pentelow object to in the way that Hester prepares it, Mrs Witham?'

'Well, for one thing, Miss Carey, Lady Pentelow doesn't like fried food swimming in grease, nor big fat sausages. She likes her bacon thin cut and crisp, and her eggs lightly poached or even scrambled. Devilled kidneys are her favourite, but I don't suppose Mrs Dodridge knows what they are.'

Hester's fingers closed around the handle of a large soot-blackened saucepan. 'You insult me, missis. We was once a wealthy family and we entertained better people than you and your mistress. You Cornish are always causing trouble.'

'For a start I am not a native of Cornwall,' Mrs Witham said angrily. 'And secondly, I am merely doing my job. I'm going to rouse Monsieur Jacques and he will prepare my lady's breakfast.'

Hester picked up the saucepan and wielded it over

her head. 'Get out of my kitchen and take your snivelling slavey with you. She made my Tilly cry and I won't have that. As for you, missis, you'd better keep out of my kitchen or I won't be held responsible for my actions.'

Rosalind stepped in between them. 'Now, wait a moment, please. I won't allow this sort of thing to continue. Mrs Witham, Hester will prepare breakfast for the family as usual, but if you wish to disturb Monsieur Jacques that is your business. I'm sure that Hester will comply with Lady Pentelow's request regarding the way in which her food is prepared, but I think it best if you keep to your housekeeping duties.'

Mrs Witham clasped her hands tightly in front of her and she stared straight ahead. 'If you say so, Miss Carey. Only I usually take my orders from her ladyship.'

'These are not ordinary times,' Rosalind said firmly. She turned her attention to the young scullery maid. 'What is your name?'

'It's Ruth, miss.'

'Well, Ruth, I want you to work with Tilly. You look to be about the same age, but Tilly has been here longer, so you must do as she says.'

Ruth bobbed a curtsey. 'Yes, miss.'

'And you, Tilly – I don't want to hear of any more disagreements. You are both paid to do a job of work and you must endeavour to get along, or you will both have to find employment elsewhere. Do you understand?'

Tilly nodded and bowed her head. 'Yes, Miss Carey.'

'I have duties to perform, if you'll excuse me, Miss Carey?' Mrs Witham backed out of the kitchen and Rosalind heard her booted feet scuttling across the flagstones in the passageway.

'You two, shake hands and then you can fetch water from the pump.' Rosalind waited until the two girls were out of earshot before turning to Hester. 'I'm sorry that you're having to put up with so much interference in your kitchen, Hester.'

'I can manage that women and half a dozen more like her.' Hester replaced the pan on the shelf. 'But I would have crowned her if she's kept on much longer.'

'I'll make sure she doesn't interfere in the kitchen. We love your cooking, Hester, but if you'd rather take over the housekeeper's position, I'll have a word with Lady Pentelow and perhaps she will send Mrs Witham back to Cornwall.'

Hester tossed her head. 'I won't be driven out of my kitchen by her or that Frenchie, or anyone. If you want to send her back to they heathens in Cornwall, please do, and I'll see to the housekeeping as I've always done.'

'Whatever makes you happy,' Rosalind said earnestly. 'We can't manage without you.'

'That's what I tell Jacob when he comes on his weekly visits. He proposed again last evening, but I says, "Jacob Lidstone, I'll marry you when I'm no longer needed at Rockwood, and that will probably be never. Go on your way, boy, and leave me be." That's what I says to him.'

'And yet he comes back again and again. How many years has he been courting you, Hester?'

'Ten year and more. But I have a job to do and I'm not giving in to his demands.'

Rosalind gave her a hug. 'You are part of the family, Hester. If you wish to marry we would have to be happy for you, although you would be sorely missed.'

'Don't worry, Miss Rosalind, I'm going nowhere until I see you wedded to a good man who'll take care of you like I have all these years. When that happens I might say yes to Jacob, but until then he'll have to wait.'

'If you're sure, Hester,' Rosalind said warily. 'But please don't sacrifice your chance of happiness for us. We love you and we all want you to have a good life.'

Hester wiped her eyes on the back of her hand. 'I'm more than content with my lot, Miss Rosalind. Now let me get on with my work, if you please. I don't want more complaints from the dining room.'

'Just one thing, Hester. I gather there was an argument between Mr Jarvis and Mr Patterson last evening. I want you to make sure that Mr Jarvis's meals are sent up to the east tower together with those for my grandfather.'

'That will be done, as usual. It wasn't my idea to stop them.'

'I'm sure of that, Hester. We will continue as we've always done. You can send Tilly up with the food when it's ready.'

Rosalind left the kitchen and made her way to the east tower where she found Jarvis preparing to give her grandfather a shave. She eyed the cut-throat razor warily. 'That looks like a dangerous weapon, Jarvis.'

A wry smile twisted his thin lips. 'In the wrong hands it could be, Miss Rosalind. Have you come to see Sir Lucien?'

'I wanted to ask you how he managed to escape last night, Jarvis.'

'It was entirely my fault, Miss Rosalind. I went below stairs to speak to Mr Patterson, and I forgot to lock the solar door. In my defence I should add that I thought Sir Lucien was asleep.'

'That I can understand, but the arguments below stairs must cease. I've just had to talk to Hester and Mrs Witham about the same thing.'

Jarvis gazed down at his feet. 'I understand, Miss Rosalind.'

'I know it's difficult for both sides, but we have to get along. However, I hope it won't be for long, Jarvis. In the meantime, just try to get along with the servants from Trevenor, no matter what the provocation.'

'I will, Miss Rosalind.' Jarvis cleared his throat

nervously. 'Might I ask if Sir Lucien will be allowed to join the family for dinner? When he's in a good phase he makes it clear that he wishes to be included.'

'Let me know when you think he would be capable of behaving normally and he may take his place at table. At the moment Lady Pentelow is under the impression that my grandfather is still unwell, but we can't use that excuse for ever.'

'Miss Rosalind, as a member of staff who has served this family for many years, might I suggest that perhaps the truth is preferable to a well-intentioned lie? Sir Lucien's condition is not of his own making.'

'Yes, I agree. The moment you think he could cope with a family meal, let me know, Jarvis.'

'Of course, Miss Rosalind.'

'By the way, Tilly will be bringing your breakfast as well as my grandfather's tray. There will be no more discussion on that subject below stairs.'

'Thank you,' Jarvis said with a ghost of a smile.

Rosalind made her way to the dining room and she was surprised to find everyone seated round the table, including Patricia and Aurelia, who were notoriously late risers.

Lady Pentelow acknowledged her with a nod. 'As you see, Rosalind, it's my opinion that everyone should have a good breakfast. I don't approve of lying around in bed until half the day is gone. I need to remind the young ladies of this, when they grace us with their presence.'

Rosalind helped herself to bacon and buttered eggs from the salvers on the sideboard. She took her place at the table. 'I agree, ma'am, but I'm surprised to see my brothers and Patsy. They are not usually up and about this early.'

'It's a simple rule, but one that I adhere to,' Lady Pentelow said smugly. 'One should start the day as one means to continue, and that includes a civilised meal.' She glanced round at her grandsons. 'What do you intend to do today, Piers, and you as well, Alexander?'

Piers swallowed a mouthful of toast. 'I thought I'd go for a ride, Grandmama. My horse is eating its head off in the stables and I need to exercise him.'

'And I'm going to go for a brisk walk,' Alexander said seriously. 'What about you girls? Do you feel like coming with me?'

Aurelia pulled a face. 'Patsy and I planned to stroll down to the village. I need some hairpins and Patsy tells me that they sell them in the village shop.'

'Yes, that's right.' Patsy crumpled her table napkin and laid it on the table. 'I warned Aurelia that Rockwood isn't much of a place, but she thinks it's high time she saw the village for herself.'

Rosalind sent her sister a searching look, but Patricia gave nothing away. If she intended to seek out Barnaby there was little that Rosalind could do to prevent her meeting him while out walking, and no real harm could come of it if she were in Aurelia's company, or so she hoped. However, the banns had been read twice and even Barnaby would find it difficult to back down now.

Rosalind realised that Lady Pentelow was staring at her. 'I'm sorry, Lady Pentelow. Were you speaking to me?'

'I included you in the question, Rosalind. How are you going to spend your morning?'

'There is always a lot to do, ma'am. Household matters take up much of my time.'

'Ah! That's where you are making a mistake. One hires a housekeeper to take over such duties, and now you have Mrs Witham to oversee matters below stairs. As we will be here for some considerable time it's only proper that we are introduced into the county society in the appropriate manner.'

'Do you want to meet our neighbours, ma'am?'

'Of course. We aren't hiding away in this crumbling castle. Piers has most generously allowed you and your family to live here, but that arrangement can be revised should the necessity occur.'

'That won't happen, Grandmama,' Piers said firmly. 'I've given Rosalind my word and that is the end of it.'

Lady Pentelow treated him to a condescending smile. 'I understand, my dear. You were always a generous little boy and that remains unchanged.

330

However, I think Rosalind and I understand each other.'

'We should have a ball here at Rockwood,' Patricia said eagerly. 'We haven't entertained for years, Rosie. Do say yes.'

'It's not very practical.' Rosalind looked to Bertie for confirmation, but he merely shrugged. 'I mean, due to financial circumstances we've had to sell the family silver and I doubt if we have more than a dozen champagne glasses.'

'Mere details,' Lady Pentelow said airily. 'You don't imagine that I would have left such valuables for that wretch Blaise to enjoy, do you? I think a ball would be an excellent idea. I'll tell Mrs Witham to organise the unpacking of all the crates and tea chests from Trevenor. You, my dear, Rosalind, will write a list of all the county families within travelling distance, and then we will go through it together.' Lady Pentelow rose majestically from her chair. 'Now, I am going to that quaint little room you call the morning parlour. Send Witham to me, if you please.' She sailed from the room, leaving a waft of expensive perfume in her wake.

Piers stood up. 'You have your orders, Rosalind. I'm sorry, but Grandmama is used to ruling the household with a rod of iron. It will take her some time to get used to the fact that this is your home.'

'If ever,' Alexander added, chuckling.

Rosalind smiled and said nothing. There was very

little she could add to the conversation in the circumstances.

'A ball would be lovely.' Aurelia jumped up from her seat. 'Come on, Patsy. Don't dawdle.'

Patricia was already on her feet and they left the room, chattering excitedly.

'I hope that Patsy isn't planning on seeing Barnaby,' Rosalind said, half to herself.

'Maybe the prospect of a ball at Rockwood will take her mind off him, Rosie. It might be good for Patsy to have something to look forward to.' Walter pushed back his chair and stood up. 'Maybe it's what we all need?'

She smiled. 'You always say the right thing, Walter. And you're right, of course. It's just that we haven't entertained for so long I think I've forgotten how such things are done.'

'Leave it to Grandmama,' Piers said cheerfully. 'She'll be in her element, and all you have to do is agree with her, and don't worry about the cost.'

'Maybe we ought to invite Blaise.' Alexander moved swiftly to the door and opened it. 'We could show him that the Blanchards are not to be beaten by a nobody like him.'

'Never mind that fellow,' Bertie said impatiently. 'You said you were going for a walk, Alex, but I'd like to hear more about army life. I thought I might have a day's fishing – are you interested?'

'Yes, why not? I'm not much of a hand with the rod and line, but I can always laze around and watch.' Alexander followed him from the room, leaving Rosalind alone with Piers.

'You won't contact Blaise, will you?' Rosalind asked anxiously. 'I don't want that man in my home again.'

'Certainly not. That wasn't one of Alexander's better ideas.' He eyed her curiously. 'Something is worrying you. What is it?'

'The idea of entertaining here is quite appealing, but there's my grandfather. We can't keep him locked away permanently. It isn't fair on him, or Jarvis, for that matter. Grandpapa isn't mad, he's just very eccentric.'

Piers frowned thoughtfully. 'Perhaps it's time to introduce him to my grandmother. I think you might find her more accommodating than you imagine.'

'I don't know about that. It might turn out to be a disaster.'

'You won't know until you try. You might attempt to keep him under lock and key, but supposing he escaped and decided to join in the grand parade at the ball? Can you imagine the scene? It would be more entertaining than any of your mama's comic operas.' Piers laughed and Rosalind found herself laughing with him.

'You're right, of course. I'll speak to Bertie, but I'm sure he'll agree, and it might be a good idea if Grandpapa were to join us for dinner this evening.'

Piers smiled. 'That sounds like a good idea. Just remember that you aren't alone now, Rosalind. You have all of us ready and willing to help you.'

'I'll let Jarvis know. I expect he'll be glad to have a night off. He'll probably go to the Black Dog with Jacob.'

'Jacob? I don't recall you mentioning him before.'

'Jacob Lidstone is Hester's fiancé. They've been keeping company for more than ten years. He lives in Dawlish, but he visits Hester at least once a week, and he keeps an eye on her aged aunt.'

'A good fellow by any standards.'

'Yes,' Rosalind said doubtfully. 'Of course.'

No matter how she tried, she had never taken to Jacob. There was something about him that did not seem to tally with his outwardly pleasant disposition. He was always very cheerful and eager to please, perhaps too much so, but whatever it was, Rosalind was always relieved to learn that Hester had turned him down, yet again.

She managed a smile. 'I'd better go and speak to Jarvis now, and then I'll write that list for your grandmother – it's going to be a busy morning.'

Chapter Eighteen

That evening everyone assembled dutifully in the drawing room before dinner. It was a custom instituted by Lady Pentelow, who insisted that it was the way that things were done in polite society. They sat round sipping sherry, although Rosalind knew very well that her brothers would have preferred a glass of ale, and Patricia hated sherry. As for herself, Rosalind was dreading the moment when Jarvis showed her grandfather into the room, even though Lady Pentelow had seemed genuinely delighted by the prospect of renewing her acquaintanceship with Sir Lucien after the passage of many years. She had waved aside Rosalind's attempt to warn her that one of the heroes of the Napoleonic Wars was not quite the man he had once been.

The ornate brass clock on the mantelshelf struck the hour and, as instructed, Jarvis ushered Sir Lucien into the room. Rosalind held her breath, and she could see that Bertie and Walter were poised, ready to spring to their feet if their grandfather decided to make a bolt for it or, even worse, to announce that the enemy had been sighted and there was a call to arms. Rosalind had given Jarvis strict instructions concerning her grandfather's manner of dress, banning his uniform in favour of a black tailcoat worn with a grey waistcoat and pin-stripe trousers.

Sir Lucien stood in the doorway, gazing vaguely round the room. A look of puzzlement crossed his face when Lady Pentelow rose from her chair, advancing on him with a determined smile.

'Sir Lucien, it's good to see that you're well enough to join us for dinner.' She held out her hand.

He shot a desperate glance in Rosalind's direction and she leaped to her feet. 'Grandpapa, you remember Lady Pentelow.'

He shook his head. 'I don't recall the name.'

'Come, sir. That's not very gallant,' Lady Pentelow said coquettishly. 'My late husband, Sir Edmund Pentelow, hosted the celebration dinner in your honour in Plymouth some twenty years ago.'

Rosalind held her breath. She could see that her grandfather was struggling and she moved swiftly to his side, taking his hand in hers. 'Lady Pentelow and her grandchildren are staying with us, Grandpapa. You've already met Piers, so may I introduce you to Captain Alexander Blanchard of the 32nd Regiment of Foot?'

Alexander stepped forward and bowed. 'Delighted to make your acquaintance, sir. Your exploits in the Royal Navy are legendary.'

'Indeed they are,' Sir Lucien said, beaming. 'How do you do, Captain?' He turned to Aurelia, who had joined her brother and was giving Sir Lucien her best smile. 'And who is this beautiful young lady?'

'This is Aurelia Blanchard, my granddaughter,' Lady Pentelow said graciously. 'We are delighted to be guests in your historic home.'

Sir Lucien roared with laughter. 'Historic, ma'am? That's a euphemism for crumbling pile of rubble, don't you think?'

'I would like to explore the cellars, Sir Lucien,' Aurelia said boldly. 'I've heard that these old castles have an oubliette where they threw prisoners and left them to die a horrible death.'

'I'm sure Bertie would have found one if it existed.' Patricia looked to her brother. 'Wouldn't you, Bertie?'

'I'd hardly waste my time exploring damp old cellars,' Bertie said, shrugging.

'But there might even be treasure hidden in a secret chamber,' Aurelia insisted. 'Trevenor is old, but not nearly as old as Rockwood. We have cellars but they are quite boring.'

'I'm sure you two can find something better to occupy you,' Piers said sharply. 'Dungeons and oubliettes were places of torture. They aren't in the least bit romantic as you seem to think.'

'This is hardly the conversation to have now, Piers.' Lady Pentelow turned her attention to Sir Lucien. 'What do you think, sir?'

'I try not to think at all these days, dear lady.'

A ripple of polite laughter went round the room, leaving Rosalind relieved but eager to steer the conversation away from the grisly history of the castle's dungeons. 'Will you take a glass of sherry before dinner, Grandpapa?'

'Sherry? I don't drink that gut-rot. Jarvis, fetch me a tot of rum and we'll splice the main brace.'

There was a stunned silence while all eyes turned to Lady Pentelow. Rosalind held her breath. If her ladyship took offence it would ruin the evening and leave Rosalind with some explaining to do, but to her surprise Lady Pentelow merely chuckled.

'You are so amusing, sir. Come and sit by me and we'll chat about the old days.' She took him by the arm and led him to a chair next to the one she had just vacated. 'Your man will fetch your drink. Now tell me everything you've been up to since we last met.'

Rosalind breathed a sigh of relief. 'Rum, please, Jarvis.'

'I tell you what,' Bertie said, grinning. 'I'll have a tot, too. What about you fellows?'

Piers nodded. 'Count me in on that. Never could stand sherry. What about you, Alex?'

Alexander nodded. 'Of course. I may be army but I'm always happy to splice the main brace in honour of our naval heroes.'

'I think I'll stick to sherry,' Walter said shyly. 'I haven't got much of a head for spirits.'

'I've never tried rum,' Patricia said eagerly.

'Nor will you, my girl.' Lady Pentelow shook her head. 'Rum is not a drink for young ladies. You girls will take sherry, or perhaps ratafia wine at a ball, but that's all, unless champagne is offered. You may drink champagne and fruit cup.'

'That's right, ma'am.' Sir Lucien slapped his hands on his knees. 'You keep the young ladies in order. My granddaughter Patricia is a handful. She runs wild, you know. Needs a firm hand. Prudence is too soft on her. Aren't you, my dear?' He sent a beaming smile to Rosalind and her heart sank. Everything had been going relatively well until this moment. She glanced nervously at Lady Pentelow, expecting her to demand an explanation, but Lady Pentelow merely smiled.

'I do remember your dear wife, Sir Lucien. Your granddaughter is so like her, no wonder you get them confused at times.'

'I do, don't I?' Sir Lucien nodded wisely. 'Yes, I'm afraid I do. That is Rosalind, not Prudence. Do you really remember my wife, Lady Pendennis?'

'Lady Pentelow, sir. It's easy to muddle names. Yes, I recall having a long conversation with Lady Carey. She was a kind and beautiful woman.'

At that moment Jarvis reappeared bearing a tray laden with a decanter and glasses. Bertie, Piers and Alexander toasted each other in rum, but Sir

Lucien was too deep in conversation with Lady Pentelow to bother. They had barely downed their drinks when Patterson announced that dinner was served.

Piers proffered his arm to Rosalind. 'That went well, I believe.'

'Better than I anticipated. Your grandmother is full of surprises. She didn't seem to think that Grandpapa was behaving oddly.'

'She's lived a long time, Rosalind. I doubt if there's anything much that would surprise her.'

'I'm very grateful to her, Piers. I hated keeping Grandpapa locked up in the tower like a madman. I think it will do him good to talk to someone about the old days. That's something we can't do.'

'And it will give my grandmother something to think about other than marrying Aurelia off to the highest bidder.'

'You don't think she'd do that, do you?'

'Not as such, but that's how it usually happens, isn't it? You're lucky in a way that you can choose for yourself without interference from your mother or Sir Lucien.' Piers escorted her to the dining room and pulled out a chair for her.

'I hadn't thought about it like that.' Rosalind sat down and he took his seat on the opposite side of the table. She caught Alexander's eye as he sat next to his brother, and the warmth in his gaze brought the colour to her cheeks. She had no doubts about Alexander Blanchard – she knew she could trust him implicitly – and she acknowledged him with a smile.

The food was served and Rosalind could find no fault with Monsieur Jacques' culinary achievements. Conversation flowed without any flights of fancy from Sir Lucien or hints of trouble below stairs. However, after several glasses of claret Sir Lucien began to nod off and was in danger of falling asleep at the table. Rosalind signalled to Jarvis.

'I think my grandfather is ready for bed, Jarvis. Do you need help to get him to his room?'

Jarvis shook his head. 'I can manage, thank you, Miss Rosalind.'

'I'll look in later.'

Jarvis moved swiftly to the head of the table and with help from Piers and Bertie, he managed to get Sir Lucien to his feet, and once on the move he seemed able to cope on his own.

'The poor gentleman has rather overdone it today,' Lady Pentelow said graciously. 'But I hope we'll have the pleasure of his company tomorrow evening at dinner. He has such a wealth of interesting stories to relate.'

When the ladies retired to the drawing room Rosalind sat next to Lady Pentelow, leaving Aurelia and Patsy to enjoy a game of piquet.

'I've looked through your guest list,' Lady Pentelow said, leaning back in her chair. 'It seems quite comprehensive but you didn't add the Knightons. Why was that?'

'I don't know that family, and surely it's too far for them to travel from Cornwall for a party?'

'The ball at Rockwood will go down in social history,' Lady Pentelow said seriously. 'I have a list of families from Cornwall, all of whom have been known to travel as far as London for a special night out. I plan to book the village inn for the night for the servants, and I'm sure we could put quite a few guests up here. My servants will help to get the rooms ready. This old castle is enormous.'

'It is but I don't think we have enough staff to make a house party feasible.'

'Nonsense, Rosalind. Leave everything to me and Mrs Witham. However, if people accept I expect most of them will make their own arrangements. I'll leave you in charge of writing the invitations, and Monsieur Jacques will be in charge of the kitchen. Your woman may assist if she's a mind to cooperate, but if not she may supervise the clearing up next day. Patterson will deal with the wine merchant in Exeter. We may need to hire more glasses, but you don't have to worry about that. We will put Rockwood Castle on the map again.'

Aurelia glanced over her shoulder. 'You will make sure that Hugo is invited, won't you, Rosie? It's a pity we can't ask Barnaby to come and help with the horses, don't you think, Patsy?'

'No, I don't,' Patricia said crossly. 'You shouldn't mention his name in front of Rosie.'

Rosalind turned her head to give Patricia a questioning look. 'I hope you didn't call at the smithy when you went to the village.'

'Of course not, Rosie. I promised I wouldn't see him again. At least, not deliberately. He happened to be walking down the main street and it would have been rude to ignore him.'

'He is very handsome,' Aurelia said, giggling. 'I can understand why you fancied him, Patsy.'

'It wasn't like that. We've been friends ever since I can remember. He doesn't love that silly little thing Lucy Warren. She used to follow him round like a shadow.'

Rosalind yawned. 'It's been a long day. I think I'll go to my room. Don't stay up too long, Patsy.'

'Aren't you going to wait for Alexander and Piers to join us?' Patricia said archly.

'I think you and Aurelia can entertain them without my help.' Rosalind turned to Lady Pentelow. 'Good night, ma'am. Rest assured I'll do all I can to help you with the arrangements for the ball.'

'And don't forget to invite Sir Michael and the girls,' Patricia added. 'I'm surprised he hasn't been here, eager to meet our guests.'

'Sir Michael?' Lady Pentelow raised an eyebrow. 'I don't think I've heard his name mentioned before.'

'Sir Michael Greystone is a very wealthy man,' Patricia said slyly. 'His land abuts the Rockwood estate and he has two daughters – my friends Christina and Sylvia.'

'You haven't mentioned his wife.' Lady Pentelow leaned forward, her eyes alight with curiosity.

'He's a widower.' Rosalind hesitated in the doorway. 'And before my sister says anything, I should add that he proposed to me and I refused. I really don't want to discuss it any further.'

'He's very presentable,' Patricia added innocently. 'Quite a catch, even if he is old.'

'Good night, Patsy.'

Rosalind did not wait for the inevitable cross-examination from Lady Pentelow. She left the room and made her way upstairs to the solar in the east tower where she found Jarvis in the anteroom, folding Sir Lucien's clothes.

'Is he all right, Jarvis?'

'Sleeping like a baby, Miss Rosalind. I think Sir Lucien enjoyed himself this evening, but he was more than ready for bed.'

'It went well, I think. I was worried, but Lady Pentelow was very understanding. If my grandfather wishes to join us for dinner from now on he must do so.'

'Quite. I understand.'

'Thank you, Jarvis. I know it must seem that we take your services for granted, but we all appreciate the devotion you show our grandfather.'

'I'm merely doing my duty, Miss Rosalind.'

'We'll agree to differ on that. Good night, Jarvis.'

'Good night, Miss Rosalind.'

She left the anteroom and instead of taking the

main staircase she opened the cleverly concealed door in the oak panelling and, holding her candle high, made her way down the spiral staircase that led to the servants' quarters, where she hoped to find Hester. As she approached the kitchen she could feel the heat from the range, and steam billowed out of the open door. She could hear the clatter of pots and pans and the raised voices of the kitchen staff, chattering together as they worked to clear up the detritus left after the evening meal.

Hester had her own private parlour, which Rosalind had made clear was to remain for her personal use, excluding the staff from Trevenor. She knew that it was not a popular decision, but Hester deserved to have somewhere to call her own. The room was furnished with slightly shabby, but comfortable, armchairs, and a small table covered with the knick-knacks that Hester had collected during a lifetime of service to the Careys. She had kept everything that the children had made for her, including the cigar boxes decorated with shells that Rosalind had collected from the beach and had patiently glued in place. There were pictures that Patricia had drawn, and poems that Walter had written from the age of five upwards. His earlier attempts were covered with ink blots and there were many spelling mistakes, but they had shown marked improvement as he'd grown older. Bertie's contribution consisted of a few pine cones and some pheasant feathers stuck in a flowerpot, but then Bertie had never been interested in art or poetry, and sitting at a desk had been torture for a boy who loved the outdoors.

Rosalind smiled as she closed the door on all these memories, but there was no sign of Hester. She was not in the servants' hall and no one seemed to have seen her for quite a while. Rosalind became worried. It was not like Hester to leave the house at night, and she was not the sort of person who enjoyed a walk, no matter what time of day it was.

Rosalind went into the courtyard but Hester wasn't there either. She walked round to the walled bailey at the front of the castle and paused, cocking her head as she caught the faint sound of voices. Keeping her distance, she remained in the shadow of the outside wall, from where she spotted Hester in deep conversation with a man. Moving closer, Rosalind realised that it was Jacob, which was a surprise in itself as he never visited in the evening, and the stable clock had just struck eleven. Rosalind was about to turn back when she heard Hester's voice rise and she sounded agitated. Rosalind's protective instincts were aroused and she marched up to them.

'Is everything all right, Hester?'

Hester spun round, her face pale in the moonlight. 'I'm sorry, Miss Rosalind. We didn't mean to disturb you.'

'You haven't. I was looking for you.' Rosalind turned to Jacob. 'You're here late, Jacob. Is anything wrong?'

He tipped his billycock hat. 'No, Miss Rosalind. I was just passing by and I thought I'd call on Hester.'

'At eleven o'clock in the evening? The only people out at this time of night are poachers or smugglers. Which are you, Jacob?'

'I don't see the humour in that question, Miss Rosalind,' Jacob said coldly. 'You told me once that I was free to visit my fiancée whenever I chose.'

'Hold hard there, boy.' Hester drew herself up to her full height. 'I am not engaged to you or any man. I think it's time you went home.'

'I thought you lived in Dawlish, Jacob,' Rosalind said, puzzled. 'I know for a fact that the ferry doesn't run this late.'

'I have a cousin who lives in the village, Miss Rosalind,' Jacob said gruffly. 'I'll stay with him tonight.'

'Then you'd best be off.' Hester shooed him towards the postern gate. 'You know I don't like you associating with those people. They always was a bad lot and nothing's changed.'

'Seth Wills is a good man, Hester. He can't help it if his brothers don't follow his example.'

'All the Wills boys were involved with the smugglers years ago. I doubt if they've changed. Saul Wills went to prison for his part in the gang.'

'He's served his time,' Jacob said sulkily. 'The old days are long gone, Hester.'

'I'm sure I remember a ship and a fight on the beach,' Rosalind said slowly. 'Was that when I had the fall and cut my head, Hester? I wish I could remember all of what happened.'

'It was an accident, and you was little more than a moppet. Now come inside, Miss Rosalind. I don't want you catching your death of cold because of this silly fellow. Go away, Jacob. Come again at a proper time or you'll find the door locked.' She unchained the postern gate and opened it. 'Out you go.'

He blew her a kiss. 'You know you love me really, maid.'

'Get on with you.' Hester slammed the gate and replaced the chain. 'Come indoors, Miss Rosalind. I'll make you a nice cup of cocoa to take to bed with you.'

Rosalind did as Hester suggested, but she sat up until well after midnight, sipping the cocoa and gazing out over the moonlit backwater. Jacob's presence so late in the evening and the mention of the notorious Wills family and their previous connection with the smuggling gangs had been unsettling. The vague memory of that dark night on the beach when she was a child still lingered in her mind, but the happenings were shrouded in a thick fog. It was very frustrating, and when she eventually climbed into bed and curled up on her side she fell asleep, only to suffer the recurrent dream. She was about to discover the identity of the strange boy and the men in the boat when she slipped and she was falling, falling, falling . . .

She awakened with a start. Maybe it had simply been a nightmare from her childhood, brought about by the tumble and the cut on her head. She sat up and stretched. This was not the time to look into the past; there was a great deal to do if they were to host a ball in two or three weeks' time, despite what Lady Pentelow said.

As the days progressed Rosalind was relieved to discover that Lady Pentelow had not exaggerated when she claimed to have had enormous experience in organising events like the ball. There were lists for everything and all the servants were given their own tasks, however small. Lady Pentelow was good at delegating and the invitations were handwritten and sent out within two days. The responses were collected and each acceptance was marked off, as were the refusals, although there were very few of these. Monsieur Jacques had drawn up a menu, which was approved by Lady Pentelow, and Rosalind had the final word, although there was nothing that she could add. Piers, Bertie and Alexander made themselves scarce in the days leading up to the ball, and Lady Pentelow encouraged them to keep as far away from the hustle and bustle in the castle as possible.

With the ball only a few days away, Rosalind was in the morning parlour checking the guest list when Patterson interrupted her to announce the arrival of Sir Michael Greystone. For a moment she was tempted to refuse to see him, but she could hear his voice in the great hall and she knew he would not give up easily. They had not met since their last encounter when she returned Gypsy to the stables and for that she was grateful, but she knew that she could not put him off for ever. She might have refused his offer of marriage, but she had a feeling that Sir Michael had not taken her seriously. Perhaps he thought that it was a female tactic to tantalise and tease him, when in fact she had meant every word. She hesitated: the temptation to refuse to see him was overwhelming.

Chapter Nineteen

Rosalind sighed. 'All right, Patterson,' she said wearily. 'Please show him in.'

'Very good, Miss Rosalind.' Patterson left, returning moments later to usher Sir Michael into the room.

'Ah, Rosalind, my dear, I'm so glad I caught you at home. You must be extremely busy with all the arrangements for the ball. My girls tell me that it's going to be the talk of the county.'

'Won't you take a seat, Sir Michael? As you can see I *am* rather busy at the moment.' Rosalind waved her hand vaguely over the pile of acceptances and the lists she had been checking.

'I'll come straight to the point then, my dear. I want you to keep the first dance for me, and the last one, also. I realise that there will be plenty of young gentlemen wishing to mark you card, so I wanted to be the first.'

'I really haven't thought about it in such detail, sir. The dance cards haven't yet arrived from the printer, so I'm afraid I can't oblige at the moment.'

'I'm sure you won't forget. After all, we have a special relationship, Rosalind. You must admit that.'

She rose to her feet. 'Would you like some refreshment, Sir Michael? I'll ring for a servant.'

He smiled. 'There is such a difference now that Lady Pentelow is in residence. Gone are the dreadful days when I used to find you exhausted and careworn from doing the menial work in the castle. I must congratulate her ladyship on helping you to right the wrongs of the past.'

'I'm sorry, sir. What do you mean by that?' Rosalind paused with her fingers clutching the embroidered silk of the bell pull.

'I simply mean that Rockwood had a certain reputation many years ago. It might have been gossip but it was rumoured that the castle was a hideaway for the spoils of the smuggling gangs.'

'That's just village gossip, Sir Michael.'

'Perhaps, but times have changed. However, I have to be aware of these things. If I am to succeed as a politician I cannot have a wife whose family connections were not quite the thing, if you follow my meaning?'

'Perfectly, sir. Now perhaps you would like to

leave me to complete my task? I have a great deal to do in a very short time.'

'I'm sure a few minutes won't make any difference, Rosalind. I was hoping to make Lady Pentelow's acquaintance before the ball. After all, we are close neighbours.'

'I'm afraid she's rather busy this morning . . .' Rosalind turned her head at the sound of the door opening and Lady Pentelow sailed into the parlour.

'Where are those lists, Rosalind?' She came to a halt, staring at Sir Michael with ill-disguised curiosity. 'I'm sorry, my dear. I didn't realise you were entertaining a guest.'

'Lady Pentelow, may I introduce Sir Michael Greystone of Greystone Park. He is our closest neighbour.'

'And friend,' Sir Michael added, bowing over Lady Pentelow's proffered hand. 'It's a pleasure to meet you, ma'am. I'm sure that Rosalind has told you about our plans for the future.'

Rosalind held her breath. The temptation to deny his claim was overwhelming, but she could hardly call him a liar in front of Lady Pentelow. She bit her lip and clenched her hands at her sides.

Lady Pentelow remained aloof. 'Really, sir? Rosalind told me that she had refused your offer of marriage.'

'But young ladies do that, don't they, ma'am? I believe it is usual to show a degree of reticence in such cases'

'What makes you think that you are special, Sir Michael? I don't know you, but I can see that you are a great deal older than Rosalind, and furthermore she doesn't seem to like you.'

'I – I didn't say that exactly,' Rosalind said hurriedly. 'Sir Michael was very supportive during our difficulties.'

'And now he wants his reward.' Lady Pentelow looked him up and down, shaking her head. 'Take my advice, sir. Find a woman closer in years to yourself – a respectable widow, perhaps. I understand that you have daughters of a similar age to Rosalind.'

Sir Michael's thin cheeks flushed angrily. 'I beg your pardon, Lady Pentelow, but this has nothing to do with you.'

'Oh, but it has, sir. My grandson is heir to the Rockwood estate and Sir Lucien has given me permission to take on the duties that would normally fall to Rosalind's parents. I would certainly advise her to think very carefully before marrying a man old enough to be her father, especially one who keeps a mistress in Exeter, and has also enjoyed a long-standing relationship with a married woman.'

'That is none of your business, ma'am.' Sir Michael's voice shook with anger and the colour drained from his face. 'If you were a man . . .'

'If I were a man, Sir Michael, I would take you by the scruff of your neck and throw you out.'

'If word of this gets out I'll sue you for slander.'

'If this becomes public property you won't stand

a chance of being elected to Parliament, Sir Michael. I think we understand each other – now leave us.'

Sir Michael made for the door. 'I'm a very wealthy man, Lady Pentelow. I could ruin you if I chose to do so.'

'Empty words, Sir Michael. Please close the door on your way out.'

He rushed from the room, slamming the door behind him.

'You were magnificent, Lady Pentelow.' Rosalind gazed at her in admiration. 'But how did you know all those things?'

Lady Pentelow shrugged. 'It was a lucky guess. I've moved in society for a long time, Rosalind. Nothing surprises me nowadays. Now let me have a look at those lists. I think we can safely cross off Sir Michael and his daughters, don't you?'

'Patsy will be sorry. She likes Christina and Sylvia.'

'She has Aurelia for company now,' Lady Pentelow said airily. 'They are exploring the cellars and dungeons as we speak. Anyway, I understand from Simms, who has been seeking information for me, that Christina and Sylvia are good-looking young women, no doubt with large dowries. I would rather not put temptation in Hugo Knighton's way.'

After the tense moments with Sir Michael, Rosalind began to relax and she laughed. 'Lady Pentelow, you are a wicked woman.'

'Yes, I am rather,' Lady Pentelow said, smiling. 'One day women might have a say in how the world is run, but I have learned how to manipulate matters so that they go my way. Now, let's check who has accepted and who cannot attend the ball.'

Despite the fact that Sir Michael had placed her in an almost impossible position, Rosalind could not help feeling a little sorry for the way that Lady Pentelow had cut him down to size. He deserved it, of course, but in the past his generosity in buying their crops at an inflated price had kept them going through a long hard winter. The worst of it was that she would now have to explain to her sister why Christina and Sylvia were not on the guest list. Her opportunity came at midday when it was time for luncheon. Rosalind entered the dining room to find Patricia and Aurelia, already seated at the table.

'Where is everyone?' Rosalind asked, looking round at the empty chairs.

'Lady Pentelow is too busy to join us.' Patricia said with a wry smile.

'Grandmama is obsessed with preparations for the ball,' Aurelia added, sighing. 'She talks about nothing else.'

Rosalind turned her head as Walter strolled into the room and took his seat. 'Where are the others? Have you seen Bertie recently, Walter?'

He reached for his napkin and shook it out with a flick of his hand. 'They're probably in the Black Dog. That's where they go after a morning's hunting or fishing. It's not what I enjoy.'

Rosalind smiled and produced a sealed letter from her pocket. 'This came for you today, Walter. I wonder if it's from Cambridge University.'

Walter leaned across the table and snatched it from her hand. 'I'm not sure I can break the seal, Rosie. What if they have refused me entry?'

Patricia snatched it from him and opened it before thrusting it back into his hand. 'Read it, you noodle.'

Walter unfolded the paper and read it in silence. He looked up. 'I'm in, Rosie. I start at the beginning of the Michaelmas term.'

Patricia leaped up and hugged him. 'Well done. You're a clever noodle after all.'

Rosalind laughed and blew him a kiss. 'Yes, congratulations, Walter. It's well deserved.'

'I agree,' Aurelia said, smiling. 'To be honest, Walter. I thought all that reading and studying was a waste of time, but it seems that I was wrong.'

'You've made him blush,' Patricia said, giggling.

'Don't tease him, Patsy.' Rosalind sent her a warning glance as the door opened and Tilly struggled in carrying a large tureen. 'Put it on the table in front of me, Tilly. I'll serve as there are only four of us.' Rosalind gave her an encouraging smile. 'Thank you, Tilly.' She ladled soup into a bowl and passed it to Aurelia. 'You have a cobweb in your hair. I hope there isn't a spider lurking in there.'

Aurelia almost dropped the bowl as she jumped to her feet. 'No, take it off me, Patsy. I can't bear spiders.'

Patricia stood up and obliged. 'It's just a little cobweb, silly.'

Rosalind served the others and herself with soup and replaced the ladle in the tureen. 'Enjoy the soup, it smells delicious. Anyway, what were you two doing in the cellars?'

'Dungeons,' Patricia said, toying with her spoon. 'They might be wine cellars now, but they were dungeons a long time ago. I'm sure we heard someone groaning. That's why we came back so quickly.'

'You mean it's haunted?' Walter asked, laughing. 'Nonsense, Patsy. It's your imagination.'

'You weren't there,' she said crossly. 'We heard it, didn't we, Aurelia? It was groaning, as if someone was in agony.'

'Then you should keep away from the dungeons from now on. Concentrate on helping with the preparations for the ball. Which reminds me, Patsy, we have to go to Exeter tomorrow morning for final fittings for our gowns. Oh, and I'm afraid that Christina and Sylvia won't be attending the ball.' Rosalind eyed her sister warily, waiting for her reaction.

'That's a shame,' Patricia said casually. 'Never mind, I believe Sir Michael is planning to outdo Lady Pentelow. That's what Christina said when I last saw her. We'll be receiving invitations to a garden party at Greystone Park with fireworks in the evening and dancing under the stars.'

Rosalind was left speechless. Once again Sir Michael had forestalled any attempt to put him in his place. He was the undisputed leader of local society and he was determined to hold on to that position. Lady Pentelow might attempt to unseat him, but Rosalind suspected that her ladyship might have met her match.

They had just finished their soup and Tilly had brought in a platter of cold meat and pickles together with a basket of freshly baked bread rolls and a dish of butter, when Alexander breezed into the dining room. He sat down next to Rosalind.

'I hoped I'd be in time to join you for luncheon, Rosie. I left the others in the Black Dog, where they're likely to remain for the rest of the afternoon.'

Rosalind greeted him with a smile. 'Tilly has just removed the tureen of soup but I can ring for her to bring it back.'

He shook his head. 'No, thank you. This looks splendid.' He turned his attention to his sister. 'Aurelia, is that a spider's web in your hair?'

She leaped to her feet. 'You said I'd removed it all, Patsy.'

Patricia shrugged. 'You'll have to look in a mirror. Most of it's gone.'

Aurelia ran from the room, leaving the door to swing shut.

'She's afraid of spiders,' Patricia said casually. 'I'm more scared of ghosts.'

Rosalind met Alexander's puzzled look with a

sigh. 'They've been trying to find the oubliette, which they think is in the cellars somewhere. Patsy says she heard groaning, but I told her that there are no such things as ghosts.'

'Then you don't know the story of the white lady who rides her grey mare through the streets of Rockwood at midnight on St Agnes' Eve,' Alexander said mysteriously. 'I heard it just now at the inn. An old man was telling the story of Marianne Carey, who, on the night before St Agnes' Day, followed the ancient rituals, by which she hoped to dream of her future husband. But something happened in that dark tower room,' he lowered his voice as Aurelia rejoined them and sat down beside Patricia. 'You should listen carefully, girls. Poor Marianne dreamed of her lover and in her sleep she walked out onto the battlements and fell into his arms – only he was just a figment of her imagination and she fell to her death. Now her ghost is seen before any tragedy in the Carey family.'

Patricia's face paled alarmingly and she clutched her hands to her heart. 'It must have been Marianne crying out that we heard, Aurelia.'

'I don't believe in spirits,' Aurelia said uncertainly. 'You're making it up, Alex.'

'I'm not, am I, Rosie? You must know the family story.'

'It's just a silly legend that grew up after Marianne Carey died in a tragic accident one winter's night in January a couple of centuries ago. I believe she

360

was jilted at the altar and some say she threw herself off the battlements, but it's just a story. You shouldn't scare them, Alexander.'

He laughed. 'It was worth it to see their faces. Of course it's just a folk tale. Forget what I said.'

'I won't sleep tonight.' Patricia pushed her plate away. 'I'm not hungry.'

'Alex is just saying it to scare us,' Aurelia said hesitantly. 'He's a wretch.'

Alexander reached for the plate of cold meat and helped himself. 'All right, I was teasing you, and to show that your fears are groundless I suggest we go down to the cellars as soon as we've finished our meal. I'll prove that it was just your imagination and there's nothing to fear.'

'But you just told us about Marianne's ghost,' Patricia protested tearfully.

'It's just a legend, as I said.' Rosalind shook her head. 'Look what you've started now, Alexander.'

'You'll come with us, won't you, Rosie?' Alexander said, smiling.

'I shouldn't humour you, but I will, if it puts a stop to this silly story.'

An hour later, armed with lanterns, they followed Alexander down the stone steps that led to what had once been dungeons, but for the last couple of centuries had been used to store wine and barrels of ale. Rosalind had not ventured into the bowels of the castle since she was a child, but the pervading smell of must and dampness brought back memories of being tormented by Bertie when she had shown fear. Bertie, of course, was afraid of nothing, unlike Walter, who had refused to accompany them. Walter lived in his imagination and had been prone to nightmares as a child. Rosalind remembered comforting him when he awakened in the night, screaming in fear after a bad dream. Bertie always slept well, untroubled by such fancies. Rosalind clutched the lantern in her hand, stepping carefully over the roughly hewn rock floor as they went deeper. The first cellar was lined with wine racks and the second with stands for barrels of beer and cider, which had only recently been filled. It was cold in the cellars and Rosalind felt the chill seeping into her bones. Stories of prisoners incarcerated here long ago had always appalled her, and even more so now. She could imagine them shackled to the stone walls and it would be easy to think that the odd sounds below ground level were caused by souls in torment. She hurried after Alexander, who had taken the lead. Patricia and Aurelia hung back, following at a distance.

They came to a halt where there seemed to be a narrow passage leading off the main chamber. Rosalind was certain she could feel a cold draught of air.

'I've never been this far before, Alex,' she said warily. 'Perhaps we should go back now.'

He turned, holding the lantern high above his

head. 'Can you feel that gust of air? It smells of the sea.'

She shook her head. 'There must been seawater seeping up underground. We can't be too far from the cliffs.'

'I'm going further. Are you coming?'

'I don't like it, Alex. What's that noise?' Patricia reached out to clutch Rosalind's hand. 'Let's go back now. I really do think this place is haunted.'

Aurelia gave her a none-too-gentle shove. 'Don't be a ninny. Maybe this goes to the beach. Perhaps it was used by smugglers. Trevenor certainly was involved in that particular trade.'

Alexander laughed. 'Don't give away family secrets, Aurelia. Anyway, I'm going on. You can follow me if you're brave enough.'

'I'm not going down there,' Aurelia said firmly. 'You must be mad.'

'I'm never coming down here again.' Patricia grabbed Aurelia by the hand and dragged her away. 'I didn't really believe in Marianne's ghost until now. Let's go back, Aurelia.'

'You two can do what you wish.' Rosalind was not going to admit defeat. 'I'm coming, Alex,' she said firmly.

She followed him, but it was easier said than done as the ground was very rough and uneven and the passage was narrow. Alexander had to inch his way between the rough sandstone walls, and it was hard to imagine smugglers hefting barrels of spirits and sacks of tea or bales of silk in such a confined space. It was as much as Rosalind could do to keep her footing as the rock beneath her feet was slippery and the walls were running with water. The further they went, the harder the going and a rhythmic throbbing sound, like the beating of a heart, grew louder as they progressed. The air was fresher as the passage widened and she realised that it was the crashing of waves on the foreshore that they could hear echoing off the rock walls.

Alex came to a sudden halt. 'We've reached the end,' he said triumphantly. 'Who would have thought that the cellars led directly to the beach?'

Rosalind looked round in amazement as she made her way to the mouth of the cave. She stepped outside and took deep breaths of the clean, salty air, shielding her eyes from the brilliance of the sun. 'So the stories are true about Rockwood being in league with the free traders.'

'They could be, Rosie. But the passage must have been excavated a long time ago. It might have been an escape route in case of siege. I imagine the castle has seen quite a few skirmishes in its time.'

Rosalind paced the damp sand, gazing up at the overhanging cliff and the rocks below, standing proud like sentries at the mouth of the cave. This was where she and Bertie had often played when they were children. Once again she experienced a sudden flash of memory of this expanse of beach on a dark night long ago. In her mind's eye she could see a ship in the bay and a jolly boat being dragged ashore.

'Are you all right, Rose?' Alexander asked anxiously. 'You look a bit pale.'

She shook her head. 'I'm fine. Maybe we ought to get back to the castle before Patsy raises the alarm. She probably thinks we've been scared to death by Marianne's ghost.'

'It would take more than that to scare a man of the 32nd Foot,' Alexander said with a wry smile. 'But it wasn't very pleasant in the tunnel. Is there a footpath up to the top of the cliffs?'

'Yes. We used to come here often in the summer, and in the winter, come to that. Bertie and I used to spend most of our free time down here. I'll lead the way.'

They arrived back in the castle bailey to find Piers waiting for them and Rosalind could see from his taut expression that he was not happy.

'What the hell did you think you were doing, Alex?' Piers demanded angrily.

'We found a secret passage and it took us to the foreshore. Why the grim face, old boy?' Alexander slapped his brother on the back. 'No harm came to either of us.'

'That passage should have been blocked off years ago. I'll make sure it's done without delay.'

'Just a minute, Piers.' Rosalind was puzzled by his attitude and she had no intention of allowing him to interfere in the running of her home. 'You have no right to make such a decision. You might be the heir to Rockwood but while Grandpapa is alive he is the head of the house.'

'You're right, of course. But the tunnel is probably dangerous and a rock fall would kill anyone foolish enough to negotiate it. That includes you, Alex. As a soldier you should know better than to expose Rosalind to danger.'

'Come on, Piers. There wasn't any risk that I could see and we're unharmed. Maybe you should inspect the passage yourself before you make such rash pronouncements.' Alex turned to Rosalind. 'Thank you for coming with me, Rosie. You're a woman after my own heart, and I mean that.'

Rosalind realised that she was blushing and she laughed. 'It was nothing, Alex. I enjoy a challenge, and I'm glad we explored the tunnel.' She shot a resentful glance in Piers' direction. 'This is still my home, Piers. I'll thank you to remember that you and your family are our guests. I assume you will be eager to get back to Trevenor if you can oust Blaise.'

'That's what I wanted to tell you. I think I might have to return to Cornwall after the ball. I want to make a deal with Blaise.'

'Can you do that while he's threatening to expose your family secrets?'

'Everyone has their price. I'm not a poor man and some things are more important than money. I'd give my last penny to see my grandmother back in her rightful home.'

'Maybe she would like to accompany Patsy and myself to Exeter tomorrow,' Rosalind suggested tentatively. 'We're going for our final fittings for new ball gowns, but it would be a day out for Lady Pentelow.'

Piers shook his head. 'I think you'll find she's too involved in her preparations for the ball. I was thinking I might take Bertie to enrol at the Royal Military Academy, but he told me that he's changed his mind. He would rather enlist and work his way through the ranks.'

Rosalind smiled. 'That sounds like Bertie.'

'I heard that the 46th Regiment of Foot were recruiting in Exeter,' Alexander said casually. 'I'd be happy to accompany Bertie there tomorrow, if he so wishes.'

'Maybe we could travel together, Alex?' Rosalind glanced at Piers, who was still stony-faced. 'Unless you have any objections, of course, Piers.'

'As you said, you are in charge here, Rosalind. It really hasn't anything to do with me.' Piers walked off in the direction of the stables, leaving her staring after him.

'I've upset him.'

Alexander laid a sympathetic hand on her arm. 'He'll get over it. That's one good thing about my brother – he doesn't hold a grudge. You put him in his place, which is something that he's unaccustomed to. It won't do him any harm.'

Rosalind watched Piers striding off and she was not convinced. But the prospect of a day out in Exeter was exciting, even if it was only to visit the dressmaker. She glanced at Alexander and saw understanding and sympathy in his eyes and she grasped his hand. 'Thank you for everything, Alex. I'm glad that Bertie has you as a friend.'

Chapter Twenty

Despite her argument with Piers, Rosalind was not going to allow their differences to spoil a day out in Exeter. Aurelia had wanted to accompany them but Lady Pentelow insisted that her granddaughter should stay and keep her company. Aurelia grumbled a little, but gave in with reasonably good grace when Rosalind told her that a trip to the dressmaker was really unexciting, and she would find a visit to a recruiting station even more boring.

Next morning, Rosalind, Patricia, Bertie and Alexander travelled to Exeter in the Blanchards' carriage, driven by Corbin, Lady Pentelow's coachman. Rosalind sat back against the padded velvet squabs enjoying the sheer luxury of being driven. It was so different from her last trip to town when she had handled the reins, driving the ancient chaise with Ajax in harness. She felt quite grand and she was aware of the curious stares of the villagers as they drove through Rockwood, heading north.

Bertie spent most of the journey asking Alexander questions about how he should present himself to the recruitment officer, and then he wanted to know what he might expect during his first few days as an enlisted man. Alexander answered candidly, describing some of the discomforts and difficulties that any new recruit would face, but Bertie remained undaunted. If she were in a similar situation Rosalind knew that she would have changed her mind about joining the army, and she could see that Patsy was equally dismayed, but Bertie was a grown man; he could decide for himself. In fact, the worse that life in the army sounded, the more enthusiastic he grew. Whatever his faults, Rosalind had to admit that her brother was never one to stand down from a challenge.

They stopped first at the dressmaker's terraced house in a back street.

'I'll meet you here in an hour,' Alexander said cheerfully. 'Whether I bring Bertie with me or not is a different matter. He's so keen to enlist that he might decide to join right away.'

'You'd better not do that, Bertie.' Rosalind shook her head. 'I want you to help out at the ball. We need plenty of dance partners to take care of the young ladies.'

'Alex is exaggerating, don't worry, Rosie,' Bertie

said casually. 'I'll be there to help out at the ball, I promise.'

Patricia alighted first, followed by Rosalind. 'I wouldn't say anything to Bertie, but I wish he'd accepted Piers' offer to take him to the Military Academy to train as an officer,' Rosalind said in a low voice. 'The enlisted men are always at the forefront when there's danger.'

'Bertie will love that. You worry too much, Rosie.' Patricia crossed the pavement to knock on the door. 'I do hope that Hugo attends the ball. Aurelia will be heartbroken if he doesn't. The Knightons did accept, didn't they?'

'Yes, they did. How many times do I have to tell you that? They're staying with the Mountjoys.'

'I know, and I wish they'd decided to come to us instead. Dorcas Mountjoy has already had a London season, and her father gives her a huge dress allowance. Aurelia will be outshone by her.'

'Don't be silly,' Rosalind said sharply. 'Hugo only had eyes for Aurelia when we were at Knighton Hall. I doubt if he'll have changed in such a short time, but if he's so fickle she's better off without him.' Rosalind turned quickly as the door opened. 'Ah, Mrs Brewer, good morning. I hope we're not too early.'

Meggie Brewer opened the door wider. 'No, of course not, Miss Carey. You'll have to forgive the mess, but I've only just got the baby off to sleep and my Eliza has been a bit of a pickle this morning.'

As she spoke a toddler rushed past her and would have run into the street if Rosalind had not caught her by the hand. She picked the child up and carried her into the narrow hallway. 'We can't have that now, can we, poppet? Close the door, Patsy. She might try to escape again if I put her down.'

Eliza chuckled and tugged at Rosalind's bonnet strings.

'Don't be a naughty girl, Eliza,' Meggie said wearily. 'The young ladies don't want to play with you. Put her down, Miss Rosalind. She'll amuse herself, like as not.'

Rosalind kept hold of the wriggling toddler. 'I'll keep Eliza occupied while Patsy tries on her gown, and Patsy will do the same while I have my final fitting.'

Neither Patsy nor Meggie looked convinced, but Rosalind sat the child firmly on her hip and followed Meggie into the front parlour.

An hour later, their gowns safely wrapped in butter muslin, Rosalind and Patricia sat in the front parlour waiting for the carriage to arrive. Eliza seemed to have decided that Rosalind was her best friend and she was sitting on the floor at her feet, playing with the laces on Rosalind's boots.

Patricia jumped to her feet. 'They're here.' She made for the door, leaving Rosalind to cope with Eliza and the ball gowns.

Meggie snatched up Eliza, holding her firmly.

'You'd better go quickly, Miss Rosalind. My Eliza won't like it that you've gone – she'll bawl her eyes out.'

As if on cue, Eliza opened her mouth and began to wail.

'The gowns are beautiful, Meggie. Thank you for all your hard work.' Rosalind struggled through the doorway, laden with yards and yards of butter muslin and silk, but Patricia breezed on ahead of her. Rosalind came to a halt, staring in surprise as she recognised Hugo Knighton standing beside Bertie and Alex.

'Look who we bumped into in town, Rosie,' Bertie said, grinning.

'Are you here on your own, Hugo?' Patricia eyed him hopefully. 'Your mama isn't with you?'

'No, I am allowed out unescorted occasionally.' Hugo took her hand and raised it to his lips. 'It's a pleasure to see you again, Patsy.' He shot a glance in Rosalind's direction. 'And you, too, Miss Carey. We're looking forward to attending the ball at Rockwood Castle.'

'It's a pleasant surprise seeing you today, Hugo. Please give my regards to your parents.' Rosalind passed the gowns to the footman, who stowed them carefully in the trunk that was attached to the back of the carriage.

'I will, of course. Might I have the pleasure of your company at luncheon? The White Hart was recommended to me by someone who knows the city well.'

'That would be lovely,' Patricia said quickly.

'I'm starving,' Bertie added. 'I could eat the proverbial horse. Joining up gives one an appetite.'

'You've enlisted, Bertie?' Rosalind made an attempt to sound pleased but she could not quite keep a note of anxiety from her voice.

Bertie gave her a quick hug. 'Don't worry, Rosie. I'll be fine. Alexander has told me what to expect and I'm prepared for anything. Besides which, I'm not going for a week or two, so I'll be there to partner the wallflowers at the ball.'

Patricia slapped him on the wrist. 'Don't be unkind, Bertie. I suppose it's all right for men to stand round chatting and drinking at such an occasion, but if a girl chooses to sit and rest for a while she's considered to be a wallflower.'

'Never mind that. Let's walk to the White Hart,' Bertie said impatiently. 'Alex, you can tell the coachman to meet us there in a couple of hours.' He strode off, Hugo and Patricia hurrying after him.

Rosalind was about to follow them when Alexander caught her by the hand. 'Shall we allow them to make a happy threesome? Come for a stroll with me, Rosalind.'

She stared at him surprise. 'We can't abandon them.'

'Why not?' Alexander met her anxious gaze with a smile. 'They won't miss us. Look, they're oblivious to the fact that we haven't moved from the spot.'

'But I should go with them to chaperone my sister.'

'She has Bertie to keep an eye on her, and I don't think she is in any danger from Knighton. I would enjoy some time alone with you.'

'That would make tongues wag. Not that I'm very well known in Exeter, but it would be my luck to bump into someone who might recognise me.'

Alexander laughed. 'Are you saying that you need a chaperone, Rosie?'

'I can take care of myself, but you know how people talk.' She eyed him curiously. 'Or perhaps you don't. I keep forgetting that you've spent so much time abroad.'

'That's true, but I did grow up in Trevenor. I know what you mean, but what harm can it do for us to take a walk to the cathedral or down to the river? We'll meet up again with the others when we're ready, and then we'll travel home together. No one will ever know.'

His smile was irresistible and she found herself laughing with him. 'You win, Alexander.'

'Alex, please. As we're playing truant we can drop the formalities.' Alexander tucked her hand in the crook of his arm. 'Corbin, you may walk the horses. We'll meet up at the White Hart in a couple of hours.'

'Are you always this impulsive?' Rosalind asked as they set off in the direction of the Cathedral Close.

'I am when it suits me. I'd like to get to know

you better, and it's virtually impossible at home. You're always surrounded by family or servants, and I never get a chance.'

She chuckled. 'Well, you have my full attention now.'

'Why do you put up with us, Rosie? I mean, the Blanchards have foisted themselves upon you. I love my grandmother dearly, but she is not the easiest person in the world to deal with and she is used to getting her own way.'

'I think she's an amazing lady,' Rosalind said earnestly. 'My grandmama died some years ago, and my mother is rarely at home. I appreciate what Lady Pentelow has done for Rockwood.'

'And you don't resent her in the least?'

'No, why should I? This situation is not of our making. I'm sorry that Bertie won't inherit the estate, but in reality he will be far happier in the military. You of all people must understand that.'

Alexander patted her hand as it lay on his sleeve. 'You are a much better person than I, Rosie. Any other woman would resent Grandmama taking charge as she does, and you have such patience with Aurelia.'

'I've had plenty of practice with my sister, so Aurelia is quite easy. At least she doesn't want to marry a man who is about to wed someone else, especially when the bride is with child.' She held up her hand as he turned to give her a quizzical look. 'Don't ask for details. Piers knows all about it. In fact, he helped me to save Patsy from making a terrible mistake.'

'That leads me to my brother. You might be forgiven for hating Piers. He turned up uninvited and claimed the home you thought was your birthright.'

'That's true, but he also saved Rockwood from bankruptcy. If Piers hadn't come along when he did we might be living in a fisherman's cottage, if we were lucky.'

'I see.' Alexander was silent as they walked down a narrow alley that opened into the Cathedral Close. 'There's a nice-looking hotel. Shall we have luncheon? You must be hungry by now.'

'I am rather, but wouldn't it be rather public? I mean, if your grandmama found out she would be very angry.'

'That makes it all the more exciting. We'll flout convention and have luncheon together, unchaperoned apart from all the other guests and the hotel staff.'

Rosie giggled. 'It does sound rather silly when you put it like that.'

'I've made you laugh. That makes our little jaunt worthwhile. You take everything too seriously, Rosie. But while you're with me you'll find life much more amusing, or so I hope.'

They walked arm in arm to the hotel where the doorman tipped his hat to Alexander, and then the manager himself greeted them with a friendly smile.

'Good afternoon, Captain Blanchard. It's good to see you again, sir.'

'Thank you, Sanderson. We'd like a table for two for luncheon.'

'Of course, Captain. Follow me, if you please.' The manager led them past the reception desk, waving aside the head waiter, to a table by a window with a splendid view of the cathedral. A signal from him caused a flurry of activity amongst the waiters and a wine list was brought, together with menus.

'If there is anything more I can do for you, Captain Blanchard, please don't hesitate to call on my services.' The manager made his way between the tables, pausing occasionally to speak to some of the guests.

'They seem to know you very well.' Rosalind studied the menu. 'You must be a regular visitor.'

'Piers is here more often that I am, but we've made a habit of breaking the journey when we travel to London. It's convenient to stay here overnight and travel on by train next morning. Now then, what would you like to eat?'

The food was excellent and the wine that Alexander selected was rich and fruity, but after a second glass Rosalind decided that she had better not drink any more. Alexander kept her amused with anecdotes of army life, which she suspected he adapted so that they were more suitable to be related in company. Even so, she had never laughed so much. She was aware that people were staring, but nothing seemed to matter when she was with Alexander. However, time passed so quickly that they had to finish their meal and hurry to join the others at the White Hart. They arrived, slightly breathless and still laughing at one of Alexander's comments, to find the carriage waiting outside the inn. Bertie was frowning ominously and Patricia was looking sulky, despite the fact that Hugo was still in attendance.

'Where have you two been?' Bertie demanded angrily. 'One minute you were following us, and then you disappeared.'

'Yes, Rosie. If I'd done that you would have been furious,' Patricia added.

'Well, we're here now.' Alexander greeted her with a beaming smile. 'I've been entertaining you sister to luncheon, Patsy. Surely you don't mind her having a little time to enjoy herself?'

'We were worried,' Bertie insisted. 'Corbin told us you had gone off together, but that's not the point.'

'Don't be so stuffy, Bertie.' Rosalind met Hugo's curious look with a smile. 'I'm sorry, Hugo. It was rude of us to walk away without a word.'

He inclined his head. 'If I were Alexander I would have done the same, Miss Carey. As it is, we enjoyed a splendid luncheon at the inn, and I look forward to seeing you at the ball tomorrow.'

When they arrived back at the castle Rosalind went straight to her room to change out of her travelling clothes and she put on a simple cotton print gown. It was late in the afternoon and it was hot and sultry with the threat of a thunderstorm in the air. There was a stillness in the rose garden when Rosalind went to pick a few blooms for the dining table, and a strange silence, as if the birds had already taken shelter. The flower room was situated next to the scullery and she went there next to find a suitable vase, but as she crossed the yard she saw Jacob deep in conversation with Abe Coaker, which struck her as rather odd. Jacob's visits had increased in frequency to such an extent that she was beginning to question his motives. If his intention was to persuade Hester to marry him soon, he seemed to be going about it entirely the wrong way.

Rosalind filled the vase with water from the pump and went into the kitchen to arrange the flowers. As she had expected Hester was hard at work, and there was no sign of Monsieur Jacques.

'I hope you're not doing too much, Hester,' Rosalind said anxiously. 'You really should delegate some of the chores to others.'

'I do what I've always done, only now there are more mouths to feed. But don't worry, I make the Trevenor lot do the hard work.' Hester wiped her hands on her apron. 'I still have you and the admiral to look after, and Sir Lucien don't want all that foreign food. He likes my pigeon pie and rabbit stew. That chef doesn't know how to make saffron buns and splits, and he'd never heard of scones and jam and cream, the heathen.'

'You're still the best cook I know, Hester. That must be why Jacob keeps coming round. I saw him in the yard just now.'

Hester shook her head. 'I don't know what's got into the boy. It used to be once a week but lately he's been here more times than I can count. I shall have to speak very severely to him. He'll be giving me a bad name.'

'You should be flattered,' Rosalind said, smiling. 'Perhaps he's going to propose again.'

Hester sniffed. 'If he does he'll get the same answer. I'm not leaving Rockwood until my services are no longer needed. If he doesn't like it, he can find someone else to pester.'

'You know we all love you, Hester. Whatever you decide, we'll always be grateful for everything you've done for us.'

'Rockwood is my home and you are my family. Nothing will ever change that, Miss Rosalind.'

'We don't deserve you,' Rosalind said earnestly. 'Anyway, I'd better put these flowers on the table. I want you to leave the hard work to the Trevenor servants. Having the ball here was Lady Pentelow's idea, but I've made sure that there's plenty of cider and ale for the party in the servants' hall afterwards. I don't know what we're celebrating, but at least Rockwood has come alive again. I suppose that's the important thing.'

Hester nodded and a wry smile curved her generous lips. 'We've been through a lot, Miss Rosalind. We keep going somehow – it's the Carey spirit. The Blanchards can claim the castle as their own, but it's the Careys who've shed their blood for Rockwood, and the village knows that. If it came to a choice, they'd take sides with the family, and the Blanchards can go to the other place.'

'Mind what I've just said and don't change the subject, Hester. If you don't take it easy I'll be forced to change your duties so that I can keep my eye on you.'

'You can send that Mrs Witham back to Cornwall, for a start. I can't abide that woman, with her airs and graces.'

'It won't be for ever, Hester. Mr Blanchard will find a way to get Trevenor back for his family. In the meantime we'll just have to rub along as best we can.'

Rosalind kissed Hester's flushed cheek and left the kitchen before Hester had a chance to find something or someone else to grumble about. She made her way to the dining room and had just placed the vase of roses on the table when she heard footsteps behind her and she spun round to see Piers enter the room.

'I thought I saw you coming this way, Rosalind.'

'Did you want something, Piers?'

'I came to apologise for my behaviour yesterday. I shouldn't have spoken out, only I was worried that you might have had an accident. It was Aurelia's fault for insisting on exploring the cellars.'

'Patsy could have said no, but she never stops to think. Anyway, apology accepted. I might have been a bit high-handed myself.'

He smiled ruefully. 'Am I forgiven?'

'Of course. I never thought this would be easy, Piers. It's a difficult situation, and not only for us. I think the servants are finding it quite hard to adapt, too.'

'I've just seen Patricia. She could talk of nothing other than having luncheon with Hugo Knighton, which made Aurelia extremely jealous – but it seems . . .' He hesitated, eyeing her warily and she knew instantly what was coming next.

'Yes, I had a meal at the Crown Hotel with Alex. I suppose you're going to tell me that it was not the done thing. Well, maybe I have a little of my mother in me after all and I am a bit of a rebel.'

'That wasn't what I was going to say. I'm not your brother or your guardian. You may do as you please, but Alex doesn't have to live with the result of his actions. He's always been able to get away with outrageous behaviour because he goes back to his regiment and there are no repercussions.'

'You make him sound like a naughty schoolboy.'

Piers shrugged. 'He never means any harm, but he can leave a trail of disasters in his wake – a bit like the storm we might expect tonight.'

His words were tempered with a disarming

smile, but Rosalind was well aware of his under-lying warning not to expect too much from his brother. She decided it would be safer to change the subject.

'Do you know where I might find your grand-mama, Piers? I've neglected her today and, with the ball tomorrow evening, I need to find out if there are any last-minute tasks she has for me.'

'I wouldn't worry about Grandmama. She is in her element when she's organising something as complicated as entertaining on a large scale. It's very important to her that it goes well, which no doubt it will. However, she was in the blue parlour when I last saw her.'

'Thank you,' Rosalind headed for the doorway. 'I'll go and find her.'

Apart from some distant rumbles of the thunder and the flashes of summer lightning illuminating the sea, the storm did not materialise that night, but next morning it was obvious that it had not gone away and the sky above the bay was a sulphurous yellow. There was a strangely atmospheric silence when Rosalind stepped outside, and not a breath of air nor the sound of birdsong. However, there was too much to do for her to be unduly worried. The servants were busy with the final preparations for the ball, and it was Rosalind who bore the brunt of any complaints and tales of minor kitchen disas-ters.

Lady Pentelow handed the guest lists to Patterson, who went about checking everything and getting in the way of the kitchen staff, who were whipped up to a frenzy of activity by Monsieur Jacques. Hester had prepared breakfast for the family and then she retired to the still room, where she had been making face cream and distilling rose water from petals collected from the rose garden by Tilly and Ruth. Hester knew when to make herself scarce and the still room had always been her domain.

Patricia and Aurelia kept to their rooms, preparing themselves for a night of romance and dancing until dawn. Piers, Bertie and Alexander were present for breakfast and then they disappeared like the morning mist. Rosalind could only imagine that they had gone fishing, or more likely would be found in the Black Dog. She hoped that the storm would miss them when it eventually made its way inland, and that the heavens would not suddenly open as the guests were arriving in the evening.

There was a time in the late afternoon when she thought that the final preparations would never be finished in time, but by some miracle the rain held off and the servants were at their stations, ready to wait upon the guests. The members of the orchestra had arrived earlier and were assembled in the ballroom, resplendent in their evening suits.

Sir Lucien, who had found out about the entertainment and insisted on being included, had donned his uniform, complete with medals, but Rosalind had managed to persuade him to remain in his room until everyone had arrived. She left Jarvis with instructions to make sure that his charge did not escape before it was time for him to make an appearance.

After a final check with Patterson to ensure that all was well in the kitchens, Rosalind went to her room to change into her ball gown. She did her hair in a simple chignon and studded it with rosebuds she had picked in the garden. There was no time to ask for Patricia's approval and Rosalind hurried downstairs to join Lady Pentelow, who was waiting in the entrance hall to greet the guests.

'You may stand next to Piers,' Lady Pentelow said firmly. 'I will greet the guests, then Piers and then you, Rosalind.'

This arrangement unsettled Rosalind at first, suspecting that people would assume that she and Piers were a couple, but he seemed to sense her fears and he moved to stand on his grandmother's right.

'What are you doing, Piers?' Lady Pentelow demanded in a low voice as the first guests were ushered into the hall by Patterson.

'You don't want people to think that Rosalind and I are engaged, do you, Grandmama?'

Rosalind smothered a giggle at the alarmed expression on Lady Pentelow's face.

'You're right, Piers. Stay where you are.'

He glanced at Rosalind and she was certain that he winked, although his attention was diverted by the arrival of Lord and Lady Knighton, together with Hugo, and close behind them the Mountjoy family, including their beautiful and talented daughter, Dorcas. Rosalind greeted them all with a smile, but she could imagine the dismay that both Aurelia and Patsy would feel when they saw the stunning gown that Dorcas was wearing. It must have been designed in London or Paris, and with her dark beauty, Dorcas was an exotic peacock amongst a flock of sparrows. She clung to Hugo's arm, acknowledging people with a gracious nod and a smile as if she were a princess. If Christina and Sylvia Greystone had been invited they would have cut the young lady down to size, but a glance at Aurelia's face was enough to convince Rosalind that there might be tears and tantrums later that evening.

When the last guest had been welcomed, Lady Pentelow made her stately way to the ballroom, where she signalled to the conductor to strike up the grand march.

'I think this is our dance, Rosie,' Piers said, holding out his hand.

'Rosalind promised the first dance to me.' Alexander attempted to edge his brother out of the way, but Piers stood firm.

'No, as joint hosts we are first on the floor.' Piers took Rosalind by the hand.

'I'm sorry, Alex,' Rosalind said softly. 'Piers is right, but I'll save the waltz for you.'

Alexander faced up to his brother. 'You have no

right to do that, Piers. Rosalind is free to choose her partner.'

'It's all right, Alex,' Rosalind said hastily. 'I don't mind.'

'But I do.' Alex clenched his fists. 'Stand down, Piers. I'm not giving in to you this time.'

'You're making a fool of yourself,' Piers said in a low voice. 'The orchestra are waiting.'

'Let them wait. This is my dance. I will lead Rosie onto the floor.'

At that moment Sir Lucien rushed into the ball room, his medal jingling together on his dress uniform. He waved his tricorn hat. 'Ship spotted to starboard. Every man on deck. We're being invaded.'

Chapter Twenty-One

A sudden silence fell on the assembled guests, servants and the members of the orchestra. Everyone stared in bewilderment, as if wondering whether this was some sort of entertainment, but Sir Lucien's continued calls to arms were undoubtedly genuine, and when Piers attempted to restrain him Sir Lucien struggled frantically.

'We're being invaded, I tell you. Let me go, you fool.'

Alexander grabbed his flailing arm. 'We'd better get him out of here, Piers.'

'Do as your brother suggests,' Lady Pentelow said faintly. 'He needs to be given something to calm him down.'

'Jarvis.' Rosalind rushed to the doorway, beckoning frantically to him. 'We need to get Sir Lucien back to his quarters.'

'I'm sorry, Miss Rosalind. I tried to stop him.'

'I know you did. He can be very wily.' Rosalind turned to see Piers and Alexander dragging a protesting Sir Lucien from the ballroom. 'Please take him back to his room. I was hoping he might have enjoyed seeing so many people and it would have taken him back to a happier time, but it seems that I was wrong.'

'There's just one thing, Miss Rosalind.' Jarvis lowered his voice. 'Sir Lucien was right about one thing, there is a ship moored in Smugglers' Cove, just as they used to be in the old days.'

Rosalind was about to question him further when she saw Jacob standing awkwardly in the middle of the entrance hall. In all the years that Jacob Lidstone had been courting Hester, he had never ventured into this part of the house, and he ought not to be here now.

'I'll leave my grandfather in your capable hands, Jarvis,' she said hastily. 'Jacob?' She walked purposefully towards him. 'Is anything wrong?'

He avoided meeting her gaze. 'Begging your pardon, Miss Rosalind. I've come to see Mr Blanchard.'

'As you can see, we have a slight problem. My grandfather has been taken ill. Won't it wait until morning?'

'No, miss. It's urgent.'

Rosalind glanced over her shoulder, but it seemed that Piers was aware of Jacob's presence and he was heading towards them. Jarvis and Alexander had Sir

Lucien more or less under control and they helped him up the grand staircase.

'It's all right, Rosalind,' Piers said with an attempt at a smile. 'I'll deal with this.'

'What's going on, Piers?' Rosalind said in a low voice. 'Jacob has confirmed what Grandpapa said in the ballroom.'

'Let me speak to Jacob. I'll handle whatever is going on and I promise you there'll be no more interruptions. Go back and enjoy the ball.' He strode over to where Jacob was waiting, without giving her a chance to question him further.

Rosalind eyed them curiously. There was something going on and she was not going to be dismissed and sent back to the ballroom. If Piers would not tell her then she was determined to find out for herself. She could not hear what passed between Piers and Jacob as they walked away, but her suspicions were confirmed when they made for the back stairs. She followed at a safe distance, thinking perhaps they were going outside to get a better view of the ship, but they headed towards the cellar steps. The light from the lantern Jacob had taken up disappeared as he went first, followed by Piers, and Rosalind snatched a candle from one of the wall sconces. Regardless of her new ball gown, she made her way down the narrow stone stairs, her slippered feet moving noiselessly. She could hear their muted voices although she could not make out what they were saying.

It was the first time she ventured into the cellars on her own and she was tempted to turn back, but she was driven by the need to know what business Piers had with Jacob and why the news of the ship in the cove had been of such importance. The cellars were deep underground and one led into another, each one going down further until they were in the ancient dungeons. She could feel the fresh air coming from the passageway that led down to the beach, but her candle was flickering and a slight breeze might extinguish it altogether, leaving her in complete darkness. She came to a halt, waiting and listening, then realised that there was another voice, which sounded oddly familiar. She took a few small steps closer, taking care to shield the flame from her candle.

'Do I have your word on it, Blaise?'

'How many times do I have to tell you, Blanchard? Give me the hoard you discovered and you can have Trevenor back tomorrow.'

'And you'll drop your claim on Rockwood?'

'My claim is as legal as yours, old chap, which means not at all. We're both cut from the same cloth, Piers.'

'Don't liken me to yourself, Blaise. I never intended to oust the family from their home, but I needed free access.'

'Look, guvs,' Jacob's irate voice echoed off the low roof, 'it's time we wasn't here. The storm is raging outside and the tide will be on the turn shortly.

If the ship sails you'll be stuck here with the goods, Mr Blaise. If the customs men get a sniff of what we've found that'll be the end of it for all of us.'

Rosalind held her breath. She was trembling with fear and indignation. She had not trusted Piers in the beginning, and now she knew that her first impression had been correct. He had used them in his quest to find whatever valuables must have been hidden on that fateful night twelve years ago. It was rumoured then that a valuable cache of smuggled articles had been skilfully hidden, but all attempts to find it had failed. Now it appeared that Piers, Jacob and Blaise had achieved the impossible. Their voices were fading into the distance. Rosalind thought quickly. The sensible thing to do would be to return to the ballroom and raise the alarm, but they might get away and she was not going to allow that to happen. Quite how she would prevent grown men from doing what they intended was not uppermost in her mind as she edged her way into the narrow passage, following the sound of their booted feet on the stone floor. A sudden gust of air did what she had dreaded and extinguished her candle. She was left in total darkness, but the air was fresher now and she knew from experience that it was not far now to the end of the tunnel. Perhaps she could plead with Piers to hand in the cache of smuggled goods. He deserved to go to prison for his involvement in the attempt to benefit from a crime committed twelve years ago, as did Blaise and Jacob, although she did not want to break Hester's heart. Blaise could look after himself.

She emerged onto the beach, which was illuminated by a vivid flash of lightning. A wind had come from the sea, bringing with it huge waves that crashed onto the foreshore, sending flurries of spume into the night air. A rumble of thunder was followed by an even louder crash. Then in another burst of light she saw a jolly boat pitch onto the shore and two men tumbled into the surf. Piers and Jacob rushed to their aid, leaving Rosalind standing transfixed. It was a scene that brought back memories of a similar event twelve years ago and she was reliving that terrifying experience.

Then a shot rang out from the top of the cliff and there was instant confusion. One of the men from the boat took a revolver from his belt and fired back, while the others dived for cover. Another flash of sheet lightning turned night into day and this time there was nowhere to hide. Rosalind shrank back towards the mouth of the tunnel, but too late: Piers had spotted her.

'Rosalind. My God! What are you doing here?' He rushed forward, bringing her to the ground with such force that she was stunned and gasping for breath.

'Don't make a sound.' A hand clamped over her mouth and she was conscious of the warmth from Piers' body as he protected her from the exchange of shots. 'Are you hurt?'

'I don't know.'

'Keep very still, maid. I don't think they saw you.'

She was eight years old again and the strange boy was holding her close. 'It was you?'

'Hush, don't say anything. These men aren't playing games.'

'You were that boy who landed from the smugglers' ship.'

'I'll tell you everything later, Rosie. For God's sake, keep your head down.'

She closed her eyes, and laid her head against his chest. She could hear his heart thundering and she was certain that its beat matched her own, but she felt safe, despite everything that she had overheard in the cellar. All she could be certain of was that this man, who had come so unexpectedly into their lives, was none other than the boy who had saved her all those years ago. It was hard to believe that it had taken her all this time to recognise him, but the scent of his body was the same, and the strength of his arms around her was as it had been when she was a child.

The gunfire ceased and Rosalind struggled to her feet. She was too angry to be afraid. The men who had recently come ashore had jumped back into their boat and were rowing furiously for the ship, battling the waves with energy borne out of necessity.

Shouted orders from the clifftop were being ignored, and there was no sign of Blaise or Jacob. The rumbles of thunder grew less frequent and the lightning danced harmlessly off the dark surface of the sea, but then heavy drenching rain fell from the sky, soaking Rosalind to the skin in seconds. She scrambled to her feet, resisting Piers' attempts to help her. 'Don't touch me.' She had to shout to make herself heard over the sound of the wind and waves.

'Rosalind, Rosie – I can explain.'

'You've lied to me all along. I heard everything you said in the cellar. You're no better than Blaise.' She backed away from him.

'You don't understand – it's not how it seems.'

'You knew that the smugglers' cache was hidden somewhere in Rockwood and that was why you went to such lengths to make yourself indispensable. Paying off our debts was to stop us turning to Blaise, who no doubt would have done the same.'

'It wasn't like that. You must listen to me.'

'Whatever was hidden must be very valuable. You would have taken Rockwood from us and you've sacrificed your grandmother's home to satisfy your greed.'

A cry from the cliff path made Rosalind turn quickly and she saw Walter making his way towards them. 'I'm here, Walter.'

He came scrambling down to the beach, sending a shower of pebbles and mud onto the sand. 'Rosie, what the hell are you doing?' He came to a sudden halt, wiping the rain from his eyes. 'Constable Burton came to the castle and the place is running with preventive officers.'

'How did you know where I was?' Rosalind said through chattering teeth.

'When we realised you were missing Bertie sent me to find you, but this is the last place I thought you'd be. If it weren't for young Tilly having spotted you making your way to the cellars, I wouldn't have known where to start. Are you all right?'

'I'm just wet and cold.'

'The police have arrested Jacob and a few others. What's going on, Piers? Why did you allow Rosie to put herself in danger like this?'

'I didn't know that she had followed me,' Piers said hastily. 'Rosie, you must allow me to explain.'

She turned her back on him. 'He's one of them, Walter. I overheard Piers and Blaise in the cellar. Piers Blanchard is a cheat and a liar, and Blaise is no better.'

'Don't compare me to him,' Piers said angrily. 'I know what you think, but it's not true.'

'Time for explanations later,' Walter said firmly. 'Let's get you home, Rosie. You need to change out of those wet clothes.'

His concern and his practical tone, so unlike him, made Rosalind smile in spite of everything. 'Yes, Walter. I'm coming.' She shot an angry glance in Piers' direction. 'I want you out of Rockwood tonight, Piers Blanchard. Your grandmother and Aurelia may remain with us until you have Trevenor ready, but you are no longer welcome here.'

'You're mistaken if you think I intended any harm

to you or your family,' Piers said slowly. 'I need to talk to you.'

'What is there to say? You tricked us into believing your cock-and-bull story. I should turn you in to the police, but you saved my life twice. Go away and enjoy the proceeds of your crime, but leave us alone.'

'I don't know exactly what's going on,' Walter said angrily, 'but Rosie's given you a second chance, so you'd better do as she says.' He took Rosalind by the hand. 'Can you make it up the cliff?'

'Yes, I can, and tomorrow I'm having that secret passage blocked up so that it can never be used again.' She was hampered by her sodden ball gown, but with Walter's help she managed to climb the steep path to the cliff top.

Constable Burton and a couple of preventive officers were about to bundle Jacob into a police wagon, together with Seth Wills, who was shackled to Dan Warren, the wheelwright, and Toby Hannaford, whose father ran the village shop. They were a sorry-looking bunch, their felt hats sodden with rainwater and their garments clinging to them. Bertie and Alexander broke away from the group and came purposefully towards them.

'Are you all right, Rosie?' Bertie demanded anxiously. 'How did you get mixed up in this? Where's Blanchard? Constable Burton informed me that he's a wanted man.'

'I followed Piers and Jacob,' Rosie said hastily. 'I

suspected that they were up to something and I was right. You won't see Piers Blanchard again.'

'You could have been killed,' Walter said angrily. 'We'd better get you indoors as quickly as possible.'

'I'm not a child.' Rosalind controlled her chattering teeth with difficulty. 'I just need to change out of these wet clothes.'

'It seems to me you're lucky to be alive.' Bertie shook his head. 'I want to know everything, Rosie.'

'I don't know what my brother has done,' Alexander said slowly. 'But if he's hurt you he'll have to answer to me, too.'

Rosalind faced him angrily. 'I find it hard to believe that you knew nothing of his plans, Alexander.'

'I promise you I am as nonplussed as anyone.'

'Your brother is little more than a criminal. He was with the smugglers when they landed their cargo of illegal goods twelve years ago.'

Alexander frowned. 'How would you know that? He would have been just a boy.'

'Bertie and I were on the beach when we should have been tucked up in bed. There was a ship in the cove, just like tonight, and when some of the crew attempted to land, there was gunfire from the cliff top. I fell onto the rocks as I tried to climb up after Bertie, and I might have been killed if a boy hadn't saved me.'

'A boy? There weren't any others on the beach with us,' Bertie said slowly. 'You had a nasty fall and hit your head. You must have imagined it.'

'No, I didn't, Bertie. Tonight I discovered that the boy was Piers, and I also found out that he's a liar, who tried to cheat us out of our inheritance.'

'Hold on there, Rosie,' Alexander said angrily. 'You can't say things like that without proof.'

'Ask him yourself,' Rosalind said wearily. 'I'm cold and wet and my ball gown is ruined. I want Hester.'

'She'll know what to do.' Walter took her by the hand. 'Come with me, Rosie. We'll go in through the servants' entrance so that no one will see us.'

'Hester needs to know that Jacob has been arrested,' Rosalind said sadly. 'I just don't know how she'll take it.'

Hester bathed the graze on Rosalind's forehead and dabbed the bruises on her arms with arnica.

'I'm sorry to bring you such bad news.' Rosalind winced as the solution of salt and water, Hester's cure-all, stung painfully. 'I don't know what part Jacob played but he's been arrested.'

'Serve him right.' Hester pursed her lips. 'Men always let you down. That's my experience, anyway. Sit still, Miss Rosalind. I can't treat you if you wriggle about like an eight-year-old.'

'That's exactly the age I was when all this started, Hester. Bertie seems to think I made it up, but you must remember the boy who brought me home that night when the smugglers landed and I fell onto the rocks. The boy slept here and next morning he had gone.'

'I do remember the boy.'

'It was Piers. He was with the smugglers then, and he was involved in what happened tonight, together with your Jacob and some of the men from the village. Blaise was in it, too.'

'Well, I never did. Who would have believed that Mr Blanchard was a wrong 'un? Have the police arrested them?'

'No, they got away.'

'But I thought that Mr Blanchard claimed to be the heir to the estate?'

'It seems that he tricked us all, Hester, as did Blaise. They are in it together.'

'I'll give him short shrift if he comes near my kitchen again,' Hester said angrily.

'The truth is that I let him go. He needs to put things right for his grandmother and his sister before the police catch him. If he doesn't make arrangements for them we'll have Lady Pentelow, Aurelia and their servants living here permanently.'

Hester put the cork back in the arnica bottle with unnecessary force. 'The old lady and her servants can all go to hell as far as I'm concerned.'

'They are victims as much as we are,' Rosalind said with a sigh. 'I just hope that they can return to Trevenor quickly.' She glanced over her shoulder at the sound of footsteps.

'Are you all right now, Rosie?' Bertie asked anxiously.

'Yes, as you see. It was just a scratch.'

'You shouldn't have gone after Blanchard on your own. If you'd told me of your suspicions I wouldn't have allowed you to do anything so foolhardy.'

'It all happened so quickly, Bertie. I didn't have time to think.'

'Piers won't get away for long. The police will catch up with him sooner or later.' Bertie eyed her worriedly. 'Are you sure you're all right?'

'I told you, I'm fine now.' Rosalind glanced down at her ruined gown. 'But I can't return to the ballroom looking like this.'

'You'll be going to bed with a hot brick wrapped in a towel, Miss Rosalind.' Hester sniffed and placed the arnica on a shelf next to the bottle of laudanum. 'I'm going to make you a cup of hot chocolate and you can take that with you.'

'That's sound advice,' Bertie said, frowning. 'You've had a shock and you might have caught a chill. Do the sensible thing for once, Rosie.'

Rosalind raised herself to a standing position. Her ribs ached where she had been thrown to the ground, but she was not going to let Hester know how much they hurt. 'I'm going to my room to change,' she said firmly. 'I'll raid Mama's clothes press to find something reasonably suitable, and then I'll rejoin the party. It's our home and I'm not going to allow the Blanchards to ruin the first ball we've given at Rockwood for years.'

'Are you sure?' Bertie did not look convinced.

'I'm going to tell Lady Pentelow exactly what I

think of her grandson, and she must leave Rockwood as soon as she can arrange her return to Trevenor, and that goes for Aurelia, too. I'm not a mean person, Bertie, but we owe the Blanchards nothing.' Rosalind closed her ears to their protests and made her way painfully to her room.

Half an hour later, with her damp, wildly curling hair confined in a chignon and her wet clothes discarded on a chair in her room, Rosalind returned to the ballroom, wearing a gown of pale blue satin, trimmed with bugle beads. It had belonged to her mother and was several seasons out of fashion, but it was still a very striking outfit and she could tell by the looks she was attracting that it suited her even better than the ruined gown.

Alexander was the first to reach her side, his handsome features creased with concern. 'Are you all right, Rosie? I wasn't expecting to see you again this evening.'

'It would take more than a few bruises to keep a Carey confined to bed,' Rosalind said, smiling. 'This is my home, Alex. Your brother has done his best to take it from us for no better reason than greed, but I am reclaiming it for my family.'

'I can't begin to understand Piers. His behaviour is unspeakable and also uncharacteristic. He isn't a bad person, Rosie.'

'You would know that better than I.' Rosalind fanned herself vigorously. It was stiflingly hot in the ballroom. Hundreds of wax candles in sconces and chandeliers sent out enough heat to warm the room and the couples dancing created their own source of heat. The orchestra was playing a gallop and the sound of laughter and happy chatter echoed off the high ceilings.

'Seriously, Rosie. I know Piers wouldn't do anything to harm you or your family.'

'Did he tell you that?'

Alexander shook his head. 'No, not exactly, but I'm certain there must be more to this.'

'Alex, I know you're being loyal, but I can't forgive Piers for what he's done. I don't want to talk about it.' Rosalind was aware that Squire Cottingham was trying to catch her attention. 'Excuse me, Alex. I have guests to attend to.'

She passed Aurelia, who was dancing with Hugo Knighton, and neither of them noticed her, which brought a wry smile to Rosalind's lips. Whatever crimes Piers had committed it was Aurelia, in particular, who would suffer greatly if his misdeeds were made public, and for that reason she was not going to report him to the authorities. Why ruin the lives of two young people who were so obviously in love?

Rosalind walked stiffly to a table and sat down. All her muscles ached but she was determined to stay until all her guests had departed. She smiled at her sister as she left the floor on Oscar Cottingham's arm. They were laughing as they strolled towards the supper room and obviously enjoying themselves. It was such a relief to see Patsy paying attention to someone other than Barnaby Yelland. Oscar was a theology student at Oxford University, and had probably been sent down yet again. Somehow Rosalind could not imagine him standing in a pulpit, preaching a sermon. He had been their friend since childhood, but Squire Cottingham was a strict father and he had not allowed Oscar to mix with the country children. At least that was his intention, which Oscar flouted on every possible occasion. He had managed to escape the schoolroom many times and had been the architect of the tree house in the woods. With his auburn hair and green eyes, Oscar was a free spirit, not unlike Patricia. In that moment Rosalind saw them as a pair who were meant to be together, and she was shocked to think that she had not seen it before.

Rosalind greeted Squire Cottingham and his wife, Glorina, who was looking oddly out of place amongst the staid matrons and youthful debutantes in their pastel gowns. With her raven-black hair and topaz eyes, Glorina had the exotic looks of her Romany ancestors. She wore an emerald silk gown trimmed with black lace, and she was flirting openly with Lord Knighton, while timid Lady Knighton looked on with a resigned expression on her plain features.

Rosalind felt a surge of pity for her. 'Lady Knighton, how good it was of you to travel so far to join us this evening. Would you like to join me for some supper? I believe Monsieur Jacques has excelled himself.'

'Thank you, Miss Carey, but I have little appetite.'

'Perhaps I could get you glass of fruit punch?'

'No, really. I am quite all right.' Lady Knighton's pale blue eyes filled with tears. 'Who is that woman, Miss Carey? She seems very forward.'

'She is the squire's wife, Lady Knighton. It's just her way – I think she likes to shock people. It is very chivalrous of Lord Knighton to indulge her like this.' Rosalind could see that her words fell on deaf ears. 'Your son is very charming, Lady Knighton. He seems quite taken with Aurelia Blanchard.'

Lady Knighton's lips tightened into a straight line. 'I've warned him against the Blanchards. They are in trade – new money. Hugo could have his pick of a dozen more suitable girls.'

'I'm sure he could.' Rosalind realised that nothing she could say would make Lady Knighton happy.

She turned away and was alarmed to see Lady Pentelow advancing on them with a determined look on her face that Rosalind had come to know meant trouble.

Chapter Twenty-Two

Lady Pentelow came to a halt. 'You weren't wearing that gown earlier, Rosalind.'

'Someone spilled wine on my skirt, so I had to change.' Rosalind hoped that the lie would go unchallenged, but she knew that Lady Pentelow had eyes like a hawk and she missed nothing.

'Strange that I didn't notice. What I did see was that you left the ballroom and were gone for a very long time. Surely that isn't the way to conduct yourself when you are here to attend to our guests, Rosalind.'

'I had to ensure that things were running smoothly below stairs.'

'Lady Pentelow, I wanted to speak to you rather urgently.' Lady Knighton unfurled her fan.

'I'm sure it can wait a while,' Lady Pentelow said grudgingly. 'I need to have words with Rosalind.'

'No, please don't mind me.' Rosalind backed away. 'I can see the vicar and his wife on the other side of the room. I haven't had a chance to talk to them yet.'

Lady Pentelow lowered her voice to a whisper. 'What is going on? Where is Piers? Did you have an assignation?'

'No, certainly not,' Rosalind said indignantly. 'What makes you think that?'

'Oh, come now, my dear. Don't think I haven't noticed the way you and Piers are when you're together. Wouldn't it be convenient if you were to trap him into marriage? You are penniless, Rosalind. You have an errant mother and a mad grandfather – do I need to say more?'

'Lady Pentelow, whatever you think of me, I'll thank you to leave my family out of this.'

'That would be difficult considering the fact that I am forced to live in this draughty ruin of a castle. Your grandfather almost wrecked the evening I have planned with such meticulous care, but luckily most of the guests seemed to think it was an entertainment, put on by a clown aping an admiral of the fleet.'

'How dare you!' Rosalind bristled with anger. 'My grandpapa is a hero. You said so yourself.'

'That was before I had to live under the same roof. Piers stressed the need to keep harmonious relations with you and your worthless brothers. Patricia is little more than a child, but I see she has the family trait of flirting outrageously. She behaves as if she's in the schoolroom, and that is where she belongs.'

'I am not continuing this conversation,' Rosalind said coldly. 'You are neglecting the one person whom you wished to impress. I suggest you look to yourself when it comes to manners and etiquette, Lady Pentelow.' Rosalind turned to Lady Knighton, who was clasping and unclasping her hands. 'I do beg your pardon, my lady. I apologise for taking up Lady Pentelow's valuable time.'

'I feel a little faint,' Lady Knighton said weakly. 'I think I must sit down.'

Rosalind was about to assist her when Lady Pentelow caught her by the arm.

'I haven't finished with you yet,' she said in the low voice. 'Don't walk away from me, miss. You will give me an explanation as to your whereabouts and that of my grandson.'

'Lady Pentelow, you will find out soon enough, but in the meantime I think you should know that Lady Knighton doesn't think that Aurelia is good enough for her son. She looks down on people who make their money in trade.' Rosalind had not intended to put it so bluntly, but she wanted to avoid explanations until the guests had departed. However, her barb seemed to have struck home and Lady Pentelow marched over to where Lady Knighton had collapsed on a chair and was fanning herself vigorously. Rosalind could imagine the conversation and she could see by the waving of hands and the expressions on their faces that this was not a cosy chat. She was tempted to find a quiet spot where she could sit and compose herself, but she had duties to perform and she made her way across the floor to greet the Reverend George Shaw and his wife, Tabitha.

It was past midnight when the first guests began to depart and Rosalind was completely exhausted, both mentally and physically. She had done her best to act as a good hostess, even though that privilege had been stolen from her, and she had managed to avoid a further confrontation with Lady Pentelow. Walter, Bertie and Alexander had danced every remaining dance and escorted single ladies in to supper as if nothing untoward had occurred. Patricia was oblivious to anything other than having fun, and Aurelia appeared to be blissfully unaware of the argument raging between her grandmother and Lady Knighton. Despite what his mother thought, Hugo had all the appearance of a young man deeply in love and Aurelia looked so happy that Rosalind could not bear to think of her distress when she realised they were facing opposition.

Even so, Rosalind found herself envying their happiness. Her own world was teetering on the brink of disaster. Perhaps she was just tired and the pain from her bruised ribs was causing her to feel melancholy, but Piers had let her down badly. She had suspected him of deceit all along, but deep down she had hoped that he would prove her wrong. She could hardly believe that the boy who had featured so heavily in her youthful dreams would turn out to be nothing but a common criminal. She managed to say goodbye to their guests, but Alexander seemed to have seen through her valiant attempt to act as if nothing untoward had happened.

'It's been a long evening,' he said sympathetically. 'Are you all right, Rosie?'

'I'm a Carey.' She smiled ruefully. 'We manage to keep going, no matter what.'

'That's no answer. You must be exhausted after everything that's happened.'

'I am a little tired, Alex. I think I'll go to my room.'

'Don't think I'm defending my brother, but Piers must have had his reasons for what he did.'

'I don't want to talk about it. I'll pay back the money he gave us to save Rockwood, if it's the last thing I ever do.'

'I'm certain that he never intended it to end like this, Rosie.'

'I've managed to avoid revealing the truth to your grandmother, but tomorrow I'm going to tell her everything. Now that there's no connection between our families I think it only right that she moves back to Trevenor.'

'I thought Blaise had taken residence there.'

'Who know what the truth is, Alex? I really don't care. Piers created this mess and he's free at the moment, so it's up to him to sort it out. I'm sorry, I'm really very tried so I'll say good night.' Rosalind walked away, heading for the grand staircase. Every step was painful and she was so tired that she could hardly drag herself up the stairs, but she did not look back, even though she could feel Alexander staring after her. She collapsed onto the bed in her room and was in the process of taking off her dancing slippers when Patricia rushed in, her face alight with happiness.

'Rosie, guess what?'

'I can't begin to imagine what it might be.'

'Yes, you can, you're such a tease. You saw me dancing with Ossie Cottenham.'

'I did, of course. I'm sure all the guests saw you two cavorting around the ballroom floor.'

'We weren't cavorting.' Patricia pouted and then she giggled. 'Well, perhaps we did cavort just a little – but it was great fun. I didn't realise how much I'd missed Ossie since he went to university.'

'Patsy, I'm very happy for you, but I'm also exhausted. Could we continue this conversation in the morning?'

'He says he loves me, Rosie. Can you credit that? I thought we were just friends, but it turns out that he's always had a soft spot for me.'

'Ossie isn't the most dependable chap in the world, Patsy. He used to be in love with Sylvia Greystone, as I recall. Then he fancied Lucy Warren . . .'

'Don't mention that little minx to me. She's taken

Barnaby from me, using her feminine wiles. I won't allow her to ruin my chance of happiness with Ossie. Anyway, you must admit that the squire's son is much more of a catch than the blacksmith's boy.'

'Patsy, I'm exhausted. I like Ossie and I'm sure that his parents will be quite happy to allow you two to get to know each other better, but please don't do anything rash.'

Patricia did a twirl. 'You are a spoilsport. I don't know where you went this evening, but for all I know you were having an assignation with Piers. It's obvious that he has feelings for you.'

'Nonsense,' Rosalind said more sharply than she had intended. 'Piers has gone and he won't be coming back here ever again. I don't even want his name mentioned.'

'Good heavens, Rosie! What did he do to upset you so much?'

'Good night, Patsy. We'll talk in the morning, I promise.' Rosalind rose from her bed with difficulty and propelled her sister from the room, closing the door behind her and turning the key in the lock. She undressed slowly and painfully, and slipped her nightgown over her head. Even though she was so tired that she could hardly keep her eyes open, she knew that she would find it difficult to sleep and she went to sit on the window seat. The storm had passed, leaving the air filled with the scent of damp earth, roses and estuary mud. The moon had emerged from the bank of clouds and its reflection shimmered on the surface of the backwater. To her surprise Rosalind could see lights bobbing up in the cove and she realised that the ship had not sailed. She could only wonder if a boat had landed to pick up Piers, and possibly Blaise as well. She might never discover the truth of their involvement, but just now she had no wish to see Piers again or to give credence to the excuses he was sure to make.

She drew the curtains and made her way back to her bed, where she lay down and pulled the coverlet up to her chin. She did not extinguish the candle, but allowed its flickering light to keep her company until she fell asleep.

Next morning Rosalind was up early and ready for a confrontation with Lady Pentelow. She had taken as much as she was prepared to accept from the imperious old lady. Now it was her turn to speak a few home truths, but first she went to the solar to make sure that her grandfather had not suffered as a result of being forcibly returned to his room last night. She found Jarvis as usual attending to Sir Lucien's needs, and she waited patiently until Jarvis left the room, taking the shaving bowl and razor with him.

'Well, Rosie, what have you to say to me?' Sir Lucien asked, smiling. 'Are you going to tell me off for my behaviour last evening? Jarvis tells me that I had one of my turns and created a scene.'

She reached out to lay her hand on his arm. 'No,

Grandpapa. Of course I'm not angry with you, but you did cause quite a diversion.'

'I'm so sorry, Rosie.'

'You were right about one thing, though. There was a ship in the bay. They had come to collect the spoils abandoned by the smugglers twelve years ago.'

'I knew that vessel had no right to be anchored in the bay. Tell me more, Rosie.'

When she had gone through all the events of the previous evening Rosalind left him with a promise to keep him informed of further developments. He might not remember what she had told him in an hour's time, but it had been a relief to talk about the deceitful way in which Piers and Blaise had insinuated themselves into their lives, purely for their own gain. She did not care about Blaise, but it hurt to think that she had just begun to trust Piers Blanchard and that her initial suspicions had been justified. As she made her way down the oak staircase with its treads worn smooth by centuries of use, she knew she must take control away from the Blanchards.

As she had expected, Lady Pentelow was seated at the dining table.

'I see that you at least are punctual for meals, which is more than I can say for your family. It seems they ate and behaved like peasants before we came to Rockwood.' Lady Pentelow opened her napkin with a flourish.

Rosalind helped herself to buttered eggs and a

slice of bacon from the silver serving dishes placed on the sideboard. She did not answer until she returned to her place at the table. 'Lady Pentelow, I don't know what has brought about this sudden change in your attitude to me and my family, but quite frankly I have had enough.'

'I beg your pardon?' Lady Pentelow stared at her in astonishment.

'You heard what I said, ma'am.' Rosalind pulled out the chair and sat down before her knees gave way beneath her. She was so angry at the injustice and the way in which Piers had lied and cheated his way into their lives that she could hardly bring herself to speak, but she kept her voice under control with a supreme effort. 'Your grandson, Piers Blanchard, is a liar. He is not the heir to Rockwood, as he claims. Neither is Ewart Blaise. I doubt very much if they are even half-brothers. Piers is and has been involved with free traders since he was a boy.'

'Stop! I won't listen to another slanderous word.'

'You are free to leave the table if you don't wish to hear what I have to say, but you will discover the truth one way or another, so you might as well sit quietly and listen.'

'This is an outrage.'

'No, ma'am. This is the truth. I heard it with my own ears. Piers and Blaise were speaking openly last evening when they thought no one was listening, but I was there and I heard every word they said. They don't want Rockwood. Their aim is to possess something even more valuable and it's hidden somewhere in or around the castle. They'll stop at nothing to get the prize.'

Lady Pentelow rose to her feet. 'Silence. Stop this wild talk at once. Piers is the legal heir to Rockwood and out of the goodness of his heart he has allowed you and your rag-tag family to remain in residence. I, personally, would have thrown you all out on the streets.'

'I'm sure you would, but now that privilege goes to me. I am giving you notice to leave Rockwood Castle as soon as your servants have packed your belongings.'

'What?' Lady Pentelow's voice rose to a screech. 'You can't do that. Where is Piers? I won't allow you to speak to me in this way.'

'Piers ran away, as he did twelve years ago when he was little more than a boy, when he came ashore with the smugglers, but the preventive men were lying in wait for them.'

'I refuse to listen to this cock-and-bull tale.' Lady Pentelow picked up the bell and rang it frantically. 'I will have you evicted from my home.'

'No, my lady. You are the one who will leave Rockwood. I have given orders for your belongings to be packed.'

'And I have told you that you have no authority in this house. I don't know where Piers has gone, but in his absence I am the senior member of the family. You will apologise to me for your impertinence. I and my family are going nowhere.'

'That is where you're mistaken.' Rosalind glanced over her shoulder as the door opened but instead of a servant it was Sir Lucien who strode into the room. 'Grandpapa, you're just in time. Lady Pentelow seems to be a little confused. She thinks that she is the head of the household.'

Sir Lucien stood very upright. 'Then I'm afraid you are mistaken, my lady. It has been a pleasure entertaining you and your grandchildren, but now it's time for you to leave.'

'But you are . . .' Lady Pentelow bit her lip. 'I mean, you have retired from society, Sir Lucien. You do not have any say in the matter.'

'Madam, I am Vice-Admiral Sir Lucien Carey, baronet. I still hold the title and I am the owner of this crumbling edifice. If my granddaughter says you and your grandchildren are no longer welcome here, then I support her decision.'

'Where is Piers?' Lady Pentelow cried frantically. 'I feel a little faint. Send for Simms.'

'Of course you may remain here until Trevenor is prepared for your return,' Rosalind said calmly. 'I haven't forgotten that you extended your hospitality to me and my sister, but until that time you are guests in our home.'

'Trevenor was taken from us by that scoundrel Blaise. I refuse to believe that Piers has anything to do with the wretch.'

'You will write a letter to Blaise, Lady Pentelow. You will inform him that his deception has been discovered and you will place the matter in the hands of the authorities if he does not comply with your wishes. Trevenor will be restored to you in the same order as when you left.'

'But you don't understand, Rosalind. Blaise has threatened to reveal the truth of his birth and create a scandal that will ruin us all.' Lady Pentelow fell back on her chair in a swoon, just as Patterson knocked and entered the room.

'Your mistress is unwell, Patterson,' Rosalind said calmly. 'Send for Simms, if you please.'

'Certainly, Miss Rosalind.' Patterson retreated, closing the door behind him.

Sir Lucien took his place at the head of the table. 'Well done, Rosie. But what will we do if this fellow Blaise refuses to leave Trevenor?'

'I will make certain that he does, Grandpapa. I intend to take the note to him myself.'

Lady Pentelow uttered a low moan. 'Now I know that you are deranged. If this fellow is so dastardly he will laugh in your face.'

'I'll take Bertie and Walter with me. I believe that some of your servants are still working at Trevenor. I'm sure they'll back us up. No one likes a bully, and that describes Blaise admirably.'

Lady Pentelow was suddenly alert. 'Are you serious, Rosalind?'

'Oh, yes, my lady. Just write the letter and I'll leave immediately.'

A timid tap on the door announced the arrival of

Miss Simms, Lady Pentelow's personal maid.

'Come here, Simms. I was feeling faint, but now I'm recovered. Fetch me my writing slope.'

Sir Lucien chuckled. 'You'd best start packing her ladyship's things, Simms. You'll be going home very soon if my granddaughter has anything to do with it.'

Rosalind stood up, leaving her food untouched. 'I'm going to rouse the boys. We'll leave as soon as possible, Grandpapa.'

An hour later Rosalind was dressed in her travelling costume with a few necessities packed in a small valise. On any other occasion it would have been almost impossible to drag her brothers out of bed, especially after attending a ball the previous evening, but when she explained her motives for travelling to Cornwall both Bertie and Walter were in full agreement. She waited for them in the grand entrance hall, but her heart sank when she saw Alexander hurrying towards her.

'Good morning, Alexander.'

He came to a halt, taking in her appearance and the valise at her feet. 'Where are you going?'

'Alex, I know this will be difficult for you, but I've told your grandmother that she's no longer welcome here. When I found out what Piers and Blaise had been planning I knew that we couldn't continue as we were.'

'That doesn't explain why you're leaving. You weren't going to tell me, were you?'

She sighed. 'I didn't want to involve you, Alex.'

'I have no idea what you're planning, but my brother has somehow got himself into a bad situation. I know Piers, and I'm sure there's an explanation, but you mustn't get mixed up in my family's problems.'

'It's too late for that. I'm trying to distance myself from them by going to Trevenor. Lady Pentelow has written a letter to Blaise ordering him to leave the premises immediately, and I'm going to deliver it in person. Bertie and Walter are coming with me.'

'Then I will, too. After all, it is my home, Rosie. You can't stop me.'

'If Piers is working with Blaise to cheat us all, you will be up against your own brother.'

'That is between me and Piers. I don't pretend to understand what's going on, but I do see the need for Grandmama to have her home returned to her. Give me five minutes and I'll be ready.'

'Very well, if you insist. I've sent for the carriage. We'll go as far as Exeter and travel on from there by train.'

'Five minutes,' Alexander repeated before hurrying off in the direction of the stairs.

Rosalind waited impatiently. She wanted to get away before either Hester or Patricia discovered her plans. She knew only too well that both of them would object, even if for different reasons. Hester would tell her to let Bertie and Walter go to Cornwall on their own, and Patricia would want to accompany them – which did not bode well.

The sound of horses' hoofs on the gravelled carriage sweep and the grinding of wheels as the vehicle came to a stop made her hurry to the entrance where Patterson, who as usual seemed to appear from nowhere, had sprung to attention and opened the door.

Rosalind stepped outside expecting to see Gurney, but her heart sank when she saw Sir Michael on the driver's seat of his curricle. He jumped to the ground and came towards her smiling, but his eyes were wary.

'Rosalind. You're going away?'

'Just a short trip, Sir Michael. I'll be back in a few days' time.'

'Might I ask where you're heading? I mean, it does seem a little strange considering you must have been dancing the night away at your ball.'

'I'll be back in a few days,' Rosalind said evasively.

'I came to apologise if my behaviour on my last visit caused you any embarrassment.'

'I'd rather forget anything that was said in the past, sir.'

'I was going to invite you and your sister to dine with us tomorrow evening, but I suppose that is out of the question now.'

'I can't say exactly when we'll be home.'

Rosalind glanced over his shoulder as Jim Gurney arrived with the ancient barouche.

'You won't get far in that decrepit vehicle,' Sir Michael said scornfully.

'We plan to travel most of the way by train. It's the up-and-coming mode of transport. I imagine the whole country will be criss-crossed with railway lines one day soon.'

'If you tell me where you are headed I might be able to help,' Sir Michael insisted. 'My landau is new and can offer you much more comfort than the old barouche.'

Alexander emerged from the doorway. 'The others are coming, Rosie.'

'Who are you, sir?' Sir Michael demanded suspiciously. 'I don't believe we've met.'

'I'm Rosalind's fiancé, Captain Alexander Blanchard of the 32nd Foot. How do you do, Sir Michael?'

Rosalind shot a sideways glance at Alex, but he was smiling confidently as he held out his hand, which Sir Michael chose to ignore.

'You are engaged to this fellow, Rosalind?'

The urge to laugh was almost too much for her, but Rosalind managed to keep a straight face. 'It's such a new development that I find it hard to believe myself, sir.'

Bertie rushed from the entrance hall. 'We're ready, let's go.' He came to a halt. 'Sir Michael, good morning. You'll forgive us if we have to rush off.'

Walter followed him into the sunshine. 'We'd best get going, Rosie. Are you joining us, Alex?'

'Yes, I can't allow my new fiancée to travel on her own.' Alex proffered his arm.

'Goodbye, Sir Michael. Perhaps we'll see you on our return.' Rosalind tucked her hand in the crook of Alex's arm and allowed him to lead her to the barouche. She climbed into the shabby interior and collapsed in a fit of the giggles.

'What's going on?' Bertie demanded as he joined them with Walter squeezing in after him. 'You two aren't engaged, are you?'

'No such luck,' Alex said, laughing. 'But I could see that the fellow was imposing on Rosie's good nature. I've met plenty like him in my travels. It was a short engagement, but one which I enjoyed very much. Maybe we could discuss it further, Rosie? What do you say?'

Chapter Twenty-Three

When they arrived in Plymouth they hired a carriage, but it was over forty miles to Trevenor and they were obliged to put up overnight at a wayside inn. Sleeping in a strange room without her sister for company seemed very odd, but it was a necessary part of their journey, and Rosalind was desperate to speak to Blaise. She needed to find out what part he had played in the deception that Piers had used to gain her trust and to insinuate himself into her family. It was humiliating to think that she had allowed herself to be taken in by the history that Piers had presented with such conviction. She should have listened to her inner voice, but he had been very convincing. Even so, there had been nothing on paper to support his story, and, in hindsight, maybe they should have demanded more proof of his claim.

These thoughts went round and round in her mind and she slept badly. The bed was far from comfortable, and the sheets smelled of the last occupant. The raucous laughter and raised voices from the taproom went on into the early hours and just as she was drifting off to sleep a stagecoach arrived, with all the clatter and noise that entailed. She was glad when dawn broke and she was able to get up and have a wash in cold water before getting dressed.

They left soon after breakfast and stopped only to change horses and enjoy a brief respite from being jolted around on rutted roads. The hired carriage was old, well used and not the most comfortable of vehicles, but Rosalind set her mind against everything other than reaching their destination.

They arrived at Trevenor in the late afternoon, only to find that Blaise was not at home. The footman who answered the door did not know when his master would return. If Alexander had not been with them Rosalind was convinced that they would not have been admitted to the house, but they were shown to the drawing room and the footman went in search of the housekeeper.

Rosalind gazed round the room, which had been furnished in the height of elegance and good taste when Lady Pentelow ruled the household. She had taken her furniture and her valuable ornaments and paintings, which was evident by the bare patches on the walls where the works of art had once hung. The only familiar items were the curtains and the

Axminster carpet, but the furnishings were sparse
and obviously second-hand. It looked to Rosalind
as if Blaise had sent the servants to scour the local
salerooms for chairs, sofas and the odd side table.
Rockwood had never looked like this, even in the
times of greatest austerity. Bertie and Walter had
not seemed to notice anything amiss and they
sprawled on the shabby armchairs set on either side
of the empty grate. Alex himself was looking round
with a perplexed expression, as if he was aware that
something was wrong, but was trying to puzzle it
out.

'Lady Pentelow took most of her belongings with
her,' Rosalind said hastily. 'They are stored in the
outbuildings at home.'

'I wondered what had happened.' Alexander
fingered the worn upholstery on the back of a horsehair sofa. 'I thought perhaps Blaise had sold
everything.' He turned his head to glance at the door
as someone knocked timidly. 'Enter.'

Mrs Phelps, whom Rosalind recognised as being
Lady Pentelow's under-housekeeper, bustled into the
room and bobbed a curtsey.

'It's so good to see you again, Mrs Phelps,'
Alexander said, smiling. 'We've come a long way to
see Mr Blaise, but I'm told he is away from home.
Would it be possible for us to stay here for the
night?'

'Of course, sir. I'm sure that Mr Blaise would offer
you hospitality if he was here.'

'Are there many of the old servants still working here, Mrs Phelps?'

'There are quite a few of us, sir, but it's not the same without the family. Not that I'm complaining about my treatment, you understand.' She glanced anxiously over her shoulder as if expecting someone to be listening to their conversation.

'Mr Blaise treats you well, I trust?' Alexander gave her an encouraging smile.

'Tolerable well, sir. Shall I have your old room prepared, and rooms for Miss Carey and the gentlemen?'

'You remember me then, Mrs Phelps?'

'Yes, of course I do, miss.'

'Well then, these gentlemen are my brothers, Mr Bertram Carey and Mr Walter Carey. I'm sorry to put you to so much bother, but I doubt if we'll be staying long. We could put up at the inn, if this is not convenient.'

'It's no trouble, Miss Carey. Leave it to me and I'll have the rooms made ready. In the meantime I expect you would like some refreshments after your journey.'

'That would be very much appreciated,' Alexander said agreeably. 'Can you tell me when you expect Mr Blaise to return?'

'I'm afraid I cannot, sir. He's been gone for nearly a week. Anyway, if you'll excuse me I'll instruct cook to make up a tray for you.' Mrs Phelps hurried from the room.

'Now what do we do?' Bertie rose to his feet and stood with his back to the empty grate. 'The fellow could be gone for days, if not weeks.'

'I grew up here.' Alexander's knuckles whitened as he gripped the back of the sofa. 'This is my home and I'll be damned if I'll let that man take it from my family. I can't believe that Piers allowed this to happen, unless of course he has some other connection with Blaise.'

'Then, if I were you,' Rosalind said thoughtfully, 'I would stay here and refuse to leave.'

There was a moment's silence as all eyes were on her.

Bertie was suddenly alert. 'I thought that Piers signed the property over to Blaise.'

'Piers is wanted by the police and the customs men,' Rosalind said pointedly. 'Maybe such a document isn't valid.'

'Perhaps Blaise is also a fraud,' Walter added eagerly.

Rosalind paced the floor, coming to a halt beside Alexander. 'If we could speak to a lawyer perhaps we could restore Trevenor to your family, and Rockwood Castle would revert to us. I remember Piers saying that he was going to consult the family solicitor in Plymouth. We should visit his chambers and ask to see a copy of the agreement.'

Alexander's brow puckered in a frown. 'That's strange. Our lawyer has always been Henry Deakin, whose chambers are in Bodmin. Are you sure that's what he said, Rosie?'

'I'm absolutely sure.'

'It seems to me that you'd better go and see the chap in Bodmin before you go careering off to Plymouth.' Bertie stretched and yawned. 'I've had enough of travelling for a day or two.'

'I agree.' Alexander nodded. 'Deakin will be able to advise us. He's a dry old stick, but he's honest.'

'Honesty seems to be in short supply round here,' Rosalind said grimly. 'It's hard to know whom to trust.'

'I'm going to Bodmin tomorrow. Come with me, Rosie. You'll think of more things to ask him than I will.'

'Of course, but what happens if Blaise returns and finds Bertie and Walter here?'

'The obvious answer is to keep the fellow out,' Bertie said casually. 'We need tactics here, Alex, old chap. You're the military man – we need to prepare for a siege.'

Rosalind shook her head. 'What if the servants side with their master? We'll have lost before we begin.'

'Parley,' Alex said briefly. 'That's what we need. I'll call the servants together. I need to discover those who are loyal to the family and the ones who support Blaise. They will have to go – it's as simple as that.'

The rattle of crockery preceded a knock on the door.

'Enter,' Alex said loudly.

Mrs Phelps manoeuvred the tray into the room and placed it on a side table.

'Thank you, Mrs Phelps. Will you stay for a moment, please?' Alex cleared his throat. 'A situation has arisen that concerns you and all the servants.'

She clutched her hands to her bosom, her eyes wide with anxiety. 'I can't afford to lose my job, sir. I have four children at home being cared for by my aged mother.'

Rosalind stepped forward. 'What Captain Blanchard is trying to say is that we intend to take Trevenor back from Mr Blaise. We believe that he seized it illegally from the family. It's their wish to return as soon as possible.'

'Oh my Lord!' Mrs Phelps eyed her warily. 'Mr Blaise won't take kindly to it, miss.'

'What we need to know is who will support us in such a situation. Are you with us in this, Mrs Phelps?' Alex asked urgently.

'Yes, indeed, Captain. I am wholeheartedly, and most of us below stairs wish that the mistress was back home.'

Alex nodded. 'Then I want all the servants, including the outdoor staff, to attend a meeting in the servants' hall in half an hour. Will you organise that for me, Mrs Phelps?'

'Gladly, sir.' Mrs Phelps ran from the room, shouting instructions as she went.

'This will be interesting.' Alexander sat down on

the nearest chair. 'Although it might cause an all-out war below stairs.'

'What have we started now?' Walter said worriedly.

'We'll discover those who are loyal to Lady Pentelow and others who wish to side with Blaise. At least I hope that's what will happen.' Rosalind went over to the tray and began to pour the tea. 'Walter, dear, make yourself useful and pass the sandwiches round, please.'

Half an hour later Alexander led the way below stairs to the servants' hall. There were fewer people there than Rosalind had expected, and it seemed that Blaise had been running the household with the minimum number of staff. That also applied to the outdoor servants, most of whom Alexander knew by name. He addressed them all, speaking briefly and succinctly and it seemed that he was understood. There were muted sounds of approval from most of those assembled, but others rose to their feet and walked out.

Alex waited until the door closed on them. 'Now I know whom to trust I'll tell you what we're going to do . . .'

Rosalind sat back while Alex outlined what was to happen. She could only hope that the solicitor in Bodmin would be able to help, otherwise their efforts might prove to be in vain and Blaise could order them to leave. The family would have lost their home for ever. It did not bear thinking about.

Alexander managed to convince the head clerk in the solicitor's office that it was a matter of urgency for them to see Mr Deakin, even though they did not have an appointment. He emphasised the fact that they were prepared to wait all day if necessary, and after an hour or so they were ushered into the solicitor's office.

'It's a long time since we last met, Captain Blanchard,' Mr Deakin said pleasantly. 'I am very busy today, but I've fitted you in. Please make yourselves comfortable and tell me what I can do for you.'

'Thank you, sir.' Alexander pulled up a chair for Rosalind before taking a seat himself. 'I'll be as brief as possible, but we find ourselves in an untenable position.'

'How so, Captain Blanchard?'

'The document that you and my brother drew up ceding the rights to Trevenor and the china clay business to Ewart Blaise – we wish to challenge its legality.'

Mr Deakin cleared his throat. 'I don't recall any such agreement.'

'It was made just weeks ago, sir,' Rosalind said urgently. 'Mr Piers Blanchard signed everything over to Mr Ewart Blaise.'

'No, miss. If such a document exists it isn't with me.

Rosalind turned to Alexander with an exasperated sigh. 'I told you that Piers went to see a solicitor in Plymouth.'

'I very much doubt that,' Mr Deakin said firmly. 'All the Blanchard family papers, including the deeds to Trevenor, are filed here.'

'Are you telling us that there could not have been such a contract, sir?' Alexander exchanged surprised glances with Rosalind. 'Are you quite certain?'

'No such agreement could have been made without exchanging the deeds or at least having had sight of them, and I can assure you that they are safely locked away here in my chambers.'

Alexander leaped to his feet and leaned over the desk to shake the startled Mr Deakin's hand. 'Thank you, sir. You don't know how much this means to me and my family.'

'Well, er, I'm glad to have been of service.'

Rosalind rose more slowly to her feet. 'Before we leave, Mr Deakin, do you know anything of the Blanchard family history?'

He smiled and leaned back in his chair, his clasped hands resting on his round belly. 'As a matter of fact I do, Miss . . .? I'm sorry I didn't catch your name.'

'I'm Rosalind Carey, and Mr Piers Blanchard claims to be related to my family. Would you know anything about that?'

'I can't say, Miss Carey. I do know that Giles Blanchard arrived from Normandy with Duke William, and was granted the land on which he built Trevenor House. The Blanchards have, to the best of my knowledge, lived there since the eleventh century. Giles married local heiress Bertha Chaldon, who was the only daughter of a wealthy landowner.'

'So Bertha didn't have a sister called Mathilda?'

'No, she was definitely an only child. Her mother died soon after Bertha was born.' Mr Deakin rested his elbow on the table, staring curiously at Rosalind. 'Why do you ask?'

'Because that is the story, as told to me by Piers Blanchard. Only in his version Giles Blanchard was given Rockwood Castle by a grateful Duke William. His wife died giving birth to twin boys, but only one survived. According to Piers, Mathilda Chaldon, Bertha's jealous spinster sister, stole the boy and spirited him away. It was Mathilda who purchased Trevenor and made it a home for them both.'

'No, that's impossible. It sounds like pure fiction to me. In fact, Bertha lived a long and happy life and had three children, two girls and a boy.'

'And would my brother know all this, Mr Deakin?' Alexander asked abruptly.

'Yes, Captain Blanchard. Most definitely. I know this because some months ago Mr Blanchard came to me and asked to look through the deed box. He said he was interested in the family history and I told him as much as I knew.'

'And the Blanchards never owned Rockwood Castle in Devon?' Rosalind had to be sure.

'Never! At least, not to my knowledge, Miss Carey.'

'Thank you. That's all I wanted to know.' Rosalind

was about to shake his hand when she had a sudden thought. 'Do you know anything about Ewart Blaise, Mr Deakin?'

He shook his head. 'Until you mentioned him I'd never heard the name before. Who is this person?'

Alexander cleared his throat. 'It's a delicate matter, sir. Blaise worked for us in the china clay mine. He came up with the story that he is our half-brother, born out of wedlock.'

Mr Deakin nodded. 'These things happen, Captain Blanchard.'

'Did my father ever make provision for an illegitimate son?'

'No, such a relationship was never mentioned.'

'Thank you, Mr Deakin,' Rosalind said, smiling. 'Thank you so much.'

He blinked. 'I've really done nothing.'

'Yes, you have, sir. You've answered so many questions. We mustn't take up any more of your valuable time.' Rosalind rose to her feet. 'We should leave now, Alex.'

'Yes, of course.' Alexander reached out to grab Deakin's hand and he shook it enthusiastically. 'Thank you for the most useful information.'

'I'll send my account as usual, only this time I know for certain that there are ample funds in the family's coffers.'

Alexander had been about to open the door, but he hesitated. 'I beg your pardon, sir? What did you just say?'

'A substantial amount of cash was handed in to my head clerk. I'm not sure who brought it but it was supposed to have come from your elder brother. He gave instructions for it to be paid into the Trevenor account, which we did the very next day.'

'But was there no explanation as to where the money had come from?'

'It was none of my business, and I didn't see the person who dropped the money off. However, it's not our business to question clients.'

'Do you know how much it was, Mr Deakin?'

'Not to the last penny, Captain. But if you call in at the bank I'm sure they will give you the details. I'm surprised that your brother didn't inform you. It was a tidy sum.'

Twenty minutes later Alexander came out of the bank building with a broad grin on his face. 'I'll say it was a tidy sum, Rosie. I must admit I'm flummoxed by the whole episode.'

'There's only one person who could answer your questions,' Rosalind said seriously. 'And we don't know where Piers is, or how he obtained such a large sum of money. Although I have a feeling it must have been the cache that Blaise was also after. Apparently it was left somewhere on Rockwood property, and has remained hidden for the past twelve years.'

Alexander proffered his arm. 'I think Blaise might have some answers. Let's get back to Trevenor and see if he's shown his face. When he hears that we've taken over I imagine he'll be back like a shot.'

Rosalind nodded. 'I agree, and I can't wait to return to Rockwood and let them all know that Piers has no claim on our home.' She tucked her hand in the crook of his arm as they walked to the livery stables. 'I imagine he will want repayment of the money he gave us. I don't know how we'll do that, but I won't rest until I've paid back every last penny.'

'He was using you, Rosie. I hate to say it because I love my brother, but he's treated us all shabbily. I hope there's a good reason for his behaviour, but we won't know until he decides to brave the authorities. I'm afraid it's more than likely that he'll end up in prison, and the money he deposited might be forfeit.'

'Do you think he's gone abroad?'

'Who knows? Piers and I used to be close, but now I feel I don't know him.'

'I can't believe that the boy who helped me to get home that night would grow up to be a criminal. I've tried to convince myself, but part of me wants to hear what he has to say, and give him a second chance.'

'If he's fled the country we might have to wait a long time. Come on, Rosie. Let's concentrate on the good news. I can't wait to see Blaise's face when he realises that he's gambled and lost.'

'He must have known that the truth would come

out eventually,' Rosalind said slowly. 'How could he be so stupid?'

'If he found what he was looking for I doubt if he'll worry about small details like that. We'd better get back to Trevenor.'

It was early afternoon by the time they arrived back at the house. Rosalind was dusty, tired and very hungry as they had not bothered to stop for refreshments. Mrs Phelps rushed round in her efforts to make them comfortable and to provide them with luncheon, which they ate on the terrace in the shade of the wisteria with its delicate purple fronds falling in jewel-like clusters from the glazed roof.

In between mouthfuls of cold meat and pickles, Rosalind told her brothers briefly what Mr Deakin had said concerning the Blanchard family history. Alexander put in a word here and there.

'Well, I'm damned,' Bertie said exultantly. 'So Piers told you a pack of lies. He's not related to us in any way and he has no claim on Rockwood.'

'Not according to Deakin,' Alexander said, spearing a pickled onion on his fork.

'But I don't understand why,' Walter added solemnly. 'Why did he go to the trouble of entering my name for Cambridge? He was willing to buy you a commission, Bertie, only you decided to join the army as an enlisted man instead. Why did he do all those things if he intended to cheat us out of our home?'

'I don't think he ever wanted Rockwood or the estate,' Rosalind said, swallowing a mouthful of food. 'It was the cache left by the smugglers than he was after, and if that sum of money he deposited in the bank is anything to go by, it seems that he found it.'

'But twelve years have elapsed since the day you first met my brother.' Alexander put his knife and fork down and pushed his plate away. 'Why was it left in place all that time? If Piers, who was only a boy at the time, knew of its whereabouts, there must be others with the same knowledge.'

'Jacob,' Rosalind said thoughtfully. 'Hester's gentleman friend. He's been courting her for years – I remember her saying that. He's been visiting her at least once a week for all that time and recently he seems to have been at the castle every day. I saw him with Piers and I followed them into the cellar. Do you suppose that Jacob knew about the hoard all along? Was he working with Piers?'

Alexander rose from his seat and walked over to the window. 'It's so unlike Piers to run away from trouble. He could clear this up instantly if he chose to return.'

'How does Blaise fit in with all this?' Walter asked, frowning.

'We might find out quite soon.' Alexander stiffened, shielding his eyes with his hand. 'Word has got round quickly. I see a deputation coming up the hill from the village.'

Rosalind jumped to her feet. 'Is Blaise with them?'

He shook his head. 'No, that looks like Jed Kitto from the Anchor Inn at the forefront, followed by Pedrick, the mine manager, and some of the servants who just walked out. I'll go down and talk to them.'

Bertie raised himself from his chair. 'We'll come with you, Alex.'

'Yes, we'll back you up,' Walter added eagerly.

'All right, come with me then, but not you, Rosie.' Alexander shook his head as she attempted to follow them.

'But we need to show them we mean business,' she protested.

'They might start hurling stones or something equally stupid. Stay here and watch from a safe distance. If things turn nasty I'll leave it to you to muster the male servants who chose to stay with us. But I hope it won't come to that.'

Somewhat reluctantly, Rosalind stayed behind. She could do nothing for now but watch and wait as her brothers and Alex made their way through the garden to the driveway leading down to double iron gates at the entrance to Trevenor. When the two sides met face to face with only the curves of the wrought-iron gate between them, she could tell by the gesticulating on both sides that the argument was heated, and she was poised to run for help, but quite suddenly the men from the village turned and walked away. She hurried to meet her brothers and Alexander as they started back up the path.

'What did they say? What happened?'

Alexander shrugged. 'It was all bluster. Pedrick threatened to send for the constable, and the rest of them, including Kitto, mumbled threats, but I told them that Trevenor belongs to the Blanchards and Blaise is an imposter. That gave them something to think about, particularly Pedrick, who could see his job vanishing into thin air, and Kitto would lose half his customers if the mine were to close.'

'You don't think they'll do anything rash, do you, Alex?' Rosalind asked anxiously. 'I mean, they wouldn't try to rush the gates and break in?'

He shook his head. 'No, they wouldn't be so foolish. Pedrick's job depends on Piers as well as Blaise, and I doubt if he'd do anything rash. Kitto is a bag of wind. He likes to think that he runs the village, but if anyone is in charge in that establishment it's his wife. I think we're safe enough unless Blaise returns and tries to raise a mob. That might cause a problem.'

'I think we should move your grandmother and Aurelia back to Trevenor,' Rosalind said slowly. 'If Lady Pentelow is in residence with all her belongings there is nothing that Blaise can do about it. He doesn't seem to have the law on his side and it's not as if he's filled the house with priceless artefacts.'

'You're forgetting that he claims to be my father's illegitimate son.' Alexander walked on, taking large strides that forced Rosalind to quicken her pace in order keep up with him. 'That doesn't mean he has a legal right to the property, but you could argue that he has a moral claim.'

'Then we need to trace his birth records and prove that he's lying,' Rosalind said eagerly. 'In which case, he has no hold over your family.'

'I think you're right.' Alexander picked her up and twirled her round until she was dizzy. He set her back on her feet. 'Tomorrow, if you're agreeable, you and I will do a tour of the local churches and check the registers of birth. It should be quite easy. Are you with me?'

Rosalind's head was still spinning and the unaccustomed close contact had made her pulse race. She steadied herself by laying her hand on his shoulder. 'I am, but how will we get away without being seen?'

Alexander smiled and brushed her tumbled curls back from her forehead with the tip of his finger. 'Leave that to me, Rosie. I grew up here. I know every inch of the estate.'

Chapter Twenty-Four

Early next morning Alexander emerged from the stables leading two thoroughbred horses. 'I'll say one thing for Blaise: he knows what he's doing when it comes to horseflesh.'

Rosalind patted the neck of a bay mare, as the animal nuzzled her affectionately. 'It seems she's chosen me.'

'Luckily there were several side-saddles in the tack room,' Alexander said, mischievously. 'Otherwise it might have been difficult for you.'

Rosalind laughed. 'I have two brothers, Alex. We used to ride every day and I never bothered with such niceties when I was younger.'

Alexander led the horse to a mounting block and held her until Rosalind was settled on the saddle. 'Just follow me.' He vaulted onto the saddle. 'I know the back way out of the estate and it takes us very near the parish church. We'll start there.'

'Lead on. This is going to be very interesting.'

The vicar was only too pleased to give them the benefit of his thirty years' devotion to God and the residents of the village. He had, he said, personally filled in every entry in the parish register in that time. He was obviously shocked by the suggestion that Ewart Blaise was the illegitimate son of Philip Blanchard, whom he took pains to stress had been a pillar of the community and had been taken from them too soon. He was so adamant that Rosalind felt guilty for thinking ill of such a good man. Alexander thanked the vicar and placed a generous donation on the collection plate as they left the church.

They mounted their horses and rode on to the next village, but the result was similar. There was no record of the birth of Ewart Blaise, nor any mention of a family bearing that name, and it was the same wherever they went: no one had heard of Ewart Blaise, nor of anyone with that surname. In the early afternoon they stopped at an inn to water the horses and give them a rest. The landlord made it clear that ladies were not allowed in the taproom and they sat at a table outside on roughly hewn wooden benches. The landlord served them with a basket of bread, a slab of cheese with a pat of butter, and two tankards of rough cider.

'I'm sorry, Rosie. This isn't what you're used to,' Alexander said with a rueful grin.

'It's a lovely day and a pretty spot. I know we haven't had any success in tracing Blaise, but it's been fun playing detective – even if we aren't very good at it, Alex.'

'I've enjoyed it too. Just being with you is enough for me, Rosie.' Alexander leaned across the table to lay his hand on hers. 'I haven't got much leave left – a week or two at the most. I'm awaiting orders. I have so much that I want to say to you, Rosie. But there are always other people in the way.'

'Where will your next posting be?' She found herself gazing into his eyes, unable to look away.

'I'm not sure, but we might be sent back to India.'

'So far away.'

'You could come with me, Rosie.'

She snatched her hand free. 'Don't say things you don't mean, even in jest.'

'I'm not joking. For once in my life I'm in earnest. Marry me, Rosie. Make me the happiest man on earth and say you'll be my wife.'

Her mouth was suddenly dry and she took a sip from her tankard. Her heart was thudding against her stays and she was sure he must be able to hear it, even above the trickling of the nearby stream and the warbling of a blackbird in a willow tree. 'I wasn't expecting this, Alex.' She replaced her tankard but her hand shook and she spilled a little on the table.

'I know it's sudden, but it's been on my mind since the first time I saw you. I know it's probably not the life you imagined for yourself, and being married to a soldier is not easy, but I love you, Rosie. I can't imagine living without you.'

She clutched her hand to her heart, as if by pressing on her bosom she could regain control her spiralling emotions. 'We came out today to solve a mystery. I really wasn't expecting you to propose.'

'Neither was I, if I'm honest. It's just that being with you for the best part of the day has been wonderful. You do have some feelings for me, don't you?'

'Yes, of course I do, but marriage is another matter. I can't give you my answer straight away, Alex. I'm sorry, but I have to think about my family. I can't abandon Grandpapa. If Bertie joins his regiment and Walter goes to Cambridge, there'll be no one to care for my grandfather. Rockwood doesn't run itself and Patsy is far too young to take on such responsibility.'

'I understand, but these problems aren't insurmountable. If we love each other we will find a way.'

'There is still so much to be done,' Rosalind said in desperation. 'Trevenor is in a state of siege and if I did agree to marry you, it would have to be done in such a rush.'

'You want a big wedding? I understand that. Aurelia has talked of nothing else ever since I can remember. We could do it – there's money in the bank. You can have everything you ever wanted.'

She smiled at his boyish enthusiasm. 'I don't want a grand occasions, Alex. It's not that.'

He leaped up from his seat opposite her and went

to sit by her side. He slipped his arm around her shoulders. 'It's too sudden, I understand. Just don't turn me down out of hand, my love.'

She edged away along the bench. 'Stop it, Alex. I can't think if you get too close. Give me time, that's all I ask. Please don't rush me into something we might both live to regret.'

He leaned over and brushed her lips with a kiss. 'You haven't said "no", and I take that as a positive "maybe", or even a tentative "yes". I don't give up easily, Rosie. I'll give you time to think it over.'

She covered her mouth with her hand. The touch of his lips, however brief, had left her longing for more. It would have been so easy to give in and allow him to fold her in his arms After all the problems she had experienced in the past it would be wonderful to lay her burdens on someone else's shoulder, but common sense won and she stood up.

'I think we ought to be getting back to Trevenor. We're a long way from home.'

'Yes, of course.' He rose more slowly to his feet, surveying the table with a wry smile. 'We haven't eaten anything.'

His words were echoed by the landlord, who emerged from the taproom with an empty tray. 'Anything wrong with the vittles, sir?'

'Nothing at all, landlord. We got talking and forgot the time. Will you have our horses brought round from your stables, please?' Alexander tossed him a coin, which the landlord caught expertly.

'Aye, sir.' The landlord stacked his tray and was about to walk away when he hesitated. 'I've been thinking about what you said earlier, sir. I don't recall a family called Blaise but old man Ewart was a shepherd and he had a son whose name I cannot recall. The boy ran away to sea when he were about thirteen.'

'How old would his son be now?' Rosalind asked cautiously.

'He'd be about the same age as my son. That would make him twenty-five, I reckon.'

'Is Shepherd Ewart still living round here?' Alexander exchanged hopeful glances with Rosalind.

'No, sir. He died of a fever five year ago or more. The same illness that took his missis.'

'Thank you, landlord.' Rosalind waited until he had disappeared into the taproom. 'I think we should call on the vicar again.'

Alexander nodded. 'I was going to say the same thing.'

If the vicar thought they were slightly mad he was too polite to say so, and rather reluctantly he allowed them to take another look at the register.

'There,' Rosalind said, pointing her finger to a faded entry at the foot of the page. 'The christening of Blease Ewart – at least I think that's what it says. It's not very clear.'

The vicar leaned over her shoulder. 'I remember the child. The mother was a servant girl from

Knighton Hall, Emily Blease, as I recall. She married Bill Ewart, the Knightons' shepherd. She's buried in the churchyard alongside her husband. Always thought herself a cut above the rest of the village, I'm afraid. She spoiled that boy and gave him ideas above his station.'

'Is that why he ran away to sea?' Rosalind asked eagerly.

'No, miss. Young Blease was caught thieving. If you want to know more about him I suggest you ask Miss Thompson. She's retired now, but she used to teach at the village school. She lives in a cottage next door to the inn.'

'Thank you so much.' Rosalind shook his hand. 'We're so grateful.'

The vicar smiled for the first time. 'To tell the truth, miss. I thought you two had come to ask me to post the banns for your forthcoming marriage, and I was going to have to refuse because you don't live in this parish. Am I right?'

Rosalind was about to tell him he was mistaken, but Alexander smiled and nodded. 'You're very astute, Vicar.'

'I've married more couples than I can remember. I can spot young love without a word being said.' He folded his hands across his chest, beaming at them.

Rosalind hurried from the cool interior of the church, catching her breath as the heat of the afternoon sun seemed to suck all the air from the baked ground. She waited for Alexander before setting off towards the lych gate.

'Hold on, wait for me.' Alexander took her by the hand. 'I know exactly where you're going.'

'Let's hope that Miss Thompson is at home. We should be getting back to Trevenor.'

He grasped her hand. 'I'm enjoying having you all to myself. Today can go on for ever, as far as I'm concerned.'

Miss Thompson's cottage was small and neat, with a well-kept front garden and flowerbeds crammed with marigolds, tall white daisies and night-scented stocks. Roses rambled across the roof of the porch, spilling over in bright pink clumps. Alexander knocked on the door and it was opened by a small, plump woman with grey hair confined in a bun at the nape of her neck. She greeted them with a polite smile and showed them into her tiny front parlour, where everything gleamed with polish and the scent of lavender and beeswax hung heavily in the air.

'Do I know you? I usually remember my old pupils, but I'm afraid I don't recall either of you.'

'No, Miss Thompson. The vicar told us that you might be able to give us some information about a boy who attended your school many years ago.'

'Do take a seat. As I said, I never forget a pupil.'

Rosalind perched on the small horsehair sofa and Alexander sat on the edge of a tapestry-covered chair.

'Does the name Blease Ewart bring anyone to mind, Miss Thompson?'

She rolled her eyes. 'That boy was the bane of my life. Totally ruined by his mother and beaten regularly by his father. As I recall, his mother made it crystal clear that she had married beneath her.'

'That couldn't have been easy for the boy,' Rosalind said seriously.

'It was rumoured in the village that Bill Ewart was not the boy's father. Of course, I don't hold with gossip, but some said that it was Lord Knighton himself. I wouldn't repeat it except for the fact that it was what Blease believed. I think that was why he took to crime at a young age. He ran away to sea when he was about thirteen. It was probably the best thing he could have done.'

'What sort of crime?' Rosalind asked.

'Petty theft, mostly. Then one day he went too far and stole from money Lord Knighton's estate manager. He would have gone to prison had he not run away from home. To my knowledge he's never returned to the village.'

'Thank you, Miss Thompson.' Alexander rose to his feet. 'You've been most helpful, but we mustn't take up any more of your time.'

'Is that all you wanted to know?' Miss Thompson turned to Rosalind. 'May I offer you a glass of lemonade, or a cup of tea? It's very hot to be out riding.'

'No, thank you. We should be setting off for home.' Rosalind stood up carefully, not wanting to knock over the small table at the side of the sofa that was covered in knick-knacks and framed daguerreotypes, mainly of children.

'My pupils,' Miss Thompson said, following Rosalind's gaze. 'So many lovely young lives entrusted to my care.'

'Except for Blease Ewart,' Rosalind said, smiling. 'Blease is such an unusual name.'

'It was his mother's maiden name. Poor Emily always considered herself to be better than other people, as did young Blease. I wonder where he is now and if he's still pursuing a life of crime.'

'He sounds like the type of person who would survive anything.' Rosalind shook Miss Thompson's hand. She was about to follow Alexander from the room when Miss Thompson called her back.

'There's one notable thing about Blease Ewart. He was very clever and good at lessons. He was convinced that his real father was Lord Knighton. Now, I don't know who put that idea into his head, although it was probably his mother, but Blease considered himself to be superior in every way.'

'Someone who fits the description you've given us has done very well for himself,' Rosalind said gently. She had not the heart to tell Miss Thompson that her former pupil was little more than a criminal, and the smile she received was worth the white lie. She left the cottage and walked down the garden path to join Alex where he was waiting with the horses.

He lifted her onto the saddle, holding her by the waist for a little longer than was necessary.

'What did she want?'

'I think she just needed to feel that Blease Ewart was not a lost cause. I told her that he had done well for himself, which is true, in a way. He lives the life of a gentleman, even if he isn't one.'

'You are too kind-hearted.' Alexander released her reluctantly. 'Now, I suppose we'd better get back to Trevenor and hope there hasn't been an all-out battle.'

Rosalind smiled. 'Bertie would enjoy a scrap. I'm not sure about Walter.'

They rode back to Trevenor, entering the grounds the way they had come in order to avoid the main gates. Rosalind had said little during the return journey. Her thoughts were occupied with Alexander's unexpected declaration of his feelings for her. It was something she had known deep in her heart, and she had been carried away by the strength of his emotions, but now, as they rode side by side through the leafy lanes, she was confused. Her feelings for Piers had been challenged by his apparent duplicity, and maybe they had been based on her childhood crush on the boy who had come seemingly from nowhere to save her life. It had come as a shock to discover that he had been planning to cheat them out of their heritage, and for that there seemed to be no reasonable excuse. She had been hurt and had felt betrayed, and then Alexander had come to her aid, and now he had proposed marriage. She did have feelings for him and she enjoyed being with him, although she was not sure whether this was a good basis for marriage. Even so the prospect of a new life as an army wife in India was an exciting challenge.

When they arrived back at the house Rosalind went straight to her room, using the excuse that she needed to change out of her dusty riding habit. Mrs Phelps sent up a maid with a ewer of hot water, and after a wash and a change of clothes Rosalind began to feel more like her old self. She sat by the open window, gazing down at the calm waters in the bay. She had seen Walter briefly and he had assured her that nothing untoward had happened in her absence. He had spent the day taking it in turns with Bertie to keep watch, and the servants had been instructed to let them know if they saw anything unusual. Walter had seemed more bored than frustrated, but Rosalind suspected that Bertie would have been longing for a serious confrontation.

She was aware of someone in the garden and when she looked down she saw Bertie beckoning to her, and she knew her moment of privacy was over. Somewhat reluctantly she rose to her feet and moved away from the window to slip off her wrap and put on a cotton print gown. She brushed her hair and tied it back with a ribbon before going downstairs to the terrace.

Bertie was standing by the low balustrade. He greeted her with a smile. 'Alex told us what you'd found out today. It's interesting, but I don't see that it helps us at all.'

'Blaise told us a pack of lies, Bertie. We won't know the whole truth until Piers decides to return, if ever.'

'In the meantime it looks as if we're about to be invaded by angry villagers,' Walter said, pointing to the gates where a crowd had gathered.

Alexander glanced over Walter's shoulder. 'That's Pedrick at the forefront. He has a good job at the mine so I can't think what he's doing. I'll go down there and speak to them.'

'They look angry,' Bertie said warily. 'And they're armed with anything they could lay their hands on. I wish I'd brought my Manton with me. A few shots fired over their heads might make them see sense.'

'I'll deal with them.' Alexander made a move towards the steps that led down into the garden. 'If it comes to a fight we have the advantage.'

'But there's more of them than us,' Walter protested.

'I mean tactically. There should be weapons locked away in the gun room. I don't suppose Grandmama would have taken them to Rockwood with her, even if she knows of their existence. They're probably ancient blunderbusses, but the protestors won't know that.'

'They must have a good reason for coming *en masse*,' Rosalind said thoughtfully. 'If you go in fighting, the trouble will escalate.' She was about to negotiate the steps leading down to the garden when Alexander stopped her.

'Where are you going?'

'I mean to reason with them,' she said defiantly. 'Don't try to stop me.'

'You're not going alone.' Alexander was about to follow her but she turned on him angrily.

'You men turn everything into a battle. Haven't you wondered why they're prepared to risk arrest by their behaviour? Let me do this.' Rosalind marched on without looking back, although she sensed that Alexander and her brothers were following at a safe distance. The afternoon sun blazed from an azure sky and the ground beneath her feet was baked dry. She could feel the heat burning through the thin soles of her shoes, and she could hear Hester's voice in her head scolding her for walking out of doors with neither hat nor gloves. The men behind the gates were shouting loudly, although she could not make out the words, but she continued walking purposefully, coming to a halt when she was just a few feet away from them. A sea of angry faces greeted her and Pedrick stepped forward.

'Go back home, maid. This isn't your fight.'

'I don't see that it's yours either, Mr Pedrick,' Rosalind said calmly. 'What is it exactly that your men want?'

His eyes widened and his scowl was replaced by a perplexed frown. 'Justice, miss. The servants from Trevenor House have been dismissed without a character and the miners haven't been paid for nearly a month. These men have families to support.'

'First, the servants were given the choice of whether to stay and work for Lady Pentelow or to walk out of their own free will. But our presence has nothing to do with the mine, which surely is for Mr Blanchard and Mr Blaise to work out.'

'Neither of them has been seen for the past few weeks, miss.'

Rosalind thought quickly. 'How much is needed to pay the men, Mr Pedrick, and yourself, of course?'

'I can't give you a figure off hand, miss.' Pedrick turned to the crowd behind him. 'Shut up, all of you. I can't hear myself think.'

'Don't let a petticoat pull the wool over your eyes, boss.' A burly miner shoved his way to the front. 'Look at the menfolk – they're hiding behind a slip of a girl.'

'What's your name, sir?' Rosalind demanded coolly.

He snatched off his cap, clutching it in his hands. 'Comer, miss. Daniel Comer. I have a wife and six young 'uns to feed and clothe.'

'It's very wrong that you and your workmates haven't been paid, Mr Comer,' Rosalind said in a loud, clear voice so that everyone could hear. 'I've just asked Mr Pedrick how much money he needs to pay you all your dues, and when he gives me an answer I will personally make sure that you all receive your wages.'

'How do we know you'm not just saying that, miss?'

Alexander moved swiftly to her side. 'You've all known me since I was a boy. I can assure you that what Miss Carey says is true. If Pedrick can give me the amount before the end of the day, I'll guarantee to have the money in the mine office before close of business tomorrow, and you will all be paid. As to the servants who chose to walk out, they will get their pay and a reference if they ask for one. Lady Pentelow might choose to take them on when she returns. I can't say fairer than that.'

A murmur of assent rippled round the group and Pedrick wiped his brow on his sleeve. 'Thank you, Captain Blanchard, and you too, Miss Carey. Can I be certain that the money will be in my hands when you said it would, sir?'

'You have my word on it.' Alexander moved closer to the gate. 'But, Pedrick, if Mr Blaise should put in an appearance don't for heaven's sake give him any money. In fact, don't let him into the office.'

'But he's part owner, sir. I haven't got the authority to keep him locked out.'

'Mr Blaise is wanted by the police and the revenue men, Pedrick. The best thing you could do would be to send for me or either of the gentlemen who are staying here at present. We'll deal with Blaise.'

'Very well, Captain.' Pedrick turned to the men. 'Back to work. We have the captain's word and that's good enough for me.' The group fragmented, the miners heading back to work and the others going their separate ways. Pedrick tipped his cap and followed them down the lane.

'Well done, Rosie,' Alexander said, slipping his arm around her waist. 'You were magnificent. Grandmama couldn't have done better.'

Bertie sighed. 'Damn it, Rosie, I was looking forward to a scrap.'

'Well, I'm glad you talked them round.' Walter started back towards the house. 'What do we do now, Alex?'

Alexander tucked Rosalind's hand in the crook of his arm. 'As soon as I know how much money we need I'll ride to Bodmin and draw it out of the bank. The mine needs to be kept in full production, not that I've ever had anything to do with the business – that was always Piers' problem, not mine.'

'Piers wouldn't let his family down,' Rosalind said firmly. 'No matter what he's done I don't believe he would desert your grandmother, Alex. There must be a good reason for all this.'

'You're too trusting, Rosie,' Bertie said over his shoulder. 'If things are settled here I vote we return to Rockwood as soon as possible. This is a lovely place but there's less comfort in Trevenor than there was in the castle when we were poor, and I miss Hester's cooking.'

Alexander chuckled. 'You are a spoilt boy, Bertram Carey. Wait until you've had to bivouac in hostile territory and in even worse weather. As an enlisted man you won't have any home comforts.'

'Then I'll work my way up the ranks,' Bertie said casually. 'I'll have to return home soon anyway or I'll be had up for desertion even before I've joined my regiment.'

'I'll leave for Bodmin first thing in the morning.' Alexander patted Rosalind's hand as it rested on his sleeve. 'Will you come with me?'

'I thought I smelled roses,' Bertie said, laughing. 'Are you courting my sister, Blanchard?'

'Certainly not.' Rosalind snatched her hand free. 'Alexander will be returning to his regiment at the same time as you, Bertie. We're just friends, isn't that so, Alex?'

He squeezed her fingers. 'I was hoping we were more than that, Rosie.'

She held back, allowing her brothers to walk on ahead. 'I asked you for time to think over your proposal, Alex. Please don't make things even more difficult for me.'

'I'm sorry, I didn't realise that you would be embarrassed by my feelings for you.'

'It isn't that. I'm not ready to make a commitment just yet. There is too much going on in our lives and I don't want either of us to make a terrible mistake.'

'But you love me, Rosie. You said as much when I told you how I felt.'

'I do have feelings for you, Alex. But I don't know whether they are strong enough to stand up to the sort of tests that life as an army wife would entail. I'm no coward, but you can't blame me for wanting to take my time. It's all been so sudden.'

'Love happens like that sometimes, Rosie.'

'Please don't say any more. Give me time, please, Alex.' She hurried on, leaving him to follow her more slowly. She knew she had hurt his feelings and she hated herself for doing so, but she had to be honest and she had to be certain. There were other matters that needed to be resolved before she could give herself body and soul to any man. The boy who had come into her life so suddenly twelve years ago still haunted her thoughts, and she needed to talk to Piers before she could make any decisions about her future.

Chapter Twenty-Five

Two days later the hired carriage drew up in the castle bailey. Rosalind had tears in her eyes as she alighted, gazing up at the grey stones warmed by a touch of gold and mellowed by centuries of south-westerly winds. Trevenor was a beautiful house, but Rockwood, for all its faults, was home. Even as her feet touched the ground, Rosalind was almost knocked over by Bob's enthusiastic welcome. He went round in circles, wagging his tail and brushing up against her so that she had to stop to make a fuss off him before he would allow her to enter the house.

'Good boy,' she said, stroking his ears. 'I've missed you, too.'

Bob gazed up at her with adoring eyes and she leaned over to give him a quick cuddle. Alex, Bertie and Walter alighted from the carriage and the coachman heaved their luggage to the ground. All was bustle around them as two footmen hurried forward to retrieve their baggage and Patterson stood in the open doorway. He managed a tight little smile as he responded to Rosalind's greeting.

'Welcome home, Miss Rosalind.'

'Thank you, Patterson.' Rosalind entered the great hall with Bob at her heels. The slightly musty smell that pervaded this part of the building, no matter how much lavender and beeswax polish was applied to the wide oak staircase, was familiar and welcoming. All the perfumes in the world could not smell sweeter than the scent of home. It was mid-afternoon, a time when the servants were least busy, and without stopping to take off her bonnet and gloves, Rosalind made her way below stairs. She found Hester, as she had hoped, in her small parlour.

'Miss Rosalind, you've come home.' Hester raised herself from her chair by the fireplace.

Rosalind gave her a hug. 'How are you, Hester?'

'All the better for seeing you, poppet.'

Rosalind smiled at the familiar term of endearment. 'I meant, how are you managing without Jacob? It must have been a terrible shock to discover his deceit.'

'He's not important. I don't even want to mention his name. That man betrayed us all, and to think I allowed him to visit me. He used me and I won't forgive him for that.'

'It's fortunate that you didn't give in and marry Jacob.'

'Well, at least I had the sense to hold back. He kept telling me that he loved me, but I never quite believed him.'

'I am so sorry, Hester. Do you know what's happened to him?'

'He and the others are going up before the magistrate at the next assizes. A few weeks in prison will do them all good.'

'You're taking it very well. I was afraid you'd be more upset.'

'Upset? No, but angry – yes. Now forget about my troubles and tell me what's been happening down there in Cornwall?'

'We've taken back Trevenor. I should inform Lady Pentelow first, so don't let on to the rest of the servants, but they will be going home very soon.'

'It can't come soon enough for me and the rest of us. I've had enough of that Monsieur Frenchie, and Mrs Witham, too. Good riddance is what I say.'

'I'm glad you're coping, Hester. Although, of course, I should have known that you would. Anyway, I'm going to my room to change and then I'll give the good news to her ladyship.' Rosalind hesitated in the doorway. 'Has my sister been behaving while I was away?'

'That Miss Aurelia is a bad influence. They maids have been in and out at all hours. I don't know why her ladyship don't tell them off, but she thinks the sun shines out of Miss Aurelia's . . .' Hester bit her lip. 'You know what I mean.'

'That sounds ominous. Do you know where I might find Patricia?'

Hester pulled a face. 'She's been out gallivanting with that Oscar Cottingham when she's not with Miss Aurelia. I told her that she's making a show of herself, but you know Miss Patricia. She don't listen to no one.'

'That's true, but I'll have a word with her, Hester. Was there anything else?'

'Sir Lucien still thinks we're about to be invaded by the Frenchies. He gave Jarvis the slip one morning and he chased Monsieur Jacques round the kitchen with a carving knife, threatening to slit his gizzard. There was such a to-do.' Hester eyed her warily. 'Lady Pentelow has a visitor. She's asked Mrs Witham to have a room made up for him.'

'Who is it, Hester?'

'I didn't see who it was and Patterson wouldn't say, so I didn't bother to pursue the matter.'

'It seems I returned none too soon.' Rosalind sighed. 'Don't worry, Hester. I'll deal with everything.'

She left the kitchen and went to her room. It was good to be home, even if Patsy was being awkward and Grandpapa was in one of his difficult phases. As to the visitor, he was Lady Pentelow's problem.

Half an hour later, washed, changed and feeling more like herself, Rosalind went to the drawing room, but the sight that met her eyes as she opened the door took her breath away. It was Blaise who sat next to Lady Pentelow on the sofa, sipping tea from a delicate china cup.

'What are you doing here?' Rosalind stared at him in disbelief.

Lady Pentelow placed her cup back on its saucer. 'Don't use that tone of voice in my company, Rosalind. Mr Blaise is my guest and I've invited him to stay for a day or two.'

'This man is an imposter, and a criminal, Lady Pentelow. What is he doing in my drawing room?'

'This is my residence now, Rosalind. Piers is the next in line to inherit Rockwood after your grandfather, who is patently unfit to be the head of the household.'

'Aren't you forgetting that it was this man who threw you out of your own home, Lady Pentelow? He isn't who he claims to be. If you don't believe me, just ask Alexander.'

Blaise rose to his feet. 'Perhaps I should go to my room, Lady Pentelow. I can see that whatever I say is going to be misconstrued.'

'How could you allow him to stay here?' Rosalind could hardly contain her anger.

'Ewart has explained everything to me, Rosalind. He feels he is entitled, as the eldest son, to inherit Trevenor, which I think is morally correct, even though society might disagree. I miss Trevenor, of course, but Ewart has told me that I am more than welcome to visit.'

'Lady Pentelow, that man is a common criminal. He's told you a pack of lies.'

'He's explained everything to me. He was duped by that man Jacob Lidstone, your cook's gentleman friend, although not so much of a gentleman, as I have learned. Poor Ewart was taken in and he's doing his best to atone.'

'It was all a terrible misunderstanding, Miss Carey,' Blaise said silkily. 'Lady Pentelow was kind enough to allow me to explain.'

'More to the point,' Lady Pentelow fixed Rosalind with a glassy stare, 'you coerced me into writing that letter to Ewart and then you left without so much as a word to me.'

'I think you need to talk to Alexander,' Rosalind said awkwardly. She could see that Blaise was enjoying her discomfort and that by some means he had won Lady Pentelow over, despite his previous behaviour. It was a relief when the door opened and Alexander entered, coming to an abrupt halt when he spotted Blaise.

'What is he doing here, Grandmama?'

'Apparently it was all a mistake, according to Mr Blaise.' Rosalind laid a warning hand on his arm. Even through the thickness of his jacket she could feel his muscles were tensed, ready for action.

'This poor man has been unjustly maligned,' Lady Pentelow said impatiently. 'He is a guest in my home and will be treated as such. Do I make myself plain, Alexander?'

'Perfectly, Grandmama,' Alexander said warily. 'But there are certain things you ought to know.'

Blaise stood up. 'I think I should leave you to sort out family matters, Lady Pentelow. I'll go to my room, if I may.'

'No, Ewart. As you explained to me, you are part of this family now. Please sit down.'

'You are too kind, ma'am.' Blaise resumed his seat, casting a triumphant look in Rosalind's direction.

She clenched her fists at her sides. It seemed impossible that a woman of the world like Lady Pentelow could be taken in by the lies that poured out of Blaise's mouth.

'Don't think you can get away with your bad behaviour, either of you,' Lady Pentelow said angrily. 'You went away without a chaperone, Rosalind. That is unforgiveable behaviour, and I blame you just as much for allowing her to do so, Alexander. Her reputation will be irretrievably tarnished.'

'Not so, Grandmama.' Alexander raised Rosalind's hand to his lips. 'Rosalind has done me the honour of accepting my proposal. We are to be married as soon as possible.'

Lady Pentelow half rose but sank back onto her seat. 'Married?'

'Yes, we're engaged,' Rosalind said defiantly.

'Allow me to be the first to congratulate you.' Blaise stood, holding out his hand. 'I wish you all the happiness you deserve.'

Alexander glared at him and there was an uncomfortable silence, broken only when the door opened to admit Bertie and Walter. They came to a halt, staring open-mouthed at Blaise.

'What's going on?' Bertie demanded. 'What is he doing here?'

'Mind your manners, Bertram,' Lady Pentelow said crossly. 'I don't know why you are all being so rude to my guest. You'll have to forgive them, Ewart. They don't know any better.'

'Why have you got your arm around my sister, Alex?' Walter asked, frowning.

'We were going to announce our betrothal at dinner,' Alexander said calmly. 'But the situation arose where we were compelled to speak out.'

'You and Rosie?' Bertie stared at them, shaking his head. 'You sly dog, Alex. But what is Blaise doing here?'

'He is Grandmama's guest. I suggest we leave them to talk.' Alexander turned to Rosalind with a meaningful look. 'I'm going to get some fresh air.'

'Yes, me too.' Rosalind turned to her brothers. 'Will you join us? It's rather stuffy in here.' She followed Alexander from the room with Bertie and Walter hurrying after them.

'What's going on?' Walter demanded.

'What is Blaise doing here, Alex?' Bertie added angrily.

'This is an impossible situation,' Alexander said in a low voice. 'Let's go somewhere we can discuss it without being overhead.'

'The library is the best place.' Walter backed away. 'I hardly ever get interrupted when I'm working there.'

'You're right.' Rosalind nodded. 'Come on, Alex, and you, Bertie.'

'Well,' Bertie said impatiently as he closed the library door. 'I'm waiting. Are you going to tell me what's going on, or do I throw the imposter out?'

'He's convinced Lady Pentelow that he is the victim and that he is part of the family, even if he was born on the wrong side of the blanket, as Hester would say.' Rosalind sank down on the nearest chair. 'She believes every word he says, although I can't think why he's risked everything to come here.'

'We'll deal with him later,' Bertie said grimly. 'You are my main concern at the moment, Rosie. Are you really going to marry Alex?'

Alexander reached out to take Rosalind's hand in his before she had a chance to answer. 'Your sister has done me the honour of accepting my proposal, Bertie.'

'Congratulations.' Bertie's frown was replaced by a smile and he slapped Alexander on the back. 'I'm happy for you both. Forget Blaise for now and come with me. We'll raid the cellar, Alex. I don't trust Patterson to select the best wine. I'm sure he keeps it for himself.'

'I always thought as much when we were at Trevenor,' Alexander said with a smile. 'Lead on,

Bertie. We'll toast our engagement when I get back, Rosie.'

Walter waited until they were out of earshot. 'Are you sure about this, Rosie? I mean, it's very sudden.'

'I think we will do very well together, Walter.' She could not deny it without hurting Alexander. It was the shock of seeing Blaise in her own drawing room and an unthinking reaction to Lady Pentelow's criticism that had made her speak out, which she now regretted bitterly.

'But do you love him, Rosie? I always thought you had a preference for Piers, but of course that's out of the question now he's proved himself to be so untrustworthy.'

'Maybe, but Piers did put all that money in the bank for his family, so he can't be all bad.'

Walter grasped her by the hand. 'Rosie, I don't usually say much, but I feel something isn't quite right here. You know I love you and I want you to be happy, but please think carefully before you commit yourself to marrying a military man.'

'I will, Walter. But nothing is arranged as yet, and Alex will be returning to his regiment in a week or so.'

'Promise me you won't do anything rash,' Walter said earnestly.

She smiled and brushed his cheek with a tender kiss. 'You are so sweet, Walter. I promise.'

Minutes later Bertie and Alexander returned clutching two bottles of claret and four glasses.

'You both look very serious.' Alexander took a corkscrew from his pocket and handed it to Bertie. 'This is supposed to be a celebration.'

'We were just saying that we need to protect your grandmother from Blaise,' Rosalind said earnestly. 'I don't know how he's managed to charm her into believing that he was falsely accused, but she needs to know the truth, and you are the only one who can do that.'

Alexander's smile faded. 'You're right, Rosie. I'll talk to her when I can get her on her own. That is, if we can prise Blaise from her side.'

'We can't tell her that she can return to Trevenor without alerting Blaise to what we've done.'

'Why not announce it at dinner this evening?' Walter said thoughtfully. 'We have proof that Blaise isn't who he claims to be.'

'It's only hearsay unless we can get a copy of the parish records.' Rosalind sat down on one of the damask upholstered chairs that Lady Pentelow had brought with her from Trevenor. 'Without proof I don't think your grandmother will believe us, Alex.'

The door burst open before anyone had a chance to speak and Aurelia rushed into the room, followed by Patricia.

'What's going on?' Aurelia demanded. 'Why are you drinking in the middle of the afternoon?'

'You are amongst the first to know that Rosie and I are engaged to be married,' Alexander said happily.

Patricia's smile faded. 'What? No, you can't be.'

'That's not fair, Alex,' Aurelia added crossly. 'Hugo has proposed to me and we were to make the announcement at a summer ball to be held at his home in two weeks' time.'

'I thought at least you might be happy for us, Aurelia.' Alexander held his glass out to Bertie. 'I think we all need a drink, old man. Except for Aurelia and Patricia: they are far too young.'

'You are a beast,' Aurelia said, pouting. 'I'm not too young to be married. Anyway, I thought that Rosalind and Piers would make a match of it, not you.'

Rosalind frowned. 'I think we need to talk, girls. Let's leave the gentlemen to their wine.' She turned to Alex with an apologetic smile. 'I'll see you at dinner, but first I have words to say to my sister and Aurelia.' She shooed them out of the library, stopping only when they were outside in the rose garden. 'That was mean of you, Aurelia. Why did you want to hurt your brother like that?'

'Alex has always been the favourite. Grandmama adores him and poor Piers was never given credit for what he did. Now you've got your claws into Alex and heaven knows what's happened to Piers. Don't you care?'

'Of course I do,' Rosalind plucked a red rose and held it to her nose, inhaling its heady scent. 'You girls have no idea what's been going on, but creating trouble between us isn't going to help.' She turned to Patricia. 'I hear that you've been behaving badly, so don't you dare criticise me.'

Patricia made a *moue*. 'You can break all the rules, but if I do the slightest wrong thing you make such a fuss about it. You're my sister, Rosie, not my mother.'

'Well, Mama isn't here at present and someone has to take care of you. Not so long ago you were prepared to elope to Gretna Green with Barnaby Yelland, and now I'm told you are flirting outrageously with Ossie Cottingham.'

'We were just having fun. Anyway, I think you have some explaining to do yourself. What were you doing in Cornwall? You didn't take a chaperone so why is there one rule for you and a different one for me?'

'That's a good question,' Aurelia said smugly. 'You led Piers on, and just because he's in a bit of bother you've decided to run away with Alex.'

'You don't know what you're talking about.' Rosalind tossed the rose into the ornamental pond and it lay on a lily pad, creating a splash of colour on the cool green leaves. She glanced from one sulky face to the other and she relented. 'If you'll stop grumbling I'll tell you what happened in Cornwall. You'll find out sooner or later, anyway.'

Patricia slumped down on a rustic wooden seat. 'Go on. Tell us what exactly you were doing at Trevenor.'

Aurelia sat down beside her. 'Yes, and I hope it won't make things difficult for Hugo and me. I want a wedding that will be the talk of the county for years to come, and I'll never forgive you if you've ruined my chances.'

Rosalind stifled the urge to tell Aurelia that she was acting like a spoilt child. She forced herself to be patient as she perched on the marble balustrade, which separated the rose garden from the deer park. 'All right, hear me out and you might feel differently.'

She related in detail all the events that had led to their hasty return from Cornwall, and the way in which Blaise had lied and pretended to be related to Aurelia and her brothers.

'How could he lie about such a thing?' Aurelia said angrily.

'Not only did he claim to be your father's love child, but he also told people that Lord Knighton was his father. Blease Ewart or Ewart Blaise, as he prefers to be known, is a cheat and a liar, and unfortunately he has managed to charm your grand-mother into believing everything he says.'

'What are you going to do about it, Rosie?' Patricia asked anxiously.

'I don't know yet. I'll have to talk it over with Alex and Bertie.'

'You'd better do it quickly.' Aurelia rose from the seat, brushing the dust off her voluminous skirts. 'If anything happens to spoil my engagement party at Knighton Hall I'll never forgive any of you.' She flounced off, tossing her dark curls so that they glinted in the sunshine.

'What a pickle,' Patricia said sadly. 'Are you really in love with Alex, Rosie? I like him a lot and I wouldn't want to see him hurt.'

'Neither would I, Patsy. You'll have to trust me on this, and you need to be careful about your own behaviour. You don't want to get a reputation as a flirt, do you?'

Patricia shook her head. 'I was just having fun.'

'I know you were, but you're a young lady now. I understand that you might find it difficult because you want to enjoy yourself, but if you want to be invited to all the best houses and balls, you will have to behave more circumspectly. Perhaps you'd like to see Christina and Sylvia again? Sir Michael won't bother me now he thinks I'm engaged to someone else.'

'You don't sound too sure of it, Rosie?'

'It's just new, that's all. I expect it takes some getting used to.'

Patricia gave her a hug. 'I don't pretend to understand, but it will be all right in the end. Isn't that what Hester always says?'

Rosalind smiled reluctantly. 'Yes, we can always rely on Hester for good advice.'

'I'll follow Aurelia. Maybe together we can find out exactly what that man Blaise has told her grandmother, and why he's returned here, of all things.'

'He's trying to take away Piers' inheritance,' Rosalind said slowly. 'We secured Trevenor for Lady Pentelow – at least I hope we did – but with Blaise changing his story every time I see him, I'm not so sure.'

Patricia kissed her on the cheek. 'Stop fretting, Rosie. Enjoy being engaged to Alexander. I know I would if it were me.'

'You like Alex?'

'Of course I do. Who wouldn't fall in love a little with a dashing soldier? And he's funny and kind – you could do worse.'

Rosalind laughed. 'You sound like my mother, not my little sister.'

'I'm growing up fast.' Patricia did a twirl and then she walked off more sedately, but with a definite spring in her step.

Dinner that evening was a strained affair. Blaise sat next to Lady Pentelow at table but conversation flagged after Rosalind's initial attempts to encourage the others to talk. Alexander said very little and Bertie was openly disapproving. The only two people at table who tried to ease the situation were Rosalind and, surprisingly, Walter, who was normally very quiet, lost in his own thoughts. Sir Lucien had kept to his solar, having once again upset Monsieur Jacques, who had declared that he was leaving at the end of the week, and no amount of persuasion could make him change his mind.

The tensions above stairs seemed to have filtered down to the servants' hall and Tilly was obviously nervous. She dropped a silver serving dish filled with roast meat on the floor, to the delight of Bob, who gobbled every last slice. Tilly fled from the room in tears and her place was taken by Ada, who seemed equally upset and spilled a jug of gravy, most of which ended up on Blaise's lap. He left the dining room muttering beneath his breath, and the atmosphere changed the moment the door closed on him. Patricia started to giggle, joined by Aurelia, and then Bertie threw his head back and guffawed. Soon everyone, with the exception of Lady Pentelow, was laughing hysterically.

'You are behaving like schoolchildren,' she said, rising to her feet. 'I refuse to sit at table with such ill-mannered people. I'm ashamed of you all.' She left the dining room, followed by Patterson, who was apologising profusely.

'Maybe we could get the servants to repeat the accident at every mealtime,' Bertie said drily. 'Then Blaise will realise he's not welcome here, because that man has a hide as thick as an elephant's.'

'How are we to convince your grandmother of his dishonesty, Alex?' Rosalind asked urgently. 'There must be a reason why he has come to Rockwood, and it isn't because he wanted to be part of the family. What does he hope to gain by this sudden turn around? Just a short time ago he was threatening to create a scandal that would ruin the Blanchards, and now he wants everyone to like him. What does that man want from us?'

Chapter Twenty-Six

Dinner was over and, to Rosalind's surprise, Lady Pentelow appeared in the doorway. 'The ladies will retire to the drawing room now and leave the gentlemen to their brandy and cigars.'

It was an instruction that neither Rosalind, Aurelia nor Patricia dared to challenge and they dutifully left their places to follow her.

Blaise had just rejoined them, having changed out of his soiled trousers, but he smiled and stood up. 'I've had a very long day,' he said pleasantly. 'If you'll excuse me, gentlemen. I think I'll go to my room.'

Rosalind stood aside to allow him to pass, but she turned her head to give Alexander a questioning look. He shrugged and held his hands palms upwards.

'Come along, Rosalind. Don't dawdle,' Lady Pentelow said sharply.

Alexander jumped to his feet. 'I think I need a

breath of fresh air. Will you walk on the terrace with me, Rosie?'

'That's out of the question,' Lady Pentelow snapped. 'Haven't you broken enough rules, Alexander?'

'I think it's perfectly proper for me to want to talk in private to my fiancée, Grandmama.'

'There's a time and a place for such things, and this is neither. Sit down, Alexander, and, Rosalind, come with me.'

'If you'll excuse me, ma'am, I think I should go to the east wing and check on my grandfather. I haven't seen him since I returned from Cornwall.'

Lady Pentelow shrugged. 'Do as you please. I don't know what's happening to young people these days. Come, Aurelia, and you, too, Patricia. We will take coffee in the drawing room.'

Rosalind did not look back. She made her way to the solar, intending to sit with her grandfather until it was time for Jarvis to help him into his bed. She found Jarvis in the small antechamber eating his supper. He leaped to his feet.

'I beg your pardon, Miss Rosalind. This is the first chance I've had to eat my meal this evening.'

'Please don't stop, Jarvis. I thought I'd spend some time with my grandfather. How is he?'

'Middling, I'd say, Miss Rosalind. But I'm sure he'll be pleased to see you.' Jarvis produced a set of huge iron keys and unlocked the door to the solar. He stepped inside. 'You have a visitor, Admiral.'

Sir Lucien was standing by one of the tall windows, holding a brass telescope to his right eye. He lowered it and glanced over his shoulder. 'Rosalind, my dear girl. It's good to see you.'

He seemed like the grandpapa she remembered from the old days and her eyes filled with tears as she rushed over to give him a hug. 'Grandpapa, how are you?'

'I can't complain, my love. Sit down and tell me what you've been doing.'

'Oh, this and that, Grandpapa.' Rosalind sat down on a high-backed wooden settle, facing her grandfather, who took his seat in a worn and rather saggy armchair.

He put his head on one side, eyeing her with a knowing look. 'Hester tells me that all is not well both above and below stairs, Rosalind.'

'You've spoken to Hester recently?'

He chuckled. 'It's our secret, Rosie. Hester is the one who keeps me up to date with family matters. She comes up to take tea with me every afternoon and has done so for many years.'

Rosalind could hardly believe her ears. 'What has she told you?'

'I know all about Lady Pentelow and her airs and graces. You see, I met Clarissa a long time ago, when we were both much younger. She was a sprightly little thing and not averse to a flirtation with a dashing naval hero like myself, even though she was married at the time.'

'I can hardly believe it, Grandpapa.'

'It's always the ones with the most to hide who become the most censorious, in my experience, Rosie. Clarissa Pentelow came from an aristocratic but poor family. She was a great beauty in her day and she caught the eye of Sir Edmund Pentelow, a wealthy merchant who was twice her age. It's common knowledge that she ran through his money with her extravagances and they say she drove him to an early grave.' Sir Lucien laughed and winked wickedly. 'Clarissa's daughter inherited her mother's beauty and she married Philip Blanchard, which is how Clarissa came to live at Trevenor.'

'Did Hester tell you about Ewart Blaise?'

'I know that a man called Blaise was here on the night of the ball. I can't remember what happened afterwards, Rosie. I'm sorry if I've embarrassed you at any time.'

She jumped up to give him a hug. 'No, Grandpapa. You don't upset anyone. We know that sometimes you are not yourself, but I had no idea that you and Hester were such good friends.'

He pulled a face. 'It isn't done, is it, poppet? I mean, apart from the fact that I'm an old man, Hester is a servant and I'm the master of the house. At least I was until that Pentelow woman foisted herself upon us.'

'Piers claims to be the true owner of Rockwood, Grandpapa. Did you know that?'

Sir Lucien lay back in his chair, closing his eyes.

'Twelve years ago, as you might remember, there was an altercation between a gang of smugglers, the men who were to receive the goods and the customs officers.'

'I do remember it, Grandpapa. I was caught up in it.'

'You were injured, and a boy brought you home. We thought you had a cracked skull, but fortunately it was only concussion. Hester brought the boy to me and he stayed here that night. We talked into the small hours and next day I sent him back to Cornwall in my private carriage.'

'You knew Piers all that time ago?'

'My dear, there's little that goes on in Rockwood that I don't know about. Piers explained his circumstances to me when we first met, and I realised that he was a good boy, far more worthy than his spineless father.'

Rosalind shook her head. Her grandfather's revelation came as a shock. 'Did you know that Piers intended to claim Rockwood for himself?'

'It was at my suggestion, Rosie. Philip Blanchard had been taking money out of the china clay company instead of reinvesting what profit he made. He was desperate, which is why he was with the smugglers that night twelve years ago.

'But Piers was also on the ship, Grandpapa.'

'The boy told me that he suspected his father was up to no good and he'd stowed away. But the gang weren't ordinary smugglers. Philip Blanchard had staged a robbery of his own mine offices in order to claim the large insurance that he had taken out, but someone reported the deception to the insurance company. The money was brought ashore, together with the contraband, and hidden on our land.'

'Did Piers tell you all this twelve years ago?'

'Most of it. The boy was worried that his father would go to prison, leaving his mother with a failing business and three children to raise on her own.'

'Did he know where they had hidden the cache, Grandpapa?'

'No, but there was a young seaman on that ship, whom Piers suspected might have that information. The boy was always snooping on the other crew members and he boasted that he knew where they had hidden their cache.'

'Was that boy Ewart Blaise?'

'I believe so.'

'You kept silent all these years. Did you know where the money was concealed?'

'If I had I might have used some of it to keep the castle from falling into disrepair. I only knew that it was somewhere on the estate, or even in the caves. Don't think that we didn't search.'

'You and who else?'

'Jacob Lidstone was part of the gang who were waiting to receive the smuggled goods in one of the caves. He's been trying to find the hoard ever since, although I've only just been made aware of that.'

'He pretended to be courting Hester. That's unspeakable behaviour.'

'I agree, and I had nothing to do with him until Hester discovered his secret. She came to me in tears, poor woman, and we decided on a course of action, with help from Piers, of course.'

Rosalind shook her head. She felt as though the room was spinning round her in concentric circles. 'So this was all a plan to trap the thieves into showing you where they had hidden the money? Piers was in it from the beginning.'

'We decided that it was the only way, and if Piers laid claim to the castle it might encourage Blaise to step forward and show his hand.'

'So it was all a fabrication? That long and complicated story about a baby snatched from its crib and taken to Trevenor was all untrue?'

'I'm afraid so, but Piers told it with such conviction that you all believed him. He had to make it sound believable to draw Blaise out into the open, which he did very successfully.'

Rosalind eyed him with concern. 'Grandpapa, you are not well. You know you have these moments when you think that we are being invaded by the French. Perhaps this is all part of your illness, and none of it really happened.'

'I do have lapses of memory, my love. But they are not as bad as I sometimes make out.'

Rosalind smiled and kissed his wrinkled cheek. 'You are a crafty old gentleman, Grandpapa.' Her smile faded. 'But where is Piers now? Why did he disappear so suddenly? What exactly is his part in all this?'

'After the girls went exploring the cellars Piers thought they might have stumbled on something. I went with him one night after everyone had gone to bed. I dropped my lamp by accident and we noticed that the oil seeped down between two flagstones. That was how we discovered the oubli-ette.'

'And the cache was hidden down there?'

'It was indeed.'

'But, Grandpapa, some of the crew on board that ship twelve years ago must have known where it was hidden.'

'They were caught, tried and transported to Australia for life. All, that is, except Blaise, who was deemed to be too young and innocent to suffer transportation. Philip Blanchard had managed to convince a jury that he was innocent, but Blaise blackmailed him into giving him work in the china clay mine, eventually making him a sleeping partner in the firm. Blaise has been taking regular dividends ever since.'

'So Blaise returned to claim what he thinks is owed to him,' Rosalind said thoughtfully. 'But where is Piers? You didn't say.'

'He is an honourable man, Rosie. He's declared

the goods to the Revenue, and he's doing his best to find the original owners of the gold and jewels that were part of the stash.'

'But where is he, Grandpapa? Why can't he do that from home?'

Sir Lucien chuckled. 'He is not too far away, Rosie. If you go to the ruined keeper's cottage in the woods you should find him.'

'We were always afraid of that place,' Rosalind said, frowning. 'Part of it was burned down in a fire and we always thought it was haunted. Why must he hide in such a dreadful place?'

'For the very reasons you've just given me.' Sir Lucien yawned. 'Now, I am very tired, Rosie. Will you send Jarvis to me? I need to go to my bed.'

'Yes, of course I will. I'm sorry, I'm being very thoughtless.' Rosie kissed him once again and hurried from the room to find Jarvis.

She made her way downstairs slowly, with all the information that her grandfather had just imparted racing round in her head. Of course, everything made sense now, except for one thing – why Piers had not trusted her enough to tell her of his plans. He had allowed her to think the worst, and she was not sure if she could forgive him for that. It was getting late and dusk was falling rapidly, even though the summer days were long. She was tempted to go looking for Piers, but it would be foolish to venture into the woods after dark. The thought of the old semi-derelict cottage still had the power to make her shudder and she decided to rise at dawn. She needed to hear the story from Piers' own lips before she could come to terms with what her grandfather had just told her.

'Rosie, there you are. I've been looking for you everywhere.'

She came to a halt on the bottom tread at the sound of Alexander's voice. 'I've just been to say good night to Grandpapa,' she said, making an effort to sound calm.

'Shall we take a walk on the terrace?' Alexander asked hopefully. 'It's a beautiful evening.'

She met his intense gaze and her heart sank. 'Alex, there's something I must say to you.'

'That sound ominous, my darling. What is it? Has Grandmama upset you? If she has you mustn't—'

She held up her hand. 'No, at least not in the way you imagine. Alex, I can't marry you.'

He stared at her in disbelief. 'What has she said to you? Don't listen to anyone else, Rosie. I love you. I want you to be my wife.'

'Alex, I love you, too – in a way, but not in the way a woman should when a man asks her to marry him.'

'I don't understand. Before dinner you were happy to agree to be my wife.'

'Alex, you rushed me into it. We both needed time to think it through properly.'

'I don't need to think about it, my darling. I know how I feel.'

'We've been thrown together, Alex. It was a lovely idea, but we hardly know each other, and I'm just not ready to make such a commitment. I'm truly sorry.'

Rosalind turned on her heel and ran upstairs, clutching her skirts above her ankles so that she did not trip and fall. She glanced over the banister rail at the bend in the stairs and saw Alexander gazing up at her with a perplexed frown. He held out his hand but she shook her head and hurried on, stopping only when she reached her room. She closed the door with a sigh of relief, but inwardly she felt dreadful. She knew she had hurt him. She did love Alex, but if she were to be honest with herself it was more the feeling of a sister towards a brother. The woman he married would have to be very much in love to survive the rigours and privations of army life, and she knew now she was not that woman. She undressed slowly and made herself ready for bed.

Next morning she was up soon after dawn and she washed, dressed and tied back her hair, taking a shawl to keep out the early morning chill. She left the castle without being seen, and Bob came bounding out of the stables where he normally slept on a pile of rugs in the tack room. He greeted her ecstatically and then ran on ahead, his tail wagging and his head down as he investigated all the exciting scent trails. Rosalind knew exactly where she was going and she headed for the woods. It was a cool morning with a heavy dew on the grass and the hem of her skirt was soon soaked, as were her boots, but she was oblivious to everything other than her intention to find and confront Piers.

The former keeper's cottage was set in a small clearing on the far side of the woods, and the brick walls left standing were charred by soot from the fire that had made it virtually uninhabitable. The sun had come up and filtered softly through the green canopy above, giving the old building a more romantic look than the frightening image Rosalind had in her mind. She hesitated for a moment but Bob did not share her reservations and he rushed towards the building, barking excitedly.

The side door opened and Piers emerged, his hair tousled and his shirt open to the waist, revealing a tanned, well-muscled torso. He blinked sleepily and shielded his eyes from the sun.

'Rosie! What are you doing here?'

'Grandpapa told me where to find you.' She was shivering, or perhaps she was trembling with pent-up emotion, and her voice shook. 'Why didn't you let me know that you were safe? You just disappeared.'

He ran his hand through his already ruffled hair. 'Sir Lucien must have explained. Come inside and I'll put the kettle on and make some coffee, although I haven't any milk.'

She followed him into the cottage, which still smelled faintly of soot, and the walls were blackened, with wallpaper hanging off in strips. However, to her surprise, the kitchen was largely untouched and a fire burned in the grate with a kettle bubbling on the trivet. A straw-filled palliasse lay on the floor, with the indentation of Piers' body still apparent, and his boots were propped up against the wall.

'Why are you living like this, Piers? Surely there's no need now that you're on the side of the authorities?' Rosalind sat down by the fire, warming her hands. She felt a chill run down her spine. 'I still think of this as the haunted house. Do you really sleep here?'

'Not very well, to tell the truth. But I've done what I set out to do. All the taxes have been paid on the goods we discovered in the oubliette. I've repaid the insurance company and the jewellery has been returned to the rightful owners. There are some things I haven't been able to trace, but I've done what I can.'

'But you paid a large sum into the bank? Was that stolen, too?'

He shook his head. 'That was from the sale of kegs of brandy and other things for which I couldn't trace the original owners.'

'Do you know that Blaise is staying at Rockwood? Your grandmother has been taken in by his lies.'

'But you didn't believe him? Sir Lucien told me

that you and your brothers had gone down to Cornwall with Alex. What did you hope to gain by that?' Piers made the coffee and set the jug aside to stand.

Rosalind met his questioning look with a steady glance. 'We took Trevenor back from Blaise and Alex paid the miners. We exposed Blaise as a liar and a fraud and Pedrick was told not to allow him anywhere near the mine.'

'You did all that for me?'

'To be honest, Piers, we did it so that your grand-mother and Aurelia could go home. They don't deserve to suffer for your wrongdoings.'

'I was involved with the smugglers by mischance in the first place, and then I made it my business to expose them and to atone for my father's sins.'

'Why didn't you tell me what was going on in the first place?'

He pulled up a stool and sat down beside her. 'I'm sorry, Rosie, but it had to be kept secret. I suspected that Blaise knew exactly where the cache had been hidden. He's clever and he's crafty.'

'Why have you waited so long to denounce him?'

'I wanted to do the right thing with the smuggled goods and return the stolen property. I knew that Blaise would demand at least half of whatever we found, and he was still holding the threat of a family scandal over my head. I knew that Hugo Knighton wouldn't come up to scratch if the truth came out and I had to protect Aurelia.'

'That was all lies. Alex and I went round the local churches looking at their registers of births. Ewart Blaise was born Blease Ewart, the son of a humble shepherd and a former servant from Knighton Park. Blease or Blaise, whichever you care to call him, went to sea when he was thirteen. That's how you first knew him, isn't it?'

Piers nodded. 'We were just boys when we met. I had stowed away on the ship, knowing that my father had joined forces with the smugglers in an attempt to hide the proceeds of the fraud he had committed. I suppose I had a vague idea that I might persuade him to return the money. It was foolish of me.'

'You were just a boy.'

He took her hand in his and raised it to his cheek. 'I'm glad you came here today, Rosie. We parted on a misunderstanding and it's been on my mind ever since. I don't want you to think badly of me.'

'I don't – I mean I never did, not really. I didn't know what to believe, but I wish you'd trusted me enough to tell me the truth.'

He released her hand, dropping his gaze. 'Yes, I'm sorry. I've been so single-minded in all this that I lost sight of what really mattered to me.'

'Blaise needs to be stopped before he tricks your grandmother into letting him back into Trevenor, or the clay mine business, come to that.'

'Yes, you're right, of course, but how did you discover his true identity?'

'It's all in the parish register of St John's church in a tiny village several miles from Trevenor. I've seen it myself.'

'I don't know why I didn't think of doing that, but my sole purpose has been to find the cache and atone for my father's criminal behaviour. I've had to live with the knowledge of what he did since that night when you were almost killed because of his involvement with the smuggling ring. I had no idea that the stash had been hidden at Rockwood until Blaise told me a few months ago. My father died, taking the secret with him.'

Piers' voice shook with emotion as he reached for the enamel jug and poured the coffee into two chipped cups. He passed one to her and for a brief moment their fingers touched. Rosalind felt the tremor pass through her body. They were so close that she could smell the familiar scent of the boy who had rescued her all those years ago, and she knew why she could never give herself to Alexander or any other man. She might have ruined her chance of happiness with Piers, but she would rather die an old maid than take second best.

Bob seemed to sense her turbulent emotions and he nuzzled her hand, almost making her spill her coffee. She put the cup down on the table. 'What will you do now, Piers? I don't know what Blaise hopes to achieve by coming to Rockwood, but we can't allow him to get away with whatever game he's playing.'

'I was planning to come to the castle this morning, and now you've given me that information about him I have the ammunition I need to send out a broadside across his bows, as your grandfather would say, and my family can return to their rightful home.'

Rosalind felt a cold shiver run down her spine. Piers spoke so calmly and dispassionately about taking his family back to Cornwall that it felt as if she had been written out of his life already. She rose to her feet, leaving the coffee untouched. 'I'd better get back before I'm missed.'

'What's the matter, Rosie? What have I said to upset you?'

She headed for the doorway. 'Nothing. I'm perfectly all right.' She ran from the cottage with Bob at her heels.

'Wait a minute.'

She hesitated and turned to see Piers striding across the uneven ground, his stockinged feet crunching on dried leaves and snapping twigs, and before she had a chance to speak he had swept her into his arms and was kissing her passionately. At first she resisted, but she found herself responding shyly at first but with increasing fervour. The strength of his arms shielded her from harsh reality, and the warmth of his body permeated her whole being. The taste of his mouth on hers was sweeter than fine wine. He put her back on her feet, but he did not release his hold, and she laid her hands flat on his bare chest. The rhythm of his heartbeats was in time with her own, and when he kissed her again their bodies seemed to merge.

He released her slowly, looking into her eyes with a tender smile. 'I love you, Rosie. I told you that once before but you didn't believe me.'

'I was wrong to doubt you,' she said softly. 'But do you blame me?'

'No, of course not. If anything, I blame myself for not being completely honest with you. I should have told you everything from the start. Can you forgive me?'

She sighed and laid her head against his shoulder. 'I love you, Piers. I think I fell in love with you when you saved me that night on the beach. I never forgot you.'

He kissed her again and this time she responded with equal passion, although she was the first to draw away. 'What do we do now?'

'I'll finish getting dressed and we'll go back to the castle together. No one will ever come between us again.'

'There something you should know,' Rosalind said hesitantly. 'It's Alexander.'

'He's in love with you. I know that.'

'He asked me to marry him and for a few hours I allowed him to believe that I felt the same way. We'd grown close during our time in Cornwall and I do love him, but like a brother. I told him that last evening and I hope he believed me. He's being sent to India in a week or so and I hate to let him go with a heavy heart.'

Piers leaned over to kiss her tenderly on the lips. 'You are so sweet, Rosie. I know my brother and, believe me, he'll get over it quite quickly. Alex is a good chap, but he's impulsive.'

A wave of relief made Rosalind smile. 'Are you saying that he didn't mean a word of it?'

'No, of course not. Alex will always have a soft spot for you – what man wouldn't? – but, if anything, he's married to the army. Alex is a professional soldier and whoever he marries will have to follow the drum.'

'Maybe we should keep our secret a little longer,' Rosalind said thoughtfully. 'Let's sort Blaise out first before we tell anyone. I'd like to break it gently to Alex, too.'

Piers nodded. 'All right, but I want everyone to know how I feel about you, Rosie.'

'I'd like to tell Grandpapa first. We had a long conversation last evening and it was he who told me the part you'd played in all this. He thinks very highly of you, Piers.'

'As I do of him. You're right – we'll tell him together, after we've sent Blaise on his way.'

'I'll go on ahead,' Rosie said, staring down at his bare feet. 'I'll leave you to finish dressing.'

'One more kiss, because it will have to last me for a while at least.' Piers pulled her to him and enveloped her in an embrace that robbed her of the desire to move, but eventually she gave him a gentle push and hurried away before he could detain her further.

Chapter Twenty-Seven

'Where have you been, Rosie?' Patricia demanded crossly. 'You must have risen very early this morning because you weren't there when I went into your room.'

'I took Bob for a walk,' Rosalind said casually.

'You don't normally go out first thing in the morning. You're very flushed. Are you sickening for something?'

'No, I've never felt better. What do you want, Patsy?'

'A messenger arrived from Greystone Park. Christina and Sylvia have invited me to stay with them for a few days. Sir Michael sent a carriage to collect me.'

'That's good, isn't it?'

'Yes, but I thought you might object.'

'I told you that you should see the girls again.

Aurelia will be returning to Cornwall very soon and you'll need your friends to keep you company.'

'I know you were supposed to be engaged to Alex, but he's very upset because you changed your mind.'

'Leave Alex to me. Get Tilly to pack a bag for you and go to Greystone Park. I assume you asked the coachman to wait?'

'Yes, I did. I was going anyway, but I prefer to have your blessing.'

Rosalind kissed her on the cheek. 'You never change, Patsy. Have a lovely time and I'll look forward to hearing all about it when you return.'

Patricia glanced over Rosalind's shoulder. 'Is that Piers?' She shot a suspicious glance at her sister. 'Did you know that he'd returned?'

'As a matter of fact I did. We're about to send Blaise packing, if you must know. I can tell you now as you're not going to be here.'

'That's why you look so happy, isn't it?' Patricia gurgled with laughter. 'You sly thing. You went out to meet him, didn't you? Don't deny it – I always knew that you were in love with Piers and not Alex.'

'Again, it's our secret,' Rosalind said urgently. 'You're right, of course, but please don't say anything.'

Patricia gave her a smug smile. 'You can trust me absolutely, Rosie. I shall have such a lot to tell the girls, but I'll ask the coachman to wait until after breakfast. I wouldn't miss the announcement for anything.' She danced off towards the staircase, leaving Rosalind in no doubt that her secret would soon be knowledge from Rockwood to Greystone Park and beyond.

Rosalind went to meet Piers. 'You didn't waste any time, did you?'

He smiled, his hazel eyes dancing with golden lights. 'I couldn't bear to be apart from you any longer than necessary.'

Rosalind checked the face of the grandfather clock, which stood ticking quietly next to a rather rusty suit of armour. 'Breakfast will be served in half an hour. Do you think that's a good time to expose Blaise as the fraud he really is?'

'Yes, I do, and I think your grandfather should take his rightful place at the head of the table.'

She nodded. 'I'll go to the solar and tell Jarvis to have him ready.'

'I should speak to Alex first and tell him about us, Rosie. I owe it to him.'

'Should we do it together?'

'I think it would be best coming from me.'

Jarvis had just finished shaving Sir Lucien when Rosalind entered the solar. Jarvis greeted her with a polite nod and hurried from the room, taking the foam-filled bowl and cutthroat razor with him.

Sir Lucien eyed her expectantly. 'Well? I can see you have good news for me, Rosie. You are so like my dear Prudence that I can read your moods like a seagoing chart.'

'Yes, Grandpapa. I found Piers and I told him what we did in Cornwall. He's here now and he's going to denounce Blaise at breakfast when everyone is present. We think you ought to take your place at the head of the table.'

'Naturally,' Sir Lucien said, nodding. 'I will be there and it will give me great pleasure to see the man exposed for the rascal he undoubtedly is.'

'I'll see you at breakfast then.' Rosalind was about to leave the room but her grandfather held out his hand.

'Before you go, there's something that we have to tell you.'

Rosalind gazed at him in surprise. 'We? Who are you referring to, Grandpapa.' She suspected that the state of affairs in the castle might have tipped him over the edge again, and perhaps he was imagining things.

'Come in, my dear.' Sir Lucien rose to his feet as the door opened and Hester walked into the room. He crossed the floor to guide her to a chair, and he stood beside her with his arm around her ample shoulders. 'This might come as a surprise to you, Rosie.'

Hester's round cheeks flushed from pink to scarlet. 'This isn't how I envisaged it would be, Miss Rosalind.'

'Now, now, my love. There's no need for subservient talk now. I won't beat about the bush, Rosie. I want you to be the first to congratulate us. Hester has long been my support and confidante and I intend to acknowledge her loyalty by making her my wife.'

Rosalind stared at them, lost for words.

'I know it's not the done thing, Miss Rosalind,' Hester said apologetically. 'But I love you as if you were my own child, and Sir Lucien has been my good friend all these years. I realise it's above my station in life, but I will always remain your devoted servant.' Hester glanced anxious at Sir Lucien, who smiled tenderly and patted her on the shoulder.

'At my age I don't give a fig for convention,' Sir Lucien said firmly. 'Hester deserves the security I can give her and she's earned respect from the rest of the household.'

'But I will not be the mistress of Rockwood,' Hester added quickly. 'I never could take that position away from you, Miss Rosalind. Nor do I even attempt to take the place of the late Lady Carey.'

'Hester, I'm delighted for you. You have kept us all together through everything and I am very grateful to Grandpapa for showing his appreciation in this way.'

'You are?' Hester stared at her in amazement. 'But, maid, I was expecting you to be shocked and appalled. I'm a simple countrywoman. I don't belong in society.'

'Hester,' Sir Lucien said sternly, 'I won't have that

504

sort of talk. You've been my friend and companion and you've raised my grandchildren when their mother took off on her flights of fancy. You deserve everything I can offer you and more.'

'Well, I am delighted.' Rosalind clapped her hands. 'Who cares what anyone thinks? As long as you are both happy, that's all that matters. In fact, I suggest you announce your engagement at breakfast this morning after Piers has exposed Blaise for the liar and cheat that he is.'

Sir Lucien patted Hester's hand. 'Then that's what I will do. It's time you took your proper place in this family, Hester, my dear.'

Piers remained out of sight until everyone was seated round the dining table. Hester had decided to stay below stairs until Sir Lucien had announced their engagement and Rosalind did not try to dissuade her. She could imagine Lady Pentelow's shocked reaction and she was not wrong. The moment the last person sat down, Sir Lucien rose to his feet. He cleared his throat.

'I have an announcement to make. It's a fact known only to a very few people, but Hester Dodridge, our cook-housekeeper, who has been with this family for forty years or more, has become my constant companion.'

Lady Pentelow glared at him. 'What are you saying, sir?'

'If you will give me a chance, ma'am. I'm trying

to tell you all that Hester has done me the honour of consenting to be my wife.' Sir Lucien looked round expectantly as he sat down.

There was a stunned silence broken by a nervous giggle from Aurelia. 'Surely this is some kind of joke?'

'A child like you might think so,' Sir Lucien said equably. 'But Hester is a wonderful woman. She has done more to keep this family together than anyone. She has been constant throughout our good times and our bad times. Moreover I am very fond of her, and I believe she feels a similar affection for me.'

Bertie raised his coffee cup. 'Well, sir. May I be the first to congratulate you? You're right. Hester is the very rock on which the castle is built.'

'I agree.' Walter nodded enthusiastically.

'Of course I think it's a wonderful thing.' Rosalind gave her grandfather an encouraging smile, which faded as she turned her attention to Blaise, who had said nothing so far. 'You are very quiet, Mr Blaise.'

He shrugged. 'I am thunderstruck, Miss Carey. Will other people be so understanding?'

'Yes, indeed.' Lady Pentelow took a deep breath. 'What were you thinking of, Lucien? You'll make the Carey name a laughing stock.'

'Perhaps, amongst ill-informed, ignorant persons, Clarissa. But you will be far away in Cornwall by the time Hester and I get married, so it will not concern you.'

Blaise glared at him. 'Lady Pentelow has signed over the estate to me, Sir Lucien. She now resides here.'

'That is where you're wrong, Mr Blaise,' Rosalind said calmly. 'We went to Trevenor and we discovered a few interesting facts. The first being that you did not have a legal agreement with Piers Blanchard, and the second being that you are a fraud. Your name is Blease Ewart and your father is a shepherd, your mother was a servant at Knighton Hall.'

'What utter nonsense,' Blaise snapped. 'I won't stay here to be insulted. You will hear from my solicitor.'

'I wouldn't do that if I were you.' Piers walked into the room. 'I know all about you and I say it's all true. You're forgetting that we were boys on the same vessel that almost came to grief in the storm, the difference being that I was a stowaway, keeping an eye on my father, and you were part of the criminal gang.'

'This is preposterous,' Blaise countered. 'Don't believe a word he says, Lady Pentelow.'

She looked from one to the other. 'Which of you is telling the truth?' She turned to Alexander. 'You're very quiet. You went to Trevenor – is what Piers says true?'

'Yes, I can only speak for our findings, Grandmama. But I can assure you that Blaise is a fraud. Piers alone knows what part Blaise took in concealing the stash from the smugglers, but I believe my brother over Blaise at any time.'

'Half of that money is mine,' Blaise said angrily. 'It's taken me twelve years to get my hands on it and I'm not giving up now. You can keep Trevenor, Lady Pentelow, and I've no interest in the china clay business, but I want my half of the proceeds and I want it now.'

'You're too late.' Piers pulled up a chair and sat down beside Rosalind. 'I've paid the tax on the smuggled goods and return the stolen articles to the rightful owners, as far as possible.'

'There was money, too. I know because I saw it when I was a lad. You don't forget things like that.'

'That money belonged to the insurance company and it's been repaid. I'm giving you a chance to be a free man, Blaise. Go now and don't come back.'

'What if I refuse? I deserve a cut.'

'Then I'll send for the constable and you'll end up in the magistrates' court. Take your pick.'

'I can't believe that I allowed you to get the better of me, Blaise,' Lady Pentelow said bitterly. 'Do what my grandson says, or face a long prison sentence or possible transportation.'

Blaise rose from the table. 'I'm going, but you haven't heard the last of me. The Blanchard family owes me something for all my efforts at the damned clay mine.' He stormed out of the room, slamming the door behind him.

'Well, what next?' Aurelia said, looking round the table. 'Aren't you glad you waited to go to Greystone Park, Patsy?'

'I think two people not a million miles from here might have news of their own to impart.' Patricia sent a meaningful look in her sister's direction.

Piers took Rosalind by the hand and she stood up. 'I'm sorry about this, Alex, but I didn't know the truth myself until an hour or two ago.'

'I'm sorry, too, old chap. But I've been in love with Rosalind since the very beginning and I'm delighted to say that she returns my feelings.'

Alexander looked from one to the other, shaking his head. 'I thought I was too lucky. But I wish you both every happiness. You're a far better man than I, Piers.'

Bertie patted Alex on the back. 'Hard luck, old fellow.'

'Are we to congratulate you?' Walter asked hopefully.

'Piers hasn't proposed to me yet.' Rosalind smiled up at him.

Piers went down on one knee. He raised Rosalind's hand to his lips. 'Rosalind Carey, I love you with all my heart. I'll spend the rest of my life trying to make you happy if you say the word.'

'Say the word then, you noodle,' Aurelia said, laughing.

'Ignore my little sister, Rosie. Will you marry me, please?'

She leaned over to kiss him on the lips. 'I think I knew all those years ago that I would marry you one day, Piers. My answer was always written in the stars. Yes, of course I'll marry you, my one and only love.'

Read on for a sneak peek of the next
book in Dilly's enthralling new series,
The Rockwood Chronicles...

*Winter
Wedding*

Coming Autumn 2021!

When she awakened next morning, Rosalind remembered that not only was it Christmas Eve, but it was the day that Patsy should have been walking up the aisle with Alex. Whereas now she would have to attend the wedding as an onlooker, there to witness their mother's marriage to Claude. Rosalind could only imagine the scene at the castle with all the family tensions bubbling to the surface, and no one in overall charge of the arrangements. She pitied Bertie and Walter having to bear the brunt of their mother's frustration when things did not go quite to plan, and Patsy's tantrums. It was the first time in Rosalind's life that she would be spending Christmas away from Rockwood and it felt very strange. She slid out of bed not wanting to wake Hester, who had still not plucked up the courage to sleep in her own room. It was bitterly cold and the fire had burned away to a pile of ash. Agathe's first chore in the mornings was to light the fires

512

but it was still early, judging by the dark sky with just a hint of dawn light filtering through the window.

Rosalind washed quickly in icy water and dressed with equal speed. She lit a candle and was on her way downstairs when she almost bumped into Agathe, who was staggering beneath the weight of a full coal scuttle.

'I'm sorry, madame. I am a little late this morning.'

'I'm up early. I couldn't sleep a moment longer.'

'I've given Monsieur Alex some coffee, madame. He called out to me as I was clearing the grate. I hope I did right.'

'Of course you did. Thank you, Agathe. I'll go to him now.' Rosalind quickened her pace, heading for the drawing room. The newly-lit fire had taken the chill off the gloomy room and she could just make out Alex's bed by the window.

Alex raised his head. 'Rosie, is that you?'

'Agathe said you were awake. Are you in much pain?'

'A bit, but she makes good coffee.'

'Sister Dominique gave me some laudanum for you to take if the pain was too bad.'

'I'm all right for now, but to tell the truth I'm starving. Does that fierce woman who keeps house allow you in the kitchen?'

'We have an understanding,' Rosalind said, chuckling. 'Not a very good one, but we've called a truce today, or so I hope. I'm hungry, too.' She moved to the bed and plumped up the pillows.

Alex caught her by the hand as she was about to back away. 'Thank you for everything, Rosie. You can't imagine how grateful I am to be out of that hospital ward.' He raised her hand to his lips. 'You smell wonderful,' he added, smiling.

'It's called soap and water, Alex.' Rosalind withdrew her hand gently. 'Perhaps you would like me to help you to wash later.'

'I think I can manage that on my own, but thank you for the offer,' Alex said with a wry smile. 'Will you have breakfast with me, please? Before Hester and Agathe take over and start ordering me about.'

'I know you love all the attention, Alex. So don't pretend otherwise.'

'I like it when you make a fuss of me, Rosie.'

She knew he was teasing, but there was a look in his eyes that she remembered only too well. 'I have better things to do than to pamper you, Alexander.' Rosalind hurried off without waiting for his response. She could still feel the imprint of his lips on the back of her hand, but a small voice in her head warned her to take care. All the old feelings she had harboured for Alex were in danger of rising to the surface, and she could tell by the warmth in his hazel eyes that she held a special place in his heart. Fate had thrown them together, but neither of them were free to resume their old relationship. She was a married woman with a sick husband who needed her, and Alex was spoken for. Rosalind made her way to the kitchen and found Delfosse sprawled in a chair at the table with his head in his arms. His snores echoed off the high ceiling, rattling the metal utensils and copper pans that hung above the range. Rosalind ignored him and went to investigate the cold room and the spacious larder. Hester had been busy the night before, plucking, drawing and preparing the geese for the table, and she had made an attempt at making a plum pudding from ingredients that came to hand. The smell of cinnamon and nutmeg filled the air with the memories of past Christmas dinners and Rosalind's mouth began to water. That aside she knew she must concentrate on making breakfast, and she remembered that Alex liked porridge.

She worked with a will and set a tray with everything they needed, including a pot of Madame Planche's strawberry preserve and thick slices of toast.

Alex raised himself on his elbow when she placed the tray on the table by his bed. 'Is that porridge? Real porridge with cream and sugar.'

'It most certainly is. I made it to Hester's exacting standards, I hope.'

'Can you help me to sit up, Rosie?'

Somewhat reluctantly, she moved to his side and he placed one arm around her shoulders. The nearness of him was even more unsettling and Rosalind had to steel herself to remain calm and unflustered. His breath on her cheek was warm and brought memories of their brief romance flooding back.

'Count to three,' Rosalind said firmly, 'and I'll try to lift you.'

He rested his head momentarily on her shoulder. 'All right. One, two, three …' he groaned with pain as their combined efforts slid him up the bed into a semirecumbent position. 'Well done, Rosie.' He leaned on her a little longer. 'Let me get my breath back.'

'It's all right, Alex. Take as long as you need.'

He made an attempt at a smile. 'I can't wait to taste the porridge.' He withdrew his arm slowly. 'Thank you, my angel. I hope I didn't hurt you.'

'No, of course not.' Rosalind moved away quickly. 'Cream and sugar, just how you like it.'

'You remember.'

'Of course. I'm the big sister. I look after everyone.' Rosalind handed him a steaming bowl of porridge.

'That smells so good. You will sit with me, won't you? I feel like a leper stuck here away from everyone.'

She pulled up a chair. 'Of course I will.'

She looked up and felt herself drowning in his gaze. Two years of happy marriage to Piers were in danger of being swept away by the resurgence of old emotions, and she realised that they were teetering on the brink of disaster. 'It should have been your wedding day, Alex,' she said abruptly. 'I wonder how Patsy is feeling.'

'She will dance at your mother's wedding and probably outdo my sister when it comes to flirting with eligible bachelors,' Alex said casually.

'Don't you care?' The question came out before she could stop herself.

'Of course I do, but I've been away a long time. To be honest, I wonder if Patsy will be upset because she wants to be my wife, or because she is no longer the centre of attention. Am I being unfair, Rosie?'

'I don't know, Alex. You could be right, but the only

way to find out is for you to be with her again. It would be too late once you are married, so maybe some time together is what you both need.'

'Are you happy, Rosie?'

The question came as a shock and she answered mechanically. 'I am, or I will be when Piers is out of danger.'

'Yes, of course.' Alex reached for a slice of toast. 'This is very pleasant, Rosie. Do you think we could rise early and share breakfast every day?'

She found herself relaxing, her anxiety calmed by his easy charm. 'I don't see why not. Although Hester won't approve.'

'That will make it even more fun. We'll go back to the lives we have planned soon enough. Let's enjoy this precious interlude.'

Rosalind smiled. 'You are a bad influence, Alex.'

Look out for Book Two in

The Rockwood Chronicles...

Winter Wedding

Coming Autumn 2021!